A PALETTE
FOR LOVE
AND

MURDER

SARALYN RICHARD

PALM CIRCLE PRESS

GENRE: Police Procedural

A Palette for Love and Murder is a work of fiction. Names, places, characters, and incidents are either the product of the author's imagination or are used fictitiously, and any resemblance to any actual persons, living or dead, businesses, organizations, events or locales is entirely coincidental. All trademarks, service marks, registered trademarks, and registered service marks are the property of their respective owners and are used herein for identification purposes only. The publisher does not have any control over or assume any responsibility for author or third-party websites or their contents.

PRAISE for *A Palette for Love and Murder*

"In the Brandywine Valley, a delicate balance exists between the very wealthy and those who serve them, but the murder of a famous artist threatens this tenuous equilibrium. In her second outing featuring Detective Oliver Parrott, Saralyn Richard offers readers a compelling story of worlds in collision. A Palette for Love and Murder probes more than the mysteries of the art world and the motives for murder. Satisfied readers will discover that it also delicately plumbs the depths of love and the human heart. Another winner for Richard." — **William Kent Krueger**, author of *This Tender Land*

"Smart, stylish and sexy, this art world caper delights with its verve and wit. The character studies are wonderful, and Oliver and Tonya Parrott are an irresistible pair." — **Ausma Zehanat Khan**, author of *A Deadly Divide*

"Richard's complex characters and intelligent story line make *A Palette for Love and Murder* a surefire hit. Beautifully written and masterfully plotted, this mystery will satisfy readers on multiple levels. I devoured it in two sittings!" — **Jill Orr**, Silver Falchion award-nominated author of the Riley Ellison mysteries

"Delightful! Saralyn Richard weaves a deeply twisty mystery around vibrant characters that will leave readers looking forward to more." — **LynDee Walker**, Agatha Award-nominated author of *Front Page Fatality*

"*A Palette for Love and Murder* is more than just an investigation of an art theft or even a homicide. Detective Parrott faces the complexities of class and the challenge of marriage, all while chasing a killer." –**Elena Hartwell Taylor**, author of the Eddie Shoes Mystery Series

*In memory of Father Frank Fabj,
lifelong inspiration and dear friend.*

In our life there is a single color, as on an artist's palette, which provides the meaning of life and art.
It is the color of love.
—Marc Chagall

CHAPTER 1

Marriage had turned out to be more. More than taking vows and sipping champagne. More than a romantic cruise to exotic islands. More than sleeping in the warmth of a lover's embrace. Tonight, Detective Oliver Parrott had another two a.m. wake-up call, but not the kind from the West Brandywine Police Station. His first thought had been of the stolen paintings he was investigating, but the punch in the kidney had come from Parrott's own true love.

"No-o-oh, oh, no," Tonya yelled, as she thrashed about in the bed next to him.

Parrott jumped out of bed and twisted around, grabbing Tonya by both wrists. "Wake up, Baby. It's just a dream. You're right here with me. Nothing's wrong."

Tonya's eyes fluttered open and closed, as she struggled against her husband's strong, tall frame. She was breathing hard.

Still holding her wrists, he murmured, "C'mon now. C'mon, Tonya."

After what seemed like an hour to Parrott, Tonya woke up and stopped resisting his efforts to calm her down. When she realized what she had done, she threw her hands over her face and doubled over at the waist. "Sorry, sorry. I don't want to have these dreams, Ollie. They just won't go away." Tears streamed down her face and neck.

Parrott thought to turn on the lamp, but decided the reflected beam from the streetlight, piercing through the curtain, was enough. He scooted to sit up against the headboard. "Come sit up here with me," he said, patting the sheet between them. "Let's see if we can make them go away."

Tonya shoved down the covers that were wound around her legs. Her white silk teddy was spotted with patches of sweat. She climbed into her husband's embrace and dropped her head on his bare shoulder.

"Now," Parrott said, snuggling into his wife's hair and smelling jasmine. "Maybe it will help if you tell me exactly what it is that has you yelling in your sleep." Every time he'd asked before, Tonya had dissembled. She hated talking about her experiences in Afghanistan, period.

"You know I can't, Ollie. Even thinking about it scares me. Putting it into words—excruciating." More tears overflowed the banks of her eyelids, and she wiped them away with quick brushes of the back of her hand.

"Yes, I know," Parrott said, "but maybe if you could say the words, finally, these night terrors would go away. That's what I remember from that psych class I took junior year." He remembered times as a cop when he'd used a similar strategy to help witnesses articulate horrible memories. "It lets the boogeyman out from under the bed."

The corners of Tonya's mouth twitched but failed to make it to smile. She was shivering, though the room was warm. "I—I don't know if I can, but I'll try." She pulled the sheet and blanket up around them both, and Parrott pressed her to him, knowing whatever he did would be inadequate.

A few minutes passed in silence, and finally Tonya glanced at the alarm clock, which said two-seventeen. She took a deep breath, and then the words began tumbling out. "Some very bad things happened when I was in Afghanistan, Ollie." Her fingers drew a pattern onto his chest. "Some things I could never tell you about."

Parrott's eyebrows rose a half inch, though this was not a revelation. "Whenever we Skyped, you said things were fine."

"I know. That was me not wanting you to worry, and, you know, all our missions were top secret. There was always the chance our Skypes weren't private. And, anyway, I thought if I didn't talk about the bad things, I could make them disappear. I know now that was foolish."

"Because now you are dreaming about them? Is that what you're saying?"

Tonya nodded. "Something happened last September when we were on a mission. It changed the way I felt about everything. I witnessed something terrible, and I keep dreaming about it, over and over."

Parrott's mouth went dry. "What is it?"

"There were six of us in a helicopter, and I was co-pilot. Five guys and me. We landed about a mile from where a terror cell was supposed to be. It was pitch black. We moved as quickly and quietly as we could, and we surrounded the place. It was little more than a hut pushed up against the side of a mountain. It was supposed to be a peaceful grab—surprise the target, cuff him, and take him back for 'treatment.'

It all went surprisingly well. No screaming, no fuss, the target looked scared, but resigned to being caught. The problem, though, happened before we took him away." Tonya's hand reached for Parrott's, and she squeezed.

"What happened, Baby?"

"The guy had a family. Wife and daughters. Two pretty young girls, maybe twelve and thirteen. Curled up on mats on the ground, two peas in a pod. They were just lying there—" A sob flew from Tonya's lips like a speeding train from a tunnel, loud and long.

Parrott pressed his wife's body into his own, trying to suppress a shudder of his own.

"—I c-can't…I just can't say any more. It's—it's too horrible." She pulled her knees into her chest and clutched tightly.

Parrott groaned, as he felt the millimeter of progress slipping away. He wrapped his arms around the human sphere that was his troubled wife, and held tight, all thoughts of sleep having vanished.

Tonya shook with emotion, her sobs finally quieting into soft hiccups.

Parrott patted his wife like a baby. His baritone voice murmured soothing syllables. When he found some words, he said, "Listen, Tonya. Whatever happened, you didn't cause it. And you can't solve it. You just need to let it go."

Tonya stared at her husband, as if he had spoken in a foreign language. "I thought you'd understand, Ollie. I see how you are with your cases. You're so focused on every detail. You're a dog with a bone. And you don't care to talk about them, either."

"That's different. Police work is, mostly, confidential. And I'm not losing sleep over my cases, either."

"That's not what you said when you were investigating the Phillips case, everyone breathing down your neck and making all kinds of threats. It don't seem all that different to me."

"All right. Point taken. I do wish you'd get some help, though. Seems like we have a bit of PTSD going on."

"I see your detecting skills are working, even at three a.m." Tonya's lips parted, showing the space between her front teeth.

In the dark, Parrott could see Tonya's expression had lost its terror, and her eyes glowed. Parrott kissed the top of her head, her eyes, and finally her lips. "We'll get through this together, my love."

"I know," she said, returning the kiss and pulling Parrott down on top of her.

CHAPTER 2

The next morning, Parrott rose early, tiptoeing around the bedroom so as not to wake Tonya. Four hours' sleep wasn't enough, but it would have to do. He had a seven-thirty meeting with the chief and a lot of paperwork to do before ten, when he would meet with the owner of an art gallery in Kennett Square. Stolen paintings weren't the most exciting cases, but that was what he had right now, and maybe he should be glad, since his mind was preoccupied with his wife.

This was one time he was glad Tonya hadn't pursued post-service employment. They'd talked about various options, including her going back to school for a master's in social work, but she couldn't make up her mind, and right now it seemed like she might just need some time to rest.

He was glad the shower didn't wake her up, and he dressed in the dark in the cramped closet they shared. He brewed two cups of joe and poured them into his travel thermos, fed Horace, the cockatiel, and grabbed a granola bar *en route* to his Taurus. The sky was eggshell tinted with streaks of blue and pink, reminding him of several of the country morning scenes in the paintings he had been studying lately.

The twenty-minute drive to the West Brandywine Police Station gave him time to consider what had transpired the night before. Three months since their wedding, two since they'd returned from their honeymoon in Galveston, and already he was worried—not about his love for Tonya. She was the prettiest and smartest damn woman he'd ever known, and he was lucky to be her husband. But was he living up to his vows? These middle-of-the-night terrors left him exhausted and helpless. Last night he had pulled out all the stops, including quoting Sigmund Freud's *On Dreams*, but that hadn't seemed to help much. Whatever happened in Afghanistan that had traumatized her so much, it didn't seem to be going away.

Parrott pulled into his parking space ten minutes early, noting the chief's car was already there. In all his time at West Brandywine, he had arrived to work before Chief Schrik only once or twice. A glance at the picture window confirmed the routine was in place—Schrik was standing there, gazing into the parking lot. Not a criticism, just a quirk. Parrott grabbed his thermos and granola bar, and sprinted into the station, ready to work.

Schrik greeted him at the door, his trademark paper clip hanging from his lips like a cigar, reminding him not to smoke. "Come on in. We've got a lot of ground to cover, just the two of us this morning."

He ushered Parrott into his inner sanctum and closed the door, although it was still early, and all was quiet. The office still smelled of pine from last night's cleaning. "How'd your interview with the artist go yesterday?"

Parrott dropped into his usual chair, opposite his boss. *Was it just yesterday?* "Stood me up. I talked to a lady, fiftyish, nice-looking. Said she's his live-in girlfriend, Elle Carmichael. Said he had a last-minute emergency with a tooth."

"Did you get a good look at his place?"

"Yeah. He's no starving artist—that's for sure. Nice place. Well-furnished. Oil paintings everywhere, and they didn't look cheap. She showed me the site of the crime, which is their studio, a converted barn. The girlfriend gives art lessons there. Lots of windows, north-south exposure for the best light, she said. No sign of forced entry, and no report of the security system breach, although the system is turned on every evening and was most likely on at the time of the theft."

"Any personal info about the lady or Allmond?"

"No, she was playing mouse. Just walked me around and pointed. Definitely not a talker. Hoping to get a crack at Allmond himself next time."

"Well, take a look at this list that just came in last night." He tossed a computer printout across the desk. "It's from the FBI."

There must have been a half dozen items on the list, each one illustrated with a thumbnail.

Parrott whistled. "So many? What's the time frame and geographic location on these?"

"All within the state, all within the last twelve months. Pretty amazing."

Parrott scrutinized the list of oil paintings, looking for patterns. First he scanned for artist names, estimated values, dates, and then locations. Finally, he looked at the tiny pictures. Printed in color, he could see enough to tell whether the painting was a landscape, a portrait of a person, or something else. "I see our two made the list," he said, pointing to the bottom.

"Yeah. Paintings like these get reported right away."

"Still, it hasn't even been forty-eight hours." Parrott's eyes ran through the estimated value column on both pages. "Look, Chief, our two paintings have the highest value. Think that's because they were stolen from the artist's own studio?"

"Could be, or maybe it's coincidence. Maybe Allmond held back on showing or selling the ones he thought were worth the most. Still, seventy thousand dollars apiece is a lot, and a big risk to the thief. Once they're reported missing and on this hot list, it's nearly impossible to fence, so why bother? That's what I want you to find out, Parrott."

"Allmond is not just a local painter. I know that. He's had shows in Kennett Square in the last couple of years, paints in a converted stable on the horse farm, but he's also got a place in New York, and his work has been shown there and in London. I'll check him out some more, and I'll talk to the cops in these other places where paintings have turned up missing. I've got a ten o'clock appointment with Rupert Brooks at The Rue Moderne. I'll include these questions. Thanks, Chief. I'm on it."

Parrott left Schrik's office and went to the break room, where he chugged his coffee and filled the thermos with more. He'd need the caffeine to stay focused on the matter at hand today. Next stop was his new office. After the Phillips case and after the honeymoon, Schrik had surprised him by upgrading his space from a cubicle-sized interior room to a larger and airier office with a window facing the park with its playground equipment and badminton net. It wasn't large, but it was comfortable, and Parrott knew it was Schrik's way of compensating him for a job well-done, a way of encouraging him to stay.

Parrott eased his body into the ergonomic leather-like executive chair and turned on his computer. His desk was as pristine and orderly as his bedroom. A cluttered environment made for cluttered thinking, and Mrs. Parrott hadn't raised any sloppy kids.

As the computer warmed up, Parrott googled Blake Allmond. He knew the artist had a second home and studio in New York. Wherever it was, Parrott figured he might learn more about the artist from that than he would from the close-mouthed community on the farm. Google did its search, pulling up several pages of entries about the popular artist, most likely the most recent first. Parrott's eyes scanned the page and clicked "next" a few times. There were pages and pages about this guy. Somewhere on the fifth page, Parrott gave his attention to the first item, something that answered a few questions and raised a few more. When he saw the headline of a twenty-two year-old news article, coffee-flavored acid burned in his chest. He scooted his chair forward and double-clicked.

CHAPTER 3

Alexander Vargas moaned as he rolled over in his bed to face the wall, tugging the covers over his head in the process. It couldn't be morning yet, despite the spidery strips of intense light straining through the aluminum blinds. Hadn't he had just crawled into bed? Just a few more minutes of sleep might stave off the nagging headache above his eyes. The taste of stale cigars and expensive gin echoed, souvenirs of last night's meeting with his Uncle Blake, a meeting gone terribly wrong.

"Guess I'd better get up," he mumbled, as he threw off the covers and dashed for the bathroom, where he hugged the toilet bowl and wished he hadn't indulged so much. Wasn't every day he was treated to cocktails and dinner at the elegant restaurant, Lacroix. Next time, he'd be more careful of his intake, if there ever were a next time.

At least he didn't have to go to work today. He'd called off yesterday, before he went into the city. He stood at the sink and regarded his nude image, the shoulder-length hair, now matted, the two-day beard, the downy patches of hair, the athletic ripples, the strong biceps decorated with pale blue veins. Not bad for twenty-nine. At least he looked better than he felt.

He grabbed his ratty terrycloth robe from the hook behind the door and slipped it on, tying the frayed belt at the waist. He ran the water till it got hot enough to soften his toothbrush bristles, then squeezed a stripe of red, white, and green paste onto them. He thought of his mother then, how she had taught him just the right way to fill the toothbrush, just the right amount. Only one of many things he missed about his mother. If she were still around, he probably wouldn't be in this mess.

Just as he started to brush, the sound of a railroad steam engine emanated from his cell phone. He let it ring while he finished brushing and did one round of spitting into the sink.

It was Veronica, his lady love, no doubt calling from the break room at Lyons Bank, where she was a teller. "Hey, honey," he croaked. "Whassup?" He glanced at the clock—11:45 already. He was supposed to call her when he got up.

"Why didn't you call me when you got up?" Her voice droned like a hornet about to strike.

"To tell you the truth, I just got up. Just brushing my pearly whites." Alexander ran his tongue around his dry mouth.

"Well, how did it go? I been waitin' to hear."

"Okay, sort of." He wished he hadn't told Veronica anything about his plan. He wished he had never even told her about his wealthy uncle. It had sort of flipped a switch in her that he couldn't flip back.

"Well, either it worked or it didn't. Which is it?" Veronica's breathing was gaspy. "Did you go through with the plan?" People were talking in the background. He hated having anyone know his business, even strangers.

Alexander examined his eyebrows and smoothed them down. "Hey, let's not talk about this over the phone, huh? Give me a coupla hours to shower and shave and grab a bite." The thought of food made his stomach clench in protest. "I'll meet you at seven at your place."

"Can't you just give me a hint? Did he come through?" More background talking, some laughing, almost like a refrain.

"Not now," Alexander replied, biting off the syllables. "Lemme go. I've got some important business to take care of." It would take some thinking to figure out a way to deliver the bad news. The scheme to lure Uncle Blake to invest in his costume business was dead in the water, and that was the least of his problems.

"Okay, okay. Leave me in suspense. I won't hold it against you. I'll be ready for the good news tonight at seven, *mi amor*. And I'll be wearing your favorite outfit, too." She dragged out the last word, ending the call in mid-syllable. It was her signature cliffhanger ending that both enthralled and annoyed Alexander.

CHAPTER 4

Blake Allmond finished with the dentist appointment in the city and returned to his condominium in Gramercy Park. Glad to have the crown cemented in, he ran his tongue over his still-numb cheek and gums. He hated that he had left Elle alone in Brandywine to meet with the detective about the art theft, but it couldn't be helped. His life, other than painting and Elle, was based in New York. Somehow the denser population and vibrant action in this elegant neighborhood made him feel more alive.

Last night's dinner with his nephew still rankled. Why had it taken so long to discover Alexander was playing him for a fool? If his banker friend hadn't tipped him off that some woman with a Spanish surname had been snooping around his financial information from a branch in South Philly, Blake might have stuck with his intention to leave a substantial portion of his estate to his dead sister's son. As much as he'd loved his sister and hoped Alexander was more like her than his good-for-nothing father, last night's dinner convinced him the young man was incapable of carrying on the family fortune and the responsibilities that went along with it.

He'd had a lot on his mind lately, and the stolen paintings had set him off, even before the call from Cecil, his lifelong buddy, who just happened to be president of the bank. "An abundance of caution," he'd said, "no harm done, but in a routine security check, we picked up a teller in another branch of the bank logging into your accounts. No transfers, just looking, but we've taken steps to protect you in the future. The gal's on probation, and, believe me, we'll be checking her computer weekly to make sure she's learned her lesson."

When Allmond had asked, Cecil said, "Her name's Veronica Espinosa. She's in the South Philly branch. Name ring a bell?"

Allmond hadn't known the name, but the Spanish surname and "South Philly" had set his mind on fire, and it didn't take a genius to figure out the connection to Alexander. In his haste to confront, he'd invited Alexander to meet him for drinks and dinner. Now the need to change his will was no longer simmering in his gut. It was boiling and rushing into his brain.

Blake kept his lawyer's number on speed dial. Not that he used it that often, just whenever he did, it was something urgent. As the phone rang, Blake thought about his lifelong friend, Gary Griffith. Images of the three of them—he and Cecil and Blake—pulling pranks at their prep school, broke the grimness from his face.

"Hey, Blakey," Gary bellowed. "How're things going in the art world these days? I meant to call you when I read about the theft. Any leads?"

"Not that I would know of. The police are just getting started. A Detective Parrott met at the house with Elle today."

"Oliver Parrott? That's the guy who handled the Preston Phillips case last year. You know the treasury secretary who died out there? Phillips' cousins, Caro and John E. Campbell. They're friends of Kim's and mine. They think a lot of him."

"Small world. Then you probably know the Campbells own one of my paintings, too. Hope theirs doesn't get lifted. Actually, I'm surprised anybody's stealing paintings these days. Ever since the heist at the Isabella Stewart Gardner Museum in 1990, the amount of scrutiny and publicity probably makes stolen paintings impossible to sell." Allmond sipped from a Long Island Iced Tea. "And why anyone would steal *my* paintings is beyond me. Fortunately, they were insured, but still. I'd planned to donate them to the National Arts Club."

"Hey, listen, I know you didn't call me up to talk about insurance companies and missing paintings. What's on your mind?"

"I wondered if you were free for dinner tonight. I want to pick your brain about a personal business matter, and I don't want to do it over the phone." Blake glanced at the antique ormulo clock with mother of pearl face on his desk. Already 4:15. "I know this is late notice, but it's important."

Gary hesitated. "It must be important if it got you off your ass to contact me. I've been complaining about your flip attitude about anything related to the law for years. So, okay. I'll meet you at eight. Where?"

"How about Maialino? I'll make the reservation."

"Right. See you at eight."

Blake hung up and thought for a minute. He'd better call Elle and tell her he was staying over a couple of days. She'd be disappointed about missing lunch at Piccolo Arancio, but he couldn't get everything done in one night, and this couldn't wait.

After he called Elle, he paced around the apartment, touching some of his parents' personal possessions. The Brandywine house was full of their belongings, but he had brought only a special few to this apartment. The clock, a pair of Georg Jensen candlesticks, the Baker etagere, and his great grandfather's gold pocket watch on a stand. Looking at and touching these objects gave him a rush, almost like the one from the Long Island Iced Tea he had nearly finished. Here, in this apartment, Blake could be himself in a way he couldn't in the larger, more opulent house.

Last night's outrage was slowly mellowing into mere anger. At least he was taking action to protect himself, and that lifted his spirits. There was just one more thing he wanted to do before getting ready for dinner. He grabbed his phone and tapped in a number he dared not put into his contact list.

When the person answered, Blake asked two one-word questions, "Tonight?" "Midnight?"

CHAPTER 5

Earlier that day, as Parrott strode down the hallway to Schrik's office, the twenty-two year-old headline he had just seen online had sent adrenaline from brain to limbs. He was already starting to make adjustments to his plan for the day and week ahead. He'd keep the meeting with the art dealer, Rupert Brooks, but now he had more than paintings on his mind.

"Parrott? What's up?" Schrik asked. "Any news about the stolen paintings?"

The rising sun cast a glare through the office window, silhouetting Schrik's burly form, and Parrott's eyes needed a second to adjust. The phone rang, too, and Parrott could hear Lucretia answering it in the distance. The office was waking up to a new day, and Parrott had a new insight he was itching to share.

"It might be nothing," he said, "but did you know Allmond's wife and kids were killed in an accident??" He paced in front of Schrik's desk. "Not only that, but he's lost his parents and his sister, too."

"Sit down, Parrott, before you wear out the carpet." Schrik leaned forward, a metallic squeak punctuating the movement. "I read somewhere about his losses. But so what?"

Parrott rubbed the sides of his head with both hands. "Just seems like a bit much. No parents, wife and kids killed in an accident, and his sister died, too? The guy's got a friggin' black cloud hanging over him."

"What are you saying? You think he's got something to do with all the deaths?"

"Not saying that. But now his paintings are being stolen, too. Nobody's that unlucky."

Schrik folded his hands over his belly and leaned back with a smile teasing the corners of his mouth. "Remember, this is Brandywine Valley. There are probably millions of people who'd love to change places with Allmond. High society, piles of money, successful in his field. Tragic about his wife and kids, but no one ever questioned that was anything but an accident. Drunk driver, I believe."

The smell of Schrik's black coffee, still steaming faintly on his desk, made Parrott wish he had brought his own thermos with him. "Who died first, I wonder, the sister or the wife and kids?"

"Good question." Schrik typed something into his computer, and then took a swig of coffee. "The wife and kids. Says the accident was—December—twenty-two years ago."

"And what about the parents?"

Schrik peered at the file, scrolling up. "Father died on a cruise ship when Allmond was twenty-five. Mother died of cancer the following year."

"So the sister died after Allmond's nuclear family."

"Right. Not sure where you're going with this. How does it relate to the case?"

"Truthfully, I'm not sure, but my instincts are telling me to follow the victim and follow the money. Even though this isn't a murder, we've got a victim—and the victim appears to have plenty of money. Why steal his *paintings*? Paintings are hard to unload, and you'd think there'd be more attractive loot on his estate."

Schrik drained his coffee cup and unwrapped a piece of gum. Since quitting smoking, he liked having something in his mouth. "I see what you mean, but I doubt the sister fits into the puzzle anyway. She's been dead for so long."

"Yeah, but sometimes dead doesn't mean 'out of the picture.' I'm gonna check her out just as soon as I talk to that art dealer. Then I'll take another crack at Allmond." Parrott rose and turned to leave. "Keep me posted, Chief."

The Rue Moderne occupied a prominent space on Union Street in Kennett Square. Parrott had chosen that one because its website featured several Blake Allmond paintings, as well as specializing in paintings by Brandywine favorite, Victor Lockwood, and his father, Paul. The Lockwood studio had drawn artists to the Brandywine Valley for three generations. Parrott had seen paintings by both the father and the son in homes where he had interviewed witnesses, and he knew they fetched a pretty penny. Now the grandson and his children were achieving notoriety, based on what Parrott had gathered from the internet.

A bell gave off a discreet tinkle when Parrott opened the door and stepped across the threshold. The faint smell of paint drifted over, and Parrott looked across the large gallery to where a woman stood at an easel, palette in hand, gazing at a wall-sized painting of a ram. The large white-walled rooms filled with framed paintings hanging everywhere made him think of a museum, instead of a store.

Soon a lanky gentleman in a gray pinstripe suit approached him, hand extended. "Detective Parrott, I presume? Rupert Brooks."

Although Parrott had arrived at the dot of ten, as planned, he couldn't help smiling at the dealer's calling him by name before he could introduce himself. It was probably a store not frequented often by detectives—or by blacks. The man's handshake was friendly enough, though. "Appreciate your meeting with me," Parrott said. "I know your time is valuable."

"Not at all," the dealer replied. "Let's go to my office." Brooks led the way, and as they passed the young artist, he muttered something like, "Nice work, Yvonne."

Her canvas, though a jumble of shapes in gray and mauve, did little to resemble the sheep painting that was her model. Parrott shrugged. One day he would try harder to understand modern art.

When they reached the cubbyhole Brooks had referred to as his office, Parrott guessed all the extravagances of the gallery had been used for displaying artwork. The room was musty and claustrophobic. Brooks sat behind a tiny desk and pointed to a wooden chair across from him.

Parrott tried to make himself comfortable, but the distance between his chair and Brooks's desk barely accommodated Parrott's long legs, and his attempt to scoot back caused him to bang against the wall. He compensated by leaning forward and placing his elbows on the desk, though he suspected that wasn't polite.

"Sorry there isn't more room. Most of our work takes place out there," Brooks said, pointing toward the door. "We could move our chairs, if you like."

"No, thanks," Parrott replied, though he gave the guy points for sensitivity. "I just have a few questions." He removed his iPad mini from his jacket pocket and glanced over the questions he had prepared. "What can you tell me about Blake Allmond's paintings from the standpoint of the gallery. How many do you have on hand, how many sold, what value do they have, how popular are they?"

Brooks ran his hand through his silvering sandy hair. "Allmond is quite popular here in Brandywine Valley. He's well-known for his technique for depicting water, you know, something the Impressionists strove to accomplish. We've sold a number of his paintings over the years. We have three small ones hanging in that gallery over there." He pointed. "Do you want to see them?"

"Not right now, but in a few minutes, yes. How about value? What do Allmond's paintings sell for?"

Brooks glanced at a three-ring notebook, but didn't open it. "I would say, depending on size and subject matter, his paintings would go for between fifty and eighty."

"Thousand?" That seemed like a lot to Parrott, but he knew those numbers to be modest in this neighborhood, and he remembered the stolen paintings had been valued at seventy.

Brooks nodded his head. "We sell his paintings on a regular basis. People like the regional subject matter and reasonable prices, and, of course, the mirror-like water. We're upset to read about the theft of his paintings. Of course, any Brandywine art heist is upsetting to us."

"Why do you think anyone would steal Blake Allmond's paintings?"

"Ah, that's the jackpot question, isn't it?" Brooks toyed with a sharpened pencil. "I don't know. Perhaps it is a fan who wants to possess the paintings, to keep them from the rest of the world, something obsessive, you know. Or perhaps someone thinks he can cash them in before they become too famous, before the price tags are in the museum range."

"Museum range?"

"Yes, once an artist achieves great fame for his body of work—and Allmond is certainly heading in that direction with his water technique—the paintings' value multiples a hundred fold."

"You mean in the millions?" Parrott said.

"Indeed. The same paintings that might sell for fifty thousand today might go for five hundred thousand or a million in time, maybe even more. The value of a painting can shoot up based solely on who collects it. Yoko Ono, for example. If she fancied Allmond's works and started buying them up, their value would shoot through the roof."

"So someone who thought Allmond's work might increase in value might steal it now, sort of on speculation it would go up?" Parrott's wheels were turning.

"Indeed. Actually, just the fact that two paintings have been stolen has caused enough of a buzz in the art world. I expect the value of his remaining paintings will go up dramatically."

"Supply and demand, eh?"

"Something like that." The dealer smiled, showing longer-than-normal eyeteeth. Otherwise, the face was rather handsome for a white guy.

Parrott shifted in his chair, failing to get more comfortable. "What can you tell me about the artist? What's his reputation for honesty? Friendships? Anyone have grudges against him that you know of?"

Brooks raised an eyebrow. "You think the thefts are personal? Well, I suppose that's possible." The dealer rolled the pencil to the edge of the desk and back to center before continuing. "I've known Allmond practically all my life, though he's several years younger. Our families were friends, and we went to the same church. I see him occasionally at art affairs. We both have places in New York. Also, he stops in here from time to time. I have no idea about his friendships or any grudges."

Parrott considered how to phrase the next question. "Since you've known the family, I wonder if you can help me get a perspective on Allmond's wealth. Does he earn a living from his paintings?"

Brooks uttered a short guffaw, then covered his mouth. "I didn't mean to react that way. It's just, your question—uh, no. Allmond's painting is more of an avocation than a vocation. He inherited the house, the lifestyle, everything from his parents. That's what enables him to devote himself to painting. He's never done anything else."

"Didn't Allmond have a sister? Didn't she share in the inheritance?"

Brooks winced at the mention of the sister. "Uh, no," Brooks stammered, his eyes glossing over. "Melanie didn't inherit. Blake got it all. And then Melanie died."

"Seems unusual. Was there a reason the parents didn't leave her anything?"

Brooks twitched in his seat, then stood, his tall, narrow frame filling much of the space in the office. He sat back down. "I suppose you'd find this out from somebody else if I didn't tell you. Melanie was engaged to be married—to someone her parents approved of—someone from her own background. She broke the engagement and ran off with a guy from Mexico. Vargas was his name. Her parents were mortified. They had her followed, begged her to annul the marriage."

"But she refused?"

"Right. She never came back, and her parents disowned her."

"Big price to pay for love, I guess," Parrott muttered. "What ever happened to her fiancé?" Parrott asked.

Brooks looked away for a moment, and when his eyes returned to meet Parrott's, he muttered, "That would be me."

CHAPTER 6

P arrott retraced his steps to Manderley, the sprawling white Colonial in the heart of Brandywine Valley, the home of Blake Allmond. It seemed just hours since he had been there for the first time, but he had more questions now, and he hoped to catch the artist at home this time. As he drove up the long, winding driveway, Parrott thought of the similarity among the approaches to these country mansions. He knew from experience the opulence and peacefulness of the setting held no power over the happiness of its residents.

Yesterday when he had walked around with Allmond's girlfriend, he had gotten the impression her life in this whale of a house wasn't exactly joyous. It wasn't anything she said or did. It was more the attitude she displayed, inward to the point of awkwardness, like a flower blooming in reverse. He hadn't pushed her to talk, thinking her impressions less important than those of Allmond himself.

Yesterday he had been expected. Today he was dropping in. It went against his sense of politeness, but sometimes the job was like that. He raised the solid brass ring and let it fall against the curlicued strike plate. That triggered the door chime that reminded Parrott of Masterpiece Theater. He waited on the porch, warm rays of the sun tickling the back of his neck. He was about to raise the knocker again when the door opened.

The same elderly gentleman who had ushered Parrott in yesterday greeted him. He was perfectly framed by the doorway, almost like a painting on the wall of a museum. His brown, wrinkled skin bespoke of heritage, age, and time in the sun, all mixed together. "How can I help you?" he asked in a neutral tone, neither warm nor cool.

Parrott remembered Ms. Carmichael's having called the man LeRoi, pronouncing it like "the king," not Leroy. Parrott held his identification at the man's eye level, chest level for Parrott. "I'd like to talk to Mr. Allmond," he said, "about the investigation into the stolen paintings."

"Mr. Allmond isn't in just now," LeRoi replied. "I don't expect him back until tomorrow some time."

Disappointed, but not surprised, Parrott continued, "Perhaps I could speak with Ms. Carmichael then?"

"Ms. Carmichael is in the studio, right now, giving an art lesson, I'm afraid. Why don't you leave me your card, and I'll make sure she calls you?"

Parrott glanced beyond the servant into the massive entry hall. Pristine and quiet, it reminded Parrott of a tomb. "Perhaps I could wait. Do you know how long she'll be?" He consulted his watch, irritated by the prospect of wasting time, but reluctant to leave empty-handed.

Consulting his own watch, the butler replied, "As you wish. The lesson should be over in a few minutes, but Ms. Carmichael usually stays a while to straighten up. My guess is she'll be back in fifteen minutes or so." LeRoi opened the door wider and motioned Parrott to enter the room to the left of the entrance. "Have a seat, Detective. May I get you a drink, some water, perhaps?"

"That would be nice," Parrott replied, wishing for some time alone in the opulent living room. "Water, no ice, please."

Almost before LeRoi departed, Parrott had his eye on the dozen or more paintings hanging in the room. This time he would examine each one. It would be interesting to find out whose paintings decked the home of the well-known artist and his artist girlfriend.

The afternoon sunlight highlighted a small landscape in an ornate frame on the grand piano in the corner. He would start there. He was no expert, but the pasture scene looked peaceful, and the artist must have used the tiniest brushes to get so much detail into such a small space. He squinted to read the signature at bottom right. M. Allmond. Melanie, maybe?

Parrott moved to where two walls met behind the piano, where a pair of oil portraits of a man in a tuxedo and a woman in a ball gown hung. Presumably they were relatives, perhaps Blake Allmond's deceased parents. Before he could check for the artists' signatures, he felt his cell phone vibrate. He reached into his jacket pocket and grabbed the phone, glancing to see who was calling.

When he saw the call was from Tonya, he knew he had to take it. She never called him while he was working.

Parrott swiped the face of the phone with his thumb and turned to face the corner, as if to mute the sound of his voice. "Tonya?" he whispered, his deep voice an octave higher than usual.

"Ollie," the voice wailed. "Can you come get me? Please, can you come get me?"

Parrott's mind raced, a million horrible thoughts of what might be wrong. "Where are you, Baby? What's wrong?"

"I'm at the Walmart Supercenter, over on Commons Drive. I passed out. They want to call an ambulance, but I don't want that. C-can you c-come?"

Parrott pulled a business card from his jacket pocket and scrawled on it, holding the phone to his ear all the while. He dropped the card onto the coffee table and let himself out. "Just leaving this house here," he muttered, as he jogged to his car, plopped behind the wheel, pushed the ignition button, and slammed the gearshift into drive. "I'm on my way." For now, paintings and artists and unavailable witnesses would have to wait.

Hearing the front door close behind the detective, Elle Carmichael appeared from the dining room on the opposite side of the house. She closed her eyes and uttered a sigh of relief. Slim and petite, she'd had no trouble hiding behind the wall while Parrott waited to talk to her for the second day in a row. Yesterday had been hard enough, but today—today, she just didn't have the strength. Hard enough making conversation with someone so vastly different—what did a fifty-one-year-old white Catholic woman have to say to a twenty-something black man at least two heads taller and half again as broad? Yesterday she had spent the better part of her afternoon teatime carting Parrott all over the house and grounds, trying to answer his questions about the stolen paintings. She had told Blake he owed her for that.

Blake had gone to New York for a dentist appointment and a meeting. He'd told her it was a dinner meeting, and it would be late before it was over. "I'll just stay in the city overnight. I'll be back here around noon tomorrow. Shall we go out for lunch at Piccolo Arancio?"

She adored the Harry's Bar Bellini and the grilled swordfish there. "Sure. I'll make the reservation. About one?"

"Fine," Blake replied, but he had been distracted. He was throwing papers into a briefcase. No need for a suitcase, since he had duplicates of everything in the New York condo. They'd kissed, a quick pressing of lips on lips, tasting less of the future than of the past.

Now Elle turned liquidy eyes onto LeRoi's sympathetic ones. "He's gone," she said, stating the obvious. She ran to the coffee table and grabbed the card. "Says he's had an emergency."

"Won't be long before he comes back. That one's full of spit and fire. The way he moved around here yesterday, not wasting a step. Like a free safety about to make a tackle."

The woman wiped at her face and sighed. "I hope he doesn't come back before Blake does. I'm not any good at talking to detectives."

"You can go on back to work now, Ollie," Tonya said. "I can manage." Her hands gripped her large handbag so tightly, her knuckles showed as pale circles on her tawny skin. "I promise I'll be all right." She was sitting on the edge of a metal chair padded in green vinyl, head held high and staring ahead, determined to be strong.

Parrott argued. "I'm not going to leave you until you've been checked out." He sat back in the adjacent chair, arms crossed at the elbow and legs akimbo. They sat in the cheerless ER waiting room at the VA Medical Center, alone except for an unkempt man, sitting by a young woman, perhaps his daughter.

"Keep your voice down, Ollie. People will think something is wrong with me, and it isn't." Tonya thought of the relaxation techniques she had learned in her training. She had been the only woman to stick it out through the brutal training to be a SEAL, something seventy-five percent of the men couldn't even do. She closed her eyes and focused inward, imagining the top of her head, her forehead, eyebrows, cheeks, nose, mouth, and jaw slackening to make way for a cool, serene river to flow through her head and neck and into her body.

"At least this VA doesn't have the strong antiseptic smell of a hospital," Parrott said, causing Tonya to lose track of the flowing river. He glanced at his watch. "I'd better call in to let Chief Schrik know where I am."

"You do that," Tonya replied. She really could deal with this herself. In fact, if no one called her in soon, she would just get up and leave. Sitting around in the VA hospital was not her idea of a way to spend a beautiful autumn afternoon.

As Parrott headed for the exit, Tonya leaned her head back and tried to recreate the peaceful scene. In Afghanistan the image of flowing water had always brought comfort, maybe because scenes like that were non-existent in the dry, harsh desert. Tonya pictured herself in a bathing suit, poised above the cool, deep river, taking a deep breath and readying her body for a perfect dive.

"Mrs. Parrott?" A short woman with graying hair escaping from a bun and a pair of glasses resting on her ample bosom held out a hand.

Tonya fought the impulse to look around for Ollie's mother. She still thought of herself as Tonya Collins. She clasped the woman's hand and rose from her seat and her reverie.

"Come with me, my dear," said the woman, whose nametag said, "Connie S." We'll go right into this room, so you can speak with the physician's assistant." She pointed to a tiny cubicle encircled by a privacy curtain.

"My husband—"

"Here I come," Parrott said, appearing from around the corner. "I'm this lady's husband," he said, flashing a toothpaste smile in Connie's direction. He held Tonya's elbow as the two of them entered the small space.

"Excuse me for asking, but I must make sure," Connie said. "Is it your wish to have your husband in the room with you when you see the PA?"

A muscle in Tonya's eye twitched, something she hoped her husband hadn't noticed. Being here in this situation, admitting she might need help, was more uncomfortable than crouching behind the wall of an enemy's hideout on the other side of the world. At least there she had felt brave and confident.

She understood Ollie's desire to protect her, his need to prove himself an attentive husband. She liked it that he was putting her before everything, even his job. But at the same time, she couldn't picture herself talking to the PA in front of him. The thought of it made her feel naked and vulnerable, as if her skin had been flayed to the bone.

Tonya looked from the woman to her husband and back. "I don't want to hurt your feelings, Ollie. I really don't. But would you mind sitting in the waiting room?" She mustered a mouth-only smile.

Parrott looked down at his hands, clasped loosely on his lap, and then met his wife's eyes. "No problem," he replied, and he stood to go. "I'll be waiting. Take as long as you need."

As Parrott retreated to the waiting room, Tonya caught a glimpse of the shine in his eyes.

CHAPTER 7

Back at the station, Parrott tapped on the doorframe of Chief Schrik's office. The chief was perusing a stack of papers. A half-eaten bowl of chili with crushed saltines sat on the desk, its spicy smell long merged with the coffee and piney cleaning smells of the station.

"Oh, hi, Parrott. Come on in and sit down." He took a long look at the detective before reaching into his mini-fridge for a cold bottle of water and handing it over.

"Read my mind, Chief. It's been a long day." He unscrewed the top and swigged a third of it down. He couldn't remember the last time he'd eaten.

"I'm just looking over a batch of paperwork brought over this morning by your friend at the Brandywine River Museum of Art. Info about Allmond." He passed the documents to the detective.

Parrott flipped through them. He'd get a better look later. "Sorry about this afternoon, Chief. I hate taking time from the job, but I had to take my wife to the doctor."

Schrik gazed at the detective under overgrown eyebrows. "She okay?"

"According to her, she is. I'm not convinced, though." Parrott rubbed his eyes. If he didn't get some sleep soon, he might have to see a doctor, himself. "Anyway, I'm glad Thea came through with the info. Anything good?"

"Bio, works, shows, techniques, even a few recent articles about the missing paintings. They do a good job with records over there. Allmond was more well-known than I thought. Matter of fact, you'll love this…guess who owns an original Allmond painting?"

Parrott shrugged and shifted in his chair. He still wasn't used to all of the wealth here in Brandywine Valley. To his way of thinking a print wasn't that different from a lithograph or an oil painting. It was all just a matter of the size of the pocketbook.

Schrik hesitated. "Your buddies, the Campbells. Preston Phillips' cousin? Something called 'Iridescent Bridge' hanging at their place here in Brandywine Valley."

"I'll get over there, see if they'll talk to me. I'm not sure how welcoming they'll be after last year. Bad memories." Parrott set the papers down and returned to the chilled water. The cool liquid lifted his drooping spirits like rain for a parched sunflower.

"Yeah, but none of them of *your* making. In fact, if it hadn't been for you, Phillips' death might have gone unsolved. They should be grateful." Schrik flicked the paper clip he'd substituted for a cigar. Parrot wished he'd get rid of it, but then it had kept Schrik smoke-free for almost a year now. "Find out anything useful this morning at the Allmond residence?"

"No, the girlfriend was in the studio. I was waiting, but that's when I got the call from Tonya and had to leave." Parrott hated to disappoint his boss. Schrik had hung in with him through rough times before, and he didn't want to lose any of the cred he'd stockpiled with him. "I did see something interesting, though. Small painting with a signature of M. Allmond. Think it could be the sister's?"

Schrik leaned back, hands behind his head, elbows out. "Talent running in the family?"

Parrott sat up straighter, remembering what the art dealer had told him about Melanie Allmond. "The guy I interviewed at the Rue Moderne told me the parents disowned her for eloping with someone beneath them. If that's true, would they have kept her painting? Or did the brother keep it? Or maybe Allmond's wife's name began with an 'm,' and she painted."

"Nope," Schrik said, flipping through pages of a file folder. "Wife's name was Susan."

"Well, none of this may have anything to do with the art theft anyway," Parrott replied, standing to go. "The case is starting to feel as dry as a snake's skin in the desert." He thumped the parcel of information from the museum and made for the door. "Maybe there'll be something exciting in here."

"Be careful what you wish for," Schrik called out, as Parrott disappeared into the hallway.

CHAPTER 8

Tonya was sitting at the kitchen table, legs crossed and tapping the air in rhythm to "Killing Me Softly." The crock pot emitted savory aromas from a pot roast that was almost ready, but Tonya was in another world, the world of Blake Allmond.

After today's fainting spell and visit to the VA hospital, Tonya felt guilty. She knew she had hurt her husband's feelings, though she hadn't meant to. She just wasn't ready to jeopardize their relationship by having Ollie seeing and hearing whatever the physician's assistant might say to her. Ollie admired and loved her for her strength. She was afraid to tarnish his opinion of her.

The PA had told her different. "Your husband obviously cares for you a great deal. Part of being married is sharing the good and not-so-good things. If you let him in, you'll see. It will lighten your load."

But Tonya couldn't do that, not yet. So she'd sent Ollie back to work, and she'd listened to what the PA said. She'd expected to get a prescription for some happy pills, and that would be that, but apparently it didn't work that way. Pills were used for some cases, but not as a first resort. Today they would do a clinician-administered screening, called CAPS-5, to evaluate for PTSD. After that was scored, they would have a better idea of what therapies would be best for treating Tonya's symptoms.

It sounded pretty scientific, routine, even, so Tonya agreed, and, all in all, it wasn't too terrible. Afterwards, she made an appointment for Wednesday, and she took a taxi back home. She checked on the roast, doing nicely, and she turned on some Lauryn Hill. Some of the guys in Afghanistan had thought Tonya resembled the hip hop diva, but Tonya couldn't see it. She liked her voice, though.

Tonya decided the best way to make it up to Ollie for calling him away from work, then excluding him from the visit with the PA, would be to help him with the art heist case.

That's why she was bent over the kitchen table, propped on an elbow, flipping through screens on the laptop, looking at Blake Allmond's life and works, trying to find the kind of information nugget that would elicit one of her husband's "you-are-just-incredible" hugs.

So far she had read numerous articles detailing Mr. Allmond's life, his painting style, the place he had carved for himself in the Brandywine Valley artists' colony. Unlike Victor Lockwood and other painters of the region who had established a pantheon of realistic paintings of rural subjects, Allmond's works reflected the interplay between light and dark used by the European Impressionists. Tonya's minor in art history provided a backdrop against which the details of Allmond's technical skills stood out. She couldn't help being impressed. His paintings sure seemed like "museum quality" to her, though she found critical reviews at both extremes.

Tonya paused in her research, standing up to stretch. Maybe a snack would do her good, replenish her energy. She rummaged through the refrigerator before settling on some carrot and celery sticks, which she dipped into the jar of peanut butter. She'd better not let Ollie catch her eating out of the jar like this, neat as he was.

When she returned to the laptop, she found an article about Allmond's personal life. Orphaned at the age of twenty-two, Allmond had inherited the 9,000 square foot home in Brandywine Valley, where he set up a studio and gave art lessons. Aspiring artists from all over America had come to learn from him. His preference for painting scenes with shining water in them led to the branding of the group of artists as the Brandywine Puddlers. He married one of the Puddlers, Susan Maycomb, and the couple had two children, a boy and a girl. When Susan and the children were killed in a car accident, Allmond went into seclusion and ceased painting for a decade.

Tonya shivered at the thought of all the troubles Blake Allmond had endured. Losing his parents, losing his wife and kids. It made a little thing like PTSD seem trivial. All of that was long ago and probably not helpful to Ollie's case, though.

She decided to search for "Brandywine Valley artists." An article in *The Hunt* magazine about the prolific artists of the Brandywine Valley caught her attention. Allmond was mentioned, and there was a photo taken last June. The artist was standing next to a petite woman with striking features. A large canvas painting of fawns bathing in a brook stood at his feet, leaning against his knees. The positioning of the deer reminded Tonya of Botticelli's three graces in the painting *Primavera*. She wondered whether that was intentional. Tonya was mesmerized by the faraway look in the artist's eyes.

The caption listed the woman as Elle Carmichael. Maybe she was the girlfriend Ollie had mentioned. Whatever their relationship, they didn't seem to be lovey-dovey in the photograph. Next she googled Elle Carmichael, crossing her fingers there would be information listed. *Wow*, she thought, as a page full of entries popped up. *So she was an artist, too.* She clicked open one of the articles, but before she had a chance to read it, the scrape of the key in the kitchen door lock announced Parrott's arrival.

Tonya ran to the door, arms outstretched for a hug. Parrott grabbed her around the waist and swung her around in a dizzying circle.

"What a greeting," he said, after three deep kisses and as many long hugs.

Tonya broke the embrace and walked over to Horace's cage. She could swear the cockatiel was leering at them. "I'm sorry about this afternoon."

"What about this afternoon?" He followed her to the birdcage and opened the door. "Hello, Horace. Bet you're glad as I am to have Tonya back."

The bird said something like, "You bet," and hopped onto Parrott's wrist.

"You know, about the fainting spell and the meeting with the PA." Tonya busied herself with testing the sweet potatoes and green beans for doneness. "Want a taste of the roast beef?"

"Let me put Horace back and wash my hands first," Parrott replied. "Mmm, that's good, and I am hun-gry." He moved the laptop to the coffee table, then cleared off the table and wiped it down with a towelette. Then he put out napkins and silverware, his evening job. "Care to tell me what the PA said? Do you think she can help?"

"She had me to do some type of psychological testing. It felt creepy, but I complied." Tonya had her back to Parrott. She was removing the roast from the cooker and placing it on the carving board. "Want to do the honors?" She handed him the knife by the handle.

Parrott started in on the roast. It was so moist, the silky layers of meat just rolled off the knife. "So what's next?"

"We'll see when the results come back. Maybe tomorrow." Tonya ladled the beans and potatoes into serving bowls and set them on the table. "Anyway, I didn't mean to hurt your feelings. I just need to do this by myself."

"Okay. No worries," Parrott said. "How about we forget about it and eat this fantastic meal?"

The couple sat down and started eating. After his second helping, Parrott told Tonya about the painting he'd seen at the Allmond house, and the pile of information he'd brought home from the station to review that night. Tonya told him about her internet research on Blake Allmond.

Parrott reached across the table for his wife's hand and squeezed. "That was so nice of you. Did you find anything interesting?"

"Probably stuff you knew already, but I was just researching the girlfriend when you came in. Let me show you." Tonya brought the laptop over and set it on the kitchen table next to Ollie's now-empty plate. "She is an artist in her own right," she said, pointing to the article.

Parrott squinted slightly as he scrolled through the article. "Oh, my gosh," he said, "look at this."

Tonya came around and stood behind Parrott's shoulder. She couldn't believe what she saw. "Well, that's pretty weird," she whispered.

Parrott put his arm around Tonya's waist and pulled her close. "Who would've ever guessed it? Blake Allmond's live-in girlfriend used to be—"

They looked at each other and finished the sentence in unison. "—A nun."

CHAPTER 9

Allmond went to his attorney's office, as planned, the next day at one to sign the papers. While in the waiting room of the boutique New York law firm, he strolled around, critiquing the artwork on the walls. Maybe his old buddy would like an original Allmond for the office. He made a mental note of the pear, gray, and lemon chiffon color scheme carried out in the furniture and carpet.

Griffith welcomed him with a bear hug and escorted him to the conference room, decorated in the same muted colors and textures. Allmond declined the offer of coffee and chocolate-dipped biscotti. The heavy thoughts on his mind would've prevented digestion anyway.

"Well," the lawyer began, as he opened a Redweld file and removed three official-looking documents in sturdy blue coverings, "I've prepared the new will exactly as you specified."

"Thanks for doing this on such short notice. I'll be glad to pay extra."

Griffith shook his wheat-colored head. Allmond was reminded of a lion, who, even in his fifties, had strength and confidence. Gary had always been the most stable of them, the leader of the pride.

"No need to pay me extra. I'm happy to help. I do want to point out, though, there's no such thing as an uncontestable will in this day and age. And with the size of your estate, I'd say the likelihood of your nephew's contesting the terms of this will is almost certain."

A stabbing in his gut momentarily paralyzed Allmond. "But I thought you said leaving a modest bequest to him would prove my intent."

"Yes," the lawyer said, pointing to the paragraph where Alexander Vargas was mentioned by name. "This paragraph proves you didn't overlook the relationship or forget to leave something to him. He can't allege that. But you know he won't be satisfied with a mere million, when so many millions are being bequeathed to others."

"Serves him right for meddling in my affairs one time too many. He and that no-good-girlfriend of his don't deserve to inherit even the one million." Allmond slumped in the client chair, thinking of how cruel a task it was for him, leaving millions of dollars to people who were not direct descendants. Would his parents have approved? Given the fact that they had disowned their own daughter, he thought they would understand.

"Oh, yeah," Allmond said, straightening up in the chair. "I almost forgot. Can you put this envelope in the file with the new will? It's to go to Elle upon my death."

"Been watching lawyer shows on TV, have you?" Gary asked, his eyebrow raised. "I can put it with the file, and hopefully many years will go by before she receives it, but you realize whatever is in the letter doesn't have the force of the law behind it."

"Understood, and maybe I'm being overly dramatic, but there are things I want her to know when the time comes."

Griffith stood and patted his friend on the shoulder. "Okay, pal. Will do. And, if you don't have any other questions, I'll gather the witnesses, and you can sign."

After signing the will, Allmond called Elle to say he was going to spend another night in the city. It was the last night of "La Boheme" at the Met, and he wanted to see it. Opera was one of his indulgences she didn't enjoy, so she hadn't pressed him. She wouldn't ask him about it, either. One of the things he enjoyed about his relationship with Elle was her trusting and easy-going nature. When he was at home in Brandywine, she was enough for him, but when he stayed over in the city, he needed more. If he had pangs of guilt for lying to her, at least they were assuaged by the knowledge he would make it all up to her in the end.

On the way back to his condo, Allmond stopped in at the specialty wine shop on Madison Avenue. Tonight he would celebrate having foiled those who had trespassed against him. He purchased four bottles of his all-time favorite, Chateau Lafitte Rothschild, 1982. It was becoming harder and harder to find this wine and vintage, so he wanted to enjoy the libation while he could.

It would go down nicely with the tournedos of boeuf au poivre he would fix for two. Though it wasn't cold enough yet for a fire, he might turn up the air conditioning and build one anyway. He'd set the table with the Venetian linens that had never been used and the fragrant Lady of the Night orchids from his bedroom. Last night had been amazing, but tonight he would pull out all the stops.

He tingled with the anticipation of all the pleasures ahead. Too bad this would have to be goodbye.

CHAPTER 10

After the results of the CAPS-5 screening came back, Vena, the PA from the Veterans' Hospital, called to give Tonya the news. She did, indeed, suffer from PTSD. Though it wasn't a surprise diagnosis, hearing the words made Tonya's face grow hot with shame. She had tried to answer the questions to avoid being labeled, but either she wasn't smart enough, or the test was foolproof.

"So what now?" Tonya asked the PA. Maybe they would give her something to stop the nightmares and the fainting spells.

"Well, I think you might benefit from some sessions with a therapist. Many of our patients have had success with Alice Ruff. She is a former soldier, too." Vena's tone of voice soothed Tonya's rancor and even gave her hope.

"Okay," she agreed. "I'm willing to give her a try."

Now Tonya was leaning on the arm of the sage-colored therapy couch, running her fingers through the braids of her hair, absentmindedly counting the beads, as she listened to the therapist's questions. So far none had been too intrusive or upsetting, but she guessed the lady was going to break her in gently, like a recalcitrant pony.

Tonya answered in a softer-than-normal voice, offering details about her tour of duty, her family, her marriage, her career plans, benign bits of information with no emotion attached. Like a first date, this session was full of polite manners on both sides.

What was different, though, was Alice's asking all the questions and Tonya's giving all of the answers. Tonya wondered whether Alice had been in a war zone, if she had herself been diagnosed with PTSD, what made her become a therapist after retiring from service. It was frustrating not to be able to ask, not to be able to turn the spotlight away from her own problems, even for a second. She caught herself squirming, and she could tell Alice noticed that, too.

Forty minutes flew by, and Alice started wrapping up—a second appointment, some homework (to keep a bedside diary of sleeping times each day, recording when nightmares occurred and what their content was).

"Am I a candidate for meds?" Tonya asked, not sure whether she wanted the answer to be yes or no.

"Not just yet, and even if I thought so, I wouldn't be the one to prescribe. I'm just a therapist, not a doctor." Alice's eyes crinkled as she replied. It was a near-smile, radiating kindness. "I do have another suggestion for you to think about, though. Some of my patients have had luck with art therapy. You know, paints, clay, that kind of thing. Self-expression through art is one way to manage difficult feelings."

Tonya thought of her art history minor at Syracuse. She had always liked the idea of drawing and painting, pounding clay, even. "How does that work? Do you give the sessions here? Are they in a group or individual?"

Alice laughed, a musical syllable floating in the air between them. "I'm probably the least artistic person you'll ever meet. We have a list of several art therapy instructors in the area for you to choose from. Most of them offer group sessions, as well as individual ones. Your insurance covers half of the cost, but obviously, individual sessions are more."

Tonya had been thinking about looking for a job, but maybe she should hold off for a while. Art therapy appealed to her, at least to try it, and appointments twice a week with Alice—she might have a chance at lifting the yoke of PTSD, after all. "Okay, I'll take the list of instructors and give this some thought."

"That's good to hear, Tonya. Every little step you take to help yourself brings you closer to regaining a normal life."

Tonya left the office armed with receipts, some reading material about PTSD, an appointment card, and the list of art therapy instructors. It wasn't until much later that she realized one of the names on the list was Blake Allmond's girlfriend.

CHAPTER 11

Alexander arrived a few minutes after seven, only to find Veronica standing behind the door wearing the red Victoria's Secret ensemble he had given her last Valentine's Day. The door was cracked a few inches, but the chain was hooked.

"Let me in?" he asked. The weight of last night's hangover was finally lifting, and he was ready for love. The outfit was a good sign.

"What's the password, Chachi?" The pout in her voice spoke volumes.

"You know I hate it when you call me that," Alexander replied. He could smell her cologne, and it gave him an instant erection. "Just open up—please?"

"Uh-uh-uh, Chachi. Password first." Her throaty laugh was annoying.

"*Hombre*," he almost shouted. "Now let me in, before I break this stupid chain from the door. What he loved about Veronica was also what he hated—she was never a sure thing.

Now, as she slid the bolt and chain open, she batted her eyelashes and moved aside for him to enter the shabby apartment. Just one bedroom, one bath, a small kitchen-dinette-living area, the place might have been cozy if someone would have invested a little time and money into it, but right now, Alexander wasn't thinking of cozy. He was thinking of how he could get Veronica to do her exotic pole dance with the bedpost.

"Well, Chachi, what do you have to tell me?" Veronica leaned forward, showing abundant cleavage, gleaming with bath oil.

Alexander took a handful and squeezed, leaning in for a long, hot kiss. When he came up for air, he said, "What I have to tell you is how amazingly exquisite you look today, how you make my heart sing." He put his arms around her as if to dance, and began moving toward the bedroom.

"Uh-uh-uh, Chachi, not yet. First you must tell me what happened with your uncle. What did he think of our idea for the costume business?" Veronica squeezed out of the waltzing embrace and plopped down on the vinyl recliner. "Business before pleasure."

He'd been afraid of this. Veronica could be quite stubborn, and she knew how irresistible she was to him. It was her ultimate weapon. He sighed and sat on the ratty sofa across from her.

"Okay. He wasn't interested in investing in a costume business. He turned me down."

"That's it? You didn't persuade him? You didn't make it attractive for him? Oh, Chachi, I'm so disappointed in you." She cast her eyes downward, the black lashes sitting on her cheeks like soft caterpillars. Alexander thought he saw tears brimming beneath them.

"For God's sake, stop calling me 'Chachi.' I hate being referred to as a little boy."

"Then stop acting like one," Veronica snapped. "You had a very easy job to do last night. All you had to do was get your uncle, your mother's precious baby brother, to give you a pittance, a pittance of what he is worth. But no, he tells you no, and you just accept that as an answer? You gave up too easy. You should have been per-sis-tent." She slapped her palm with each syllable.

"I did try to convince him. I gave him all of the arguments we planned together, but he kept saying, 'I'm an artist, not a businessman. I'm just not interested.'"

"Not int-e-res-ted?" She slapped again. "We don't need him to be interested. We just need his mo-ney. Did you tell him the Mummers would be our first clients?"

"Yes, and even that didn't impress him. He wondered what made me interested in a costume business, when I didn't know the first thing about the textile industry. And—and I mentioned your

background as a seamstress, your experience in theater, and—"
Alexander put his face in his hands.

Veronica stood and lifted a fuzzy coverlet from the sofa and wrapped it around herself. "What did he say then?"

Alexander's gaze fell on the open window, where he heard a neighborhood dog barking. A sour taste crept into his throat, and he turned back to look at his girlfriend, covered in the plaid blanket. "Veronica, tell me something. Have you been snooping on my uncle's bank accounts?"

Veronica dropped the afghan, exposing most of her left breast in the process. "Why do you ask such a thing?'

"Just tell me the truth. Did you or did you not look at Blake Allmond's bank accounts from your computer at the bank?" He realized he was holding his breath.

"There's no way anyone could tell. I've been very careful."

"Evidently, not careful enough, my love. The bank president at the Manhattan branch has noticed 'excessive hits,' or some such activity from the South Philly branch. He's my uncle's good friend and told him all about it. Told him they are protecting him, watching his accounts." Alexander ignored Veronica's squeal and went on. "You'll be lucky if you aren't fired for this."

Veronica's mouth twitched, as if she were going to say something, then thought better of it. Then she thrust her chin out and said, "Okay, so what if I looked? I found out a lot. Your uncle is way wealthier than I ever could have imagined. He's got dozens of different accounts. His money is earning money each month, more than you and I could earn together in a lifetime." She swallowed. "And what's more, there are no joint tenants on any of the accounts. You are his closest relative, Chachi. When he dies, you will be a very, very wealthy man." She opened her arms, holding the afghan out like wings, and she swooped over to where Alexander was sitting and wrapped her arms around him, afghan and all.

Alexander stood and pushed her away. "That's where you're wrong, my love." His voice gained a bitterness that hadn't been there before. "My uncle has put two and two together. He saw through the costume shop scheme, and he knew I had a girlfriend who worked at Lyons Bank in South Philly. Because of this 'interest in his accounts,' he is changing his will."

"Changing his will? But how could he? He loved your mother, his sister. Half of his money rightfully should have been hers, should be yours. Why—"

Alexander spoke through his teeth. "He has every right to change his will. My mother abandoned her inheritance when she married my father. The only right I have to any of that money is through my uncle's goodwill, which, thanks to you, has evaporated. You shouldn't have done it. You will probably lose your job over this, too."

Veronica collapsed on the sofa, her head in her hands and loud sobs piercing the air. "I thought I was helping you, Chachi. I love you, and I wanted to help you become rich."

Alexander glanced at his beautiful lover, curled up into a wet, sniffling ball of emotions, and his heart yielded to pity. "If you love me, then stop calling me 'Chachi,' once and for all. We'll get through this together, and we haven't really lost anything that we ever had." He patted her on the shoulders and back, and soon they embraced and held each other tight.

A few hours later, when dusk filled the room, and they crawled out of the messy bedsheets, Alexander murmured, "Love is all I need. My mother didn't care about money, and neither do I."

As he headed for the bathroom, he didn't hear Veronica's mumbled response, "You might not need money, but I do."

CHAPTER 12

Parrott was on the road to Bucolia, the country mansion of Caroline and John E. Campbell, the site of Preston Phillips' demise and the beginning of Parrott's own first murder investigation. His windows were down, and he felt at one with the scenery. The leaves had morphed into a panoply of colors, and the morning sun backlit the landscape with dramatic beauty. A tinge of coolness in the air hinted at the coming of winter. Last year this time Parrott was a single man, waiting for a substantial case to investigate, naïve about the way rich people lived.

Now the thought of seeing the Campbells brought a surprising amount of familiarity, if not pleasantness. How ironic that they had a Blake Allmond painting at Bucolia. They had certainly been friendly when Parrott set the appointment to see the painting and to talk about it. Maybe Mrs. Campbell would even offer him those delicious Madeleine cookies, as well.

Before he reached the winding path to their home, his cellphone rang. The word, "Ma" popped up on the screen. Parrott steered the car with his legs as he enabled the Bluetooth, and rolled up the windows so he could hear better.

"'Morning, Ma. Beautiful day, isn't it?"

Exhaling, Cora Parrott said, "What's goin' on with Tonya?"

Parrott's heart skipped a beat. Tonya had been in the shower when he'd sneaked in a kiss and left for work just a half hour ago. "What d'ya mean?"

"I just called her to chat about Thanksgiving. I know it's early, but I like to get started ahead of time. I thought Tonya and I had a good relationship, and all, but—"

Parrott suppressed a groan. Tonya would not want her new mother-in-law knowing all about the PTSD, but in his experience, there was no hiding anything from his mother. She was clairvoyant when it came to reading people, especially him. "You *do* have a good relationship, Ma. What happened?"

"Well, first she called me, 'Cora.' I'd asked her to call me Ma, just like you. My friends call me Cora, but she ain't friends, she's family."

Parrott detected a snort, and he pictured a mama elephant readying herself for a confrontation. "She *is* family, Ma, and she's very fond of you. Maybe it's hard for her to call anyone but her own mother, 'Ma.' She took her mother's death really hard."

"But that's been years ago. I'd think she'd be glad to have a new mother, 'specially with holiday times comin' up soon. I no sooner brought up Thanksgiving than she cut me off and asked if she could call me later. Said she had an art class to go to, and she was running late."

Parrott was approaching the turn to Bucolia. He would soon have to end the call, as well. "Don't take it personally, Ma. I know Tonya wouldn't hurt your feelings for the world. She has a lot of respect for you. She probably really was running late, and today *was* her first art class."

"What kind of art class is she taking, anyway? It just seems odd to me. Nobody I know takes art classes unless'n they're retired or disabled or somethin'. I thought she was thinking about gettin' a new degree, not fritterin' away her time in an art class."

Parrott feared the way this conversation was going. "Listen, Ma. Tonya needs some time after being in Afghanistan all those years. I'm supporting her in taking some time off, and you should, too. I know she'd appreciate it, and maybe she'll get around to calling you Ma one of these days, as well."

Parrott drew up in the circular driveway at Bucolia and came to a stop. Before he could cut off the engine, he heard his mother say, "Sounds like you just got where you are going, son. I'll talk to you again soon."

"Love you, Ma," he replied.

"Love you, too."

A pumpkin, purple chrysanthemums, some ears of dried corn, and an assortment of colorful squash graced the stoop outside of Bucolia. Parrott put away his thoughts about his mother and Tonya and Thanksgiving and rang the doorbell. So much of this job required him to compartmentalize.

Instead of a servant, Caroline Campbell opened the door and stood, smiling. Neatly dressed and poised, she was a perfect picture of the landed gentry. The disdain Parrott had once felt for the Campbells and their friends had eroded long ago, but remnants of awe surfaced.

"Welcome, Detective," Caro said, extending her hand warmly. "It's good to see you again."

Parrott almost said, "And under better circumstances this time," but decided not to remind her of the sadness surrounding her cousin's death the previous year. Instead he nodded and thanked her, as she led him to the family room and offered him a seat across from the spotless fireplace. The room had been redecorated.

"John E. will join us in a few minutes," Caro said. "Can I get you some coffee?"

"Thank you, ma'am," Parrott replied. "I take it black."

"I remembered that," Caro said with a Mona Lisa smile. She left him alone to get the coffee.

Parrott wasn't sure whether his presence was more of a nuisance or a visit, whether he was viewed as family enemy or family friend, but he perked up when Caro returned with a tray of steaming black coffee and some miniature cream puffs.

Footsteps on the basement stairs signaled the approach of John E. He entered the room, a little grayer around the temples, but otherwise unchanged. Parrott stood and extended his hand.

"Hello, Parrott," John E. said, gripping the detective's hand. "I hear you're on the Allmond art heist case. Good for you."

Caro turned and said, "Oh, there you are, John E. Shall I get you some coffee?"

"No, thanks, dear. Come and sit down." John E. patted the loveseat next to him.

Parrott had never liked eating or drinking alone, but it would be rude not to indulge after his hostess had gone to the trouble of serving him, so he picked up the coffee mug and took a swallow. Probably Keurig-brewed, it was delicious, strong and woodsy, and almost scalding, just the way he liked it. "Great coffee," he said, and popped a pastry into his mouth.

Caro scooted back into the loveseat and nestled into the arc made by her husband's arm. "So, we were distressed to hear about the paintings stolen from Blake's studio. We've only recently purchased this one," she said, pointing to the large squarish landscape on the wall across from her. Framed in silver, the subjects of the painting were a nest of robins in a willow tree, looking down at a rock-filled stream of silvery-pink and blue water. The birds'-eye perspective and the virtual shine of the bed of water made for a stunning effect, even to Parrott's relatively unschooled eye.

"It's quite beautiful," Parrott commented, taking another swig of coffee and setting the mug down on a napkin. He could see now that the room's new furniture had been chosen to complement the colors in the painting, and for a second, he flashed back on his mother's comment about Tonya's having signed up for an art class.

"We think so," John E. replied. "Of course, we've known Blake for years, followed his career. He's known for the way he portrays water—he started that when he was quite young—but it's only lately I think he's hit his stride as an artist."

"Why do you say that?" Parrott asked. Rupert Brooks had seemed to think the water technique was Allmond's main claim to fame.

"It's just one man's opinion," he replied, exchanging glances with his wife, "or one couple's opinion, but we think Allmond is moving on from the typical Brandywine landscape motif. This painting, for example, is not just a depiction of nature. The birds' perspective could represent something Platonic, something other-worldly." John E. chuckled a little. "Guess I sound like an art history professor, don't I?"

"I see what you mean," Parrott said. He took out his iPad and opened it to the questions he had prepared. "Can you tell me where and when you purchased this painting?"

Caro chimed in. "We bought it in Kennett Square at the Rue Moderne. It was sometime last spring, wasn't it?" She looked at her husband for confirmation. "Do you want me to give you the exact date?"

"If it wouldn't be too much trouble," Parrott replied. "Is that Rupert Brooks's place?"

Caro nodded, apparently impressed at Parrott's familiarity with the art gallery.

"Do you mind telling me what you paid for the painting? It's relevant to the investigation, or I wouldn't ask."

John E. scratched at his goatee and looked at Caro before replying, "I can get you a copy of the appraisal we submitted to our insurance company, if you'd like. I think it was upwards of $28,000."

"Is $28,000 what you paid for it, then?" Parrott asked, remembering Brooks's comment about the expected increase in value of "museum-quality paintings."

John E. gave an indulgent smile, as if Parrott were a freshman student in his art class. "New art appraisals are the same as the purchase price. Fine art usually appreciates, so re-appraisals usually show a jump in value."

Parrott thought about reasons people insure art. "So how much might you expect the value to go up in, say, a year's time?"

"Maybe ten to fifteen percent," John E. replied, "but it's not what you're probably thinking. People wouldn't intentionally buy art to have it stolen or damaged, so they could cash in on the insurance policy. First, that would be illegal, and who would risk that? Secondly, you could only do that once and get away with it, and why do it with a painting worth as little as $28,000? Thirdly, the insured amount represents a replacement value, but if the art appreciates, the owners won't recover full value unless they reappraise often."

"I understand," Parrott replied. He reeled from the comment that $28,000 wouldn't be that valuable. He picked up the coffee mug and drained it. "Let's change the subject a bit, if you don't mind. You mentioned you've known Blake Allmond for years. When did you meet him, and how?"

"Didn't the Bakers introduce us to Allmond?" John E. asked his wife.

Caro replied, "Yes, it was back when you were teaching at Princeton. Allmond is a distant cousin of Andrea's, I think. Stan invited us all to a dinner party when Blake was there."

"Approximately what year might that have been?" Parrott was mentally calculating the Campbells' ages against Allmond's. Allmond was certainly younger.

"Oh, somewhere around the late '70's or early '80s. We were in our early thirties, I think."

"Did Allmond bring his wife to those parties?" Parrott asked.

Caro and John E. looked at each other, and Caro shrugged. "It's a long time ago, but I don't actually think so. But—"

Parrott picked up on the odd expressions. "Is there some reason Allmond wouldn't have been there with his wife?"

John E. took over. "Maybe his wife was with him. Far be it from me to judge anyone else's marriage, and I don't like to engage in gossip. Especially now the poor woman is dead. It's just tragic."

Parrott was intrigued but decided not to probe too much. After all, Allmond was the victim of this robbery, not the perpetrator. "Perhaps people in the art world, even here in Brandywine Valley, lead sort of unconventional lives."

John E. and Caro exchanged glances again. "Unconventional is a good word, I'd say," was John E.'s reply.

"One more thing before I go," Parrott said. "I've been gathering information about the Brandywine River artists, and it seems to me, compared to Victor Lockwood and his father, Blake Allmond's paintings have far lesser value, although Allmond's water technique is much admired and copied by the Lockwoods. Do either of you have any theories about that?"

More exchange of glances. This time, Caro replied. "It's my opinion Allmond's paintings exceed those of either Lockwood in both technique and in meaningful subject matter. Of course, it's a matter of taste, and a painting's value is often relative to the way it resonates with the potential purchaser. I've always felt the senior Lockwood's paintings are inconsistent. Some are outstanding, but others, just so-so."

"Did the younger Lockwood and Allmond know each other, then?" Parrott asked.

"Oh, yes," Caro said. "Allmond studied under Lockwood, but if you ask me, the pupil in this case did more to teach the teacher."

John E. squeezed his wife's knee, and Parrott made a mental note to look into the relationship and influence of Lockwood and Allmond on each other.

Driving back to the station, Parrott reviewed what he had learned from the Campbells—about appraisals and values of individual pieces of artwork, about Allmond's relatives, his marriage, and his relationship with the famous elder artist. None of it was clear yet, but he had some ideas for further study.

He was almost in the station parking lot when he got a call from Chief Schrik. "Where are you?"

"Two minutes away. What's up?"

"Get in here quick," Schrik hollered. "I just got word from NYPD. Blake Allmond's dead."

CHAPTER 13

Parrott's mind was zooming faster than mc2 even as he observed the speed limit on his way back to the office. Allmond's death ratcheted up his interest in the art heist case. A vision of Allmond's girlfriend, Elle Carmichael, so shy and small, floated before his eyes. She would take this hard. He was kicking himself that he hadn't interviewed the artist in person, not that he hadn't tried. Now, depending on the circumstances of the death, solving the art theft may become way more important. The thought filled him with energy.

He parked and sprinted into the station, winking and waving at Lucretia through the plate glass separating the public entrance from the hallway to the offices. He went straight to Schrik's. The chief was doing laps in the tight oval track near the window, where footsteps had worn a path in the carpet. The pacing alone spoke volumes.

"So Allmond was killed?"

Schrik stopped and nodded. "Shot at close range. Body was found staged on the bench in his shower. One of those fancy deals with rain, sun, steam, music."

"You said NYPD. I knew Allmond had a place there."

"Yeah. A condo in Gramercy Park."

"When did the call come in?"

"About a half hour ago. Police were called late this morning. Vietnamese housekeeper walked in and heard the shower running. She was expecting the place to be empty, as usual. Got the shock of her life when she saw the vic, naked and wet and a hole in his chest."

"ETD?"

"Not yet. Hot water from one of those tankless, perpetual heaters. Kept cooling at bay."

Parrott dropped into one of the chairs facing Schrik's desk. He rubbed the sides of his head. "I gotta tell you, Chief. I hate to hear about anyone dying before his time, especially when foul play is involved. But I'd be lying if I didn't admit having a murder—not just an art theft—on our hands is making a big old light to shine in my brain. I'm itching to find out more."

"Wait a minute, hold it." Schrik's gravelly voice pierced the air, and he lowered himself into the chair facing Parrott. "The murder's not our case. It happened in New York, out of our jurisdiction."

Parrott grinned. "Just seeing if you were paying attention, Chief. Still, knowing the artist was murdered makes solving the art theft way more interesting. Maybe there's a connection." He stood and walked to and fro in the small space in front of Schrik's desk. "Speaking of New York, what made them call you?"

"They were looking for somebody to notify the next of kin. When I told them we were investigating an art theft at the Brandywine house, you could hear the cylinders click. You know how New York is. They want you to fall all over yourself giving them information, doing them favors, but when it comes to sharing, they play the stingy older brother. Anyway, you want to do the honors?"

"Tell the girlfriend, you mean?"

Schrik nodded. "And a nephew in Philadelphia. I told 'em we'd do both."

Parrott winced and thought of so many deaths he'd experienced in his twenty-seven years—his dad's, Grandma Sharon, some friends, his cousin. "Murder is always a helluva thing. I don't think I'll ever get used to it."

Schrik came around the desk and clapped the detective on the shoulder. "Nope, and you shouldn't. The day you become immune to the shock and upset of an unnatural death—that's the day you've become ineffective in this career. Hating crime, having the outrage of it boiling in your gut, that's what separates the best cops from the worst ones."

When Parrott pulled up the long, winding driveway to the Allmond place an hour later, five cars were parked in a gravel patch about 500 yards from the front door. Would he be interrupting a party? A second glance confirmed the cars were nondescript, Fords, Chevys, Toyotas. One of them reminded him of Tonya's, well-used, but well-taken care of. Probably not a party. Maybe the servants' cars? But wouldn't there be a servants' entrance somewhere else? Parrott shook his head. The gravity of his errand weighed on him, like concrete casing, poured and drying.

As before, LeRoi answered the door, a slight upturn of his thick lips as he recognized Parrott. He fumbled with the front door, but opened it wide. "Come on in. Miss Elle isn't available right now, though."

Parrott nodded as he entered the giant entry hall. "Do you know how long? It's a matter of importance."

The elderly butler pointed to the living room. "You can wait here. She's out in the studio, teaching. Class ends at three. She cleans up afterwards. Usually back here by 3:30."

Parrott consulted his cell phone. It was 3:10. He didn't want to interrupt the class, and he certainly wouldn't give her the news in front of students. Waiting twenty more minutes couldn't hurt anything.

LeRoi pointed at the window facing the front of the house on the west side. "If you look out that window there, you'll see them leaving. Their cars are right over there." The butler turned on a stained glass lamp and made for the doorway. "May I offer you refreshment while you wait?"

"No, thanks." Parrott flipped through the latest edition of *The Hunt* magazine without registering any of the content on the glossy pages. A coffee table book entitled, Brandywine River Valley Art, and featuring a cover photo of Victor Lockwood, caught his eye. He supposed there would be a chapter about Allmond inside, but he'd have to check later. Right now, he had a one-track mind.

No cop enjoyed the task of notifying relatives, but someone had to do it. It was even harder when the deceased had met his end violently and by an unknown person. There might be hysteria.

There'd surely be questions. And Parrott would need to gauge Elle's reaction for its emotionality, its sincerity. He couldn't predict how she would take the news, but one thing he knew. No matter how he phrased them, his words would cause a paradigm shift. Once they were uttered, there'd be no going back.

He glanced at his cell phone and out the window. Ten more minutes. He stood and walked around the perimeter of the room. He stared at the painting by M. Allmond and thought about the discussion he'd had just a few hours ago with the Campbells about art. What had they called the painting with the birds? Otherworldly? Well, this painting could be labeled otherworldly, too, with its phosphorescent clouds and misty outcroppings of trees and bushes. Talent ran in the family, along with a tragic sadness, becoming even sadder.

Voices and activity outside the window drew Parrott's attention. A pair of women seemed deep in conversation as they moved across the gravel to their cars. Another two women followed the first pair. No one seemed to be rushing to leave. Finally, a fifth woman came into view, and Parrott couldn't believe his eyes. Surely, he was mistaken, but this woman was black and wore braids just like Tonya's. She had the same shape as Tonya, too, and she walked toward the dusty blue Corolla, Tonya's car.

Parrott flashed to the phone call from his mother that morning. Tonya was on the way to an art class. Was Tonya taking art lessons from Elle Carmichael? Why wouldn't she have told him?

Parrott felt as though two worlds were crashing into one another. His first impulse was to run outside and confront his wife. But what would he say, and how would she react? It wasn't as if he had caught her in an infidelity. He didn't want to seem unsupportive of her steps to deal with PTSD. Also, he was here to do a job, and Tonya's presence could do nothing but distract him from the grim task ahead.

No, he would stay inside and watch Tonya start up the Corolla. He would go to the barn and do what he had come here to do. And when he was finished, he had a similar errand in Philadelphia.

It would be several hours before he would come face to face with his beautiful wife. That would give him plenty of time to figure out whether to mention having seen her here or how to bring it up. He was about to turn from the window and head for the studio when a scrunching caused him to jerk his gaze back to where the Corolla spun out of the gravel and onto pavement. He could just make out his wife's head staring back in the direction of his Camry as she took off.

CHAPTER 14

Parrott remembered from his previous visit that the art studio was a converted barn, bright, high-ceilinged, spacious, and comfortable. The space included a reception area with loveseats, lamps, a huge area rug, and a kitchenette/bar. It wouldn't be the best place to break the dreadful news, but it wouldn't be the worst either.

He asked LeRoi to accompany him and remain in the room while he spoke with Ms. Carmichael. "I think it's best in case she requires extra support once she hears what I have to tell her."

The butler's wrinkled eyes met Parrott's, and a grimace froze his other features into a mask of pain, but he kept silent. He motioned to Parrott to follow him along the path to the studio. Parrott noticed the rust-colored tinges on the leaves, a nip in the air, and the smell of hay in the distance, all made more vivid by the mortal weight on his shoulders.

As he walked, Parrott dismissed an errant thought comparing the old man to Virgil, leading the way through the levels of Dante's hell. It wouldn't do to over-dramatize this. Notifying next of kin was just another part of the job.

The two men entered the studio through an unlocked door. They walked through the reception area to the largest room, where a small grouping of tables and chairs and easels had been set up. Soft music was playing, something classical, and the scent of apples and cinnamon floated in the air. Parrott could see why the class was considered art therapy. The environment reminded him of a scene from a classic Christmas movie.

Elle was putting the last few objects into a metal cabinet. She shut the cabinet with a scraping sound. She picked up a rag and started wiping off the tables. LeRoi cleared his throat, and she looked up with a start. "Oh," she said, and the single syllable faded into the high ceiling. She folded the rag and walked with it toward the servant, a question in her eyes.

"Ma'am, Detective Parrott is here to see you again. Shall we meet with him in the front room, where we can sit?"

Elle looked past LeRoi, and when her eyes met Parrott's, he looked away. "Is this about the stolen paintings?"

Parrott found his voice and said, "No, ma'am. Not this time."

Elle sighed. "All right, then. Let's sit down, and you can talk to me." She wiped her hands on the rag, and she trudged into the front room, perching on one of the loveseats.

Parrott sat opposite her in the other loveseat, but LeRoi remained standing at his mistress's side.

Elle gave a lop-sided smile and said, "Okay, let's have it."

Parrott's planned words turned into mush as he looked into the clear green eyes of Allmond's girlfriend. That she had been a nun hovered in his mind. "I wish I had good news to give you, but the fact is, I have some very bad news today."

She crossed herself, and her green eyes began to fill.

"I'm sorry to have to tell you Mr. Allmond has died in his condo in New York. His body was found a few hours ago by the housekeeper."

Elle uttered something between a gulp and a scream, and her face crumpled before she covered it with both hands. LeRoi placed a hand on her shoulder.

"I know this is coming as a shock, the worst kind of shock. I'm sure you will have questions, and I'll do my best to answer them." Parrott and LeRoi exchanged glances. The petite woman was now shaking uncontrollably, her surprise and grief both palpable and genuine.

Once she was able to breathe sufficiently, Elle uncovered her face and spoke. "H-how did it h-happen?"

"He was shot. His death was instantaneous. I'm sure he didn't even have time to register pain." Parrott fidgeted. "Perhaps that is a comfort to you."

"K-killed? B-but w-who? Who would want to kill B-blake?" She grabbed onto LeRoi's hand and held it for a few seconds, then let go and clasped her hands in her lap. "He told me he had business in the city. He was supposed to come home t-tonight."

Her child-like tone was typical of someone struggling with shock and disbelief, and Parrott was patient. "The New York Police Department will be investigating, and I'm sure you'll hear from them in the next few days. They'll be doing everything in their power to make sure whoever did this is brought to justice."

"New York?" Elle repeated. "Will you be investigating, too?"

Parrott took the question as a compliment. "I'll continue to investigate the art thefts, but Mr. Allmond's murder, because it occurred in New York, will be an NYPD case. Of course, I'll be happy to help out when I'm needed. That's why I'm here this afternoon."

"Oh, oh," Elle cried. "This is just horrible. I never—"

"No one ever expects something like this," Parrott said. He couldn't help feeling sorry for the woman. She seemed so alone in the world, and a blow like this could be overwhelming. He pulled out his card and a pen. He wrote on the back and handed it over. "Don't feel you have to go through it all alone. I've written my personal cell phone number on the back. Feel free to contact me any time, day or night. I might not be able to answer your questions, but I'll help get you to the people who can." He stood, and nodded at LeRoi.

Elle stood, too. Shaken and pale, she resembled a mouse at the foot of a giraffe, but she held out her hand and murmured a thank you. "I'll be okay, Detective," she said, as he turned to go.

Parrott's eyes, as he turned back to look at her, were wet with an unnamed emotion. He didn't know why he felt so moved by this woman. Perhaps it had to do with her having been a nun. As he opened the door to leave, he said, in his deep baritone voice, "I have every faith you will."

CHAPTER 15

usk was tiptoeing in as Parrott left the studio, and he wanted nothing more than to head for home. He hadn't eaten since breakfast, and he'd burned off every calorie and then some. He wanted to go home, grab a bite, give Horace some out-of-the-cage time, and hug his wife, not necessarily in that order.

But none of that could happen until he notified Allmond's nephew in Philadelphia, Alexander Vargas. He climbed into his car and punched up Vargas' address in his GPS. It was a forty-five-minute drive, and it was already past four p.m.

Driving on US1 toward 322, he passed scenic properties, country estates secluded by trees and winding roads, but he paid no attention to the lush landscape or the occasional glimpses of deer. He thought about the expression on Elle Carmichael's face as the news of her lover's death had registered. His instincts told him her reaction was spontaneous and genuine. Without knowing much about her relationship with Allmond, he didn't believe she'd had anything to do with his violent death.

By the time he'd reached I95N, he was ruminating over what the Campbells and Rupert Brooks had told him about Allmond's paintings. Was Allmond's murder, coming so closely on the tail of the theft, a coincidence? Or were the two crimes linked in such a way that solving one would be solving both? Parrott's experiences with the Preston Phillips case had taught him, the 135 miles of geography between Brandywine and New York represented a world of difference. Still, he could already tell Allmond's death and the theft of his paintings were going to intertwine, no matter how much the powers that be might try to keep them separate.

The streets of Philadelphia, too, presented a stark contrast to the roads and paths in Brandywine Valley. When he pulled up to the Vargas townhouse, Parrott shook his head. The nephew and the uncle certainly led different lives. The corner building faced Sedgley Avenue in an enclave occupied mostly by immigrants. The deep red brick and white stone edifice may have been chic a century ago, but now it needed a good power-washing, and maybe some tuck-pointing, too. The windows showed grime, and one had aluminum foil covering the pane.

All he knew about Vargas fit into a concise paragraph, inside a folder on the passenger seat. Twenty-nine years old, son of Francisco Vargas and Melanie Allmond Vargas. Lived here with his mother until her death, five years ago. Works for a construction company that builds industrial and commercial.

Parrott parked on the street across from the unit and watched for signs someone was inside. It was just five o'clock, so Vargas might not have arrived home from work yet. Parrott popped the glove compartment, where Tonya had stocked an unopened box of protein bars. He grabbed one and ripped open the wrapper without examining the flavor—any would do—and bit off a huge chunk. He was still chewing when he heard and then saw a rusty Dodge Charger pull into the narrow driveway next to the townhouse and screech to a stop. Parrott stuffed the second half of the snack into his mouth, as he watched a slender dark-haired guy alight from the car and slam the door.

Vargas ran a hand through his longish hair before pressing his key fob to lock the car with a loud honk. He climbed the five steps to the front door landing and let himself in with a key from the same holder. Once inside, he turned on a series of lights, giving the home the appearance of coming to life in the deepening gloom.

Parrott folded the empty wrapper into halves until it fit unobtrusively into his right pants pocket. He would dispose of it at the first opportunity, but he liked to keep his car neat. He got out and stretched. He noted some activity in the neighborhood, a few dogs, another person arriving home, lights on here and there. As shabby as it was by comparison to Brandywine, it was still better than the streets where both he and Tonya had grown up.

It felt good to dash across the street and hustle up the few steps. Too much sitting was going to put a layer of flab on his middle if he didn't watch out. He rang the doorbell and waited. It only took a few seconds for Vargas to flip on the outside light and crack the door a couple of inches.

"Can I help you?"

Parrott showed his badge. "Detective Oliver Parrott, West Brandywine Police Department. Are you Alexander Vargas?"

Vargas gave a slight nod, causing a lock of hair to fall over one eye, almost eclipsing the frown lines that appeared like an eleven between his brows. "Why, what's happening, man? What's goin' on?"

"May I come in? I have some information to give you, and I don't expect you want to hear it out here." Parrott gave a perfunctory smile, aiming for casualness.

"I guess so," Vargas muttered, as he led the detective to a combination living room, dining room, kitchen. Clothes, dishes, and empty food containers littered the room, and an odor of bacon grease mixed with stale beer. Vargas cleared the top of the breakfast table. "This okay?"

Parrott pulled out one of four ice cream parlor chairs and sat, motioning to Vargas to do the same.

Vargas bounced his thigh, tapping the floor with his heel. "What's this about? Is it about Veronica?" Before Parrott could reply, he said, "No, wait a minute. Did you say Brandywine?"

"Who's Veronica?" Parrott asked. He wasn't here to interrogate, but he couldn't help asking. This guy gave off too many strange vibes. He stared at Vargas' leg.

"Look," Vargas said, "if you're from Brandywine, you must have been sent by my uncle. Blake Allmond. The famous artist." He stared into Parrott's eyes as if he could read his fate through them. "If it's something about him, why doesn't he just tell me, himself?"

Parrott gave him a temporary pass for not having answered the question about Veronica. He uncrossed his leg and planted both feet on the floor, both forearms on the table. "Well, it's like this," he said. "The New York Police Department asked me to notify you of your uncle's death. He died in his New York apartment sometime last night or early this morning."

Vargas lost all color in his face and gasped. "Died?" His leg ceased moving, and he bent over, elbows on knees, as if he were trying not to faint. When he raised his head again, he asked, "Are you sure? Blake Allmond, the artist? There must be some mistake. I—I just saw him, and he was fine."

Parrott shook his head. "It's no mistake. I'm sorry to bring you the bad news."

"But—but what happened to him? He wasn't sick, but now he's *dead*?" A look of horror overcame him, whether out of guilt or fear he had been exposed to a deadly disease, Parrott couldn't surmise.

He touched the nephew's arm to stabilize him, to ready him for the next shock. "He was killed, Mr. Vargas. I know this is upsetting to you. You were probably very close to your uncle, and on behalf of the New York and West Brandywine police, I give you our deepest condolences."

Vargas pushed on the table with his arms and stood up, his head hanging down. "Close? I don't know how *close* we were. We shared the same genes, and we both loved my mother, but I wouldn't say we are—uh, were—especially close."

"And yet you say you just saw him?" Parrott replied.

Vargas's dark eyes shifted, and the eleven appeared above his nose again. "Yes. We went out to dinner last night? No, two nights ago. I met him in New York—" His voice broke off into a sob. "Omigod, you don't suspect I *killed* him, do you?"

Parrott raised his voice to match the volume of the outburst. "Please sit down, Mr. Vargas. I'm merely delivering the bad news to you, as Mr. Allmond's next of kin." Lowering his voice, he said, "I'm not here to accuse, or even interrogate you, although you might consider telling me where you were last night."

Vargas sat again and ran his hands through his hair. "I was with my girlfriend. Veronica Espinosa. I'm with her most evenings, either at her place or mine. Last night was at hers." He thought for a minute. "I have some questions, too. Like who would have killed my uncle? It's not like he was in the Mob or anything. Why?" His leg began its rhythmic pounding again.

Parrott responded in a measured tone, his eyes on Vargas' face the whole time. "As I told you, Mr. Allmond's body was found in his Gramercy Park apartment. The who and the why are questions the New York PD will be answering in the days to come. I'm sure they'll want to talk to you, especially since you were one of the last people to see your uncle alive."

Vargas put his face into his hands and groaned. "Was it a robbery? Was anything taken from the apartment?"

Parrott replied, "If so, it wasn't mentioned to me. Of course, there were some paintings stolen from your uncle's Brandywine studio last week. I've been investigating that crime, but the murder, having taken place in New York, is not my case."

"Jesus Christ," Vargas cried, and he grabbed a tissue from a box on the table and blew his nose. "I never expected anything like this. It's true, we weren't that close, but my uncle has always been the one person I could count on. The whole rest of the family is gone, and my father's side—they aren't there for me."

Parrott couldn't help feeling sorry for the guy. Parrott's family didn't come from wealth or have famous artists in their midst, but there were lots of them, and when the chips were down, they were always there for each other. "You may want to get in touch with Ms. Carmichael, your uncle's partner. Perhaps the two of you can comfort each other."

Standing and preparing to leave, Parrott reached into his pocket, past the folded wrapper, for his card case. He pulled out a card and handed it to Vargas. "If I can help you, feel free to call me on my cell phone."

Vargas sniffled and muttered, "Thanks, man," as he led Parrott the few steps to the door.

Parrott suddenly felt suffocated by the grief and clutter and staleness of this place. How could a person live in such squalor? He made for the door. It was only as his eyes swept the room in a farewell glance that he noticed the one saving grace in the whole place. Centered on the wall over a shabby vinyl sofa hung a beautiful oil painting—depicting a Brandywine Valley scene, and in the foreground he could swear was Blake Allmond's house.

CHAPTER 16

The next evening, Elle Carmichael knelt beside her bed in the much-too-spacious mansion she had called home for more than twelve years. Anyone who might have walked by and seen her petite frame, her hands pressed together in prayer, and her straight, glossy hair, half-covering her face, would have mistaken her for a child.

A candle burned in a brass candlestick on the nearby desk, filling the room with an other-worldly glow and a waxy perfume.

Elle tried to focus on the words of the prayer she was repeating in a slow, soft, almost mechanical voice. The Sisters of Mercy had taught her how to pray, not like a lay person, but how to block out the profane worries of the world, how to achieve a blank mind, and then how to fill the mind with sacred and holy thoughts, peaceful thoughts. Always the artist, Elle had likened it to prepping the canvas to ready it for new colors and textures.

That had been sinful, she knew, to think secular thoughts when praying.

"It's like baking a cake with the wrong ingredients," Sister Octavius had told her.

Elle had wanted to ask, "How can art be wrong?" So much of what had drawn her to the convent to begin with was art—glorious Renaissance paintings of the Madonna and Child, techniques that made the ethereal real. In a way, she had imagined joining the convent as stepping into a sacred and mysterious painting.

Perhaps that had been the wrong kind of thinking, a harbinger of the greater sin she would make in leaving the convent, turning her back on her vows. The guilt welled up, filling her eyes and nose with stinging nettles.

Now as she tried to pray, her thoughts zigzagged from present to past and back again, and then to the future. Where would she go? What would she do? She had given up everything for her art, for Blake. She had loved the wholesomeness of being a nun, using her energy to serve others. She had even loved the asceticism, the denial of material things. It had made her feel pure and worthy. She had rejoiced in the ability to bring light into the lives of the good children she served, ignoring their disabilities, teaching them to sing and play and paint.

The painting, though, had been her undoing. Little by little, as she worked with her pupils, her hands on theirs as they held paintbrushes, an insidious niggling in her brain grew stronger and more insistent, causing images to flash before her eyes. She wanted—no, needed—to paint.

She had confessed these guilty impulses to Father Frank, accepted her penance, but still couldn't reconcile her need to paint with the restrictions of the convent. While she prayed for cessation of the distractions from her mission, she also researched Saint Catherine of Bologna, the painter and manuscript illuminator. Couldn't she also find a way to appease her desire to paint with her desire to serve the Lord?

Seeing her passion for art could not be quenched, Father Frank had instructed Sister Octavius to set up a makeshift studio in the corner of a back porch. At the end of each weekday, before night prayers, Elle could indulge in painting for a blessed hour.

That single break in protocol, though, had led to others. Elle's paintings had been true works of art, too beautiful to keep cloistered. Eventually they had been shown, then sold, the proceeds going to the Church.

It was at one of the art auctions that Elle had been touched by Blake Allmond's art, and then by Blake himself. The attraction was immediate, a bolt of lightning surely sent by God Himself.

And now thirteen years later, Blake was dead, and Elle could not go back to being a nun. Her seduction to worldliness had led to a dead end. This house, the huge studio she shared with Blake, the small group of acquaintances she had met in the Brandywine art colony—all of these belonged to Blake and not to her. She felt like a counterfeit artist, an interloper in Blake's world.

The art therapy class was the only part of her life she could call her own. She loved the way her students responded to her instruction. Like teaching the good children years before, she focused the lessons on allowing the artist's spirit and yearning for peace to shine through. Each of her current students was battling some kind of demon, and Elle saw her mission to facilitate a victory of good over evil as something holy. But how could she continue to teach? So much of her strategy was bound up in the studio with its extraordinary sunlight and airy space.

The stolen paintings preyed on her mind, also. It was easier to think of that loss than this fresher one. She had been the one to discover the theft, to call the police, to walk around the property with the detective. Blake had turned it over to her to speak with the insurance company, as well. He'd said he was tied up with a new project. He'd tell her all the details soon. She'd assumed it was a commissioned work of art, but maybe something sinister had been going on, something related to his murder.

Elle couldn't imagine anyone wanting to kill Blake. No kinder, more generous person walked the planet. The thought of his being found in the shower, shot in the chest, sent renewed trembling from her midriff to her limbs. Whoever it was who'd snuffed the life from Blake had also wounded her. Until she knew who it was and why it was done, she'd never have a moment's peace. Perhaps whoever it was would be coming for her next.

She'd packed a few belongings in a single suitcase earlier in the day, but the truth was, she had nowhere to go. Tears spilled onto her bosom as she abandoned all pretense of prayer. She was utterly alone.

A creak in the floorboard outside of her room brought her to her feet. She eased her body against the closed door, listening.

"Miss Elle? You still awake?"

LeRoi's gravelly voice reminded her she wasn't entirely alone. "Yes, I'm just c-catching up on some reading."

"I thought you might could use a bedtime snack. I've got some Ovaltine and madeleines for you."

Though she wasn't hungry in the slightest, Elle was touched by the old man's thoughtfulness. He, too, must be feeling at loose ends by Blake's sudden death. She brushed away imaginary wrinkles in her silky top and drawstring pants and threw a robe on over the outfit before opening the door. The butler held a tray of elegant goodies.

She forced a smile, hoping it was convincing. "Thanks, LeRoi. You're a good man. How about if I come downstairs and we enjoy the snack together?"

CHAPTER 17

By the time Parrott arrived at home after making the notifications of Allmond's death, the slivered moon and several other heavenly bodies were shining in the inky sky. He was hungry and bone-tired, so, as much as he yearned to be with Tonya, he was dragging his heels. He wasn't equipped for the scrimmage he expected to have with her over having seen her at Manderley.

He wasn't angry, exactly, more hurt that she wouldn't have told him about the art lesson and the teacher. It was starting to feel like they'd had better communication when she was overseas in Afghanistan than they did now, and that scared him.

Tonya's Corolla was on the street, a peace offering. With only a one-car garage, someone's car had to stay out overnight. By parking on the street, she was telling him to pull into the driveway and garage tonight. Cheered by the thought, Parrott put away his car and his angst and let himself in through the kitchen door.

The aromas of chili and cornbread slapped him in the face, and he began salivating before he could get a word out. Tonya was at the stove, stirring the pot in that sexy way of hers, where her whole backside rotated with the spoon. At the sound of the opening door, she turned around, her braids swaying behind her.

Parrott could tell instantly she had been crying. Her eyes were puffy and sunken. The thought flew through his mind that he had seen her cry more in the few months since they'd been married than in all the years of dating.

He dropped his keys on the table and went to her, encircling her curves in his arms. Holding her was better than any elixir to make the stress of the day disappear. He went in for a kiss, at the same time reaching to turn off the burner under the pot of chili.

"Hey, Oliver, what're you doing?"

She never called him Oliver, except when she was upset. "Whaddya mean, what'm I doing? I'm trying to hug my beautiful wife."

Horace the cockatiel clung to the door of his cage, hanging at a thirty-degree angle and calling, "Beautiful wife. Beautiful wife."

"I know that," Tonya said, "I meant why are you cutting off the flame? I thought you'd be coming in here famished after such a long day. Don't you want to eat dinner?" She wriggled out of his embrace and lit the gas under the flame, adjusting it. She returned to stirring as if her life depended on it.

" 'Course I do," Parrott said, in his throaty register. "I just thought we could spend a little time being man and wife first." Not used to being rejected, he turned to the bird cage and opened the door. "Come on, little fellow." Horace flew out and landed on Parrott's shoulder.

"Are we going to eat dinner with Horace on your shoulder?" Tonya snapped the knob into the off position and grabbed a bowl. "The chili's ready now."

Parrott felt they should be talking instead of eating, but his digestive system thought otherwise. He led Horace to the corner where his perch and toys were, and the bird hopped off. At least somebody was acting normal.

Why is Tonya so edgy? If anyone should be uptight about both of us being at Manderley at the same time, it should be me. How can she be upset with me for doing my job?

He set out the napkins and silverware and filled two tumblers with iced water. He had learned from the long separations when Tonya was in the Navy, sometimes it was best to let the lady do the talking first.

Once the dinner was on the table and his wife was sitting across from him, he lifted his glass of water in the gesture of a toast and waited for her to reciprocate.

She hesitated, but lifted her glass, a pained look taking over her face. "Oh, Ollie, I know I'm acting bitchy. I can't even explain why, except I know you saw my car at Elle Carmichael's house. I went there for art therapy, but I didn't want you to know."

"For God's sake, Tonya. We're husband and wife. Why do you need to keep secrets from me?"

"How about we eat first, then talk? I haven't eaten all day." She picked up her soup spoon and dug into the bowl of chili.

"Okay," Parrott replied, realizing he was famished, himself. "Only thing I had since breakfast was a power bar from the glove compartment. Glad you put them in there." Shoveling a series of spoonsful into his mouth in progression, Parrott hummed with pleasure. He'd never tasted anything so delicious in his life. He broke off a piece of cornbread muffin and buttered it on all sides. The salty, greasy morsel tasted like heavenly ambrosia. "Delicious," he murmured between bites. "Thank you for this mighty fantastic dinner. It's just what I needed."

Tonya nodded. She continued eating, too, until all but a few scraps were left in her bowl. She started to clear the table, but Parrott grabbed her wrist and said, "Sit down, honey. I'll do the cleaning up. Let's clear the air between us instead."

She sat back down and put her hands over her face. She choked out a sob. "I don't know what you want from me, Ollie, but whatever it is, I don't think I can give it to you."

"Baby, don't say that. Why are you saying that?" Parrott pounded the table. "What is this about?"

"I can't stand the person I am since I've been back. I'm jumpy and nervous all the time. I look around for trouble, even when I'm doing the simplest things. I wear myself out 24/7." She grabbed a tissue from her pocket and blew her nose. "I can't sleep. I can't relax." She stood and started putting the empty dishes in the sink. "Sometimes I think I should go back."

"What? Tonya, you aren't making sense. Why would you go back to the place that gave you this problem to begin with?"

"Don't you see? That's what I'm used to. It's my comfort zone to be on guard, adrenalin flowing. Yeah, it was dangerous, but I got used to the danger. Now I can't get used to the peace and quiet."

"Well, what does all this have to do with the Allmonds?"

"I'm trying to deal with this PTSD on my own. It's important to me to be strong and independent. When I saw Allmond's girlfriend on the list of art therapy teachers, I thought how cool would that be? An ex-nun for a teacher, and maybe I could help you with your case, too."

"Honey—"

"No, listen. I knew you'd discourage me from stepping into your world, so I gave my name as Tonya Collins. Wrote the check from the account I haven't changed over yet. Today was the first class, and it did me a lot of good. That is, until I saw your car there. I know it's irrational, but all I could think of was you'd ruined the one good thing I'd done for myself in weeks."

Parrott rubbed the sides of his head and thought hard before he spoke. "I'm sorry you felt that way. To be truthful, I probably *would* have discouraged you from taking your lessons there. Conflict of interest, tainting the case, whatever you'd call it—it's not usually a good thing to mix business and family, especially when you're a cop."

Horace squawked, "Oh, dear, a cop," causing both husband and wife to chuckle.

"I was waiting in the living room to speak to Ms. Carmichael. I had no idea you'd come walking out of there, just as I was preparing to go in. What upset me most is you not telling me. It hurts my feelings you shutting me out like this." So far no mention of Blake Allmond's death, so Tonya probably didn't know. And Parrott was afraid to tell her.

Another sob wracked Tonya. "Sorry I keep hurting your feelings. It's all I seem to do is hurt people's feelings. Even your mama's. She called this morning, and I barely could even talk to her. I'm just a bad luck charm, Ollie. You should dump me before I break your heart entirely."

Parrott wanted to rush over and put his arms around Tonya, tell her how precious she was to him and always would be. But something told him she needed her space right now, so he sat in his chair, leaning back against the wall. His stomach was full, but his heart was empty. "I'm not going to do any such thing," he said. "And you aren't a bad luck charm. When I was working on the Phillips case, it seemed the whole world was out to stop me. If I hadn't had you, your picture, our Skypes, I don't think I could've survived."

"But that was before. When I was on duty, I was a different Tonya Collins. Every day I had to prove myself. I had to be tough and sharp, and I was. It was hard work, but I slept better at night there than I have any time since I've been back."

"Even on our honeymoon?"

Tonya nodded, and somehow that wounded her husband more than anything. What had she been doing while he'd slept like a baby?

"I really connected with Ms. Carmichael—she told us to call her Elle—today. She's the calmest, most serene person I've ever met, and her love of art radiates from her. If I could emulate her, I believe I could find that person I used to be."

Remembering how distressed Ms. Carmichael was when he left her, Parrott realized he needed to tell Tonya about Allmond's death. It would be in the news, and Ton-ya would be furious with him if she were to find out from another source. He cleared his throat. "Um, I'm happy to hear that, honey. I believe in you, too, and if Ms. Car—Elle—inspires you, I'm a hundred percent behind it."

Tonya's eyes grew rounder, and the corners of her mouth hinted at a smile. "So you're okay with me taking classes there? It won't ruin your case or anything?"

"Nah. If we get to a place where it becomes a problem, we'll talk about it then." It would've been a good time for a hug, except for the glob of bad news paralyzing Parrott's throat. He needed to get it out. The moment was now, but the question was how. "There is something I need to tell you, though."

Perhaps it was the gravity in her husband's tone that made Tonya freeze in her place at the table. Hands, head, and braids were absolutely still, and eyes were riveted on Parrott's.

"The reason I was at Manderley today wasn't the art case. I mean, I'm still investigating that case, and all, but that's not why I was there this afternoon." He cleared his throat again. "I was waiting in the house until class was over, so I could talk to her privately. The reason I was there was to notify Ms. Carmichael that Blake Allmond had passed."

"Dead? You say he's dead?" Tonya shook her head, disbelief written all over her face. "But how? Why?"

Parrott went to her then. He stood behind her in her chair, resting his hands on her shoulders. "He had a place in New York, stayed there overnight. His housekeeper found him in the shower. He'd been shot in the chest."

Tonya jumped up, the force nearly toppling her chair, despite Parrott's standing there. She turned around, tears shining in her eyes. "Oh, no. That poor sweet lady." She looked about the room, as if solace could be found in a corner somewhere. "You see what I mean, Ollie? It's me. I'm the bad luck charm. I'm the one who brought this trouble to Manderley."

With that, she grabbed her car keys from the tray on the counter. "I've got to get away and be by myself." She was sobbing as she threw the door open and crossed the threshold. "And don't you dare come after me, either." She slammed the door behind her.

Parrott clenched his fists, his mind suffused with worry and pain. Horace flew onto Parrott's shoulder, and the two of them dashed to the window, watching as their lady-love took off, burning rubber.

CHAPTER 18

When Parrott left Alexander Vargas' townhouse after notifying him of his uncle's death, Vargas closed the door and locked it with the security chain. His hands were shaking, and his mind was being processed like a Margarita. The dinner he'd shared with his uncle two nights before would be branded in his memory forever, and there would never be a chance to repair their relationship now. Would Allmond have had time to change his will, as promised, in the short period afterwards?

Alexander's first impulse was to call Veronica. She wouldn't believe this news. *She'll probably want to break out the confetti and champagne, maybe even don the red negligee.* The image caused Alexander to hesitate. His feelings toward his uncle had always been complicated, but he didn't feel like celebrating the older man's death. It was going to take some time to sort out his thoughts and emotions. The detectives in New York would surely come after him, and maybe after Veronica, too, now she'd been caught accessing Allmond's bank statements. He was going to need a plan, the sooner the better, and he had the feeling Veronica shouldn't be a part of it.

Alexander looked around his living space, seeing it through the eyes of the detective. *When did it get so filthy, so cluttered?* He moved around the room picking up empty cans and bottles, pizza and Chinese food cartons. When his hands and arms were full, he dumped everything on the kitchen counter and went back for more. After several minutes he had filled a dozen plastic bags from the supermarket with trash, and he hauled them out to the garbage can in the driveway.

Next, he started washing dishes and silverware, putting the clean items in the dish drainer on the side of the sink. He vowed not to let things get so out of hand again. The police were certain to be back, but next time, he wouldn't come off looking like such a lowlife.

The house still needed several hours of work, dusting, mopping, vacuuming, and more, but hunger pains were piercing through the adrenalin. He opened the refrigerator to see what leftovers might tame the gurgles in his gut. There wasn't much. He hadn't eaten at home since before the dinner with his uncle. Pulling out the hydrator, he found some cheese, Colby and Monterrey Jack, and two cans left from a six-pack of Bud. A half-empty box of crackers was on the shelf, too, kept in the refrigerator to avoid attracting weevils. A couple of dill pickles, and it would have to do as dinner.

He took a newly-washed plate from the drying rack and wiped it off with his sleeve. He was in the process of cutting cheese and placing it on the cracker rounds when his cell phone rang. It had to be Veronica, he thought, and when he saw the caller ID he decided to let it go to voicemail. He had never done that before, and he considered he might be crossing a line in the relationship.

He opened a can of beer and took a long swig. When the phone stopped ringing, he gave it time to record a message, debating with himself all the while about whether to call her back immediately. Caution won out, though, and when the two-tone ding sounded, indicating a new voicemail, he called in to pick it up.

"Hi, Chachi, it's me. I thought you'd be home by now, but you're not answering. I cancelled dinner with my brother tonight. I told him I had a migraine. So do you want to come over? *Crazy/ Beautiful* is on tv. I know how you love that movie. We can watch it, and then we can watch each other." A long pause gave Alexander time for another swig. "Anyway, call me. I hate talking into these things."

Alexander disconnected and wondered how long he could go without calling her back, without going back to the well. He still loved her, was crazy for her, but he had to admit sometimes she scared him, and that imbecile brother of hers scared him even more. Her obsession with his uncle's wealth had left a bad taste in his mouth, too. The fact that she had violated bank policy to snoop into his uncle's accounts—without discussing it with him first—concerned him. If she would do that, what else would she do?

He chewed on a cheese-topped cracker and wondered, if he couldn't trust Veronica, whom could he trust? He remembered his mother's telling him repeatedly, "Your mother is your best friend." Once he had asked her, "Was your mother *your* best friend?" She had frowned, and her eyes had filled. After a few seconds, she had replied, "There was a time when I didn't think so, but now I see she was. Your mother always has your best interests at heart."

Alexander wished he could have his mother back, just this once. She would be able to advise him about what to say and do. He finished his makeshift meal and washed the dish. He thought he might turn on the TV, distract himself from his worries. On the way to the corner where it stood on a dusty table, he passed by the sofa. The painting his mother had done of Manderley caught his eye, and he stopped to stare at it.

The sprawling mansion had been in the Allmond family for generations. His mother had told him stories about her childhood there. She had been happy growing up with servants and horses and luxuries. Despite whatever had prompted her to chuck it all and run away with his father, she had painted it, years later, with an ethereal glow. It looked heavenly with its white pillars and open gates.

The detective had told him to reach out to his uncle's partner. Maybe his mother was telling him the same thing through the painting. He didn't know much about Elle Carmichael, except she had been a nun. He didn't know how much Elle knew about him either. It wouldn't hurt if he could get her on his side, get her to trust him. At least it was worth a try.

As he made up his mind to go to Manderley soon, he fixated on the upstairs front window in the painting. Maybe it was the effect of the two beers, or the stress of his uncle's death and Veronica's phone call, but he could swear he saw something move, like a hand letting go of the curtain.

CHAPTER 19

Bad luck, bad luck. The words repeated in Tonya's mind like a refrain from a frightening fairy tale, and her heart pumped the rhythm through every artery and vein. As Tonya drove through the residential streets and onto the highway, she thought of all the destruction she had been a part of, all the deaths.

Only eleven when her mom died, she had taken the loss as a personal indictment. If she had only been a better daughter, her mom would still be here. She should've done more to help around the house. The heavy load of working and taking care of a daughter must have caused her mother to become ill in the first place. And then there was Granny, a dear friend in high school who'd had sickle cell, and all those people overseas.

Tonya's eyes burned, as the accusatory phrase thrummed in her head. The clock on the dashboard said 08:22, but she just kept going. She took an exit without realizing where she was heading. It wasn't until she passed the quaint old mill that she realized she was retracing her path to the Allmond house. It was as if her car were taking her where *it* wanted to go, instead of the other way around.

No streetlights shone over the narrow road, and the car's headlamps threw two inadequate dots of illumination ahead. Tonya rolled down the car's windows and breathed in the cool night air and the woodsy smell. She considered turning around and going home, but the patter in her head and the pounding in her heart drove her on. When she pulled up to the gates of Manderley, she screeched to a stop and parked in the grass at the side of the road. From here the mansion was a dollhouse, sitting at the top of acres and acres of rolling countryside. Star-like glimmers shone in a couple of windows, but most of the estate was cloaked in shadow. *Bad luck* echoed in Tonya's brain, and she imagined the overwhelming scope of the grief she had brought to the home's inhabitant this night. She should never have signed up for Elle's art therapy. She should have known she would bring a curse wherever she went.

Tonya covered her face with her hands and cried out. Her breathing was heavy, a stone moving inside every time she exhaled. What should she do? Where should she go? As much as she loved Ollie, how could she go back to him, live with him? She would taint him with bad luck, too. She pictured Ollie, putting his arms around her and soothing her. "It's not your fault," he would say, but he would be wrong. How many people would have to die around her before he would see the truth?

She pulled up to the circular driveway, determined to ring the doorbell and confess her thoughts to her teacher. PTSD sucked. It took every molecule, every morsel of energy, just to navigate through a single day. After the art class, a seed of hope had sprouted in her. Maybe she could immerse herself in the pleasantness of the setting and the kindness of the instructor. Maybe she could soak up the sense of relief from tension the two hours provided, and it would grow and multiply within her. That was what she was thinking when she'd walked to her car after class. But then she'd seen Ollie's car, and it was as if a pinhole had formed in the balloon, and air was escaping.

Now that Allmond was dead, poor Miss Elle might cancel the remainder of the classes, and it would all be Tonya's fault. She wondered why Ollie hadn't called her, begged her to come home, but a glance at the passenger seat told her she had left her cell phone at home. She didn't have her driver's license either.

The night chill enveloped her, and she started up the car and closed the windows. Sitting out here like this wasn't doing anybody any good, least of all her. She needed to get back home, take some Ibuprofen, try to get some sleep. Tomorrow she would call Vena at the VA hospital. She was ready to take drugs or whatever the next step was. She had to do something drastic, or she would lose her mind. She rubbed her eyes. The lids felt swollen and thick.

Tonya jerked the gearshift into drive and proceeded down the service road, back toward the highway. She stomped on the accelerator, in a hurry to get away from the gloom. Her eyes didn't see and her ears didn't hear the hundred-pound doe until it crashed into her bumper, flew several feet above the ground, and landed in a bloody heap on the side of the road. The impact had brought the Corolla to a dead stop, deploying the airbag, and jolting the driver with its sheer violence. When Tonya heard the screaming, she was too shocked to realize it was coming from her own throat.

Elle and LeRoi sat at the breakfast room table, drinking pomegranate tea and talking quietly about the Allmond family history. LeRoi had served Blake's parents in this house, so he was a wealth of information about the people Elle had never met. The stories of childhood escapades, friendships with well-known people, and a multitude of celebrations kept Elle connected to Blake and diverted her mind from his death.

LeRoi had cracked the windows in all the rooms on the first floor, so a pleasant cross-draft sauntered about the two of them, cooling feverish thoughts, and dispersing the aroma of dampened grass and leaves inside the house. The plate of Madeleines had been hardly touched, but LeRoi was refilling their cups, and Elle was asking a question about Blake's sister, Melanie, when a firm bang-bang-thump caused Elle to stop in mid-sentence.

"What was that, do you think?" She jumped up and darted to the living room window, pushing her way through the thick layers of drapery fabric. "I'm sure I heard something."

LeRoi, whose hearing had been diminished by almost eighty years of use, followed. He opened the drapes and peered out into the darkness alongside his mistress. "Can you see anything?"

"No. But that's a human scream, I'm hearing. I'm sure of it." Elle grabbed the butler by the arm. "Someone's hurt. Get flashlights, and let's go. Someone needs our help."

"Better call 911, too, Miss Elle. Do you have your cell phone? I'll get the flashlights and jackets. It'll be chilly out there."

Elle and LeRoi, flashlights in hand, trudged down the sloping grounds of Manderley, fifty yards down the driveway. Elle crossed herself and mumbled prayers, as she walked. Dried leaves clung to the hem of her robe, which billowed behind her like a train. "Be careful, LeRoi. It's slippery." Elle wished for a heavier pair of shoes and a flashlight with a bigger diameter. The stars and the moon provided only a modicum of light. Whoever decided street lights would ruin the country charm of these roads must never have answered a night-time call for help. Likewise, the only sounds were those of nature, wind rustling leaves and a distant owl, muted by the human sounds of respiration and locomotion.

Elle reached the scene first, and she shone her flashlight left and right. The narrow stripe of light landed first on a bloody deer at the side of the path, motionless, then on a car. Both were about ten yards ahead. She called over her shoulder, "I see it. An accident. Looks like a car hit a deer pretty hard." She picked up the pace, leaving LeRoi behind. She prayed whoever was in the car was still alive.

When she reached the scene, she ran first to the car, an old model Toyota. She shone her flashlight into the driver's window, but the glare obscured most of the view. A single passenger, a deployed airbag, a coating of dust—no movement. Elle tried to open the car door, but it wouldn't budge, whether because it was locked, or damaged, she couldn't tell.

She ran around to the passenger side and tried the door, but no luck. She looked up to see LeRoi approaching, the glare from his flashlight swinging with each step. "Maybe we can see inside better if you shine into the driver's side, and I stay here," she called.

LeRoi did as his mistress suggested. The light coming from two angles helped them see into the car. The punctured airbag took up most of the space between the dashboard and the seat, pinning the driver in an awkward position. It was so dark inside, except for the glistening white powder.

Elle could barely make out the outline of a driver, who was stirring and moaning. Were those braids? Beads? A woman then?

The face was obscured by the airbag, and she didn't seem to be aware of the pair of flashlight beams dancing around her.

The whine of a siren split the air, and then another. "Hang on," Elle shouted into the car window. "Help is coming." Did the driver respond, or was her own pounding heart teasing her? Unable to help the car's driver, she turned to examine the deer, a doe. Clearly it was dead, its lifeblood pooling around it like a cushion. Somewhere nearby, Nature was grieving, and maybe some fawns, too. Elle could identify.

As the sirens approached, LeRoi examined the damage to the front of the car. The impact had smashed the left front bumper in, and the hood resembled an accordion. "Whew," he mumbled, and it came out like a whistle. "One little deer can sure do a lot of damage. I hope this lady'll be all right."

Within seconds, the driveway filled with sounds and lights, as EMS, followed by a patrol car, pulled to the side and screeched to a stop. Both turned off their sirens, but left the lights flashing. The patrolman swept Elle and LeRoi off to the side, next to the deer. Elle saw the two EMS workers checking the car doors. She called out, "They're locked," but no one paid attention.

"Think you need the cutters?" one guy asked of the police officer.

"Nah, I can just break the glass here. Toyota is shatterproof." With a single swing, the patrolman bludgeoned the back window on the driver's side. Elle grabbed LeRoi's arm and jumped backward as the sound of the metal-on-glass filled the air. Just as predicted, the window cracked into a thousand little hexagons. If it hadn't been so frightening, Elle might have likened the pattern to a modern portrait of an angel. It glistened and reflected the colored lights from the emergency vehicles. Then the patrolman knocked it in.

In a matter of seconds, he had the door unlocked, and after a struggle with the dented metal, he swung the door open and pulled the partially deflated airbag out of the car. The peculiar smell of powder mixed with polymer floated in the air. The EMTs stood behind him with oxygen, a blood pressure cuff, and a stretcher with IV fluids ready. The patrolman stepped aside to give them access. "She's alive, fellas. Not sure if she's conscious though."

Elle watched from the sidelines as the professionals did their jobs, feeling as if she were in an episode of "Nightwatch Nation," which Blake watched on A&E. *Oh, Blake*, she thought. The EMTs bent over the driver, taking pulses, blood pressure, whatever initial assessments they did, blocking Elle's view. She couldn't hear much of what they were saying either.

After a minute or two, the patrolman, whose nametag said Barton, rolled the gurney up to the side of the car, and the EMTs extracted the woman from the car and placed her on her back with a pillow under her head and a sheet and blanket over her feet and torso. The transfer was so fluid, so smooth, except for the patient's moaning and turning her head from side to side.

Patrolman Barton climbed into the now-vacant car. Amid the beads of glass and airbag powder, he searched the seat and the floor of the front and back seats. "I don't see anything, no handbag, no ID," he called out. "We'll have to take her in as a Jane Doe."

When he stepped out of the car and closed the car door, Elle had her first glimpse of the woman on the gurney. Something about those braids and beads looked familiar, and Elle uttered a cry. She ran across the road to get a better look, confirming her hunch. "I know who this is, Officer."

Barton turned to look into the tiny woman's green eyes. "You do? You know her, you say?"

"Absolutely. This is my new student. Her name is Tonya Collins."

CHAPTER 20

Once Tonya was identified at the scene of the accident, things moved quickly. Officer Barton had teamed up with Parrott often in the past, and hearing the name Tonya Collins caused him to examine the victim's face. "Mrs. Parrott," he repeated, "can you hear me?"

Tonya stirred, opened her eyes, but didn't focus. Her blood pressure was 80/40, and oxygenation was 78%. "We're taking you in to Brandywine Hospital ER," one of the EMTs said.

"And I'm calling your husband to meet us there," Barton said, pushing buttons on his cell phone.

Elle and LeRoi, who were standing at the side of the road, exchanged glances. Elle asked, "Did you say, 'Parrott'? Do you mean Detective Parrott?"

Barton didn't answer, but he didn't have to. After a few seconds, he said into the phone, "Parrott, it's Barton. Your wife's hit a deer out here by the Allmond house. She's got some injuries, and EMTs are taking her to Brandywine's ER."

Up until then, Elle hadn't minded the cool night air, but now she began to shiver. The day had been too much for her, and she couldn't wrap her mind around this accident. *Why is the detective's wife taking my class, and why isn't she using her married name? What is she doing out here at this time of night?*

LeRoi took off his jacket and wrapped it around Elle's shoulders. "Miz Elle, I think we should go back home. These folks are leaving, and there's nothing more for us to do here."

Officer Barton ended his call and turned to shake hands with LeRoi and Elle. "Thanks for the quick response. You might have saved this lady's life. Detective Parrott told me to tell you he's very grateful." The EMTs were loading Tonya into the ambulance, and Barton was set to follow them, when he stopped. "Oh, I almost forgot. My sympathy to you in your loss." He extended his hand to Elle.

"Thank you, Officer. And take good care of Mrs. Parrott. She's one of my art students."

"Wait a minute," Barton said. "Your hand is mighty cold. I think you two better get in my car and let me take you back up to the house. We can't have you getting sick after this act of heroism."

When Elle returned home, she wrapped herself in a plaid afghan and sat in the library with a cup of tea. It was late, and she'd sent LeRoi to bed. She wouldn't be able to sleep. Knowing Blake would never again share the bed made her reluctant to climb into it. The library had always been one of her favorite rooms in the house. It was roughly twenty by thirty feet, and all four walls were lined with bookshelves and books, all the way up to the twelve-foot ceiling. It put the convent's library to shame with its showy gilt-edged tomes, many of them first editions and autographed.

The carpets were thick, the furniture was comfortable, and the lighting was strategically placed to facilitate long, luxurious reading sessions. She would miss this room if she left. *Why am I thinking "if"? Of course I will have to leave.*

Elle threw aside the afghan and walked around the room, eyeing certain books by favorite authors: Colleen McCullough, Harper Lee, Andrew Greeley. She lingered at the shelf containing family photo albums. Blake had never shown her these. He had never looked at them, himself, as far as she knew. Probably it would have dredged up too many memories. Even good memories would have been painful. Now Blake was gone, and who would care about the photographs that chronicled the history of an extinguished family?

Elle pulled a gold-embossed oxblood leather album from the shelf at random. It still had a buttery feel and a pleasant smell from the tanning process. She sat down with it in the comfy chair and began turning pages. The photos were professionally taken, the setting an elegant party at a hotel ballroom.

At first she thought it was a wedding reception. The table decorations and food and orchestra were more elaborate than anything Elle had ever seen. People were dressed in formal attire, too, but she didn't see a bridal gown in the crowd. There was Blake, all of about twelve years old, dressed in a tuxedo. He was already handsome, despite the braces on his teeth.

Elle scanned the photos for faces she might recognize. There was a picture of Blake's parents, lifting champagne glasses in a toast. Next to them stood Blake's sister, Melanie. Elle had known Melanie before she died, but she had never seen her as sparkling and vibrant as she looked in this photo. She was standing next to a slim young man with sandy hair and high cheekbones. He reminded Elle of someone she knew, perhaps someone in the art world.

Of course! This had to be Rupert Brooks, and the party must have been the ill-fated engagement party. Rupert carried a lot of Blake's paintings in his gallery, an arrangement Elle had thought odd, since his engagement to Melanie had ended so badly. When she had asked Blake about it, he'd said, "Why shouldn't I give him the business, just because my sister changed her mind about marrying him? Besides, I bear some responsibility for Mel's change of heart, so maybe I can make it up to him this way."

Elle touched the face of the twelve-year old boy who would change her life. How could he have influenced his sister's decisions, when she was already an adult? What had caused Melanie to break up with Brooks and break her parents' hearts? She looked so happy in these photographs, so whatever it was must have happened later.

The second-to-the-last photo in the album gave her a jolt of surprise. It was a picture of Victor Lockwood, holding a Tiparillo cigar in the air, his other hand resting on Blake's shoulder. The famous artist would become a major influence on Blake's work, and even on Elle's. She hadn't realized Blake knew him that many years ago.

Her head nodded as she bent over the photograph. She rearranged her legs under the afghan and turned sideways in the ample chair, so her head rested on its arm. With thoughts of Blake floating in her head, she thought she might close her eyes for a few minutes.

Her last thought was of Tonya Parrott. She crossed herself and prayed Tonya would be okay, and finally she drifted into some semblance of sleep.

CHAPTER 21

Having raced to Brandywine Hospital, Parrott arrived at the same time as the ambulance. He parked his car and dashed to the circular driveway, where the paramedics were unloading the stretcher. Tonya had been given an IV, and she had regained consciousness. Tears pooled in Parrott's eyes as she emerged, head first, and her eyes connected with his.

"Hello, Detective," she murmured. Her voice, normally so robust, was wispy and weak. "Sorry—for all this."

Parrott wanted to take her in his arms and comfort her. He wanted to tell her no need to apologize, everything would be okay. But he couldn't do any of these. His chest was paralyzed with roiling emotions: anger, worry, hurt, and love. He touched his lips and then the stretcher next to her face.

The ER protocols for a motor vehicle accident took four hours. At the end of all the blood tests, x-rays, and CT scans, the doctor popped in to say they were going to admit Tonya for observation, since she had lost consciousness. Otherwise, she had a broken right shoulder, multiple contusions, but, all in all, suffered no other significant damage. Her physical strength and stamina from the Navy had stood her well in this situation, and they expected her to make a full recovery.

They had given her pain medication before setting the shoulder and putting her into an immobilizer. Parrott held her other hand as he walked alongside the gurney. By the time she was settled in the semi-private room, with no one sharing the other side, it was almost three a.m. and the first time they'd been alone together since dinner.

Tonya was hooked up to monitors, a blood pressure cuff, and an IV, in addition to the immobilizer. Her discomfort showed in her eyes and the awkward position of her neck and torso, but her streak of determination showed in the set of her lips. "Ollie, I never should have—"

"Sh…let's just get us some rest now. Plenty of time to talk tomorrow." Parrott pulled the guest chair closer to the bed, angled so he could see his wife's face. Despite everything, she was the most beautiful woman in the world. He found an extra blanket on the closet shelf, and he covered himself. "A few hours' shuteye will do us both a lot of good."

Tonya nodded. "Love you."

"I love you, too." Parrott marveled at how much simpler life had been just twenty-four hours before, when all he had to worry about was an art heist.

Worries had kept Alexander awake for much of the night, too. Not wanting to tell Veronica about his uncle's murder, he had avoided answering calls or replying to texts. He'd finally wrapped the phone in a bath towel and shoved it to the back of a cabinet in the bathroom. After that, he worried she might drive over to see what was wrong, or even worse, send her brute of a brother.

A week ago, news of his uncle's death might have been cause for celebration, at least in Veronica's mind. She had never been shy about reciting fantasies about living in the mansion in Brandywine, hobnobbing with Philadelphia's elite. None of her imaginings had inspired Alexander, though. He hadn't been raised with champagne taste. The more his girlfriend fixated on material things, the happier he was his uncle was alive and well, a buffer between Veronica and her wild dreams.

If Uncle Blake had carried out his threat to change his will, Alexander would be disinherited now. He could live with that, but could Veronica? She had already pushed him to say and do things his mother wouldn't have approved of, and she would push him to fight tooth and nail to contest the will and fight for what was his.

He didn't like the position this put him in with the police. His head was telling him to break it off with Veronica before it was too late, but the very idea of living the rest of his life without her made his heart throb with desire.

The clock said 3:05. He needed to sleep, or he'd be no good at work. He took a picture of Veronica from his wallet, the one he'd taken of her last summer, sunbathing on the bank of the Brandywine River, naked from the waist up.

He lay down on the sofa and closed his eyes. Before long, he crossed over into a dreamless sleep.

CHAPTER 22

The next morning, the sun poured its thick, golden rays through the breakfast room window of Bucolia. They formed a warm rectangle on the table where Caro Campbell opened the New York *Times*, looking for the daily crossword. As she turned pages in the news section, Caro stopped to notice this headline:

Brandywine Artist, Blake Allmond, 54, Dies in Apparent Homicide; Known for 'Mirror Technique.'

Blake Allmond, 54, was found unresponsive yesterday at his second home in New York, the victim of an apparent homicide. The son of society parents, Alexander and Blanche Allmond, Mr. Allmond made a significant name for himself among the Brandywine River artists of the Victor Lockwood school. Mr. Allmond's "mirror technique" has distinguished his career and caused his paintings to be admired and imitated. No details have been released by the police at this time.

Caro's first instinct was to tell John E., but he was out riding with Stan Baker. Her thoughts flew to the conversation they'd had with Detective Parrott about the stolen paintings, and she walked over to the original Allmond, hanging over the mantle in the dining room. The "mirror technique" held her in awe, as it always had. She had always fantasized about having the artist over for dinner, so they could dish over the painting together.

Remembering that Allmond was a cousin of Andrea Baker's, she picked up the phone and hit speed dial. The phone only rang once before Andrea picked it up.

"Caro, hi. What's up?"

"You sound busy. Did I disturb your writing?" When Andrea was in the throes of a crime novel, she usually didn't answer the phone. "Have you seen the *Times* this morning?"

"No, I read it online, but haven't gotten around to it yet. Why?"

Caro shifted in her chair. "I hate to be the bearer of bad news, but there's a short article about Blake Allmond. Seems he's been killed."

"Blake Allmond, the artist?" Andrea's voice rose an octave. "Are you sure?"

"It says, 'Brandywine artist,' killed in his New York apartment. Didn't you tell me he is a cousin?"

"Yes, a third or fourth cousin, or second twice removed. Whatever that means. I haven't seen him in ages. I'm so sorry to hear it."

"Me, too. I can't imagine why someone would want to kill such a talented artist. And something odd, too, Detective Parrott was here just two days ago. He's investigating the theft of Allmond's paintings, apparently taken from his studio."

"Hmm, wonder if the theft is related to the murder," Andrea replied. "My crime writer's mind is always at work." She snickered, but stopped short of laughing. "How tragic this is. Blake is younger, but his sister Melanie was my age, and we grew up together."

"Was? Are you saying Melanie is dead, too?" The thought gave Caro chills.

"Yes, but worse than that. Both parents are gone, Melanie's gone, and Blake's wife and children died in an accident. The whole family's wiped out, one tragedy after another."

Caro thought she detected a catch in her friend's voice. "No heirs then?"

"Um, I think Melanie has a son. She ran off with a guy and married him, it must be thirty years ago. Broke her parents' hearts. Broke her engagement, too, after her parents had given her a blowout engagement party at what was then the brand-new Rittenhouse Hotel in Philadelphia."

"Sounds like a Romeo and Juliet scenario."

"Closer to the truth than you think. The fiancé was high society, and the boyfriend was an immigrant. I think he was related to the Allmonds' gardener. I remember a big hubbub in the family at the time, and then again when she died. Everyone blamed the husband for her death, even though it was lung cancer that killed her." Andrea paused, and it sounded like she took a sip of something. "Oh, I'm *so* sorry to hear about Blake."

"Me, too, and not just because he's your relative. Ever since we bought one of his paintings, I've wanted to meet him, have him over for a dinner or something. I'd been meaning to talk to you about it, but Preston's death has thrown me off-kilter, and I kept putting it off."

"Well, don't beat yourself up about it. I don't think it ever would've happened anyway. They weren't very social."

"They? Did he remarry, then?"

"No, not that I know of, but he had a live-in girlfriend, another artist. Considering we live in the same few hundred square miles, you'd think we would have spent more time together, but Stan is older, and Blake is younger, and I always had the sense he and the girlfriend were rather reclusive." Andrea sniffed. "I'm sorry. I just never expected to hear this kind of news about Blake."

"Don't apologize. If anyone knows what it feels like to lose a cousin so unexpectedly, it's me."

"That's true." Andrea blew her nose. "Say, do you think Parrott will be investigating? Maybe I'll give him a call."

"He's investigating the art theft, but the murder happened in New York."

"Oh, yes. You did say that. Well, maybe I'll give him a call anyway. He's such a sincere young man. Maybe I could help him in some way."

"As a member of the family, you probably could." Caro doodled a series of stars on the note pad in front of her. "Are you thinking about paying a condolence call to Blake's girlfriend?"

Andrea sighed. "I suppose I should at least offer. It would be the right thing, although I feel awkward about it."

"Would you like me to go with you? I have a couple of cakes and pies in the freezer that we could take."

"Thank you. That sounds wonderful. Let me see," Andrea said, her voice tapering off as a page-flipping sound filled the silence. "I'm looking for contact information, but I don't even have the woman's name here."

"Well, that gives you a reason to call Detective Parrott. I'm sure he can tell you her name."

After Caro hung up, she remained at the table, drawing stars and circles on the margins of the newspaper. A familiar stab of pain reminded her she hadn't gotten over her cousin Preston's death yet. Now Andrea would have a similar hole in her heart. It was bad enough when someone died like their friend, Gerald Kelley, of natural causes, but when the life of a family member was cut short like this—it changed a person forever.

CHAPTER 23

That same morning, Veronica stormed into the South Philadelphia branch of the Lyons Bank in the nick of time for work. When she reached the teller counter where she had worked for the past eighteen months, she found the bank's security guard sitting in her chair. *This can't be good*, she thought.

"'Morning, Hector," she said, attempting a breezy tone. "How's the family?" She lifted the hinged countertop and passed through to the teller's side, hoping Hector would vacate her seat, so she could grab her till, and carry it to the central safe. She had to transfer money into it before she could take her first customer, and there were already several people pulling into the parking lot. The other two tellers were at their stations and ready. Nobody liked it when people had to wait. She had already seen the fish eye from Maggie, the girl to her left.

She reached for the drawer handle, but Hector's rotund middle blocked her access. "Hey, I'm running late. Let me in, please." She flashed a brilliant smile, hoping it didn't look fake.

"Sorry, *mi amiga*," the guard replied. "Orders from the boss." His fingers encircled her wrist and pressed hard, preventing her from reaching the drawer.

"Ow," she cried. "What's going on here?" Her thoughts flew to Alexander's warning, "You'll be lucky if you don't get fired." *Oh, where is Alexander when I need him, and why didn't he call me back last night?*

"Potfiller is waiting for you in his office, and he ain't smiling." Hector whispered, but Veronica suspected the two other tellers heard every word. Each of them was only a few feet away, and the office gossip quotient was high at this moment.

Potfiller was Reginald Philpot, so nicknamed when he was the chief loan officer. The number of "pot" jokes associated with banking likely hastened his promotion to Branch President. It certainly wasn't his affability with customers or employees that got him there. Veronica crossed herself and grabbed her purse from the floor under the desk, where she had flung it. Without a word to Hector or the girls, she marched down the hall, holding her head high.

The traffic pattern dead-ended at Edith's desk. A stocky, middle-aged woman with a graying bun, Edith served as Cerberus to Mr. Philpot. Veronica couldn't remember the last time she had approached Edith's desk. The woman's staunch appearance and authoritative voice reminded her of the Wizard of Oz's admonition to Dorothy to go home. A queasiness rose in Veronica's throat, but she tamped it down.

"Mr. Philpot wanted to see me?" She pointed to her name tag, which had "Espinosa" in large letters, "Veronica" in smaller ones underneath. She hoped the tiny tremor in her voice went undetected.

Edith rolled her steely-grey eyes toward the office of the president. "I'll tell him you're here," she said, and she lifted the receiver to her ear and tapped an extension into the telephone keypad. "Ms. Espinosa is here to see you," she said in a tone that implied, "prepare the chopping block." After a second or two, she said, "Very well," and disconnected. Her eyes met Veronica's, and she said, "You may go in."

Veronica nodded, and turned toward the closed door. As she walked away, she thought she heard Edith mumble, "Good luck."

Heart thumping in her ears, Veronica tapped on the door, wishing she could run away and never come back. She considered whether she had stepped on anyone's toes, aggravated any customers, come up short at the end of a day. No, the only thing she could think of was the bit of research she had done on Blake Allmond. What had started out as a simple fact-finding mission, to learn about her boyfriend's uncle, now caused every fiber of her being to be on guard. If Philpot asked her why she had done it, she would say it had been an innocent mistake. She had keyed in an account number in error, and when she had seen whose account came up, she recognized the name and took a closer look. No big deal.

"Come in," boomed a voice through the solid door. Veronica turned the knob and pushed. What she saw inside nearly caused her to faint, not just Mr. Philpot, but a woman and man in uniform. As she approached the desk, she had the impression of being pinned on a stage with a white-hot spotlight.

Her boss pointed to the third chair, and she lowered herself into it as if it were a life raft in a stormy sea. It was then she noticed the two gold badges on the visitors' waistbands. *Holy shit! They were NYPD.*

In all her twenty-five years, Veronica had never been more frightened. She willed herself to breathe, in, out. She clutched the arms of the chair for dear life, until she let go and folded her hands in her lap. She crossed her long legs at the ankle the way she had seen Meghan Markle do. Finally, she made eye contact with Mr. Philpot and gave him a tentative smile.

"Miss Espinosa," her boss began, "let me introduce you to Detectives Rayburn and Coleman from the New York Police Department." He paused to straighten the small stack of pages in an open folder on his desk. "They are here to talk with you about one of the bank's customers, Mr. Blake Allmond."

Here it comes. Chachi was right. I'm not just busted—I'm probably fired. Veronica braced herself for whatever.

"Before I turn this over to them, I think you should know one of our officers in the Manhattan branch, a personal friend of Mr. Allmond, noticed someone without authority had accessed Mr. Allmond's accounts. This apparently occurred not once, but several times." He exchanged glances with the police before continuing. "I'm sure you're aware everything you do under your sign-on leaves tracks, and since Mr. Allmond was not a customer at our branch, your actions raised some red flags."

Veronica inhaled and opened her mouth to reply, but before she could utter a word, Mr. Philpot said, "Please. Don't say anything yet. I'm going to turn this over to the officers. I'm sure they have some questions for you."

With that, Officer Coleman scooted his chair forward and sideways at an angle, the better to make eye contact. "Miss

Espinosa, before we get started, I'm going to read you your rights. You have the right to remain silent..."

Omigod, I'm going to be arrested. Veronica shut her eyes and blocked out the rest of the Miranda rights. When Alexander had warned her that her snooping had been noticed, she had googled misdemeanors related to bank records. Having found none, she had relaxed. It wasn't as if she had embezzled or committed fraud. She had just looked at them. *But why are the New York police here, and why are they reading me my rights?*

She forced herself to pay attention. She would demand a lawyer if need be. She wouldn't fall into a trap.

"Miss Espinosa," the lady cop said in a tone probably meant to soothe. "I'm Officer Rayburn. Officer Coleman and I want to ask you some questions about your connection to Blake Allmond, specifically, why you checked his bank accounts five times in the past month."

Veronica found her voice, though when it came out, it was little more than a squeak. "Am I under arrest?" The word "arrest" nearly stuck in her throat.

"No, ma'am. We are just trying to get a sense of why you were so interested in Mr. Allmond's bank accounts."

Veronica looked at her boss, and back at Officer Rayburn. She seemed to be pleasant enough, professional. "I—I stumbled upon the wrong account by accident, transposed two numbers or something like that. When I saw the account balance, I got curious and checked to see if there were other accounts in the same name. I was fascinated a local artist could have so much accumulated wealth."

Officer Coleman interjected, "So are you saying it was merely an accident that you went into the account the first time?"

When Veronica nodded, he said, "And the fact you are dating Blake Allmond's nephew has nothing to do with your spying on the accounts?"

A fist squeezed Veronica's heart. *They know about Alexander. And what else?* She took a deep breath and screwed up her courage. "What's the big deal? So I looked at the account balances. As far as I know that's not a crime."

"Perhaps you are right, Miss Espinosa," Coleman responded. He exchanged glances with his partner, who jumped in.

"I think you should know before we go any further, we are investigating Blake Allmond's murder."

The "M-word" caused the room to spin and chilly pinpricks to sting her arms and legs. Before she could respond, she fell forward and toppled to the floor in a dead faint.

CHAPTER 24

Morning came early at Brandywine Hospital, when the sharp voices and clanging of breakfast carts filled the hallway with unwelcome efficiency. Parrott sat up and checked his cell phone. He had slept for less than three hours.

He glanced at Tonya, who remained impervious to the noise. She looked as if she hadn't moved a millimeter. The pain meds must have done their magic.

A hand flipped the overhead lights on, and a voice called, "Good morning," as if they were guests at a surprise party getting underway. The covered breakfast dish smelled like something lukewarm and bland.

When the food service worker saw Parrott, she jumped. "I didn't know there was a guest in this room. Want me to bring a tray for you, too, Mister?"

"No thanks." Parrott glanced at Tonya, who was rubbing her eyes with her left hand. "Want some breakfast, honey?" he asked. Tonya's disability was starting to sink in. With her dominant hand immobilized, how would she feed, dress, or bathe herself? She certainly wouldn't be able to drive, cook, or go to her art lessons.

He had to work. How would she manage by herself? Maybe he should ask his mother to come help.

Tonya stretched her free arm over her head and winced. "Doesn't smell very appetizing."

She tossed the covers aside and tried to sit up. "Think I'd better go to the bathroom."

Parrott put a hand out to stop her. "You need to call for help. You're still hooked up." He pushed the call button on the remote control, and when he caught the stern look, he said, "Listen, I know you like to be self-sufficient and all that, but you've got to give yourself time to heal. As long as your shoulder is out of commission, you're going to have to accept help. Period."

When the nurse's aide came in to help Tonya get to the bathroom, Parrott stepped out into the hall and called Chief Schrik. "I'll be in a little late this morning."

"I heard about your wife. She needs you more than we do right now, so take your time."

Not for the first time, Parrott appreciated the kindness of his boss, but he had an independent streak of his own. Very few of his friends had landed positions like his, and he meant to stay worthy of it. "If they release her this morning, I'll get her settled at home, and then I'll come in. I have some ideas of next steps for the case."

"Think about it this way, Parrott. You worked hours of overtime yesterday, notifying Allmond's next of kin. You could take the whole day off today, and you'd be entitled."

An hour later, Dr. Hwang visited and explained the results of all the tests. "You are a very lucky woman. Your brain scans look good, and there are no signs of fractures anywhere but in the shoulder. You're going to be bruised and sore for several days, but I'm sending you home."

Tonya exhaled and grinned, showing the space between her front teeth. She resembled a bird sprung from a cage.

"Hold on a minute," the doctor said. "I didn't say you could start doing everything you're used to doing. Your arm has to stay immobilized for six weeks. No showering, no driving, no using it for anything. This will be very hard on you." He frowned. "You are right-handed?" When Tonya nodded, he said, "Even harder. You will need help at home. If you don't follow instructions, you'll probably need surgery."

Now it was Tonya's turn to frown, but only for a second. "I'll be a good patient, I promise. I made it through Navy SEAL training. After that, I'm pretty sure I can endure anything."

Parrott interjected. "Maybe I can get my mother to come stay with us for a few days, just to get you settled in, cook some meals and freeze them. Do the laundry."

"Please, Ollie. Let me try on my own. If I can't manage, then we can call your mother."

Parrott knew when to concede a battle. One of the things that attracted him to Tonya was the same thing that confounded him at times—her ability to handle things in her own way. The past few weeks the PTSD had seemed to erode her strong spirit. Ironically, with this injury, it seemed to be reemerging. Maybe having a physical ailment to deal with would take her mind off of her mental ailment. If it did, it would bring blessed relief.

"Okay, sweetheart. We'll do it your way," Parrott said. "Now, what do you say we head for home? I know a bird that's missing us by now."

CHAPTER 25

The chair in the library had proven to be an ideal place to sleep. Its over-sized seat and padded arms cradled Elle's petite frame. The thickness of the walls muffled outside sounds. The single picture window, covered in heavy wood shutters to match the bookshelves, faced west. So it was after ten a.m. when LeRoi knocked on the door and woke her up.

"Pardon me, ma'am," he whispered. "I've been looking for you, and I have a breakfast tray ready in the kitchen."

Elle scanned the room, her eyes landing on the open photo album on her lap. It all came back to her with a punch, Blake, the accident, holing herself up in the library. She wished she could go back to sleep and escape the harsh reality.

Still dressed in the pants and top and robe she had worn outside, she rolled onto her feet and began straightening up.

"No need to clean up. Gives me something to do." The servant's dark circles and bleary eyes gave away his own grief.

"Okay, then," Elle replied. "I think I'll go upstairs and shower." She thought of Blake's clothes and toiletries, waiting in vain for his return, and a boulder formed in her throat. "We have some difficult tasks ahead of us."

LeRoi followed Elle out of the library and into the foyer, where she headed for the stairs. "Yes, ma'am, and you've already had some phone calls this morning. I believe they went to voicemail."

Elle imagined who might be calling once news of Blake's death got out—lawyers, bankers, police—she would have to make funeral arrangements today, too. The enormity of it weighed her every step. She supposed she would have to cancel her art classes for this week.

She turned and called to LeRoi from the staircase. "Please remind me. I want to send flowers to Tonya Parrott."

After showering and donning clean clothes, Elle went down to get something to eat. It was almost noon, and breakfast had lost any appeal after sitting on the tray for hours. Sounds of the vacuum cleaner wafted through the house, and Elle didn't want to interrupt, so she foraged through the pantry for something to fill her stomach, if not her spirit. A can of SpaghettiOs with meatballs, fit the bill, something she'd considered "comfort food" from her childhood on. She added a sprinkle of parmesan cheese and heated it up in the microwave. A glass of iced tea and a chocolate-covered biscotti rounded out the meal.

While she was nibbling the dessert, the phone rang, filling her with dread. She prayed for the strength to handle the trials ahead, and she answered the phone.

"Ms. Carmichael, Gary Griffith. You remember we met a couple of years ago at a charity benefit in New York? You were auctioning a painting, if I remember correctly?"

Elle recalled the evening. Gary was one of Blake's buddies from high school. He had sparkling blue eyes and a kind face. "I remember," she said. "You've heard about Blake."

"It's in today's newspaper. You have my deepest sympathy, and I want to help you however I can. Blake was a good man, a true friend." He paused as if to wipe his eyes or fold his hands in prayer. "I called earlier and left a voicemail message."

"I apologize. I was just about to listen to messages. I, uh, overslept this morning."

"No need to apologize. I just wanted to inform you of a few things and set up a time for us to chat. Blake was in my office just before he—uh, died. He changed his will and gave me instructions to be followed upon his death. I never dreamed it would be so soon."

"What? Blake changed his will? I wonder if he had a premonition. I keep turning it over in my mind. Who would have wanted Blake dead? I was unaware that he had any enemies."

"I know the feeling. Blake was always everybody's friend. Before all the tragedy, he was the most light-hearted and fun-loving of us all. Even after, he'd give you the shirt off his back."

Another pause. "Anyway, I want to schedule a time to meet with you, and also with Blake's nephew. We can wait until after the funeral, but I don't want to wait too long. The end of the year will be here before we know it, and there are tax considerations."

Elle imagined she would have to leave Manderley before the end of the year. It was only right the home remain in the family. She chided herself for having been so unprepared for something like this. Her life with Blake, though, was still in its youthfulness, or adolescence. They were barely middle-aged. Her voice, when she found it, was reedy. "I haven't even thought about a funeral yet. Blake never discussed his wishes with me." Tears stung her eyes and nose.

The lawyer's voice took on a gentler tone. "Perhaps I can assist you. The Allmonds have always used Terry Funeral Home in Downington. You may remember Melanie's funeral was there."

"Yes, I remember now. It's in that lovely two-story house on Lancaster. I'll contact them today."

"You probably need to talk with the New York police first, to see when they'll release the body. In fact, I'm surprised you haven't heard from the police before now."

"They may have called and left a voicemail. I can see I've got my work cut out for me. Why don't I work on the voicemails, contact the police and the funeral home, and get back to you? I appreciate your help more than I can say."

Elle ended the phone call and pulled a pen and notepad from the desk drawer. She started a list: Gary Griffith, Terry Funeral Home. Then she listened to voicemails.

The first one was from 9:02 a.m., a woman's voice. "This is Detective Rayburn from the New York Police Department. I'm trying to reach a Miz Elle Carmichael. Please give me a call at your earliest convenience."

Next was the call from Griffith. The third voicemail was from Tonya Parrott. Elle put down her pen and listened. "—I just wanted to tell you I'm sorry for your loss. And also I'm okay. I'm sorry for disrupting your evening like that. You must think I'm a lunatic. It's just, I enjoyed your class so much yesterday. You're a really cool lady and a great artist. When I heard about Mr. Allmond I flipped out, and I got in my car and started driving.

It was a surprise even to me that I ended up at your place. I never even saw the deer. Anyway, I've got a broken shoulder, but I'm at home. Just wanted you to know I'm thinking of you. Let me know if I can help with anything."

Elle made a note to look up Tonya's address from the class enrollment form and send her some flowers. She'd email the five students about cancelling the class. The SpaghettiOs gurgled in her stomach, but she ignored their familiar notes. It was time to face a different sheet of music. She dialed the number of the New York Police Department.

CHAPTER 26

By the time Parrott got Tonya settled at home, and he'd warmed up the leftover chili and cornbread for their lunch, it was almost two. Tonya picked at her food, apparently lost in pain or thought. Parrott ate quickly, all the while considering whether to express his anger, worry, and concern about Tonya's rash behavior. None of this had to have happened.

He washed out the dishes and put them on the rack to dry, cleaned Horace's cage and fed him, and checked for voicemail messages. The Toyota dealership had confirmed receipt of Tonya's car. They would have three days to get the insurance company to assess the damage.

"You can go on to work now, Ollie," Tonya said. "I'm gonna find me a movie, and maybe take a nap." She held the remote and clicked.

"You sure? I don't have to go in if you need me here."

"Why should you sit here doing nothing? You aren't the one who needs to heal. I'll be fine, and if I need anything, I'll call." Charles Laughton in *Witness for the Prosecution* filled the screen.

Parrott hesitated, but said, "Listen, baby, we don't have to talk about this now. You can heal physically first. But at some point we need to address what happened last night. Not dealing with it will only make it worse."

Tears peeked from the corners of Tonya's eyes, and she hung her head. "Okay," she whispered.

Parrott leaned in for a kiss before leaving. "I'll pick up a pizza from Rocco's for dinner. See you around 7." He marveled at Tonya's calmer disposition since the accident, how suddenly the switch could flip from frantic to calm and back again. It pained him to know this was not normal, and, as much as he loved her, his wife was going to need more help than he could offer.

When he got to the office, Lucretia handed him several messages. Andrea Baker had called. The crime writer had helped him solve the Phillips case. Whatever she had to say, he was glad to hear from her.

Another call had come from the Galveston Chief of Police. While they were honeymooning on Galveston Island, the Parrotts had gone deep sea fishing. The police chief and his wife were on the same excursion. They'd struck up a friendship and shared some opinions about a thorny case down there. *Maybe he's calling to tell me they've wrapped it up. Sure hope so.*

All of these could wait, though. Parrott needed to get back to the stolen art. Allmond's death didn't change the fact that Parrott had an active case. If anything, it made the case a whole lot more interesting. He wanted to drop in at the Rue Moderne this afternoon. He'd assembled some questions for the gallery owner.

Parrott swung by the chief's office to give him an update on Tonya and tell him his plan. "I'm glad to see you, Parrott. I just got off the phone with New York. The autopsy's done, with a TOD between 12:30 and 2:30 a.m. on Wednesday. Allmond had eaten dinner, probably had alcohol, too, but toxicology isn't back yet. With a gaping hole in his chest concerns about poison are minimal anyway."

"Any suspects yet?"

"If there were, we'd be the last to hear about them. Only reason they told me that much is courtesy, since you notified the next of kin. Saved them a trip. They'll be releasing the body for burial. Oh, and they asked me if you've developed a relationship with Allmond's girlfriend."

"Why do they care about that?" Parrott wasn't sure whether Schrik knew about Tonya and the art therapy class, but he would need to disclose it. He'd rather Schrik hear about things from him first.

"Keep their options open if they need you to facilitate a Q&A. They'd never admit it, though, and they'd never give you credit for anything in their case, even if you delivered the solution to them on a silver platter."

"That reminds me. I don't know whether Randy told you Tonya's accident was on the roadway in front of Allmond's house." Schrik smiled. "He did, and I was sure you'd give me an explanation whenever you got around to it." Parrott rubbed the sides of his head. "I'm not sure I can explain it, but I'll try." He summarized yesterday's events, starting with the art therapy class and ending with hitting the deer. "Tonya seems to be taken with Ms. Carmichael, and apparently the feeling is mutual."

"I'd say you have indeed developed a relationship with Carmichael then."

"I was worried you'd think it was a conflict of interest, Chief." Schrik pushed his chair back and stood. "I might have," he said, "if we were investigating the murder, especially if we thought the girlfriend was a viable suspect. But the stolen paintings? Nah. Tonya's friendship might even give us an advantage."

"Well, I'm glad you know about it. Any thoughts before I head out to Rupert Brooks's shop?"

"None you haven't thought of already, I'm sure. Just remember, Brooks is one of *them*."

After the Phillips case, Parrott knew exactly what that meant.

There was a stiff breeze rustling the leaves on the trees outside of Rue Moderne, blowing some of their fallen brothers in circles outside of the doorway, already cast in shadows by the waning sun. The bells jingled when Parrott opened the door. Otherwise, the room was quiet. Parrott strode through the first room and into the museum-like room where an easel was set up, but no artist. *All of this expensive art on the wall and no one to prevent someone's walking off with it? Probably security cameras everywhere, though.*

"Hello, hello," came a familiar male voice from the direction of Brooks's office. The lanky art dealer hurried into the room. Red-framed readers bounced on his chest, and as he approached, Parrott could see the miniature paintings, serving as occasional beads on the eyeglass chain.

Was it Parrott's imagination, or did Brooks frown when he realized who had entered the shop? "Sorry to come without calling first. I thought of a few more questions, and I was in the neighborhood."

Brooks hesitated for a second, then said, "Sure. Come on back." He led the way to the tiny office and motioned for Parrott to sit in the narrow space. The room smelled of paper and ink. "I was just working on a new exhibit we're going to have in February. Victor Lockwood's granddaughter's first, and she's quite talented."

"It must be a *coup* to have a first Lockwood exhibit in your gallery," Parrott said. "Are you close to the family then?"

"The exhibit won't be here, although I'm the organizer. It will be in New York." He fingered the red glasses on his chest. "You could say the Lockwoods and Brookses go back a long, long way. My father helped Victor get started. There are artists and artist-wannabes in many of the Brandywine families, you know."

Parrott gazed at Brooks's high cheekbones and patrician nose and remembered what Chief Schrik had said about him. "Actually, that dovetails with one of the questions I have. As I've looked into the paintings taken from Blake Allmond's studio, I've learned there were many other beautiful paintings there, on the wall and stored. I've seen, for example, Allmond's sister Melanie was an accomplished painter, as is Allmond's significant other, Elle Carmichael. There may have been other paintings of value there, as well." Parrott attempted to lean back. "So my question is this, do you think the thief targeted Allmond's two paintings specifically? And, if so, why? What would that tell us about the person who stole the paintings?"

Brooks scratched the side of his nose. So far no one had mentioned Allmond's death, but it was the elephant in the room. "Well, Detective. You've asked three questions, not one, and I'm not exactly sure how to respond. I am an art dealer, not an art thief."

"Of course, I didn't mean to imply—"

"—And furthermore, I'm sure you are aware Mr. Allmond is now deceased. I'm surprised you didn't ask whether I thought the same person who stole the paintings murdered the artist."

Parrott nodded. "I may have gotten around to that. However, Mr. Allmond's death, er, murder, doesn't negate the fact that a crime was committed by stealing the paintings, doesn't diminish our obligation to solve that crime, and, if possible, make restitution to Mr. Allmond's estate."

Brooks blinked.

"Shall I repeat the questions?"

"Not necessary. My guess, although I am no expert in art theft, is Allmond's paintings were the targets. Melanie was a fine artist, and so is Elle, for that matter, but neither made a name for themselves with the Brandywine artists, as Blake did. What I think that tells you is the thief is someone who knows something about art, maybe even knew Blake personally." He paused to clear his throat and polish his glasses with the hem of his sweater. "Of course, this is pure speculation on my part."

"I understand, and I appreciate you humoring me. So, let's carry the scenario a bit further. If the thief knew the value of Allmond's paintings and pre-selected which ones to take, what do you think he plans to do with them?"

Brooks shook his head. "That's really puzzling. Anyone who knows about fine art knows stolen art is almost impossible to fence. No reputable dealer is going to buy it, and black market buyers wouldn't offer enough to make it worth the while to steal it. So that points to an amateur. In my opinion, of course." Tiny dots of perspiration appeared on Brooks's upper lip. "Listen, I hate to rush you, but I've got to finalize these plans, and it's getting late."

Parrott gave what he hoped was a sympathetic smile. "I won't be much longer. I just want to follow up on the idea you mentioned earlier about the theft and the murder being connected. Do *you* think they are connected, Mr. Brooks?"

"Did I mention that? I thought you were the one who brought that up." Brooks fidgeted. "I'm sure I couldn't venture a guess about that."

"One more thing. Last time I was here, you told me you had been engaged to Melanie Allmond. After the engagement was off and Melanie married someone else, did you remain close to the family, or did hard feelings get in the way?" This was the question Parrott came to ask. The others were just throwaways.

Brooks took a deep breath before answering. "Hard to answer. I guess in the short term, there were hard feelings, but Blake and I reconnected, both being in the art world, and all, and I would say we are still—uh, were still friendly. You know I carry his paintings."

"If you don't mind my asking, why *did* Melanie break off the engagement?"

Brooks looked at his watch. "That, Detective, is something you would have to ask her, or maybe her little brother, if only either of them were available. No one was kind enough to share that information with me." He patted his hair and stood. "I'm sorry, but I have an appointment in New York this evening."

Refusing to take the hint, Parrott shifted gears. "I *am* curious about something else that I think you could help me with. When your customers purchase expensive paintings, other than hanging them on the walls of their homes, what do they do with them? There's only so much wall space in a person's home, yet people collect art throughout their lifetimes. I'm trying to get a feel of what happens to a work of art once it's purchased, or even stolen."

"Great question." Brooks sat down again. He seemed to be more relaxed to talk about this subject. "Many collectors rotate the paintings displayed in their houses. They may hang a painting for six months or a year, then exchange it for another. That way they don't tire of looking at the same painting."

"I get that, but where do they store the unhung paintings?" He leaned forward, putting him almost face to face with the dealer. "They must have concerns about the paintings being damaged or stolen. Wouldn't their insurance companies want to know, as well?"

"Yes, there are temperature-controlled storage facilities, highly secured in terms of protecting the paintings, fully insured, and very expensive. A good number of paintings end up there when they aren't being used. In fact…" Brooks paused to look at his fingernails.

"In fact?"

"Some purchases are shipped to these art warehouses directly, without ever having been displayed by the new owners."

Parrott scratched his head. "Why would someone buy a painting, just to hide it in a warehouse?"

"Could be a number of reasons, but the most common is taxes."

"Taxes?"

"Let's say you bought a Lockwood painting from me, here in Kennett Square, for fifty million dollars. Six percent state tax comes to three million."

Parrott whistled.

"If you wanted to avoid paying the tax, you could have the painting packed and shipped to a warehouse in Delaware. No state tax there, and you wouldn't have to pay the taxes until you shipped it back to your home in Pennsylvania."

"No kidding. People would really do that to avoid paying tax."

Learn something new every day about how the rich people live.

"So who keeps track of what paintings are stored in a warehouse? Someone must."

"Art warehousing is a business, just like all of the other art-related businesses. The only difference is ninety percent of that business is discretion. The locks on the warehouses are strong, but the locks on the people's mouths are even stronger."

"Maybe Allmond's stolen paintings are sitting in a warehouse," Parrott said.

"Well, good luck finding them, if they are. It'd be like finding a needle in a haystack."

CHAPTER 27

By the time he left Rue Moderne, the sun hovered over the horizon, and indigo clouds were dragging the cloak of evening over Kennett Square. While he was inside with Brooks, Parrott had put Tonya out of his mind, but the instant he crossed the threshold into the approaching evening, anxiety encroached on his thoughts, and he decided to skip going back to the office.

He punched speaker and called home as he hurried to the car. Tonya answered on the first ring. "Hello, Detective," she answered, her voice groggy from sleep or drugs or both. "You'll never guess what I received today."

Relieved by her tone, he said, "I'll bite. What?"

"A gorgeous flower arrangement. Mostly roses and chrysanthemums. The delivery man had to bring it in and put it on the table."

"Who's it from?" Parrott asked, kicking himself for not thinking of something like that, himself. "A secret admirer?"

"You won't believe it. I'll read you the card." The rustling of fabric filled the pause. "Here it is, 'Heal fast, so you can return to class soon. –Elle Carmichael.'"

Parrott made a mental note to pick up a box of chocolates on the way home. "That's really nice of her, especially since she's got some healing to do, too," Parrott said. "How are you feeling?"

"Not too bad. I've slept off and on most of the day. Horace keeps me company with his sweet singing. We watched a movie together."

"I'm on my way home now. What do you want on your pizza, the usual?"

"Sounds great."

"*You* sound great. Be there in a few minutes."

Parrott disconnected, called in the pizza order, and checked his office voicemail, thankful for Bluetooth, which allowed him to do everything by voice. One motor vehicle accident in the family was more than enough. As he drove, he skimmed through the messages until he reached one that made him smile.

"Hello, Detective Parrott, this is Andrea Baker. I'm sure you remember me. I'm Caro Campbell's friend. Any-way, I hope you are doing well these past few months. I wonder if you could call me. It's about Blake Allmond, who happened to be my cousin. I understand you're investigating over there..."

Andrea had helped him solve the Phillips case last year, something for which he would be eternally grateful. Her experiences as a crime writer had come in handy, and she was a pretty down-to-earth person, too, especially compared to some of the others he had met from the Campbell party. He figured he owed her. He voice-activated the call-back code, as he drove.

After they exchanged pleasantries, Andrea said, "So, you've got the missing paintings case? I can't think of any-one better to look for them."

"Thanks for the compliment, but the case has been slow going."

"Now Blake has been murdered, it may be even slower, don't you think? The more heinous the crime, the more attention and effort. I know better than to ask whether you've got suspects."

"The murder is a New York case, you know, but I imagine there might be some crossover. Anyway, how can I help you?"

"Well, you might think it odd, but even though Blake was a cousin, I didn't know him all that well. His sister Melanie was my age, and Blake was about ten years younger, a huge difference when you're kids. We crossed paths once in a while here in Brandywine, but he kept a low profile, and we didn't run in the same circles."

"Understandable. He painted, while you wrote."

"Yes, and he wasn't part of the horsey crowd either. Anyway, I attended the funerals of Susan and the kids and Melanie, and I may have met Blake's significant other a time or two over the years, but I can't remember her name. I'd like to call her and offer my sympathy or even help with the funeral arrangements. I was sure you would be able to tell me."

"Sure. Her name's Elle Carmichael. Nice woman. I'm sure she'd appreciate your call."

"Happen to have her number?"

"Not with me, and I won't be back in the office till tomorrow."

"I can wait until then. Do you know whether she has family or a group of friends to support her? I keep thinking of how I might feel in her shoes."

"I'm sure she's in shock, and grieving, but hopefully she'll recover in time." Parrott pulled into the parking lot of See's Candy and climbed out of the car. The aromas of chocolate and marshmallows filled his nostrils, even before he opened the door.

"I can tell you've gotten where you were going, so I'll let you go. Thanks for calling me with Elle's number when you have it."

"Sure thing." He hung up and thought for a few seconds about the Baker-Carmichael connection. He'd make sure with Ms. Carmichael it was okay to give her phone number to Allmond's cousin. Knowing another person associated with the Allmonds could only help him, and it couldn't be a better person if he had picked her himself.

CHAPTER 28

Alexander had felt guilty all night over not calling Veronica back. Now he was at work, having a hard time concentrating. He hadn't gone this long without talking to her since they'd met eleven months ago. Hearing about his uncle's death had changed his paradigm, though. It had made him afraid. He knew it was bad not to take her calls—it didn't bode well for the relationship, but he also knew he couldn't keep avoiding her.

When he was a little boy, about eight or nine, he had been addicted to jelly beans. His mother took him for a dental check-up, and he had seven cavities. His mother had taken away the jelly beans. Alexander understood the jelly beans were no good for him, and he tried to stop craving them, but before long he couldn't stand being without them, and he managed to get some, stash them away, and resume his habit.

Veronica was his current jelly bean. Some of her ideas scared the shit out of him, but he knew his taste for her wouldn't go away, so he might as well give in. When he got home from work he would clean up and go over there, maybe even take her some flowers. When she asked him why he hadn't answered the phone, he'd tell her he'd left it at work by mistake. When she asked him why he hadn't come over anyway, he'd tell her about Uncle Blake. She would have a million questions, and he would do his best to dodge every one of them.

With so many thoughts swirling in his head, it was a wonder he was able to concentrate on his work, but Alexander pushed them aside and focused on things that could be measured, hammered, and drilled. Before he knew it, it was quitting time, time to shed the hard hat and put away the tools. Today he had been framing windows in an apartment building, new construction. Normally, he'd be chomping at the bit to leave, but today there was lead in his feet. On the other hand, he couldn't wait to get his arms around Veronica's waist and pull her close. *Oh, man, I'm totally lost.*

He only worked twenty minutes away from home. As he drove through the gathering evening, *Crazy in Love* came on, and he turned up the radio to blaring. Who ever thought being crazy in love could be so complicated?

When he turned onto his street, Alexander hit the brakes. Veronica's silver Chevy Cobalt was parked in his driveway. He squinted to see if she was sitting in the car, on the stoop, or on the steps to the side door, but there was no sign of her. His heart raced, from worry or excitement, he didn't know which.

He pulled up to the house and parked on the street, leaping out of the car. He felt like shouting her name at the top of his lungs, something he might have done even a week ago, but now he tamped his emotion. He peered into the Chevy's windows—no Veronica. There was nothing to do but go inside and call her cell phone.

When he got to the front door, he found it cracked open. Warm air greeted him as he pushed against it, head first. "Veronica?" he called into the dim interior.

"Over here," she answered, her voice muffled by nasal overtones. She was lying on the couch surrounded by crumpled tissues.

Alexander slammed the door behind him and rushed to the sofa, throwing his arms around her in an awkward embrace. Their lips locked in a passionate kiss that lasted until she gasped for air. "Honey, what are you doing here? How did you get in?" He had intentionally not given her a key, and he hadn't accepted the key to her apartment when offered. That was a level of commitment they hadn't quite reached.

"Oh, Chachi, I've had a terrible day. I've been here over an hour, waiting for you to get home." She clung to his waist and wailed.

He brushed her tears away, letting his fingers play in her dark tresses, the inevitable desire resulting. "What happened?"

Veronica sat up and stared into his eyes. "Before I tell you, why didn't you call me back last night? You still love me, don't you?" He pulled her close and said, "Yes, I love you. Can't you tell?" A long moment passed before he asked again, "What's got you so upset?"

She grabbed his face in her hands and asked, "Do you know what happened to your uncle, Chachi?"

The question filled him with dread. He wasn't planning to keep it a secret, but he had expected to have time to tell her, himself. "How did you find out?" he whispered.

"The police. They were waiting for me when I got to work this morning. It was like you said. I called attention to myself by breaching his accounts."

Alexander stood and began pacing around the small room. "I was worried that would happen. You should never have done that in the first place." A bad feeling overtook him. "Did they ask you about me?"

"Not at first, but after they told me he was d-dead, m-murdered, well—I fainted."

"You fainted? That's not good."

"I know. I think I was in shock, worried they had come to arrest me. When I came to, they brought me water. Then questions. What was my connection to Blake Allmond, what made me so interested in his money?"

"What did you tell them?" Alexander held his breath.

"I had to think fast. If I made up a lie, surely I'd be caught up in it, and I'd look guilty. If I told the truth, I'd still look guilty, just maybe a tad less so. So I told them we were friends. I saw you at a party, and you mentioned you were the nephew. I got curious and decided to see if Allmond was a customer, see if he was as rich as you'd said."

"What else did they ask you?"

"What I did with the information, what I intended to do with it, stuff like that. I told them, 'Nothing.' I told them I didn't tell anyone what I saw. They asked me a lot of personal questions, too."

"How did the bank handle it? Did they fire you?"

Veronica shook her head. "No, but they weren't happy. It doesn't look good for the bank to have the New York police investigating one of its employees. I get that."

Alexander exhaled the breath he hadn't realized he was holding. "They're not going to forget about this, you know. The police and the bank. They're going to be watching your every move. Hell, they're probably going to be watching me, too." He sat and leaned forward, elbows on knees, staring at a spot on the wall. This was what he was afraid of.

"By the way," Veronica said, looking around the room, "you cleaned up. It looks nice."

He ignored the compliment. Dark thoughts crowded his brain.

"I feel better telling you about this, Chachi. It's strange. I've fantasized about your uncle's death, wondering how much you'll inherit, what it could mean for us. But now he's dead, I can't even think about the money. All I can do is worry."

"Listen, my love. We are going to have to be very careful. I don't think we should be together for a while, till all this dies down. You said we were friends, but the police will try to make more of our relationship. They may have even followed you here today."

"Do you think so?" she asked, darting to the window and peering out at the leaf-strewn street. "It looks quiet."

"You can't tell by looking. They have ways of tracking people without being noticed." The thought of being apart was chewing at his insides, but the thought of being together frightened him more.

"What about talking on the phone? Can we text at least?"

"They can tap our phones, see our emails."

"Oh, Chachi." Desperation crept into her voice. "What if we sign up for emails using fake names?"

"Too easy to find, and that makes it look like you have something to hide." He rubbed his face, thinking.

"But what if something happens? How can I get a message to you without being caught?" Tears were forming in her eyes again, and she choked back a sob.

"How about this? Tomorrow I'll get a burner phone. I'll call your cell phone to register the number on caller ID. Don't answer the phone for any unknown numbers. I'll call twice in a row, so you know it's me. You do the same thing, and we'll have each other's emergency numbers. Understand?"

Veronica nodded.

"But only for an emergency. It's too dangerous to contact each other otherwise."

"How long do we have to do this, Chachi?"

"As long as it takes." He took her into his arms and nuzzled the spot behind her ear where neck met shoulder. "I will miss you, my love."

She climbed on his torso, wrapping arms and legs around him, and squeezing tight. "Not as much as I'm going to miss you."

A few minutes later, he said, "I love you, but you'd better go now."

She put on her jacket and gathered her pocketbook and keys, staring at the floor.

"One more thing," Alexander said. "How did you get into my house this afternoon?"

"Oh, that," she replied. "I picked the lock. I learned how from my brother Alonzo."

CHAPTER 29

The next morning Elle received three phone calls in a row. The first was from Tonya Parrott, thanking her for the flowers.

"You're quite welcome, my dear. It's the least I could do. I'm glad to hear your injuries aren't worse. That was quite a large doe you hit."

"Tell me about it. The funny thing is, I didn't see her at all until I hit her. I feel bad for taking her life, and I apologize for worrying you, as well. It's not as if you don't already have a lot to deal with. I also wanted to tell you how much I enjoyed your class on Monday. It was exactly what I needed, and now I guess I won't be painting for a long time."

"I could tell you enjoyed the class," Elle replied. "Some of the students come in expecting to become professional artists in six weeks' time, and some come expecting to find joy and peace. You fall into the latter category."

"Is it that obvious? That I'm a total mess?"

"You aren't a total mess, dear. In fact, you are quite talented and very much in touch with your feelings. I could see that right away. For me, art is a pathway to everything good—serenity, soulfulness, enlightenment, and spirituality. I try to help my students find those things, too."

"I think you're an amazing person, amazing teacher. Subconsciously, I wish I could somehow make things better for you. *I* should be sending flowers to *you*."

"You can help me by healing and coming back to class. I'm going to postpone the next class until after Thanksgiving. That'll give me a chance to attend to business and get *myself* together. I'll be in touch."

Elle had no sooner hung up the phone with Tonya, than it rang again.

"Ms. Carmichael, this is Detective Rayburn of the New York Police Department. I'm calling for two reasons. First, we've completed Mr. Allmond's autopsy. We still have some toxicology tests to finish but we are ready to release his body. Am I right in assuming Mr. Alexander Vargas is Mr. Allmond's next of kin?"

Elle's reply came out as a peep. "Yes, Blake and I were never married."

"Have you and Mr. Allmond's nephew made arrangements?"

A wave of nausea mixed with chills washed over Elle at the thought of burying Blake. She imagined he would have wished to be cremated and buried next to Susan and the children at the cemetery in West Chester. His parents and grandparents were there, too. "I don't have the details yet, but I can work on them this morning. Can I get back to you in a couple of hours? I've already spoken to Terry Funeral Home, but we were waiting to hear from you before proceeding."

"That would be fine, but I suggest you speak with Mr. Allmond's nephew, since the body will be released to him. We appreciate your help."

At least the Detective is a woman, and she sounds sincere. "You said you have another reason for calling?"

"Yes, ma'am. Detective Coleman and I would like to interview you, to learn more about Mr. Allmond, as part of our investigation. We know this is a difficult time for you, so we are prepared to come to you. Would sometime today be convenient?"

"Today?" Elle clenched her hands in her lap and closed her eyes. Of course she had known this was coming, but the thought of having her relationship with Blake scrutinized and possibly made public made her want to crawl in a hole. She had always been a shy and quiet person. Her background and the years in the convent had intensified her need for privacy. Blake's murder would put her and their life in a harsh spotlight. She had neither the will nor the taste for it, but how could she say no? These people had a job to do, and they needed her input. "I suppose so."

They agreed on two p.m. Elle looked at the clock, agitated. *I've got four hours and a million things to do.* She pulled a notepad and pen from the desk and started making a list: contact funeral home, cancel classes, call Gary Griffith, the attorney. She'd wanted to beef up the security system on the art studio after the paintings were stolen, but Blake had convinced her to wait until he got home from New York. Blake had taken care of all the bills and services. She guessed these kinds of things would fall to her now, at least until Blake's will made it clearer. The hammering of a headache was gathering strength in both temples. She wanted nothing more than to mix up a palette of pastel colors and sit before a blank canvas in her studio. Only there did she feel competent and in charge.

If only she had some close relatives—or some of Blake's—to guide her on this lonely path. It was hard to think like a widow when she had never been a wife.

This time, when the phone rang, she jumped. *What now?* She considered letting it go to voicemail, but relented on the third ring.

"Ms. Carmichael, do you remember me?" The husky voice belonged to a young man. "My name is Alexander Vargas. I'm Blake Allmond's nephew." Something about the way the words tumbled out triggered a memory.

"Hello, Alexander. I believe we met a couple of Christmases ago, before your mother died. Weren't we at the 1906 at Longwood Gardens for lunch?" He hadn't been much more than a teenager then. *And then, at Melanie's funeral, of course.*

"Yes, ma'am. My mother thought a lot of you. She thought you were perfect for her brother at this time of his life."

"Thank you for sharing that. Actually, quite the reverse was true. Your uncle was perfect for me."

"I'm calling—to give you my sympathy. I just saw Uncle Blake two days before he was killed. I...I didn't have the chance to tell him how much he meant to me, and also to my mother." His voice broke. "I just thought, maybe, we could talk and share some of our feelings. I'd be happy to help with making arrangements or anything you need."

Elle crossed herself. Hadn't she just wished for a relative to help? And the fact was, Alexander, as next of kin, had more authority for signing documents than she did. She knew Blake's relationship with Alexander was complicated. He hadn't been around for much of the boy's childhood. Though Melanie had kept in loose touch with Blake after being disowned by her parents, she had raised Alexander in South Philly, away from the family's wealth and position in Brandywine Valley. It was only after Blake's parents had died and then the kids and Susan, that Melanie had reconnected with Blake. Melanie's life had been a struggle, and Elle had been sympathetic. The two women had connected through their art, too, and though they hadn't been close, they had shared a mutual respect.

"I appreciate your call, Alexander. Things are a bit overwhelming at the moment. Let me extend sympathy to you, as well. It must be hard to lose another member of your family." She thought for a minute. "Actually, I was going to call you. The New York police must have called you about releasing the body."

"Yes. They wanted to know what funeral home I wanted to use. That's part of why I needed to talk to you."

Elle filled him in on the inquiries she had made at Terry Funeral Home. "They are going to expect you to sign papers for everything, but I'll take responsibility for paying the expenses, if that's okay with you. Can we meet there to arrange everything together?"

"S-sure, I guess that would be okay." Alexander cleared his throat. "Truthfully, I'm not any good at funerals. Uncle Blake took care of my mother's."

After making plans to meet at the funeral home, Alexander added, "Would you like to get together sometime after the funeral? I'm happy to help with anything you might need on the property. I work construction, you know, and I'm pretty handy at all the trades."

"That's very good of you, and I might take you up on it at some point. Why don't we agree to keep in touch? I have a feeling we will have some things to discuss along the way."

When Elle disconnected, she held onto the receiver. For all she knew, Alexander would be moving into Manderley, and she'd be moving out. If those were Blake's wishes, she would understand.

She had never expected any more than what he had given her—love, freedom, respect as an artist. And nothing could ever take those away. At least she hoped not.

CHAPTER 30

That morning when Parrott arrived at his office, he found a bombshell on his desk in the form of a ten-inch security envelope with a New York postmark and a handwritten address. What made it a bombshell was the insignia where the return address should be. Lucretia, who had probably tossed the mail on his desk, would have had no idea that the overlapping cursive letters, "BA," were the way Blake Allmond signed his paintings.

Undoubtedly, the thick envelope had been handled by many in its journey to his desk, but Parrott didn't want to add his fingerprints to the mix, and, unsure of why Allmond wouldn't have emailed him whatever was inside, he decided to call the district attorney's crime scene forensics technicians to come examine it.

While he waited for them to arrive, he avoided touching anything on his desk. He did gaze at the postmark, though. It had been mailed three days ago, the same day Allmond was killed. Six "forever" stamps decorated the upper right corner, which Parrott took to mean Allmond had stamped the letter himself, rather than taken it to the post office counter.

When Jerry showed up from forensics, he apologized for taking so long. "Hate to hold you up like this."

Parrott looked at his watch with *faux* concern. "A whole thirty-five minutes. The chief might be upset, but me, I just enjoyed two coffee breaks in a row. No problem at all."

Jerry got right to work, using a ninhydrin solution on the surface of the envelope. It didn't take long for purplish fingerprint ridges and patterns to show up. "Looks like the envelope was handled by two or three different people, but that's to be expected. We can run the prints to compare with the ones we got last week at Allmond's studio. You want me to take the envelope to the lab to open it under controlled environment?"

Parrott was itching to see what was in the envelope, but patience was a virtue his mother had taught him. "Yeah, I think it's best. How long do you think it'll take?"

"Things were pretty slow when I headed out. If nothing new has come up, I could have it ready for you in under an hour. I'll call to tell you when it's ready."

While he waited, Parrott busied himself with returning phone calls and emails. First he called the Galveston Police Chief, Armando Gonzalez. After announcing himself, he waited a few minutes before a booming voice filled the airwaves. "Hey, Parrott. How's it going up there? How's that knockout wife of yours?"

"Just fine," Parrott said, "except Tonya had an accident, hit a deer and broke her shoulder."

"Ouch. Sorry to hear that, man. You guys shoulda stayed down here. No deer on the island. Nothin' bigger'n a coyote." Parrott thought of how relaxed and casual their time in Galveston had been, and he thought maybe Gonzalez was right. Then he remembered Tonya had said she wasn't sleeping well, even then.

"How're you and Michelle doing? Did you eat up all that fish you caught?"

"Nope. Still got some in the freezer. Some of yours, too. Thanks again for giving us your catch."

"No problem. It was that or throw it back. I don't believe in wasting nature," Parrott replied. "Hey, did you close that beauty queen murder case we talked about?"

"Yeah, that's why I'm calling. Your advice really panned out."

"You mean about the Big Chief Bill Orange tattoo on her buttocks?"

"Exactly. She'd broken up with a guy, came down here for spring break to get away from him. He followed her down, tried to get her to change her mind, and when she wouldn't, he strangled her."

"So how'd it help to know the ink was Syracuse's former mascot?"

"Turned out they were both from Syracuse, and his name was Bill. He has the identical tattoo on his butt. None of us had ever seen that cartoon figure before, so you cracked the case for us."

"Glad to help," Parrott said, a warm satisfaction curling inside. "Sometimes all it takes is another pair of eyes and ears."

"Return the favor anytime. Let's keep in touch."

Parrott hung up, and found himself whistling as he called Andrea Baker. He had a lot to be happy about at this moment. Tonya seemed better mentally, despite her physical disability, and the pain meds were helping her sleep better. He had actually had a full night's sleep last night. Being thanked by the chief of a police department fifteen hundred miles away was like the gumdrops on top of the gingerbread house, not essential, but oh, so sweet. And the anticipation of finding what was inside the envelope Allmond had sent him created a pleasant pounding in his temples. It wasn't even ten o'clock, and he already felt he'd won the Triple Crown.

No answer at the Bakers', so Parrott left a message that Elle would welcome a call from Andrea. He swung by Schrik's office to tell him about the letter from Allmond, but the chief was elsewhere, so he went to the break room to fill his coffee mug for the third time. He was basically killing time until he heard back from Jerry.

He sat at the table, where today's *Times* was open to the want ads. He wondered who, here, would be looking for another job. He closed the paper and folded it into its original creases. Sipping his coffee, he unfolded it again, flipping through pages and skimming the headlines.

The clock on the break room wall, which usually ran five minutes fast, said eleven. *Close enough*, Parrott thought, and he pulled out his cell phone to call Jerry.

"Hey, Parrott. I was just about to call you. Fingerprints were Allmond's all right. Contents are clean, except for more fingerprints, nothing suspicious. Looks like a hand-written note and copies of insurance policies. Want me to bring it all back to you, or do you want to come get it?"

The blood rushed faster in Parrott's veins as he contemplated reading what Allmond had sent him. "My turn to do the driving, Jerry. I'll come get it."

He jumped in his car and headed toward the Chester County CSFU. He rolled down the window to capture the cool breeze and the earthy smells. The sun blazed through the windshield, filling the car with warmth and cheer. Parrott couldn't remember the last time he'd felt this energized.

CHAPTER 31

After Elle spoke to the funeral home director, she sat in the breakfast room, staring at the mural of cows, painted in muted grays and greens. The sting of fresh tears assaulted her eyes. The impressionistic rendition, a nod to the home's history as a dairy farm, had been her idea, her artwork.

She fiddled with the corner of the persimmon-colored placemat. The aroma from the nearby bowl of walnuts nauseated her. Blake's body was on its way to Brandywine, and she would have to shore herself up to view it.

"You don't have to," the soft-spoken Mr. Levy said. "When someone has met with a violent death, it's often better to remember him the way he was in life."

But Elle didn't feel right not saying goodbye to Blake. He had meant too much to her. He deserved to have someone who loved him by his side, speaking tender words and giving him a final caress. She would want that for herself when her end came, as well.

She put her head in her hands, praying for strength to get her through the challenges ahead. LeRoi entered the room, his steps hardly making a sound. When he saw his mistress, bent in distress, he touched the back of her chair and cleared his throat.

"Miss Elle," he said, his voice at once gravelly and mellow, "can I get you something?"

Elle raised her head and attempted a smile. "No, thanks, LeRoi. I'm just dreading the next few days. I've never been good at saying goodbye."

"Mind if I sit with you for a spell?"

"Not at all. I'd appreciate the company, and any insights you might have."

The old man winced, as if singed by her words. "It's strange, but I had this same conversation with Mr. Blake when it was time to bury Ms. Susan and the children. It was a mighty hard thing to deal with."

"I'm sure it was. A lot of sorrow in this house through the years." She brushed at her eyes.

"Yes, ma'am, but some beautiful memories, too. Nothing is all bad. The Allmonds were good people, smart, compassionate, kind. When times were good, they shared their good fortune with others. When times were bad, they never complained. Mr. Blake was that way, too."

"I wish I had known them all. It seems I've come so late to the party that I don't belong. The burden of making final arrangements for Blake is almost too much to endure."

"Hate to hear you talk like that, Miss. You brought a lot of sunshine to this house after Mr. Blake lost his wife and sons. Seems to me you lifted him up, too. Helped him get back to painting again." He bent to examine the surface of the kitchen counter. "Seems to me Mr. Blake would want you to be the one to care for him at the end. Whatever becomes too much, let me help you with. You aren't grieving alone."

Elle sighed and moved to the other side of the table, bending to embrace the old man's shoulders ever so lightly. "You're a good man, LeRoi. That's exactly what I needed to hear." She straightened her posture and walked over to the sink. "I'm not really hungry, but maybe we should get a bite to eat before the police arrive. They'll be here at two."

"Yes, ma'am. There's a bowl of Dijon egg salad in the fridge. Mr. Blake's favorite. Shall I fix you some?"

Elle marveled at how every single thought, every sentence, reminded her of Blake. "He used to call it 'Heavenly Egg Salad.' That will be perfect." She sat down at her place again, noticing for the first time the neatly folded New York *Times*. She opened it and scanned the headlines. The world continued to rotate on its axis, it seemed. Blake's obit wouldn't go in until tomorrow. As she turned pages, she noticed a headline on page eight about the Lockwood art exhibit. She and Blake had been looking forward to that.

She choked down the egg salad. Not that it was bad, but everything was hard to swallow right now. She put away the newspaper and went upstairs to shower and get ready for the next hurdle.

At two o'clock on the dot, the doorbell rang, and LeRoi ushered the visitors into the living room. Voices drifted up the stairs, and Elle steeled herself. Her black pantsuit and muted blue scarf didn't offer much in the way of armor. She remembered something Sister Octavius had quoted, "For God has not given us a spirit of fear and timidity, but of power, love, and self-discipline."

The detectives, a burly, bearded man and a slim, caramel-skinned woman, stood when Elle entered the room.

"I'm Detective Coleman," the burly one said. He reminded her of the subject of "The Black Pope," a Charles White painting she admired. "And this is my partner, Detective Rayburn." Rayburn looked more like a model than a detective.

"May I offer you something to eat or drink?" Elle said, motioning the officers to sit and taking the chair opposite them, herself.

"No, thanks," Detective Rayburn replied. "Your butler already asked." Her smile revealed teeth that were braces-perfect and gleaming. If this woman had a rough side, and she probably did, it certainly didn't show.

Coleman said, "Ms. Carmichael, we are sorry for the intrusion at this sad time. You have our sympathy for the loss of Mr. Allmond." He removed his cell phone from his jacket pocket. "Of course, we are charged with the task of identifying the murderer and bringing him or her to justice. You can help us do this job by answering some questions for us today." He paused to make eye contact. "Would you mind if I recorded our interview?"

Elle shook her head. She couldn't imagine what she would say to impact their investigation. She couldn't tell them the slightest thing about who murdered Blake.

He set the phone on audio record and put it on the coffee table, and a whiff of his woodsy cologne stuck in Elle's throat, suffocating her. He stated the date, time, location, and participants, including that all parties had agreed to being recorded. Next, he said, "As a formality, I'm going to read you your rights, Ms. Carmichael. We routinely start our interviews this way."

Elle bit her lower lip, but remained stoic. It hadn't occurred to her she would be a suspect in any sense of the word. She had nearly worshipped Blake, and who would ever think a former nun as the killing type? Barely hearing the words, Coleman was reading, she imagined the intonation of prayer instead.

Detective Rayburn took over. "Let's start with your relationship with Mr. Allmond. How and when did you meet?"

Elle recounted the story of her painting while in the convent, noticing not even a raised eyebrow in the faces of her listeners. *They must have already researched me.* "One of my paintings was being auctioned at a fundraiser for St. Joseph's University in Philadelphia, and some of Blake's early paintings were there, too. I fell in love with his paintings first. I had never seen landscapes portrayed with such vitality.

It was after the tragedy of Blake's family, so when I met him, he had stopped painting. There was a sadness in him, a suffering. It colored his face, his voice, his posture. I was mesmerized."

"So how did you, er, end up together?"

Elle indulged in a brief smile. "Do you mean, what kind of courtship happens between a famous artist and a cloistered nun? It wasn't a torrid romance, if that's what you're thinking. I don't know exactly what Blake saw in me, but I think he was looking for tranquility, and my art spoke to him. He bought my painting and hung it here at Manderley.

Blake was connected to the secular art world in a way I could never have dreamed of being, and he started recommending me as an artist worthy of attention. I received invitations to have my work shown at benefits and galleries. The Church didn't approve, even though every time I sold a painting, the earnings went to them. Father Frank could see that, more and more, I was straying from my vows. My faith was still strong, but the art world seduced me with its lures of freedom of expression, beauty, and acclaim."

Detective Coleman removed his glasses and polished them with a handkerchief. Elle wondered whether he was bored.

"Anyway, Blake became a mentor, a friend, and eventually I left the convent and moved here almost thirteen years ago."

"You never married?" Coleman asked.

"We never needed to. There wouldn't be children, and we had both been married—he to Susan, and I to the Church. Our life together was dominated by art."

Coleman looked around the room, presumably noticing the original works of art and other artifacts displayed. "Pretty nice home you have here. Probably a far sight fancier than the convent."

Elle bristled. It wasn't what he said, but how he said it that got her Irish up, but she clenched her jaw, determined not to show it. "It's a lovely home that has been in Blake's family for generations. I just happen to live here at the moment."

"At the moment?" Coleman said. "Do you expect to move out any time soon?"

Elle felt heat rise up into her face, but before words could form a retort, Detective Rayburn intervened. "I understand. Your world has been turned upside down, and nothing seems permanent to you right now."

Elle nodded, grateful to be saved from losing her temper. "Do you have more questions?" she asked Detective Coleman.

"Oh, yes, ma'am, we do. For one thing, what can you tell us about your, uh, about Mr. Allmond's trip to New York. Do you know why he was there the night he was killed?"

"Blake often spent a day or two in New York, especially during the week. His apartment there was comfortable and well-located. He had friends there, and business contacts, people who owned galleries, customers. I thought nothing of it when he said he was going there for a few days."

"He didn't mention any specific appointments he might have had this time? Were there any particular worries or problems he had that you knew about?"

"He had a dentist appointment and a dinner meeting. He was supposed to come back the next day and take me out to lunch. Then he called to say he needed to stay in the city a second night. I didn't question him."

"What were you doing while he was in New York then?"

Annoyance festered in Elle's mind at the implication, but she answered in a mild tone. "What I always do. I am an artist and a teacher. I spend most of my time in my studio, either painting or planning lessons for my art therapy students."

"Where is the studio?"

"Right here on the grounds behind the house. Would you like to see it?"

"That won't be necessary at this time. Is there anyone who can corroborate you were here on the property the entire time Mr. Allmond was in New York?"

"Yes, LeRoi lives here in the house, and he and I see each other frequently in the course of a day."

"Or night?"

"Yes, even at night."

"So you wouldn't have left the house at night, maybe after saying good night to LeRoi, and driven to New York?"

"Heavens, no. I don't drive at night, and I don't drive to New York at all." Elle lowered her voice. "I would have had no reason to in any case."

"Not even to check up on him?" Coleman shot a look at Rayburn.

"It wasn't like that at all," Elle said. She might as well have been standing on a precipice. The insinuation pushed her over the edge. "I don't appreciate your implications. You come into a house of mourning and talk this way." She looked to Detective Rayburn for understanding. "I know you have a job to do, and I'm trying to help you, but you need to stop maligning Blake, and our relationship, if you want my cooperation."

Clearly the "good cop," Detective Rayburn held out a hand like a crossing guard holding back traffic. "I'll take over now. And we just have a few more questions." She scooted forward on the sofa and leaned forward. "How well do you know Veronica Espinosa?"

Elle was perplexed by this sudden shift in topics. She strained to associate the name with a face, but came up blank. "I don't believe I know anyone by that name," she replied. "Who is she?"

Rayburn ignored the question, continuing, while Coleman busied himself with checking that the recording was still on.

"What about Mr. Allmond's nephew, Alexander Vargas? What is your relationship with him?"

"Alexander? Why, he just called me this morning. He offered condolences, and we made plans to meet to plan the funeral." Elle supposed the police would interview Alexander and ask about her.

"Was it unusual for him to call you, or do you speak with him often?"

Something told Elle to be on her guard, even though Detective Rayburn's questions were easier to take. She wished Blake were here to deflect attention from her, and then she shrugged. If Blake were here, the detectives wouldn't be. "Alexander rarely calls here, and when he does it's not for me. He and his mother were estranged from the family until after Blake's parents died, so the ties aren't especially close. Still, they *are* blood relatives, and I think both Blake and Alexander felt some affinity from that." She thought of her own estrangement from her family. She wasn't any more certain of an affinity with her own relatives.

As before, Rayburn didn't comment, but rolled off another question. "Did you and Mr. Allmond ever discuss what might happen after one or both of you passed?"

Elle shook her head. "I wish we had. It might have helped me make decisions right now. I keep trying to divine what Blake would have wanted."

"I meant, in terms of his property. Are you in line to inherit?"

Rising from the chair, Elle walked around the living room. *Why does everything always come down to money? Blake could have been a starving artist, living in the street, and I still would have been drawn to him.* "I have no idea," she finally replied. "Death seemed a long way off, and we never talked about things like that. I don't even know if there's a will."

Rayburn made eye contact with Coleman. "Would you like to take a break, Ms. Carmichael? I have just a few more questions, but I need you to sit down."

As polite as the lady-detective seemed on the surface, Elle felt trapped. She understood they were on a mandated fishing expedition, but she didn't enjoy being on the hook. Nevertheless, she sat.

Coleman took over. "Thank you, Ms. Carmichael. Can you give us a list of Mr. Allmond's friends and any regular contacts? Also, were there any arguments, business problems, disagreements of any kind with anyone?"

Elle pondered before answering. How could she explain theirs had been a quiet, contemplative life? "I can give you a list of people. In fact, I can give you a copy of the list of people we invited to Blake's last exhibit in April. Mostly friends, patrons, other artists, gallery owners, people associated through the arts. I save those lists as Excel documents. We usually invite the same people every time."

"And what about the enemies?" Detective Rayburn asked.

Elle's eyebrows and corners of her mouth pulled downward. "I don't know of any enemies. Blake was a genuinely good person— friendly, kind-hearted, generous—I never heard anyone say a bad word about him. The only problem—"

Both detectives perked up. "Problem?"

"—the only problem was the theft of the two paintings. Those were paintings Blake intended to donate to The National Arts Club. It's located in Gramercy Park, across from Blake's apartment. He'd wanted to become a member for a long time, and donation is part of the application process." Elle started to rise from the chair, but sat down again. "Do you think the theft could be related to Blake's murder?"

Coleman replied, "Anything is possible, but the theft isn't our case. I assume there's an ongoing investigation."

"Yes," Elle replied. "Detective Parrott of the West Brandywine Police Department has been investigating. He's quite thorough. Have you heard of him?" Maybe this was a question they would answer.

Coleman muttered something unintelligible.

"If not, I suggest you give him a call. He might be able to help you with the case. He's got a fantastic reputation around here." *And he could teach you a thing or two about questioning a witness.*

CHAPTER 32

His foot heavy on the accelerator, Parrott arrived at the DA's forensic unit in record time, fifteen minutes. He couldn't wait to see what was in the envelope Blake Allmond had sent him.

When he arrived, Jerry was gone, already working on another matter. "He left this for you, though," the receptionist said, waving a sealed manila envelope in the air.

Reading the name on her name tag, Parrott said, "Thanks, Mindy." Receptionists came and went faster than county cases. Parrott took the envelope to his car and sat in the parking lot with it in his lap. He should take it back to his office to open, but the package felt like a firecracker, ready to explode, and he didn't think he could wait another fifteen minutes.

He ripped at the envelope seal, but Jerry had used clear tape on top of the brads. Not wanting to rip any of the contents, Parrott removed the Swiss Army knife from his pocket and slid the blade into the edge. When he pulled out the contents, he saw Jerry had put everything back the way he had found it.

Parrott turned the envelope, now stained purple, over in his hands. He opened the flap with the knife and pulled the tri-fold of papers out. The first was a typed letter.

Detective Parrott—
My apologies for not meeting with you. It occurs to me you may think me rude at best, and irresponsible at worst, for leaving Elle to deal with your questions about the stolen paintings. I assure you I don't intend to be either.

I do wish to cooperate with you in investigating the theft. The two stolen paintings were to be donated to The National Arts Club in Manhattan. I left them on a table near the entrance, intending to deliver them the next day when I went in for a dental appointment. The fact that someone came onto the grounds of my home, breached the lock and security system on my studio, and made off with these two paintings, favorites of mine, troubles me. I hope you are able to apprehend the thief and recover them.

Enclosed are copies of insurance policies covering the stolen paintings. I thought perhaps they would help you in your investigation.

I'm quite sure Elle was able to answer any logistical questions you have about the studio. She actually uses it more than I do.

I've spent the night in New York, and although I intended to come back to Manderley today, I've some wrinkles I must iron out before I return. Whatever questions remain for me, I will be happy to answer upon my return.

Yours sincerely,
BA

The signature consisted of the same interlocking initials as on the return address, and Allmond's trademark signature on his paintings. No premonition of death in this letter. Allmond clearly planned to be back at Manderley soon. The "wrinkles," though, might shed some light on one or both of the crimes being investigated.

Parrott started the ignition, heading back to the station. On the way, though, he stopped at Freddy's to pick up a steak burger, onion rings, and a frozen custard. While he stood in line, he called Tonya to see how her appointment had gone with the PTSD counselor. She had refused to let him go with her, insisting she could handle getting there and home in a taxi.

She sounded groggy when she picked up.

"Did I wake you?" Parrott asked. The smell of beef, sizzling on the grill, made his mouth water.

"No, I'm just worn out. Physically and emotionally. It took me over an hour just to dress myself and deal with the cab. I'm not complaining, though. I keep telling myself this is nothing compared to basic training as a SEAL."

"I wish you'd let me help you. How was the counselor?"

"Good. She explained how any little thing might trigger an attack. A sound, a flash of light, a dream, a person's face—even the fact that I'd committed to starting counseling—anything that might remind me of Afghanistan."

"Did you tell her you've been sleeping better since the accident?"

"Yeah, but she says another trigger can happen any time. She thinks the art therapy is a good step, and when I said that was pretty much out now because of my shoulder, she said to keep going. She said I could do the art with my left hand. The main point is the therapy, and so what if the product is abstract and uncontrolled?"

Parrott's order number was called, so he stepped up to the counter, juggling phone, wallet, and keys.

"Sounds like lunch is served," Tonya said. "We can talk later. I'm going to try to take a nap. Love you."

"Luh you, too," Parrott replied. He'd already bitten into a puffy, hot onion ring, and he hadn't even left the counter yet.

When Parrott got back to the station, Chief Schrik was at his desk. Parrott stuck his head in the door, and Schrik called him in and asked him to sit down.

Parrott showed him the letter from Allmond and watched his face while he read it.

"Well, whaddya know?" Schrik said. "The artist wasn't blowing us off, after all." He played with an open paper clip. "How does it feel to get a letter from a dead guy?"

"It does feel strange. It makes me want to solve the murder more than the art heist."

"Uh-uh, Parrott. I don't have to remind you. Not our case." He popped the paper clip in his mouth, and it hung over his lips like a cigar. "We should share the contents of the letter with NYPD, though. The 'ironing of wrinkles' statement may be a lead."

Parrott groaned. "How come we're always accommodating New York, but New York doesn't give a flip about us?"

"Nature of the beast, Parrott. You know the age-old story of the city slicker and the country bumpkin? Well, we're the country bumpkin in this game, and no amount of brains or experience is gonna change that. Even if you worked for Philadelphia PD, New York would treat you like a second class citizen."

"Well, anyway, I've got a few ideas from this letter and the insurance documents. I'll be in my office if you need me."

Parrott had no sooner sat down at his desk when his phone rang. The caller ID said, "Andrea Baker."

"Thank you for paving the way for me to call Elle Carmichael. I'm going to call her later today."

"No problem, and I think she's looking forward to hearing from you. Nice of you to reach out."

"My pleasure," Andrea said. "Listen, one of my friends saw something today on Craigslist that might interest you. It's an original painting by Blake, dated in the late 1970s, asking $50,000. Shall I send you the link?"

"Sure," Parrott replied. He didn't think the missing paintings would turn up there. Whoever stole them would know there were a lot of people looking for them right now. On the other hand, you never could tell where a bit of information would lead, so he didn't want to discourage anyone from sharing.

"I just wonder if the person who's selling it realizes Blake is dead. Wouldn't that make his paintings increase in value? If so, then the seller would be better off to wait. Anyway, that's your bailiwick, not mine."

Parrott thanked Andrea and disconnected the call. He thought about her last comment, though, and filed it away to ask Rupert Brooks the next time he saw him, maybe at the Lockwood exhibit. And speaking of Lockwood, he wanted to learn more about the "Father of the Brandywine River Artists." He had a hunch knowing more about Lockwood might open up a new perspective on Blake Allmond.

CHAPTER 33

The South Philly branch of Lyons Bank had been a flurry of activity all day long. One of Veronica's fellow tellers said business was always brisk in the weeks before the holiday season, and today had been a killer.

Even though she spent most of the day sitting behind the counter, Veronica's feet ached. She kicked off one spiked heel and rubbed her foot. Her hands were rough and dry, too, and she'd snagged two fingernails. Normally, these petty ailments wouldn't phase her, but normally, she would have an evening with Alexander to look forward to.

The prospect of having days and nights on end without seeing her *novio* was driving her crazy. There were only so many tv movies she could watch alone in her bed. It had only been two nights, and already she was losing weight from the stress. The belt she wore to work had to be cinched a notch tighter.

Last night she had received two hang-ups in a row on her cell phone. She was sure they had come from Chachi, and she had memorized the number of his throwaway phone. Today her brother Alonzo would bring her a new phone with an unlisted number, and tonight she would return the signal. It would kill her, though, not to let the phone ring through and be answered. *Was missing him with all her heart an emergency?* She knew he wouldn't think so.

It was hard to keep her mind on her work, as well. Every time she looked up to see a young male in line, she did a double-take to see if it was him. She hadn't interacted much with her manager since the police interview, but that whole mess had left her self-conscious and more than a little paranoid. She even resented the looks from the other girls behind the counter. How much did they know?

Now she'd had some time to think about things, she realized Blake Allmond's death wasn't exactly a good thing. Even if Alexander did become a multi-millionaire, the money would cast a huge tent of suspicion over them. Her stupidity in using her position at the bank to research Allmond's money haunted her, day and night. She also worried she might have tipped police attention toward her brother, and that wouldn't be good for any of them. What had seemed like a sparkling fairytale now felt like a dark labyrinth.

Alexander was standing in line at Bebe's after a full day of decking a roof, and experiencing a withdrawal similar to Veronica's. Without his lady love, two days felt like two decades. Last night, when he had signal called her, he had almost broken down and called a third time, letting it ring until she answered. He missed her sultry pout, her salty expressions, even her crazy ideas.

As much as he missed her, though, there was a small voice in his head, crooning a melody of freedom. Bebe's, for example. Alexander loved Bebe's, but Veronica detested everything on the menu, deeming it low-class food. Alexander inhaled the aroma of his bacon double cheeseburger and fries, as he set it on the passenger seat of the car. He couldn't wait to dig into it.

When he walked into his tidy apartment, he marveled at how disciplined he had become. It had only been a couple of days, but still, the counters and tables were clear of trash, and no clothes were strewn around. He took a beer from the refrigerator and clicked on the TV. *Gladiator* was on tonight, something he'd never be able to watch with Veronica around.

He was halfway through the feast and glued to Russell Crowe and Joaquin Phoenix when his regular cell phone rang. He reached into his jeans pocket and glanced at the caller ID, which said, BLAKE ALLMOND. A surge of surreality prickled his skin, but when he heard the musical female voice, he realized who was calling—Elle Carmichael.

He clicked the volume button on the remote, and Russell's voice went mute.

"I hope I'm not disturbing you," Elle said.

"Not at all. How are things going over there?"

"Still hasn't hit me, I don't think, but we're making some progress. I called to tell you my thoughts regarding the funeral. We could have it Friday afternoon at one o'clock. Terry Funeral Home in Downington. I thought Blake would want to be cremated with his ashes buried in the family crypt in West Chester. Your mother is there, too, isn't she?"

Alexander's eyes flew to the painting of Manderley, over his sofa. "Yeah. She couldn't abide her family in life, but she wished to be buried with them."

"Maybe she came to realize love of family was stronger than petty arguments. People outgrow their anger sometimes—if they're lucky. Anyway, what are your thoughts about those plans?"

Alexander grew silent, thinking of his mother's generous spirit at the end of her life and feeling incompetent to evaluate Elle's suggestions. "Thanks for asking me about the funeral plans, but I have no idea what my uncle would want. You can decide."

"Uh," Elle said, "there are a few other things. Would you like to ride in the limousine behind the hearse with me? It seats six to eight people, but there are only three of us, you, me, and LeRoi, our house man and friend."

Alexander's prickles returned, as his last evening with his uncle replayed in his head. "I, uh, I'd be honored. Thank you for asking."

"Is there anyone special in your life you'd like to ride with us?"

Veronica popped into his mind, and he shook his head from the irony. She would have loved to be front-and-center at his rich uncle's funeral. If only they could turn back the clock by a week. "No, I guess not. Nobody that close, anyway."

"Would you like to give a eulogy?"

Cheeseburger swirled around in his stomach, along with conflicted thoughts. "I don't know what I would say." He'd never considered being given such an honor, and he didn't feel worthy of it. It wasn't as if he had grown up celebrating holidays together, or as if his uncle had mentored him in some way. Their relationship had been relatively distant, and tenuous.

"Maybe your mother shared some things with you about her baby brother," Elle said. "It wouldn't have to be long, just a few sentences."

Alexander didn't want to disappoint Elle. This was the first time he could remember being included in an Allmond family ceremony, and he was touched. Or maybe he was feeling guilty—all he knew was he couldn't say no. "Okay, I'll think of something."

"Wonderful," Elle replied, her voice actually sounding something like happy. "I'm sure that would make your uncle very proud."

Alexander wondered whether Uncle Blake had ever spoken about him. She was treating him as though he were an important member of the family, instead of the son of the cast-off sister, a third-class citizen, at best. He wished he could undo the last few exchanges he'd had with his uncle, too. It filled him with shame that he had succumbed to Veronica's plan.

It's funny how life can turn on a dime, he thought. *A few days ago, Uncle Blake was sitting on top of the world—professionally, financially, and personally. And now, now he'd been brutally murdered, and no one left to mourn him but a sincere girlfriend and a schmuck of a nephew.*

CHAPTER 34

After several hours of research, including talking to people familiar with the art world, Parrott was ready to call it a day. He'd started with the Brandywine River Museum, where a curator referred him to some websites and gave him names of people who had personal knowledge of the Lockwoods. One contact had led to another, and he had compiled pages of notes that may or may not become important.

The most surprising bit of information came from a source who asked not to be identified, an older woman who was part of the artsy community in Brandywine Valley. She claimed Victor Lockwood had been bisexual. She said the renowned painter had courted her son, also an artist. Parrott didn't know how this might help him find Blake Allmond's stolen paintings, but you never knew.

The light coming in from his office window had waned to a pale gray flannel, and from the looks of the tree branches, the wind had kicked up.

Parrott filed his computer notes in folders within folders, and his handwritten notes into hanging file folders in his desk. He grabbed his coat from the hook behind the door and shoved an arm into a sleeve. Turning off the light, he started to close the door behind him, but changed his mind.

Maybe Tonya would like to see the color copies he'd made of the two paintings stolen from Blake Allmond's studio. Her recent interest in art and her friendship with the artist's partner made it likely. He opened his desk drawer and pulled out the 81/2 x 11 pictures he'd received from the National Arts Club. They'd been part of Allmond's application for membership.

When he got to the car, he called home to see if he could pick up something for dinner. After two rings, a familiar voice, but not Tonya's, answered.

Parrott flinched. "Ma? What are you doing there? Is Tonya okay?" Recent events had put him on edge whenever anything out of the ordinary happened.

Cora replied with a smile in her voice, warm and syrupy. "She's just fine, son. She's in the bathroom prettying up right now. I think she's ready for you to come home."

"Did she ask you to come over?" Parrott would be surprised as hell if that were the case, but maybe the discomfort and boredom had gotten to her, and she didn't want to bother him.

"No, son, quite the opposite. You've got a very self-sufficient wife. But you've got a mother who loves to cook and wants to make things a little easier. I brought dinner and some meals for the freezer. I'll just stay here till you get home, so's I can get a look at you and give you a hug."

"Why not stay for dinner or spend the night? It's already dark, and I don't like you driving now." Since his father's illness and death, Parrott fretted over his mother.

"Can't do. I've got my book club tonight at Aunt Lorraine's house, and I'm bringing dessert, cherry cobbler. Don't worry—I brought some for you, too."

Parrott laughed. "You know me so well, Ma." The thought of seeing Tonya, Horace, *and* his mother had him stepping on the accelerator a little harder, and he could already taste the warm cherry cobbler.

After dinner, Parrott reached for his wife's free hand and held it, rubbing circular motions around her knuckles. "You look mighty beautiful, Mrs. Parrott."

Tonya chuckled. "It must be the light from the candles your mother set the table with. She was determined to give us a romantic dinner."

"Any dinner with you is a romantic dinner." He leaned over and kissed her, careful not to budge her shoulder. "How are you feeling? Did it help to take a nap this afternoon?"

Tonya shifted in her chair, as if she couldn't quite get comfortable. "I actually couldn't sleep, so I spent the afternoon on the Internet, until your mom showed up, that is."

"Funny, I was on the Internet, too, researching Brandywine artists. In fact," he said, retrieving the printed pages from the envelope on the counter, "I brought you some pictures." He cleared the dishes from Tonya's place at the table and set the photos of Allmond's stolen paintings there. "I bring you, 'Brook Graced by Irises,' and 'After Harvest Blues.'"

Tonya studied the paintings with the intensity of a radiologist, looking for spots and shadows. After many seconds she looked up, her eyes shiny. "They're really good. The composition, perspective, lines, colors—even these printer copies are rather mesmerizing, aren't they?" She held one up at arm's length. "I hope you can recover these paintings, Ollie."

"I hope so, too." He cleared all the dishes and began to wash them.

"Wish I could help you."

"And ruin my husband points? No, my broken-winged angel. I've got this." He rinsed a pot and turned it over on the rack to air-dry. "So, what were you researching on the Internet?"

"Promise me you won't laugh." Tonya walked over to Horace's alcove. She made a kissing sound, and the cockatiel jumped onto her outstretched index finger.

"Okay."

"I was researching nuns."

"Don't tell me you're thinking of joining a convent," Parrott replied, raising an eyebrow.

"Not exactly." Tonya giggled. "I was trying to figure out what makes nuns so serene."

"Miss Elle has made quite an impression on you, hasn't she?"

"She has. Here she is with her life crumbling around her, and she sends flowers to me. Did you know there were studies of nuns done in the '80s and '90s? They found nuns' attitudes lead to healthier and more emotionally stable lives."

"Impressive."

"I think I can learn a lot from Elle Carmichael—and I don't mean just about art."

Parrott dried the last dish and wiped off the table. "Sounds like, between therapy and reading about nuns, you've had a full day of introspection." He grinned and wiggled his eyebrows. "Just don't tell me you're going to make it a habit."

CHAPTER 35

The Allmond obituary ran in the New York *Times* and in the local Chester County *Press*. A Friday afternoon funeral would mean closing the store, but Rupert Brooks would have to bite the bullet. There was no way he could skip it. Too many people knew of the connections between his family and the Allmonds, and his absence would cause tongues to wag.

Tongue-wagging, in Brandywine Valley, was a contact sport. He understood that more than most, having been battered and bruised often over the years. As much as he tried to maintain a low-key profile, people thrust their noses into his business, asking personal questions, creating innuendo.

Being the only son of the well-heeled Brooks family, carrying on the Rue Moderne's tradition as a beacon of the art world, and maintaining the family estate in Chadds Ford had been benefits that came with responsibilities. The fact he had never married, especially after the debacle with the engagement to Melanie Allmond, had been the single most disappointing factor in his parents' judgment of his success. At sixty-six years of age, he didn't have many regrets, but he still cared what people thought of him, and he hated himself for it.

He wrote down the time of the funeral on his desktop calendar and circled it. A half-eaten roast beef sandwich with pepperoncini sat next to it. The store phone rang, diverting his self-absorbed thoughts. He dropped the pen to answer.

A gruff voice said, "This the art gallery?"

Something was off, both in the voice and the word choices. This didn't sound like the typical Rue Moderne client, and caller ID said, "Restricted." "How may I help you?"

"You sell paintings by Blake Allmond there?"

Brooks picked up the dropped pen and snatched a note pad from the corner of his desk. "Yes, Mr. Allmond is one of our artists. He's featured on our website. Are you interested in purchasing one of his paintings?"

"Hah," the voice said. "Are *you* interested in purchasing one of his paintings? A friend of a friend has one or two of them to sell."

This was not the first time Brooks had received a call like this, someone testing the waters, someone disposing of estate furnishings, or possibly someone trying to unload hot merchandise. But it had been a long time, and he'd never had someone ask about one of Blake's paintings. Maybe something by an unknown artist, something that might sell for $300 or so. Given Blake's murder, Brooks was on high alert.

"I might be interested," he said, working to keep emotion out of his voice. "Is your friend's friend in the Brandywine area?"

"He could be. How much would you be paying for one of his paintings?"

Brooks's mind was sprinting, and the path it was taking wasn't pretty. He jotted, "1-2 BA," and "How much you paying?" on the notepad. He said, "That would depend on a number of factors. Why don't you have him bring in the paintings, so I could look at them?"

"What kind of factors? My friend's just looking for a ballpark number."

Hmm, a friend of a friend has just become a friend. Brooks played along. "There are quite a few factors that play into a sale of fine art. The reputation of the artist, the number of paintings he has in circulation, the value of the artist's other paintings, the size, the medium, the frame, the painting's provenance—"

"Provance? What's that?"

Brooks wrote, "Provance." He said, "Provenance is basically proof of ownership." He thought of a way to soften it. "After all, we can't sell something we don't own, right?"

"What if the person got it as a gift?"

"Ah, that happens quite often. We would just need to see documented evidence of the gift. But we are getting ahead of ourselves, aren't we? Why don't you—uh, your friend—bring the paintings in, and we can get the process started?" Brooks wrote, "Gift," and underlined it three times. "In fact, why don't you give me your friend's name and contact information, and I can talk to him directly?"

"He ain't much for talking. He asked me to find out."

"Well, how about giving me your name and phone number? I can do some research into current prices for Mr. Allmond's paintings, and I can call you back." Brooks held his breath, not expecting much.

"I'll tell my friend what you saying, and I'll call you back." A click and a dial tone confirmed Brooks's expectations.

This caller was uneducated about art and galleries, and it couldn't be coincidence that two of Blake's paintings had been stolen recently. A headache formed at the bridge of Brooks's nose and radiated upward.

Brooks should call Detective Parrott immediately, but his mind was paralyzed, as he thought through this development. He tried to convince himself there was nothing significant about this phone call that he could give to the police. Maybe it wouldn't hurt to wait, see if another call came in. On the other hand, if he didn't report the call, and it came out later the thief had called, it would look bad for him. As much as he wanted to distance himself from anything having to do with Blake Allmond, his thoughts kept circling around to the fact that he already had one foot in the quicksand.

Opening the pencil drawer of his desk, Brooks flipped through the dozen or so business cards he had collected, but not filed away. Landing on Parrott's, he examined the card on both sides, as if he might find something useful. He tapped the card against the edge of the desk and considered. Once he opened a new conversation with Parrott about this, there would be no going back.

He picked up the receiver and started to dial the number Parrott had given him, but before he had punched the last number, the bells on the outside door jingled. Brooks startled and dropped the receiver back into its cradle. No one could blame him for giving preference to a customer. He could call the detective later.

Brooks strode out of his office and into the main gallery, eager to help whoever was there. As he walked, he clenched his hands, and perspiration tingled his forehead and upper lip. He tried to tell himself he wasn't nervous.

CHAPTER 36

Friday morning, the day of the funeral, dawned with a lavender sky and minute flurries drifting through the air. The weatherman had predicted a light snow in the morning, increasing in density throughout the day, and letting up by nightfall. Unusual for this time of the year, but not unheard of.

No one liked standing out in the cold at the cemetery, where no buildings stood to break the wind's force, so, with Alexander's cooperation, Elle had arranged for the entire service to take place at the Terry Funeral Home. Blake's ashes were going into the mausoleum at St. Agnes' Cemetery anyway. The plan was for guests to convene at one o'clock, visit with the mourners until two, have a celebration of life service, have a brief ceremony at the cemetery, and return to Manderley for a late afternoon reception. Elle had wanted Blake's home to be a part of the memorial.

Blake had been raised as a Methodist. Like Elle, he had allowed art to draw his spirituality away from religious dogma, but unlike Elle, he had broken from the church completely. Elle couldn't imagine he would have wanted a religious ceremony now.

She and LeRoi pulled up to the 1804 Jug House, as the funeral home building was known. The gray limestone building had once been a luxurious Gregorian-and-federal-style home, and its entrance still had the ambience of hospitality. A wood-burning fireplace gave off the scent of pine and hickory, and Elle paused to gaze at the lithograph above the mantle, Victor Lockwood's.

Despite the warm greeting from the funeral director, the occasion settled on her, like a medieval suit of armor, with all of its weight, but none of its protection. She held her gloved hand out to LeRoi, who escorted her toward the chapel. They had both been here before. As they passed an antique mirror, Elle observed what a striking pair of opposites they made. Age, size, shape, and skin color were different, but they had the same sad and tired look about the eyes.

The funeral director interrupted her thoughts. "Your nephew is inside the chapel, waiting for you."

Elle didn't bother to correct him. For today, at least, Alexander could be her nephew. As the trio stepped inside the chapel, a wiry bundle of long, dark hair and muscled biceps rushed to greet them. Alexander bent to hug his uncle's partner, and shake hands with LeRoi, murmuring, "I'm sorry for this sad occasion." Elle caught a whiff of cigarette mixed with mouthwash.

"It's a sad day for us all," she replied, examining Alexander's face for similarities to Blake's. Something across the eyes and brow line resembled the Allmond family, perhaps the wide-set eyes and long lashes. Her artist's mind strove to memorize them. Blake had never had the slight twitch in the right eye that his nephew had, though.

Elle and LeRoi shed their coats and handed them to the funeral director. The room was set up for forty or fifty people. A table at the front was draped with cloths and held a gold and green urn. An aisle led to the table, next to which the family would stand to greet the guests. Elle picked up the urn and held it close to her heart. The three of them would represent Blake's family, though none of the three was related to the others.

"This is where we are supposed to stand," Alexander said, striding across the space next to the table. "I remember from my mom's funeral." His rapid movements suggested nervous energy. "I don't know that I'll recognize anyone, though."

The first guests appeared in the doorway at the back of the chapel. Detective Parrott and his wife Tonya came down the aisle. Tonya was wearing the immobilizer for her broken shoulder, but otherwise, she looked healthy and attractive.

Tonya expressed her sympathy to her art teacher, reaching out with her free hand to give a half-embrace, half-pat-on-the-back. "Ms. Elle, your kindness has meant a lot to me. I will be here for you, too."

Within a few minutes, the room started to fill with well-wishers. Cecil Pennington, President of Lyons Bank, and his wife Simone were among the first. Cecil and Blake and Gary Griffith, Blake's attorney, had a long history dating back to boarding school days. Gary and his wife Kim were there, too, and Gary pulled Elle and Alexander aside.

"Would it be possible to have a few minutes after the reception for a brief meeting? Rather than bringing you both into New York, I thought we might read Blake's will at the house after everyone leaves."

Hairs stood on the back of Elle's neck, and she noticed the way Alexander's eye twitched at the mention of the will. She supposed they might as well fill the day's bucket with an even larger emotional burden. At least it would save a trip into the city, and by day's end, she would know much more about her future.

All of Elle's other art therapy students were there, apparently having come together. Several artists and gallery owners, as well as people from the Brandywine Conservancy and Museum were there. Some of the people who worked with Alexander were there, and quite a few people from LeRoi's church. Before long, the room was filled, and the funeral home personnel were bringing in more chairs.

In her peripheral vision, Elle caught a glimpse of Detectives Coleman and Rayburn in black clothes, talking and looking around. If it weren't for them, she could pretend Blake had just died, and forget about how.

Taking advantage of a small break in the line of guests, Elle strolled over to greet the choir director of LeRoi's church, who would lead the church group in a hymn following the eulogies. While she was thanking Pastor Wilson, she noticed the back of a tall, slim man, standing at the table where Blake's urn sat. She walked over to see who it was, and when she got to the other side of the table, she was surprised to see it was Rupert Brooks, the owner of the Rue Moderne.

"Hello, Mr. Brooks," she said. "So nice of you to come."

Brooks leaned over to shake Elle's hand. "Please don't thank me. I've known Blake nearly all my life, certainly all of his. My heart goes out to you."

"Thank you. I know you and Blake go back a long way. As a matter of fact—"

Elle had been about to mention the photo album with pictures of him and Melanie, but she caught herself. Perhaps it wouldn't be appropriate to bring that up. She looked up to see three people coming toward her, two women and a man. "Please excuse me," she said, turning to greet them.

The taller woman, smartly dressed in leather, cashmere, and a colorful scarf, led the way, arm extended. "Elle," she said, her voice warm as spiced cider, "I'm Andrea Baker, Blake's cousin? We spoke yesterday?"

Elle shook her hand. "Yes, of course. I remember. Thank you for coming."

Andrea brushed what looked like melted snowflakes from her hair. "These are my dear friends, Caroline and John E. Campbell. They own one of Blake's paintings, and they wanted to meet you and pay their respects."

After shaking hands with Andrea's friends, Elle noticed the New York detectives staring at her. *Why are they here, really, and why are they so focused on me?* The answer, when it came, caused the room to spin like an amusement park ride she had ridden as a child, but hated. All of the voices blended together into a cacophony of words. Dizzy and nauseated, she started for a chair, aiming not to topple over onto the patterned carpet.

The next thing she knew, Tonya Parrott stood at her side, staring into her eyes and offering her a cup of water.

Elle sipped. The cool liquid went down like a sweet elixir. "Just what I needed. Thank you." Relieved she'd recovered her equilibrium and composure, she felt like hugging Tonya.

"No problem," Tonya replied. "You looked like a flower in the desert."

Elle was relieved not to have all eyes and ears on her. "I d-don't know wh-what happened." She glanced in the direction of the detectives, who continued to stare.

Tonya held her hand and squeezed. "Maybe you're feeling a little like the way I felt the other night, when I drove to your house and hit the deer. There's a whole lot to take in here with all these people. I think you'll be okay now, though. And I'm staying right here by your side."

The celebration of life service was brief. Cecil and Gary, Blake's oldest friends, each gave a eulogy, praising Blake's artistic talent, his dedication to family and community, and his sense of humor. Vignettes about adolescent pranks from their days at boarding school lightened the tone, and no one mentioned the artist's gruesome end.

Alexander spoke about how his mother had viewed her baby brother, how proud she had been of his success, and how, especially when times were rough for her, Uncle Blake had reached out and offered help. "When she died, Uncle Blake was equally kind to me. I wish I had shown my appreciation more than I did."

Elle took a turn at the podium, but all she could manage was to share that Blake had left a permanent imprint on her mind and her heart. "I will carry his legacy there until the end of my days." She asked the guests to join her in a prayer.

The funeral director asked other guests to share memories of the deceased, and a few others spoke, echoing the messages of Allmond's art, his contributions to the Brandywine art community, and his generous nature. A final eulogy was given by LeRoi, the person who had known Allmond the longest.

The old servant walked to the podium with stooped shoulders and a worn demeanor, but his voice was clear and strong. "My name is LeRoi Hawkins, and I've worked for the Allmond family almost my entire life. No better people anywhere, they treated me like family. I remember Mr. Blake as a little boy, 'bout three years old. I'm not much for speech-making, but I need to remind you all, if anyone needs reminding, of just a few things about Mr. Blake. First of all, he was a born artist with God-given talent. When he was nothing but a little pipsqueak, he was collecting pretty things and arranging them this way and that. He was smart enough to do anything he wanted in life, but what he wanted to do was art. Painting gave him joy, but it also brought joy to many others. Seems to me he has left a big legacy through his paintings.

Mr. Blake had a lot of hardships in his life, and he took them hard. Burying his parents, his wife, his son and daughter, and his sister—even one of these losses could break a man, but sometimes troubles prepare ordinary people for extraordinary things, and when Mr. Blake met Ms. Elle here—well, I knew he was going to be okay, and I knew together they would bring a special light to the world.

I never met anyone kinder or more generous than Mr. Blake, and I'm sure going to miss him."

While the church choir was singing, "I Watch the Sunrise," Detective Rayburn sidled over to Parrott and nudged him, tilting her head toward the exit.

"Be right back," Parrott whispered to Tonya. Something told him the slender light-skinned woman was a cop, even though she was dressed to fit in with the crowd.

The lobby was empty, but Rayburn led Parrott to the vestibule outside of the main entrance. It was snowing harder now, and the area was chilly, but private. "Are you Detective Oliver Parrott with West Brandywine?"

Parrott nodded. It came as no surprise that New York PD would send homicide detectives to the funeral to observe.

"I thought I heard someone say your name earlier. Thanks for helping us out with notifying next of kin. We appreciate it."

"No problem," Parrott said. He knew she wouldn't have brought him out here just to thank him, but he was a patient man with no need to talk first.

"How's your investigation going on the theft?" Rayburn's casual pose was belied by the piercing look in her eyes.

"Moving forward, but slow." Parrott scratched the side of his head. "Allmond's murder kind of put a brake on things."

"You on duty today?"

"Not really. Not like you. My wife takes art lessons from Elle Carmichael. I'm here as a guest."

"Mind if I ask what your take is on Carmichael?"

Parrott's eyebrows shot up, but he kept his voice even. "My wife likes her a lot. She's been cooperative with me, too. You know she's a former nun."

"Yeah, with the accent on former."

"You think she's dirty?" Parrott knew enough about human nature to accept that almost anyone was capable of doing anything under certain circumstances, but if Elle turned out to be a murderer, he'd never be able to console his wife.

"Well, let's say she would have abundant motive."

"You mean money?" Parrott shook his head almost imperceptibly. "She doesn't strike me as particularly greedy. Her lifestyle was fine enough with Allmond alive."

"True, but it's *his* lifestyle I'm talking about."

"*His* lifestyle? What do you mean?"

"Not for publication, but Allmond was having affairs in his New York apartment. For years."

Parrott's mouth went slack, and he uttered a single word, "Huh." A few seconds later he asked, "So you think Allmond was going to leave Elle for another woman?"

Rayburn stared into his eyes and shook her head. "Not another woman, Parrott. Allmond was having affairs with men."

CHAPTER 37

After the funeral, guests dispersed to their cars, some going back to their regular lives, some heading to the cemetery. Parrott and Tonya had decided not to go to the cemetery, but to grab a cup of coffee somewhere and hang out for about an hour before going to the reception at Manderley.

The weather had worsened. Thick curtains of snowflakes had turned the afternoon into evening before its time.

Rayburn and her partner returned to the city. When Parrott had asked if they would be at the reception, she said they didn't want to intrude on what would likely be a smaller gathering, and, besides, they didn't want to be on the highway in heavy snow at night. "Glad you're going, though. You can fill us in if anything comes up."

The Parrotts drove to the Starbucks in Thorndale, inside the supermarket. Tonya's shoulder was aching from the cold weather, and she wanted to buy an analgesic, as well. When they finally sat down to sip their coffees, Tonya asked, "Who was the lady you left to talk to? A cop?"

Parrott winked and grinned. "Can't pull anything over on you, Ms. Collins. They teach you how to sniff out cops in the Navy?"

"Nope, I learned it growing up in the 'hood. Except I never knew any female cops, and for sure none that pretty. I hope she observed the wedding ring on your left hand."

"I'm quite sure she did, and she also probably checked out the stunning woman I was standing with. No one can hold a candle to you, sweetie." He leaned over to give her a peck on the cheek.

Tonya took another sip and leaned back, closing her eyes. "I suppose I shouldn't ask you why she wanted to talk to you."

Parrott took his wife's free hand in both of his. "You know I can't talk about cases."

"Well, I hope they find whoever killed Blake Allmond and put him away."

Parrott considered what Detective Rayburn had told him about suspecting Elle, and he wondered whether Ton-ya would feel that way if her friend turned out to be the killer. "Do you feel like going on to the reception, or do you want to go home and rest that shoulder? This has already been a difficult outing for you."

Tonya gazed at him, and he admired her long, curled eyelashes. "Oh, no, Ollie. We have to go to the reception. I promised Elle we would be there for her, and I intend to keep my promise."

The long roadway, the circular driveway, and the additional parking areas had been plowed, and car parkers were giving out tickets and taking keys from guests as they arrived. Parrott turned his Camry over to a guy whose jacket said, "Alonzo," and he rushed over to assist Tonya as she entered the house.

The Campbells and Andrea Baker had walked in to Manderley ahead of the Parrotts. Caro and John E. were carrying several cakes and pies, handing them over to a young woman in a black and white maid's uniform.

Several couples milled about the living room, looking at the paintings on the wall and talking in hushed tones. A table by the French doors held a display of photographs, framed newspaper clippings, gallery programs—souvenirs from Allmond's successful life in the competitive world of art. Parrott didn't know any artists before now, but he compared it to guys he knew from football who'd made it big in the pros. The ratio of wannabes to successes made his respect for Allmond multiply.

Tonya found Elle in the breakfast room and sat down next to her, while Parrott walked around, observing. Despite the house full of guests, flowers, and food, the atmosphere at this reception was off. Even for a funeral reception, it was too quiet, too cold. Whether Elle was overwhelmed with grief, or she was overly shy, she certainly wasn't playing hostess.

Parrott saw LeRoi, standing in a corner with the choir director from the church. Approaching them, he extended his arms for a man-hug. "Great eulogy you gave, man. Heartfelt."

LeRoi lowered his eyes, and for a moment Parrott thought he might cry. "It's mighty difficult to bury somebody younger than you. Mr. Blake always told me he would take care of me. Now I'll be looking after Miss Elle, I guess."

Parrott murmured something about how Mr. Blake would likely appreciate that, and he moved on, walking from one room to the next. He spotted the Campbells, Andrea Baker, and Rupert Brooks, huddled in a corner in the family room. As he approached, they stopped talking, a reminder that he wasn't, and never had been, a part of the one percent. He wasn't one to judge, but he wasn't one to stand around and talk about works of art, when there were people grieving, either. He said hello and left to swing back to the breakfast room to check on Tonya and Elle.

This time there were three at the table: Tonya, Elle, and Allmond's nephew. They made quite a picture of diversity, but he was glad to see them smiling. This reception could use a little more sunshine.

"Is this seat taken?" Parrott asked, pulling the fourth and last chair away from the table.

"You need a password to join this table," Tonya said with a wink. "We were just laughing about cows." She pointed to the mural on the wall opposite them. "Elle painted that. Isn't it lovely? Did you know this property used to be a dairy farm?"

Parrott must have looked perplexed, because Alexander said, "I'll explain what's so funny. I was telling the story my mom told me about what she did with Fanny, her favorite of the cows her parents kept at the barn. One day she decided it was too cold outside for Fanny, so she brought her inside the house and coaxed her up the stairs to her bedroom."

So far Parrott didn't see what was so funny. He looked from one to the other.

"Fanny got spooked and started running all over the upstairs, but she wouldn't come back down. My mom didn't know that cows won't walk down stairs. Their legs don't move that way."

Elle piped in. "They had to build a makeshift ramp, sedate the cow, and slide her down the stairs. But before they could do all that, Fanny had made herself quite at home upstairs. It took months to get the stench out of the house."

"And that was the end of keeping cows on the property," Tonya added. "From then on, the Allmonds bought their milk at the store like the rest of us."

Parrott guessed you had to be there to get the humor, but he was glad for anything to lighten up the somber day, so he chuckled and said, "Great story."

Elle stood and stretched. "I think I'd better go talk to some of the other guests. I wouldn't want people to think I'm as out of place here as Fanny was."

That was the signal for everyone to rise from the table and find another conversation. Tonya asked Parrott to accompany her to the bathroom and stand outside the door. Managing her nature breaks with only one hand had been a challenge, and Parrott didn't mind.

The first-floor bathroom was small, compared to those in more modern homes. It fit into the space under the staircase Fanny had climbed. Parrott followed Tonya to the bathroom and looked around. He could tell many guests had used the toilet and sink. The linen towels were wet and wrinkled, and the waste can was three-quarters full with crumpled paper ones. The toilet paper roll was down to the last half-sheet of tissue, certainly not enough.

"Let me get you a new roll," Parrott said. The most logical place would be under the sink, but he couldn't open the cabinet until Tonya stepped outside, and he sat down and slid his legs to the side. Feeling like a contortionist, he yanked on the cabinet door and leaned over at an angle to reach in, feeling around for the familiar soft paper cylinder. The plastic covering of the multi-pack slipped from his grasp, and his hand knocked against something hard and cold, that clattered to the floor of the cabinet.

Afraid he was making a mess inside the cabinet, worse than Fanny the Cow, he stood, pushed himself into the corner, held in his stomach, and bent over in front of the open cabinet. He saw the package of toilet paper rolls he had knocked over, but he also saw the item he had dislodged by accident. Lying at the edge of the opening was a black-and-silver object half-wrapped in what looked to be a white pillowcase. It didn't take Parrott two seconds to recognize what it was—a .380 semi-automatic Beretta Pico pistol.

CHAPTER 38

Throughout the funeral, Alexander had wandered about, feeling like the black sheep that he was. He had nothing in common, really, with anyone there. The couple of guys from work looked as lost and out of place as he felt. The only person he knew well was sitting in an urn at the cemetery. Still, people were treating him with the politeness of Brandywine Valley society. When he gave his eulogy, they had hung on to every word. It was almost as if he, the last surviving descendant of the distinguished Allmond family, might soon be living in their midst, so they might as well get to know him.

Whatever kindness they showed him, though, felt as unearned and uncomfortable as the starched shirt and silk tie irritating his neck. He could hardly wait for the day to be over, so he could go back home, ditch the clothes, and veg out in front of the TV.

He wondered what Veronica was doing. Certainly she was aware of the funeral, and it probably chafed her that she wasn't able to attend. He imagined what it would be like to have her there with him, dressed to kill in something showy, and hanging on his arm like the society lady wannabe she had always been. He missed her, but having her here with him would have made him feel even more different. He looked around at the distinguished men in fancy imported suits. Surely there were bank presidents, attorneys, physicians, and other important people here, probably even police detectives. The thought made him itch.

Though the crowd at the cemetery was more intimate than at the funeral home, Alexander had remained on guard. The Allmond mausoleum held his mother's remains, and at one point, when his uncle's urn was set next to hers, he'd almost lost it.

On the way to Manderley afterwards, he allowed himself to think about the family fortune. Not that he was expecting anything. Uncle Blake had made it clear he was disenchanted with him. And not that he was desirous of anything. He couldn't imagine himself living anywhere besides South Philly, in the townhouse his mother had left him, or working anywhere but in construction. He had carved out a niche for himself, and it wasn't in this stratified atmosphere of Brandywine.

As he pulled into the roadway leading to Manderley, though, he gasped. It had been years, and he had forgotten how regal it looked, sitting at the top of a winding drive. The blowing snow added to the fairyland impression, and his mom's painting of her ancestral home flashed before his eyes. Though he had never lived there, she had, and that gave him an emotional bond to the property that he couldn't explain in words.

A burly guy in a hooded parka opened his car door outside of the entrance to the house. *Car parkers, how incredibly high class.* He wouldn't complain, though, in this weather. When he got out of the car and started to hand his keys over, he noticed the name on the parka, "Alonzo."

He examined the face beneath the hood to confirm it was indeed Veronica's brother, and he froze. "What are you doing here?" he muttered between clenched teeth.

"Don't get your balls in an uproar. I ain't gonna ruin your chance for the golden ring. I'm just doing what I do—shoveling snow and parking cars. And the rest of the year, I'm one of the groundskeepers."

A cauldron-full of dread filled Alexander's long body from feet to neck. This couldn't be coincidence. What started out as a light-hearted romance with Veronica had magnified and intensified far beyond his ability to control it.

"Does Veronica know you're working here?" he hissed, hoping the answer would be no.

Alonzo let forth with a guffaw, jerking his head in the direction of the parking pad. A slim guy in a navy pea coat, scarf, knit cap, and boots approached, carrying the keys to a Mercedes. When he got closer, and made eye contact with Alexander, his face broke out in a gleaming smile. "Hi, Chachi."

CHAPTER 39

Parrott didn't tell Tonya what he had seen under the sink in the bathroom for a couple of reasons. First, he'd read the sight of a gun was a common trigger for a PTSD episode. Tonya had been doing so well since her accident. A gun in a pillowcase might be enough to set her back, and it might also create pandemonium throughout the house.

"Hey, baby," he said, instead. "How about getting Elle to help you in another bathroom?"

"Why, what's the matter with this one?" Tonya asked, trying to look around Parrott into the bathroom.

"Out of toilet paper."

"Why don't you come with me then, to find another bathroom? Why do I need to bother Elle?"

Parrott struggled to come up with something. It wasn't easy having such a smart wife. "I need to call the chief right away, and I need the privacy." He gave what he hoped was a winning smile and leaned out of the doorframe to grab the handle. "I hope you understand."

Tonya shot him a look that she wasn't buying it, but she nodded and walked away.

Parrott closed himself in and pushed the lock button. His fingerprints were already all over the tiny room. He closed the seat of the toilet and sat, speed-dialing Chief Schrik's number into his cell phone.

When Schrik answered, he cut to the chase. "How fast can we get a warrant to search Manderley?"

"Three or four hours, presuming we have probable cause. Why? What's going on there?"

"I stumbled on a pistol wrapped in a pillow case under the sink. I didn't touch it, and I'm securing the scene, but we can't call forensics out without the owner of the house consenting, and Blake Allmond is unavailable."

The chief gave Parrott an atta-boy but cautioned him not to get too far ahead of things. "Who knows you found it?"

"Nobody yet, but it'll be hard to keep under wraps. It might be good to know what the ballistics on Allmond's shooting showed, in case there's a match."

"Parrott—"

"Yeah, I know. That's not our case. But if this turns out to be the weapon, New York will be on it like brushstrokes on canvas. Meanwhile, I'll protect the chain of custody."

"Okay, I'll get the paperwork started. Let me know if you need backup. Looks like a long night ahead."

Parrott stepped out of the bathroom, closing the door behind him. He remained in place in the hallway, looking and listening for LeRoi or Elle. He heard people saying their goodbyes, and he was torn between dashing to the front door to prevent anyone from leaving and standing guard for what might turn out to be important evidence. *The operative word here is* might, he thought. *How can I stop people from leaving, when we don't know anything about this gun yet?*

As if in answer to a prayer, LeRoi walked through the breakfast room into the kitchen, several feet away from where Parrott was protecting the bathroom. When he saw Parrott standing in front of the closed door, he broke stride and headed in Parrott's direction. "You waiting for the bathroom? There's another one back there." He pointed toward the library wing.

"Actually, no," Parrott replied. "I need your help in closing off this bathroom, so nobody goes in. Might be for several hours. Meantime, can you help me block it off, and as quietly as possible? I'd rather not cause any more commotion than necessary."

LeRoi was a treasure. Not only did he manage the barricading of the door, but he did it efficiently, effectively, and without asking a single question about what was going on. Parrott could have hugged him.

Meanwhile, guests were saying their goodbyes in the living room and foyer, keeping Elle and Alexander occupied and away from the bathroom. Tonya, however, was a different story. She'd apparently managed to go to the other bathroom, but she needed help tucking her blouse in, and worry lines were drawn above and beside her eyes. As she turned the corner, she came face-to-face with her husband and the butler, who were lifting a bombe chest and nestling it against the door, just under the door knob.

"What's going on, Ollie?" Tonya asked, obviously more curious and less discreet than LeRoi.

Parrott held his index finger parallel to his nose and uttered a quiet, "Sh." He looked around for a spot for them to sit, where he could keep an eye on the door. When he pinpointed the breakfast room table, he asked LeRoi, "Can we move that table a little to the left, so we can watch from there?"

After Parrott and LeRoi adjusted the table and chairs, LeRoi went to check on things in the other rooms, and the Parrotts sat down. Tonya tried to start a conversation again, but Parrott was already typing into his iPad mini, totally engrossed.

"Ollie, I need to know what's going on. I'm starting to get anxious."

"Okay," Parrott said, closing his notepad and putting it away in his pocket. "I'm sorry, baby, but I'm trying to get a search warrant. I don't mean to ignore you, but this could turn out to be pretty important."

"What did you see in the bathroom?"

Parrott was pondering how much to tell her when Elle came into the breakfast room, looking for Tonya.

"Oh, good," she said, when she laid eyes on her student. "You didn't slip out when I wasn't looking." She leaned down to examine Tonya's face. "You look tired, though. Has this been too much for you?"

Before Tonya could reply, Elle caught a glimpse of the furniture, pushed up against the bathroom door. "What's this?" she asked, looking from Tonya to Parrott and back toward LeRoi, who was supervising the help in the adjoining kitchen.

Parrott replied. "We've had to block off the bathroom, Miss Elle. I saw something in the vanity when I was looking for a new roll of toilet paper. I'm working on getting a search warrant, but it might take hours, and we can't have the room contaminated in the meantime."

The color drained from Elle's face as she took in this news. She collapsed into a chair next to Tonya. "What in the world—what did you see?"

Parrott kept his voice soft, not knowing who might be lurking around the corner in the next room. "It was a pistol. Were you aware there was a pistol on the shelf in that cabinet?"

Elle choked back a sob. "What in the world is going on around here? No, I wasn't aware there was a gun in this house. Neither Blake nor I keep—kept—guns. We didn't believe in them." She put her head down on her arms and took some deep breaths. "Who would have brought a gun into this house? Why?"

Parrott used his most soothing voice. "It's too early to speculate. Let's wait until we get in here to investigate, and maybe we'll have more answers. Meanwhile, do you mind if Tonya and I stay here? We won't get in your way if you have other things to do."

Elle started to reply, but the lawyer who had spoken at the funeral entered the room. "Oh, here you are. I've been looking for you. Alexander is waiting in the library. Would this be a good time to go over Blake's will?" The sandy-and-gray-haired Gary Griffith pushed his wire-rimmed glasses up on his nose and looked from Elle to Parrott to Tonya.

The muscles in Elle's neck were ropy and tight, and her eyes were wet. She looked at Parrott as if one more decision would cause her to crumble. "I—I—"

Having heard the word 'will,' Parrott perked up. If Allmond's will bequeathed the house to Elle or Alexander, he could ask permission to search from the presumptive new owner and eliminate the need for a warrant.

He stood and faced the attorney, hoping the six or so inches he had on him height-wise didn't intimidate. "Am I correct in assuming the will names the person who will inherit Manderley?" When Griffith nodded, he turned to Elle. "If you aren't too exhausted, I think it would be a good thing."

Griffith sat down in the chair vacated by Parrott and spoke to Elle directly. "Elle, are you all right? We can always arrange to do this at a later date, but I thought it would be more convenient for you and Alexander to do it here."

Elle looked from one to another. "Thank you, Gary, and all of you. This is a horrible time for me, and I don't know what I'd do without you, and LeRoi, and even Alexander." She squeezed Tonya's free hand. "Has everyone else left?"

"I'll go look," Parrott said, taking off through the kitchen. He made the circuit around the rooms where the reception had taken place, meeting up with LeRoi at the front door. The last of the servers and car valets had left.

Parrott and LeRoi returned to the breakfast room, and LeRoi confirmed everyone was gone, except for those present and Alexander, who was still waiting in the library with Kim Griffith, Gary's wife.

Elle turned to the attorney, her eyes fixed with resolve. "Is it all right with you if we all adjourn to the library together?"

Griffith hesitated. "Usually we discuss the will in a private setting with just the beneficiaries present. Those would be you, Alexander, and LeRoi."

"But there's no prohibition for having others in the room, is there?"

"Well, no. But why, may I ask, do you want this?"

Elle's mouth formed a straight line, and her chin resembled an immovable boulder. "The circumstances of Blake's death have turned it into a public spectacle. Everyone is soon going to know the contents of Blake's will, so when I hear them, I might as well be surrounded by friends and people I trust."

"Okay, then," Griffith replied. "If Alexander and LeRoi agree, we can all assemble in the library."

While the attorney went to check, the group in the breakfast room remained quiet, each apparently lost in his or her own thoughts.

Parrott's mind was racing over the gun, the possible scenarios for its having been left there, and the people attending the reception. Even if the gun had nothing to do with the murder, it raised some significant questions. If it turned out to be the instrument of Allmond's death, the gun might carve the path to a lot of significant answers, as well.

He excused himself to call Schrik. "Hold off on the warrant. We're about to find out who owns Manderley." As he walked to the library, he considered the possibilities. Perhaps selfishly, he was hoping it was Elle.

CHAPTER 40

The library at Manderley might have been the coziest room in the house. A pine-fragrant fire was blazing yellow and blue in the fireplace, and two rows of chairs had been arranged near it. Gary Griffith had set one of the chairs and an end table to face the group. A thick Redweld file sat on the table, drawing Parrott's attention like a magnet.

We certainly are a motley crew, Parrott thought. *Old, young, black, white, male, female—and the only true relative is Alexander.* He imagined what Allmond must have gone through in writing the will, perhaps grieving for his wife and children all over again. If what Detective Rayburn had told him about Allmond's affairs with men was true, none of those lovers were going to inherit. As he observed the faces of the three incipient heirs, Elle, Alexander, and LeRoi, only LeRoi's features weren't drawn into a mask of tension. Behind them, Tonya and Kim Griffith sat, flanking Parrott. He wondered whether they felt, as he did, like they had second-row seats at a drawing room play.

The crackling of the fire was the only sound in the room, until Griffith cleared his throat and opened the Redweld, extracting a document and an envelope. He set the folder on the floor and the envelope on the table. He smoothed his thick mustache and stroked his chin, perhaps stalling as he thought of how best to begin.

Tonya put her hand on top of Parrott's. Hers was ice-cold, despite the warmth of the fire. It had been a long, stressful day, and he should be taking her home, but the gun in the bathroom would make the day even longer. To make things worse, his stomach broke forth with a long, loud burble that caused the three on the front row to turn around and stare.

"Shall I get you something to eat?" LeRoi asked. "There are plenty of leftovers."

Parrott shook his head. He didn't want to delay this meeting a single minute.

Griffith held up the thick document and proclaimed, "This is the last will and testament of Blake Milton Allmond, signed and witnessed in my office." He looked from one person to another. "As you know, Blake was a dear friend. We go back a long way, and he trusted me to make sure his wishes were represented herein." He pressed the will to his chest before opening to the first page.

"Blake had a previous will, which I also drafted, but he asked me to draft a new will recently, renouncing the first one."

Parrott, sitting directly behind Alexander, watched Allmond's nephew squirm. Tonya must have noticed it, too, because she squeezed his hand and tilted her head toward the young man.

"As you all know, Blake Allmond was a man of substantial wealth, some inherited from his parents, and some earned as an artist. Throughout his life he was a good son, brother, husband, father, uncle, life partner, and friend. This last will and testament reflects his desires to distribute his property and possessions." He paused to stare at Elle, Alexander, and LeRoi. "We don't usually talk about wills so soon after the funeral and in the home of the deceased, but I offered to do so for Elle's convenience, and she accepted. As it is a long and complicated document, I have brought copies for the three of you to read at your convenience. In the interest of time now, I'll summarize the contents for you.

To begin with, Blake owned two homes, the co-op in New York and this home, Manderley, the Allmond family estate. The co-op in Gramercy Park has been left to the National Arts Club. The contents, though, are not part of this bequest, so the co-op will have to be cleaned out relatively quickly.

Let's start with you, LeRoi Hawkins. Blake was grateful to you for your long and faithful service to him and to his family before him. It was his express wish that you, LeRoi, continue to have a home at Manderley for as long as you wish. He also has left you a cash sum of $250,000, as well as his Patek Phillipe wristwatch and several other personal items."

LeRoi gasped, mumbling something like, "Aw, I'm honored," and he wiped his face with a handkerchief.

"Alexander," Griffith went on, "your uncle wanted you to have something to remember him and your mother's family by. He bequeathed you a cash sum of one million dollars. He also wanted you to have your great-grandfather's gold watch and chain."

Alexander choked back a sob, presumably because he was emotional about the generous bequest. From Parrott's vantage point behind and to the side, Alexander's leg-tapping was in full force.

"Elle, with a few exceptions of donations to charity organizations, Blake wanted to leave the remainder of his estate to you. That includes Manderley, all of his unsold paintings, his automobiles, furnishings, antiques, jewelry, and other possessions. Of course, Manderley, for all practicality, cannot be sold as long as LeRoi chooses to live here, and I believe it was Blake's hope that you would continue to live here, as well. It will take some time to assess and value the estate, but based on recent values of stock holdings, insurance policies, and other investments, and not including the value of Manderley and the home in Gramercy Park, their contents, and Blake's unsold paintings, you will inherit a cash sum in the neighborhood of six million dollars."

"My God," Elle said. "I had no idea of Blake's wealth. Believe it or not, we never talked about it. Th-this is almost too much to fathom." She rose and ran out of the room, raising Parrott's adrenalin, as he thought about the gun in the powder room. He thought about running after her, but she returned a few seconds later with a box of tissues. "Would anyone else like one?" She returned to her seat and dabbed at her eyes.

Tonya leaned forward and placed her hand on Elle's shoulder. Parrott considered the irony that Elle needed consoling for inheriting a fortune. He wondered what Alexander and LeRoi were thinking.

Griffith glanced again at the will and continued. "Every will has an executor whose job it is to make sure the terms of the will are adhered to. Blake named you, Elle, as executor, but you need not carry that responsibility without advice and counsel. There are many excellent and experienced law firms who would be glad to work with you."

Elle's eyes darted from person to person in the room, as if searching for a trustworthy face on which to land. "What about your firm, Gary? You knew Blake the best and know what he wanted. Can't you do the work?"

Griffith smiled, the crinkles on the sides of his eyes reminding Parrott of Santa Claus. "Of course I can, but I wanted you to know you didn't necessarily have to hire me. We can do the paperwork in the next few days to get the will on file with the Registrar of Wills of the Orphan's Court in Chester County and start carrying out its terms."

He passed out the copies of the will to the three beneficiaries. "My card is inside, so feel free to contact me with questions or comments. Oh, and two more things—the will makes it very clear Anyone who contests the will and loses will forfeit his or her inheritance." He looked from Elle to LeRoi to Alexander to make sure they understood. "And secondly," he said, as he handed an envelope to Elle, "Blake left this letter to you, Elle, to be read after his death. You can open it and read it privately. I do not know the contents."

Elle took the envelope and held it to her heart with one hand, while she patted at her eyes with the other. Everyone seemed to be frozen in place, as if unsure of post-will-reading etiquette, but Parrott had work to do. He positioned himself in front of Elle's chair and shook her hand. "Now we know who the new owner of Manderley is, do we have your permission to call forensics to conduct a search?"

CHAPTER 41

A lexander couldn't wait to get away from Manderley. Sitting here in the library was suffocating, and not just because of the fire, the emotional day, and the uncomfortable suit. He felt like a ceramic piggy-bank filled to capacity with pennies. One more, and he would explode into smithereens.

His uncle's death, even without the specter of murder, had sent his thoughts on a backwards path to his own origins. It was true he hadn't been raised at Manderley and hadn't known his Allmond grandparents, but he had been close to his mother, who had, so it wasn't as if he were raised in a separate solar system. The painting of the home had hung in their living room for as long as he could remember, tethering him to a past he had experienced mostly by osmosis.

He had admired and respected Uncle Blake, too. The fact that he hadn't done enough to show it bothered him a lot. But that wasn't all.

When that attorney spoke about the change of the will, Alexander's cheeks had blazed with heat. *He* had been the reason for the change, and he was deeply ashamed. In addition, it begged more than a few questions.

Uncle Blake had been furious with him, first because of Veronica's snooping into his bank accounts, and secondly because he'd asked him for seed money for a costume business. *Now I see how transparent that was—why should I leave a good career in construction for something like that? It was obviously ill-conceived.*

O, Veronica. Alexander couldn't think of her without an electric tug shooting through him. It had only been a few days since their separation, but it felt like a year. Seeing her today, disguised as a valet parker, had set the clock back to zero, filling him with sheer physical need. What was she doing there? Had she gone to such extremes just to get a glimpse of him? Or was she up to something?

Sitting there in the front row for the reading of the will had been almost excruciating. Uncle Blake had threatened to cut Alexander out of the will, so he hadn't expected any-thing. But the lawyer had specifically named him as an heir, so, what the h—?

Once he heard the lawyer say, "a million dollars," it was as if cotton had clogged his ears. Those three words kept repeating themselves in his head, beating a drum that was delightful and scary at the same time. A person could do a lot with a million dollars. If a million dollars was punishment for his scheming ways, what might his inheritance have been before? No, he would not allow himself to think about that.

A million dollars was enough to shine a light on him as someone who would benefit from his uncle's death. He turned to glance at the detective, only to find Parrott's eyes boring into his own. He realized his heel was tapping and his heart was beating to the rhythm of a million dollars.

What would Veronica say when she heard he was a millionaire? The thought terrified him, but not as much as the subsequent thought—what would Alonzo say? Alexander would never be able to trust Alonzo. He knew in his brain, his heart, his Allmond-genes, it had been a mistake ever to get mixed up with him, and therefore with Veronica, as well.

By the time the attorney had stood to pass out copies of Uncle Blake's will, Alexander had renewed his resolve to break off with Veronica. He had to think of himself—there was no one else to guide him. Given her antics in coming to Manderley today, he would have to be extra-careful not to encourage her.

He started to feel better, more in control. He took a deep breath and went over to say his goodbyes to Elle, but before he could, Detective Parrott intervened, asking for permission to bring forensics in to search the premises.

That could only mean trouble. Alexander didn't know that much about crime, but he had watched a lot of movies and TV shows. Parrott's wanting to search the premises meant he already knew there was something to be found.

Alexander panicked. Whatever happened next, he didn't want to be anywhere around.

CHAPTER 42

As soon as Elle gave permission, Parrott went back to the breakfast room to call the forensics lab. He was vaguely aware of Alexander and the Griffiths saying goodbyes, but it was late, and he hoped to catch Jerry if he hadn't left yet. There was always someone on hand to take calls, but Parrott valued Jerry's professionalism and sense of humor.

As the phone rang, Parrott crossed his fingers mentally. His eyes wandered to the barricaded bathroom door. When Jerry's voice greeted him, he said, "Hate to call so late in the day, but I found a weapon in the bathroom at Allmond's house."

"That's what I like about you, Parrott. If you're not finding evidence, evidence is finding you. Don't worry about the hour. I'll come with a team."

Parrott gave him the address, assuring him he hadn't touched the gun, except to knock it off the shelf, and he'd secured the bathroom. Manderley was a good forty-five minutes from the DA office and lab in Bethlehem, maybe an hour in the snow.

LeRoi was in the kitchen, putting together a light meal, while Elle had gone upstairs to change clothes. Tonya had returned to the breakfast room with Parrott, but the tightness around her eyes and lips told him she was in pain again. He should take her home, but he had to keep an eye on the bathroom, at least until Jerry arrived.

"I'm sorry about keeping you here so long," he said. "You could probably take another couple of Ibuprofen now."

Tonya waved away the suggestion. "What's really bothering me is the fact someone put a gun in that bathroom. That's been chewing away at my brain the whole time we were in the library. What if you hadn't gone looking for toilet paper? What if you hadn't found it? Would that person have come in here blazing bullets?" Her voice was growing in stridency and had almost reached screeching.

Parrott's own anxiety bubbled in his gut. Torn between duty to his wife and duty to his job, he was paralyzed to do right by either. Calling upon what he had learned in a class on de-escalation, he made eye contact and touched his wife's arm. "Instead of playing, 'What if,' let's stick to the fact none of that has happened. There could be a thousand explanations for the gun to be there, and we are doing the right thing to have forensics tell us the facts, instead of imagining the worst."

Tonya's eyes were fixed on her lap. Her upper lip glistened. "I can't help it, Ollie. I know you're right, but weapons make me nervous, especially in a house of a person who was murdered. My heart is flapping so loud I can barely think."

"Let me get you some water. I wish I could take you home so you could rest."

"Okay. Maybe I'll take the Ibuprofen, too." She sucked in a string of cleansing breaths and focused her attention on a spot on the opposite wall. Parrott had seen her practicing this type of breathing after her counseling sessions. By the time he brought the water and Ibuprofen, her breathing had returned to something resembling normal. "I understand you needing to stay here. People depend on you to do things right, and you can't be catering to me when you are on the job. I get that."

"We could call a taxi."

"No, I can gut it out. How long does forensics usually take for something like this?"

"Depends on what they find. Could be anywhere from forty-five minutes to two hours." Parrott lifted Tonya's hand and kissed the palm. "I can leave as soon as they get here, though. All I'm obligated to do is babysit this barricade to make sure no one contaminates the scene any further."

"Let's play that by ear." Tonya sniffed. "Do you smell that? Mmm."

LeRoi walked in with a tray. On it were two placemats, soup bowls and plates, soup spoons, and rolled linen napkins.

"Mushroom barley soup. Homemade. There ain't nothing that isn't made better by mushroom barley soup."

"I'm sure that's right. Won't you join us? And what about Elle?" Tonya asked.

"There's plenty more on the stove. Miss Elle will probably be down in a few minutes. No point in rushing her. You go ahead and eat it while it's hot."

Parrott thanked LeRoi and watched Tonya lift a spoonful of soup to her mouth with her left hand. "You've gotten pretty good at that."

"Must be all the practicing I'm doing when I'm not attending funerals and babysitting guns."

Parrott grinned. LeRoi must have been right about the powers of mushroom barley soup. For the time being, he had his wife back.

CHAPTER 43

Elle had run upstairs to her bedroom on the pretext of changing into more comfortable clothes, but truthfully, she was shaking all over. She couldn't remember a single time in her life when so many emotions had swarmed about her like honeybees, promising sweetness, but threatening stings. She flung the door open and eyed the bed. Oh, if she could only climb under the covers and not come out.

Closing the door and pushing the lock button, she leaned her warm forehead against the cool frame and closed her eyes. She moved to the closet, removing the black knit dress and houndstooth jacket that would forever remind her of this sad day. She hung them up in the closet and slid her hand along the rack of possible options. Clothes had never been her thing, but Blake had insisted she build a wardrobe. Many of her outfits he had purchased without her. She stepped into a charcoal gray pant suit with large buttons and pockets in the jacket.

She opened the top dresser drawer and gazed at the collection of rosary beads. She chose the ivory-colored ones from the Holy Land. She knelt by the side of her bed and tried to clear her mind of worldly matters. She thanked the Blessed Mother for the many joys of her life, and then she allowed herself to cry.

After praying, she lay on the bed in the dark room, staring at the ceiling. Her rumbling stomach reminded her she hadn't eaten all day. She reviewed the events of the day, starting with the funeral, the eulogies, the cemetery, the reception, and the meeting in the library. It was all a blur, but two facts stood out. She wouldn't have to leave Manderley, and there was a gun in the bathroom—both unbelievable, but for different reasons. She never could have imagined in her past life, when she was Estelle Carson, that she would end up in this situation.

But here she was, Elle Carmichael, artist, teacher, and heiress to a fortune. *Thank you, Blake Allmond.* She rose and smoothed the wrinkles in her pant suit. Maybe she should wash her face and comb her hair, too.

First she'd open the envelope Gary Griffith had given her. She had dropped it on the corner of the night table when she first came into the room, so overwrought that she couldn't deal with it. Now that she'd had a few minutes of quiet, though, it was drawing her like iron filings to a magnet. She switched on the bedside lamp and picked it up. This would be her last communication from Blake—she was eager to read it, but dreaded it at the same time.

She held the envelope, staring at Blake's perfect penmanship on the front. She carried it with her to the windows, where she lowered the blinds and closed the curtains. Propping pillows against the headboard, she created a comfortable space, lit by the soft light of the single lamp, and she slid her forefinger into the flap, pulling the seal open as neatly as possible.

Dear Elle,

By the time you read this letter, you will most likely know I've named you as executor of my estate and heir to most of my property and possessions.

As the person dearest to my heart, this is most appropriate. I am grateful to you for giving me a reason to live after unspeakable tragedy. You are my muse, my inspiration, my love. I trust you will follow my wishes and use the inheritance wisely. Do what brings you joy and satisfaction.

There is another purpose for this letter, something that will come as a revelation to you, something I have kept as a secret for many years.

You know, I'm sure, my path as an artist began when I was very young. My mother saw I had a natural talent, and she encouraged it. She persuaded my father to arrange for lessons with the already up-and-coming Victor Lockwood, who was a family friend. I was the luckiest kid in the world. Lockwood took me under his wing and taught me many things. I was in awe of his ability, his skills.

I wanted to be like him—to be him. The amazing thing was, he adored me, too. He convinced me I would be the next Monet. I had been studying with him for five years, and I was fourteen years old, before I realized his adoration had a price.

I was Lockwood's young lover. We had a sexual relationship for over ten years, until he became ill and reclusive and stopped painting. At first I was forced, but later I was a willing participant.

You may or may not be aware there were other such relationships among men in the Brandywine art community, and probably there always will be. I am no one to judge, and I know you are one who is quick to understand and slow to condemn.

I hope you can forgive me for not telling you about this part of my life and this side of my nature. It has been a source of self-consciousness, and I have endeavored to keep it a secret, even at times from myself."

Elle dropped the letter to her lap and gasped. How had she lived with Blake all these years and not known? Heat rushed to her face at the thought of how naïve she had been. The unworldly former nun.

Why, you may ask, am I disclosing this to you now, when it would be simpler to take it with me to my grave? The reason is this—Victor Lockwood gave me an original oil painting as a token of his love and appreciation. This was many years ago, when I was in my twenties. I doubt he realized how valuable the painting would become.

I loved the painting—technically, it was a masterpiece, and I was honored by his beneficence. But even then, I couldn't tell anyone about it, even my parents. It would raise too many questions, and I was never comfortable with that. So I hid the painting. It has had many hiding places over the years. On the one hand, it's a shame the world is denied its beauty and brilliance, but I could not bring myself to acknowledge it publicly, given the circumstances under which I had come to possess it.

Enclosed in this envelope is the letter of provenance Lockwood gave me with the painting, along with a letter from me, conveying the painting to you. You should have no trouble proving the painting's authenticity and your legal ownership of it.

As much as you love and value art, I recommend you sell the painting at auction through one of the fine auction houses. It should fetch a hefty price, but, more importantly, it belongs in the open, where others can study and appreciate it. It has remained in a hidey-hole for far too long.

I have taken every precaution to ensure you are the only one to know how to find this painting, but one never knows into what hands this letter may fall. I also have reason to believe there are people who are still alive who know of its existence and covet it. Therefore, I will not spell out the location of the painting. I will only say you will find it if you look in the right place. It is in a place neither too cool nor too hot, surrounded by Hawthorne, sunsets, and my favorite artist's happy place.

I hope you understand this story of my past in no way diminishes the love I've had for you and for Susan before you. As artists, we share the joy of making others see the world through our eyes. I had lost my ability to do that when I met you, and you gave it back to me.

Thank you for sharing your spirit with me, my love. I have every faith you will carry on in a way that would make me, and all of the Allmond family, proud.

Blake

Elle brushed a few tears away and closed her eyes. She wished she could brush away the feeling Blake had been controlling her, was still controlling her, despite his generosity. He had loved her, though. That had always been apparent. She could picture Blake, sitting at his desk in Manhattan, writing these words with the same care he used in painting a landscape. She glanced at the letter from Victor Lockwood and the second letter from Blake. Everything had been done with precision, and now it was up to her.

Elle folded the letters and put them back into the envelope. She looked around for a safe place to hide it, finally deciding upon slipping it between the pages of an old sketch pad she kept in the closet.

To say she was depleted, physically and emotionally, was an understatement, but she had guests in the house, and the aroma of comfort food had drifted up the stairs. Maybe she could get Tonya to join her in a good, stiff drink, as well.

She wasn't sure where the painting was, but she had some ideas of where to start looking. Finding it wasn't the only worry, though. She kept coming back to the fact Blake had been murdered. Even worse, a gun had been hidden at Manderley. What if the Victor Lockwood painting had been the motive for Blake's murder? If so, the painting carried a terrible curse. And, as the new owner of the painting, she might be its next victim.

CHAPTER 44

After finishing the mouth-watering soup, and still waiting for forensics to show up, Parrott had an idea. "I'll be back in a few minutes," he said to Tonya. "I'm going to chat with LeRoi in the kitchen."

The butler was at the oven, removing a tray full of hors d'oeuvres reheated from the reception. The kitchen was steamy and filled with smells of meat and pastry. Parrott's mouth watered, as he offered to help arrange the various delicacies on the serving platter, but LeRoi waved him away.

"Well, can I ask you a few questions while you work, then?" Having grown up around people who served others, Parrott had a special place in his heart for them.

"Sure." LeRoi closed his eyes and leaned his elbows on the counter for a few seconds. Recovering quickly, he said, "I 'spect you have quite a few."

"I noticed you are the only Manderley employee who was named in Mr. Blake's will. A place this size must have many more people who work here. Can you explain?"

Spots of color appeared on LeRoi's cocoa-colored cheeks. "I'm grateful to Mr. Blake for honoring me. There are quite a few other employees who keep this place running—three housekeepers, a part-time cook, a maintenance and repairs guy, four groundskeepers, and a chauffeur. There used to be nannies, too. Nobody lives here but me, though, and nobody's worked here much longer than three or four years, 'cept me."

"How long have you been here?"

LeRoi paused in covering the tray with aluminum foil. "More'n fifty years. Seems like my whole life." He lifted the lid of the soup pot and turned the flame off. "Mr. Blake was only a tyke when I got here."

Parrott looked around the kitchen, a room he'd never seen before. A light from the alarm system winked at him from the corner of the ceiling. "I guess the other employees will be upset if they hear you were named in the will."

"Maybe they won't find out. Anyway, knowing Miss Elle, nobody's going to be fired for no reason. Mr. Blake knew how kind-hearted she is."

"Who's kind-hearted?" Elle asked, as she entered the kitchen and looked from LeRoi to Parrott. She peeked under the foil and withdrew a petite puff pastry filled with lamb and mint jelly. Popping it into her mouth, she murmured, "Mmm, mmm," and moved to the stove, lifting the lid on the soup pot. "Guess I'm hungry. It seems like days since I've eaten."

"Glad you're getting your appetite back," LeRoi replied. "Why don't you sit down with Miss Tonya, and I'll bring you some of everything. You, too, Parrott."

Parrott glanced at his watch. "Forensics should be getting here any minute, but, sure, I'll sit down with you."

Elle and Parrott walked into the breakfast room, where Tonya had fallen asleep at the table, her braids forming a natural frame for her face and neck. Once they saw her, they tiptoed and pulled their chairs as quietly as possible. But when LeRoi followed them, carrying the tray of hot hors d'oeuvres, the aluminum foil rustled, and she woke with a start.

"Sorry if I woke you," LeRoi said, pulling the foil from the tray and setting the serving tongs down at an angle. He looked at Elle. "I'll be back with soup."

Tonya sat up and rubbed her eyes. "I guess those Ibuprofens knocked me out."

"Not surprising," Elle said. "This has been a long, hard day for you with your shoulder. Would you like to lie down in a bedroom?"

Parrott was pretty sure this was the first time Tonya had been invited by the landed gentry to take a nap in a bedroom of a huge mansion, and he caught the smile playing on her lips. What an unlikely friendship this was, but a friendship, nonetheless.

"No, thanks," Tonya replied. "But I will have some of these yummy appetizers."

LeRoi arrived with a bowl of steaming soup for Elle, as well as a decanted bottle of Malbec and three wine glasses. He placed a china tureen on the center of the table, as well, "in case anyone wants seconds."

Parrott's stomach growled, and he ladled more soup into his bowl. "Do you have the recipe for this?" he asked Elle. His mother was a fine cook, and one of her specialties was soup. He bet she'd love to try this one. Before she could answer, the doorbell rang. "That will be Jerry and the boys." He jumped up to run to the door, but LeRoi was already ambling toward the entry hall. "I can let them in. Why don't you sit down for a minute?"

"No, sir. My job."

The snow had stopped long ago, but the wind had kicked up. Jerry and two other guys were dusted with tiny crystals of snow. The circular driveway was cleared to the pavement, but powdery drifts had landed here and there, making the view look more like January than November.

The technicians stomped their feet on the doormat before entering the house, where they removed their jackets. LeRoi led the parade down the long entry hall to the breakfast room, where Parrott introduced them to Elle and Ton-ya. "These are the same men who examined the studio a few days ago. They're the best in the business."

After securing Elle's permission to examine the bathroom and whatever other areas of the house might be indicated, Jerry and his assistants put on gloves and booties. Parrott suggested the trio of diners move supper to another room.

As they all pitched in to carry one or two items to the dining room, Parrott observed blinking lights from the alarm system again. He had wanted to ask Elle about the security system, but so much had happened to derail his investigation. Now seemed as good a time as any. Once they were settled in the dining room, he said to Elle, "I'm seeing motion detectors in the ceilings of every room. What can you tell me about your home security system?"

Elle chewed on a bacon-wrapped chunk of filet before answering. "It's U.S. Security. Every room on the first floor has multiple wirings."

LeRoi had returned to the kitchen wing to be accessible in case the forensics team needed anything. Low rumblings of voices served as background rhythm to the conversation in the dining room. Elle reached for the Malbec and poured a glass for herself. "How about some nice wine?" she asked Tonya and Parrott, who declined, one because of the Ibuprofen, and the other because he considered himself on duty.

"Are there cameras, too?"

"No cameras. It's an old system. After the paintings were stolen, Blake talked about upgrading."

"What about the alarm system in the studio?" Parrott was kicking himself for not having gotten this information sooner.

"It's wired, too."

"Do you set both locations from one keypad, or are there separate keypads?

"Two keypads in each location, each with its own code."

"Didn't you tell me the night the art was stolen, you had set the alarm in the studio?"

"Yes, we set both alarms every night. Things are pretty peaceful out here, but you never know, and there are valuables in both places."

"If someone broke in while the alarm was on, what would happen?"

"The keypad would beep for sixty or ninety seconds—I forget which—and then a solid alarm would sound. We would have another sixty or ninety seconds to disarm the alarm and call the service, but if we didn't do that, they would contact the police to come out."

"And none of that happened on the night the paintings disappeared?"

"Right. It was as if the alarm hadn't been on at all—which we know wasn't true. No beeps, no solid alarm, no police. It's a mystery."

"Who, besides you and Mr. Blake, knows the alarm code?"

"LeRoi knows it. He's the one who puts it on most of the time and turns it off the next day. But it doesn't matter who knows the code, because if someone who knew the code opened the door to the studio, the keypad would beep, and it didn't even do that."

Elle took another sip of her wine and set the glass on the placemat. "May I change the subject, detective?" A vein in her forehead was pulsing, and lavender circles under her eyes had become prominent.

Tonya placed a hand on Parrott's knee under the table, and Parrott covered it with his. "Of course," he replied to Elle. "We can talk about burglar alarms anytime. What's on your mind?"

"I'm more than a little upset about there being a gun in the bathroom. Since I'm quite sure neither Blake nor I put it there, and I seriously doubt LeRoi did, either, I can only conclude someone brought it here and stashed it in the bathroom." She took another sip. "But who would do that, and why? The only thing I can imagine is someone wants to make things look bad for me—"

"—Who would do that?" Tonya asked, her voice heavy with indignance.

"I don't know who, but I'm sure I know why. As the major beneficiary of Blake's estate, I'm an easy suspect for having murdered him. Am I right, Detective?"

Parrott wanted to allay Elle's fears, but there was no getting around the fact she would be a suspect, weapon or no weapon. "The New York detectives have probably put together a list of suspects by now. Yes, your name is probably on the list, and yes, if this turns out to be the weapon that killed Mr. Allmond, NYPD will be extremely interested in how it got here. That's why we've got forensics here. Their work will provide good information."

"But if I had killed Blake, why on earth would I put the gun in my own bathroom?"

"You didn't kill anyone," Tonya said. "I'll bet you don't even kill flies or spiders."

A flicker of a smile showed on Elle's face. "Actually, I don't. All of God's creatures deserve to live their lives."

A tap on the doorframe caused all three pairs of eyes to focus on LeRoi. "Excuse me for interrupting, but the gentlemen have finished in the bathroom, and they'd like to talk to Detective Parrott."

Parrott excused himself and strode to the breakfast room area, where Jerry had set up a makeshift work area, using the table. The gun had been placed in a sealed plastic bag. The white pillowcase it had been in was now black, and it was also in a sealed bag. The bathroom vanity, was black from the powder used to elicit fingerprints, especially under the sink. Smudges were everywhere, and certain prints and partial prints were obvious, too. "Looks like you've struck oil," Parrott said.

"Plenty of prints, if that's what you mean. Probably too many in the bathroom. The gun we're bagging, tagging, and we'll hold it until you tell us what you want to do with it." Jerry rubbed his palms together, as if trying to remove traces of the soap and water he had used to clean them. "We'll hold onto everything in case it leads to a match up later."

"You've worked way past closing time, and I appreciate it."

Jerry started packing the objects into a large carrying case. "We took a lot of photos, and we're taking some towels and a soap dish, too, in case there might be skin." He pointed toward the bathroom, which resembled a tattoo-covered giant. "Sorry for the mess, but, you know, it comes with the territory."

"I know—it's unavoidable. I'll explain to the lady of the house. Let me know what you find, and thanks for coming out."

"By the way, we just finished the report on the studio in the back. No fingerprints anywhere, not even on the keypad. The perp was definitely gloved up, and either the alarm wasn't set, or he used one of those USRP N210's to disarm it. Sophisticated thief. We did, however, pick up a couple of hairs and flecks of skin. Assuming they don't belong to the people who belonged there, you might get some mileage from them."

"Hey, a lead is a lead, even if it's a hairy, flaky one." Parrott chuckled. "I've run into those software-defined radios before—they seem to be the hottest thing for serious home burglars. Anyway, thanks again. You and your guys are the best."

By the time Parrott saw the forensics guys out and he and Tonya said their goodbyes to Elle and LeRoi, it was after nine p.m. The night air was crisp and cold, and the sky was freckled with stars.

Parrott drove, while Tonya leaned her head back, eyes shut.

"Go ahead and take a nap, honey. You've earned it."

"I'm not sleeping. Just thinking about poor Elle. Her and LeRoi in that huge house by themselves. I don't think I could handle it if something happened to you."

Parrott reached over and squeezed her hand. "Exactly how I feel about you."

Tonya squeezed back and sat up straighter. "Ollie, what's your gut feeling about that gun? You don't think Elle hid it there, do you?"

"No, but it doesn't matter what I think." As he left the country roads for the highway, he hit the accelerator, both physically and mentally. His thoughts were on the conversation he'd had with Detective Rayburn, the guests at Manderley, and the terms of the will. It was a whole week since the paintings had been stolen, and he was no closer to finding them. Allmond's murder had completely derailed his case.

"Why do you say that?" Tonya asked, still holding his hand.

"If anything, the gun may be tied to Allmond's murder—not the stolen paintings—and that, my love, is not my case."

CHAPTER 45

Now, as he drove back to South Philly after the reading of the will, Alexander drew energy from the clear, cold evening and the patches of snow dotting the landscape. Thanksgiving would be here soon, and he had a lot to be thankful for.

A million dollars, properly invested, would give him a comfortable cushion for the rest of his life. Of course he would keep his job. There was no reason not to. But a million dollars in the bank gave a man options. His mother had walked away from it. He owed his very existence to that. She had raised him without the luxuries, but he did okay. It would take a while for the concept of being a millionaire to sink in.

Even though he had declared himself free of Veronica, he imagined what she would say when she found out about the inheritance. Snooping into Uncle Blake's accounts had given her a bottomless lust for money. And now she'd seen Manderley, albeit from the outside, she'd be carping about how unfair it was the estate wasn't going to him. She would probably push him to contest the will and risk losing it all.

Not my problem. He realized for the first time Veronica was a glass-half-empty girl, and he was a glass-half-full guy. Why hadn't he seen that before? And then there was Alonzo.

Alonzo had given him the creeps from the first time he'd laid eyes on his boxer's face and muscular body. A broken nose and facial creases too prominent to be ignored gave him a sinister look, even when he was smiling.

Veronica had mentioned Alonzo's job as a landscaper in Brandywine Valley, but she'd neglected to mention specifically where he worked. That was no oversight, Alexander understood now, and he shivered with the realization he had been a pawn in some obscure game of chess, where Manderley had been the kingdom, and Blake Allmond had been the king.

Thinking back to the day he and Veronica had met at Cookie's Tavern, the way she had sidled up to him, wearing that low-cut red dress with a slit up the thigh—he'd thought he hit the jackpot. When he'd introduced himself, she'd seemed to know his name already. She'd said something like, "You're *the* Alexander Vargas?" He'd been flattered. Maybe she'd heard of him from the neighborhood soccer team he'd played in, or the Habitat for Humanity work he'd done last year.

Now he shivered with suspicion that Alonzo had used Veronica to target him, stalk him, even. What he'd thought was true love had been nothing more than a calculated plot. He had played into their hands over and over again. What he had done for love could not be undone.

Alexander pulled off the highway. A thick copse of woods surrounded a creek, known to him since childhood. He got out of the car, leaving the door open, and ran in the rising light of the moon, about fifty yards, where the creek seemed fullest. He removed the burner phone from his pocket, checked to make sure it was the right one, and threw it into the frigid-looking water.

It felt good to divest himself of Veronica's means of contacting him, but only for a moment. His real cell phone was scorching him through his other pocket. If she couldn't get him through the burner phone, she wouldn't hesitate to break their pact and call him on the original phone. He hesitated for a moment, thinking of the pictures stored on this android and the hassles he would have to go through to get a new number.

He remembered his mother's saying, "There are times in life when you've got to make a break, even if it's painful." He scrolled to his favorite picture of Veronica and tried to memorize the details. Then he shut off the phone and threw it into the inky water.

He stumbled back into his car and drove home, to his clean and neat condo. Tomorrow he would get a new cell phone, and he would start a new life. It was too late for Uncle Blake, but maybe it wasn't too late for him.

CHAPTER 46

After the funeral reception, the Campbells' Mercedes SUV pulled out of the driveway *en-route* to dropping Andrea off. "Thanks for coming with me, you two. I really didn't want to go by myself."

Caro turned to offer a gesture of comfort. "It's too bad Stan is out of town, but we were glad to help out. Heaven knows you were a help to us last year with Preston. It was nice to meet Elle, despite the circumstances. To think we live so close, but we've never run into each other."

"That's Brandywine," John E. said. "Everyone is stuck in some niche, but the niches don't mix. Kind of a shame."

"It was nice to see some of the artsy crowd there. Did you recognize Benjamin Lockwood, Victor's son? He had glasses with royal blue frames."

"Was that Lockwood? We actually have one of his paintings in our family room."

"Yes, and the NYT art critic, Helen Masterson, was there in the salmon and gray tweed suit. She's a heavy hitter."

John E. interjected, "Personally, I enjoyed meeting Detective Parrott's wife. Even with her arm all trussed up, she's a good-looking woman. They make a nice-looking couple."

"Yes, she served in Afghanistan as a Navy SEAL. I didn't know there were women doing that."

"Oh, and Rupert Brooks. He seemed kind of harried, I thought. Gave me the bum's rush, and I've given him quite a bit of business over the years."

"He probably had to get back to the gallery. This is the time of year people purchase art, so they can have it up before the holidays. Did you get his postcard advertising Sophia Lockwood's first exhibit in February? I'd like to go."

"Maybe Stan and I will go, too. In fact, maybe I'll invite Elle to go with us and make a day of it, get her out and back into the art world."

"That's thoughtful of you."

John E. pulled the car into the Bakers' driveway and shifted into park. "Tell Stan we said hello."

Andrea leaned forward to air-kiss Caro and John E. "Will do, and thanks for the ride and the moral support." After she let herself in, she watched them drive off through the glass panel of the door. She couldn't stop thinking about her cousins from Manderley. Who would have dreamed all that had befallen them?

She ran through her mind all of the people who had been at the funeral or at the reception, many she had known, and several she hadn't known. Her experience with writing about crime told her at least one of the "guests" had been a plain-clothes detective.

As she hung up her coat and headed for the kitchen, she remembered times spent at Manderley. She and Melanie had played together as children there and here, in her home. In fact, a pair of portraits hanging in the staircase might have been of common great-grandparents.

Andrea regretted not knowing Blake better. She wondered about the paintings stolen from his studio. Who would have taken them, and why? More importantly, was the theft linked to Blake's murder? She couldn't imagine a scenario that would connect the two crimes, but she couldn't imagine pure coincidence allowed for them in such close proximity. Another thing she wondered was why the bathroom she'd wanted to use before leaving was barricaded. She wasn't crass enough to ask, but she was curious, just the same.

One thing she was certain of—she hoped whoever had killed her cousin would be found and given whatever he—or she—deserved.

CHAPTER 47

Early the next morning, Tonya was sleeping, but Parrott had to go to work. He closed the bedroom door and tiptoed into the bathroom, taking clothes, shoes, and cell phone with him. Not entirely unexpectedly, he got a call from Chief Schrik. "Listen, I'm going to call Jerry and put a halt on processing that gun."

Parrott gave one last swipe of the razor and wiped his face with a towel. "Really, Chief? Did New York find out about it already? We don't know yet whether this gun was used in our crime or theirs, or neither one."

"Yeah, but I slept on it, and decided we don't need the aggravation of them saying we messed up their case down the line."

"Well, I'll admit the weapon's more likely to be theirs than ours, since ours was a person-less crime. Too bad, because I trust Jerry more than anyone to do a clean job." Parrott sighed. Mentally adjusting his agenda for the day, he continued, "Who's calling New York about the gun?"

"You want to do the honors? It's the least I can do after taking away your latest Easter egg."

"Okay. I'm sure they'll be on it like a dog with a filet mignon. At least I hope we get credit for preserving the scene. Maybe they'll share info with us in return."

"Don't count on it." Schrik paused to sip something, making Parrott wish for coffee. "What they will do is ask millions of questions about *your* case."

"And we will go all out to help them." Parrott couldn't help thinking how unfair it was.

"That's just how it is. They've got priority any way you look at it. Don't you want to see Allmond's killer brought to justice?"

"Don't ask rhetorical questions, Chief." Parrott walked into the kitchen to start the coffee, cell phone sandwiched between shoulder and ear. "Some news from Jerry on our case—no prints, but some skin flakes—could be significant. Whoever took the paintings is no amateur. Used expensive equipment to get past the alarm, and wore gloves to do it."

"How much traffic goes in and out of that studio? We'd have to rule out legitimates."

"One of which is my wife. I think there are five or so students who take art lessons there. I'll talk to Elle after I call NYPD."

When Parrott called Detective Rayburn's number, a deep, husky voice answered. "Coleman here, how can I help you?"

Irked, he replied, "Parrott from West Brandywine. Thought I was calling Rayburn."

"She's indisposed. I'm phone-watching. You got something on Allmond?"

Definitely not the chatty type, but that's okay. Two can play at this game. "Possibly. Found a pistol in a pillowcase in a bathroom at Manderley. Secured the scene. Chester County forensics came out and took it. Thought you'd be interested."

Parrott could hear the squeak of a chair, as he imagined Coleman sitting up. "Really? What kind of pistol?"

".380 semi-automatic Beretta Pico."

"Bingo. More than interested. Tell me again who's got it?"

"So you recovered something that matches? Glad to hear it." Parrott stalled. "Chain of custody's clean from the time I found it. Ask for Jerry at Chester County on Market Street in West Chester. There was a full house there yesterday at the funeral reception. No idea who stashed it there."

"Wouldn't be surprised if it was the girlfriend. Smart of her to put it there on a day when lots of folks would be using the bathroom."

"She doesn't seem the type to me," Parrott replied.

"There's more than meets the eye there. Did you know her legal name isn't Elle Carmichael? Not saying that's significant but could be. Anyway, I can't wait to get that piece to our forensics lab. This could be a big break."

The detective sounded more animated than Parrott had ever heard him. "Good luck. Jerry is expecting to hear from you."

A click and a dial tone sounded in Parrott's ear. *Not even a thank you.* Parrott hoped he would never be so wrapped up in himself or his case as to hang up on someone who'd just helped him.

Elle had slept sporadically. Dream fragments about money and paintings and guns subverted attempts to clear her mind. Her body ached from weariness—her eyes burned, and her neck and shoulders felt stiff.

She looked at the green digits of the alarm clock—3:41. Much too early to get out of bed for the day, but she wanted to re-read Blake's letter. She turned on the portable reading lamp kept on her bedstand and padded to the hiding place in her closet. Clutching the letter against her chest, she returned to bed and pulled the covers up around her. She shivered again, reading about the Victor Lockwood and the way Blake had come to own it. The revelation had aroused sympathy, but not revulsion. She had always known Blake was a complicated person with a difficult past, but she had also known he had immense talent and a good and kind heart. For her, those traits trumped everything else.

The uncirculated Lockwood painting would indeed fetch a fortune, but more than that, Elle wanted to see it. She wanted to drink in its beauty, its technique. Owning a Lockwood was so far out of her realm as to be laughable, to make her giddy, but own it she did—if she could only find it.

"It is in a place neither too cool nor too hot, surrounded by Hawthorne, sunsets, and my favorite artist's happy place." Of course, the painting was somewhere indoors. Too much heat or cold might harm it. It could be in a temperature-controlled storage facility, but Elle didn't think so. That would involve a contract and a key, and there was nothing in the letter to indicate either of those. Her hunch was it was somewhere at Manderley. Blake would have had more control over it if it were here.

But Manderley was huge, nine thousand square feet, and that didn't count basement, attic, or outbuildings. All of the rooms at Manderley had paintings, and some had collages of paintings hanging on the walls. She hadn't examined the artists' signatures on all of them, but she was certain she would have known if a Lockwood was "hiding in plain sight." Besides, Blake said he had hidden it away.

The best place to store paintings was the studio, but Elle was familiar with all of the inventory there, and there were no Lockwoods—she was sure of that. There were closets and pantries throughout the three stories of the house, and there were several rooms that had access to attic space. At least four generations of Allmonds had lived here, and heaven knew what was stored where.

The entire house was surrounded by hawthorn bushes, though she thought the plant's name was spelled without the final "e". Or maybe the painting was surrounded by other paintings with hawthorns and sunsets as subject matter. And who was Blake's favorite artist? Over the years he had collected paintings by various artists, both local and foreign. She wished this riddle were less obscure, but wasn't that the point? Blake had wanted his instructions to be complicated enough so that no one could crack them, but her.

Elle shoved the covers aside and slid her feet into soft, pink slippers. She looked out the window at the broad expanse of Manderley. It was four a.m., and the sky was still dotted with twinkling stars and moon. Wrapping her robe around her and tying the belt, she padded out into the hallway and down the stairs.

She was sure LeRoi couldn't hear her from his bedroom on the third floor, but she stepped slowly anyway, avoiding a couple of squeaky boards she knew were there. Once she reached the first floor, she walked to the extreme north end of the house. Her mission was to cover every first-floor room, examining it for closet or cabinet space, where a painting might be secreted.

She hadn't gone through more than five or six rooms, though, before she realized what a massive undertaking this would be. She had so little information. How large was the painting? Was it framed or unframed? Signed or unsigned? What was its subject? Lockwood was known for his landscapes, but this early painting might not be. What exactly was it she was looking for, and would she know it when she saw it?

She sat on the piano bench in the living room and counted the paintings in the room. There were eighteen, including two of Blake's, two of Melanie's, and one of hers. She'd never thought there was such a thing as too many paintings, but now the magnitude of the task overwhelmed her.

Something else bothered her. Blake had said he had reason to believe others knew about the painting and might look for it. What others? What if this valuable painting had something to do with Blake's murder? A sob worked its way from the pit of Elle's stomach to her throat, and she thought of the gun hidden in the bathroom.

For thirteen years, Manderley had been a peaceful, pleasant place to live. It hadn't concerned her that she and Blake weren't married or that she didn't have ownership in the mansion. She had enjoyed the freedom to paint and teach, and she had left practical concerns to Blake.

Now Blake was gone, and Manderley was hers. Along with it came a seemingly infinite number of responsibilities and worries, one of which was this—would whoever killed Blake now come after her?

CHAPTER 48

The morning after the funeral, Veronica showed up at Lyons Bank at the stroke of nine, as usual, but this time Hector halted her at the door, grabbing her by the upper arm.

"Let me go, or I'll be late."

Hector tightened his grip. "It's too late already, *mi amiga*. Orders from Potfiller—you're to clean out your desk and leave."

She jerked away from him. "What? I'm fired? Why?"

"Nobody's telling me, and they probably won't tell you either. Maybe it has something to do with your not being here yesterday. This place was a zoo, lines around the corner and out the door in the morning. Not a good day to be sick."

"B-but I couldn't help it." Panic rose in her throat. "Let me talk to him."

"I can't, *muchacha*. He gave me strict orders. Clean out your drawer and your counter and vamoose."

Veronica shook free of the security guard and ran toward Philpot's office. So close to Thanksgiving, she needed her job. The chief loan officer's door was closed, and the blinds were closed. There was nothing to do but go with Hector to get her few belongings and leave. The other tellers would probably enjoy witnessing her comeuppance, but she wouldn't give them the satisfaction of carrying on about it. She tossed her dark tresses behind her shoulders, held her head high, and marched to her counter, as if she were a queen who had decided to move from one throne to another.

After packing her extra pair of stilettos, emergency makeup kit, sewing kit, and a framed photo of her and Alexander, she handed over her lanyard and ID and left. Her cheeks burned with a mixture of fury and shame. Taking off from work yesterday to masquerade as a valet parker had been foolish. What had she been thinking? Seeing Alexander for one minute hadn't been worth losing her job.

This bank job had been her most respectable ever. She'd enjoyed the contact with people, the responsibility of being accurate, and especially being around money. She'd hoped to move up, maybe become a manager or an officer one day. She'd built relationships with some of the customers, and she would miss hearing about their families and their jobs.

But she had blown it. She trudged out of the building and into the parking lot, ignoring the chilly wind that whipped at her ankles and blew her hair back from her face. She wanted to call Alexander now more than ever, but after the way he had ignored her yesterday, she was leery. Maybe after five, she'd call on the burner phone. Surely this qualified as an emergency. She wondered whether any mention had been made about the disposition of Allmond's wealth. So many questions she had, but no one to ask.

Thanksgiving was in two days, and her rent was due four days after that. Nothing had gone according to plan, nothing. She started her car, glancing at the gas gauge—she had an eighth of a tank left.

Alonzo had let her keep the tips from parking the cars yesterday. Mostly five dollar bills, they were crinkled up in her coat pocket. She took inventory and found she had a little over a hundred dollars. She drove to the nearest gas station and pumped ten dollars' worth. When she went to pay, she tossed a newspaper and a pack of gum onto the counter, as well. Might as well spend the morning reading the want ads. Maybe she'd luck out and find something where she wouldn't need a reference from her last employer.

When she arrived at home, she threw her purse and the box of items from her desk onto the dining table and trudged to the kitchen. She turned on the burner under the kettle to make herself a cup of instant coffee. After a couple of minutes, it was ready, and she took a sip of the watery liquid. It was all she deserved.

She opened the newspaper to the classifieds and started reading as she swallowed the bitter-tasting beverage. There weren't more than a couple of pages of listings, and she hardly knew where to begin. "Administrative assistant" was as good a place as any, but the words swam in front of her eyes.

Veronica pulled out her cell phone, searched for Alonzo's contact number, and pushed the green icon. When her brother answered, she raised her voice, though there was no need to. "Hey, it's me, your unemployed sister."

"Unemployed? What's happened?"

"Who knows? They don't have to give a reason, so they don't. Maybe they didn't like my calling off yesterday, or maybe they're still mad I got into the records. It don't matter. I'm out, and there's no going back." She leaned her elbow on the table and covered her eyes with her palm.

"Sorry to hear it. Maybe your boyfriend can help you get a new job. Seems to me he's riding high now his rich uncle is gone. Bet he's inheriting a bundle."

"Yeah, well, I can't even call him, thanks to you. I should never have listened to you about snooping into the bank records. And it was a dumb idea to dress up like a man and park cars yesterday, too."

"You're the one who had to see lover boy. Don't lay that on me."

Veronica stood and paced, waving her arm around as she talked. "Whatever. The bottom line is I need money. I don't have savings, and I don't have a cushy job like you."

"Hey, there's nothing cushy about my job. I work hard for what I get, little sister. You're the one who hasn't held up her end of the bargain. You figure out a way to marry that weasel you're so in love with. Get yourself pregnant if you have to, but once you're Mrs. Vargas, it won't matter whether you have a job or not. We'll be set."

Veronica hung up the phone and swallowed the last of her coffee. It might as well have been hemlock.

CHAPTER 49

Elle's meanderings through Manderley had been unproductive until she landed in the music room, where she found a California landscape with the signature of C. Hawthorne. Her heart leaped at the first clue word from Blake's letter. She took the painting down from the wall and examined it, front and back. She looked around the room for cupboard or closet storage, attic or basement access, anyplace the Lockwood might be hidden, but there was none.

She hung the painting back in place and snapped a picture of it with her cell phone. She walked back to the study and sat at the roll top desk that had belonged to Blake's great grandfather. Her laptop had been shut down for the funeral, but she started it up now. While waiting for the homepage to come up, she took a pen and notepad from the desk drawer. She had so many things to do—it was best to make a list.

She wrote, "Bank accounts, life insurance, credit cards, Gramercy Park." Searching for a hidden painting seemed almost frivolous compared to these important tasks, but Blake had set her on this treasure hunt, so it meant more to her than all of the rest, combined.

When her homepage lit up, she typed C. Hawthorne, artist, into the browser and waited for it to search. Within seconds she had a hit. Charles W. Hawthorne was an early twentieth century artist. Known as "a painter's painter," he'd founded the Cape Cod School of Art in 1899. The painting in the music room was a beach scene in Maine, beautifully rendered and quite moving. Maybe there were other Hawthorne paintings in the house.

She shut down the laptop and stood to proceed to the next room in this wing, but a shuffling in the hallway meant LeRoi was up and moving.

"Good morning, Miss Elle. I saw the light on and came to see if you were ready for an early breakfast."

She loved that about LeRoi. No questions about why she was wandering around in the music room before five in the morning. The world could use more people like him. "You know what? Breakfast sounds good. Let me go upstairs and shower first. Give me twenty minutes?"

"Waffles and sausage?"

"Great, or whatever you have on hand. Don't go to any trouble."

"Also, the cook is due to come today. I'm sure she was planning to prepare for Thanksgiving, which is only two days away. Do you want me to call her not to come?"

How odd that the world continued to move forward without Blake. Elle was in no need of a Thanksgiving feast, or even the cook's services for just herself and LeRoi. On the other hand, this was no time of the year to interfere with Fern's livelihood, and maybe having some hearty food in the house would make the holiday less dreary. "No, let's keep everything in its usual routine. We'll find a way to use the food. If we don't eat it, we can donate it to one of the shelters in Philadelphia."

As she ascended the stairs, she wondered whether Alexander had plans for Thanksgiving. Or what about the Parrotts? Tonya wouldn't be cooking with her broken shoulder. Fern usually cooked enough for ten, even though they rarely had company for the holiday. Elle was interrupted in her thoughts by a loud rumble in her stomach. Right now waffles and sausage seemed like a good first step for the day.

After breakfast, Elle sat down to make her phone calls. She figured Alexander was at work, but she could leave him a voicemail. She called the cell phone number he had given her, but instead of ringing, it went straight to voicemail. At the end of the message, a voice added, "This customer's voicemail box is full. Please call back later."

That's odd. Alexander doesn't strike me as the type to let his mailbox clog up. But then again, he probably shut his phone off all day yesterday for the funeral, so maybe he took a lot of messages. She hung up and punched in the number she had for Tonya Parrott, who answered promptly on the second ring.

After asking about Tonya's well-being, Elle got to the point. "I know it's late, and you've probably made other plans, but I'd love to have you and your husband join LeRoi and me for Thanksgiving dinner. Nothing fancy, but you shouldn't be cooking, and Fern does make an outstanding turkey and dressing."

"How nice of you. We were just talking on the way home last night about how Thanksgiving has crept up on us this year. We were all supposed to fly to Ollie's Aunt Rachel's in St. Louis this year, but with my shoulder, we had to cancel. No flying with this immobilizer."

"So will you join me? I'd be grateful for the company." Elle hated the way that sounded, so pitiful, but it was the truth. It was starting to hit home that the peaceful, but reclusive life she and Blake had led had yielded few connections and even fewer friends.

"How kind of you. Let me ask Ollie, and I'll get back to you. What time, and what can I bring?"

"Just bring your appetites. I hope to see you Thursday." Elle headed to tell LeRoi, but the doorbell chimes stopped her. Who could it be? She followed LeRoi toward the front door, but when she got to the long foyer, she ducked into the bathroom and listened.

It was the NYPD detectives, and LeRoi was ushering them into the living room. Elle held her hand to her chest. Her heart was pumping so fast, and perspiration formed on her upper lip. Why had they come back today? How many times would she have to submit to their questions and insinuations? Maybe she should discuss this with Gary Griffith, but it was too late now. They were already in the house.

She and LeRoi walked back into the kitchen, where she poured herself a glass of iced water with lemon, trying to calm her nerves.

"They say they just have a couple of questions. Do you want me to stay in there with you, Miss Elle?"

"That's what they always say, apparently." She sighed. "I appreciate the offer, but that might raise suspicion. Maybe you could stay close by, in case I call for you?"

Without waiting for the answer she knew would come, Elle walked into the living room. Coleman stood, leaving the book he was looking at open to one of Victor Lockwood's early paintings. Elle shivered to think another masterpiece was somewhere nearby, waiting for her to uncover it. Now was no time to think of that, though. She had to focus. "Hello, Detectives Rayburn and Coleman. How may I help you today?" She took a seat and motioned for Coleman to do the same.

The burly detective brought out his tape recorder and set it on the coffee table. "If you remember, we recorded our last interview with you. Is it okay to do the same today?"

Elle nodded. She didn't see how it could hurt anything, and she didn't want to be impolite.

He pushed the start button and taped an introductory statement with the time and place, reminding Elle she had been Mirandized earlier, and her rights were still in effect. "We're in Chester County to pick up the weapon found in your bathroom, so thought we'd stop by while in the neighborhood."

"Yes, I was shocked when Detective Parrott found it. Blake and I don't keep guns in the house."

"Unusual for people living out here in the country, don't you think?"

"Possibly, but we are—uh, were—peace-loving people. There were some antique guns on display here from generations ago, and we got rid of them."

Detective Rayburn leaned forward. "Miss Carmichael, do you have any idea who might have put that gun in your bathroom vanity?"

"I've fretted about it. There were a lot of people in the house yesterday. Anyone could have used the bathroom without raising any suspicion whatsoever. Do you think that's the gun that was— was used—to—to kill Blake?"

"We won't know that until our lab has examined it, but it's a possibility. Do you think you could give us a list of names of everyone who had access to your bathroom?"

"I could try, but some of the people here were friends of Alexander's or LeRoi's, or people Blake knew, but I didn't."

"We'd appreciate it very much if you could do that. Also, why do you think someone might hide a weapon there?"

Elle had the feeling of being in third grade and sitting in the front row, where Sister Agnes called on her constantly. "I don't know. To get rid of it? To make it look like it belonged to someone in this house? Or maybe to use it?" She gave a sarcastic laugh. "Whatever the reason, it spells trouble."

Coleman took over. "Had you ever seen this gun before?"

"No, indeed. And I barely looked at it yesterday. I have an aversion to guns. They make me uncomfortable."

"Ms. Carmichael, do you know if Mr. Allmond left a will?"

"Y-yes, he did." She knew she needed to answer these questions, but each one felt like a violation of hers and Blake's privacy. Murder, she supposed, had laid bare all of their secrets. Still, she disliked Coleman's manner.

"Do you know where we can get a copy of that will?"

"Blake's attorney is Gary Griffith. His office is in midtown Manhattan." She crossed her arms and then uncrossed them, when she remembered that was an unfriendly pose. "I can call to authorize Mr. Griffith to make a copy available to you, if you'd like."

As if she surmised what Elle had been thinking about Coleman, Detective Rayburn broke in. "Thank you. That would be lovely. Just a couple more questions for today, and I apologize, because these may be delicate ones."

Elle braced herself for whatever was coming, but at least the asker had framed them in a compassionate way.

"Are you aware Mr. Allmond has been having sexual relationships with men?"

Elle gasped. Whatever she had expected, this was not a question she was prepared for. Twenty-four hours ago, she never would have believed what the detective implied. But after reading Blake's confession about his relationship with Victor Lockwood, she didn't know. At first forced, but later consensual. It seemed the letter—more than his paintings, more than Manderley and all of his possessions—would be a roadmap to Blake Allmond.

Both detectives were staring at her, waiting for a response. "I—uh, no." A vacuum-like swishing took over her solar plexus and moved upward. Inarticulate as it was, that was all she could say.

Rayburn replied, "I see it has come as a shock to you, and I apologize, but we feel this is pertinent to Mr. Allmond's murder."

"I—I understand." Perhaps they were expecting her to ask questions, like who, when, and where, and perhaps those questions would come later. Right now, Elle wasn't sure she wanted to know.

"I know this is a personal question, but I need to ask it. Was your relationship with Mr. Allmond Platonic?"

Elle cringed, and her face grew warm. She had been raised not to talk about sex, and her vow of celibacy had reinforced that rule of propriety. The strength of her love of art and for Blake had exploded her world, made her bold and eager to embrace a different life. Now this had become police business—it felt like a knife scraping away at her soul—but she answered. "No. It was not Platonic."

The realization she had been living with a bisexual man and not known it created a major shift, not so much in the way she viewed Blake, but in the way she viewed herself. Was she so naïve and unworldly as to believe their relationship to be monogamous? Had being sheltered from knowledge of sexual behavior made her oblivious to signs that her partner enjoyed, maybe even preferred, sex with other men? Had Susan been equally oblivious, or had Blake been straight during his marriage? Had they both been exposed to diseases?

Detective Rayburn is scrutinizing me. I'm a slide under a microscope. "Do you have more questions?"

"Yes, I'm afraid I do. You seem to be surprised by Mr. Allmond's relationships, yet you knew he had a second residence and spent a considerable amount of time in New York."

"Is that a question? Blake had that place in Gramercy Park long before he met me. As an artist, he found it beneficial to spend time in New York. That's where the business of the art world takes place—museums, galleries, exhibits, and shows. And that's where our agent, banker, attorney, and other business people live and work. I never questioned Blake's motives for going to New York."

Detective Coleman began pacing, apparently bored or dissatisfied with taking a back seat. Elle wished she could get up and walk around, too. She had the feeling she would never be able to shake the mantle of inquisition.

Rayburn pushed on. "I just have one more question for you, and then we have to get back to the city. Something has perplexed us—something only you can answer. Why did you change your name?"

The question seemed to reverberate in Elle's ears. All the other questions had stung, but this one was a sword in the gut. It signaled with clarity that the detectives' interest in her was more than in the role of Blake's partner. They'd done research on her. They considered her a suspect.

She remembered the Miranda rights they had read and reminded her of. Now they had two interviews tape recorded, and she had answered their questions so freely. She had been naïve with Blake, and now with the detectives. For some reason Tonya's bravery in the face of adversity flashed before her, and she made a decision to be naïve no more.

Elle replied in a calm, firm voice, "Stop the tape recorder. I'm hiring a lawyer."

CHAPTER 50

Two days before Thanksgiving, and Rupert Brooks slapped his briefcase and aluminum coffee mug onto the desk in his cramped office, his mind in cyclone mode. He'd lost the better part of a day's business yesterday in order to attend the funeral and reception. Inconvenient timing, but it couldn't be helped.

Today he'd opened the gallery two hours earlier than usual, not that he expected customers, but he had so much to do to get ready for the big show in New York, and time was running out to advertise the full complement of paintings. His original deadline had already passed.

Introducing Sophia Lockwood's art to the world had been his brainchild. He'd never organized a show in the big markets before, but representing the granddaughter of Victor Lockwood translated to a sure thing. At least he'd thought so.

He'd convinced his friend and New York gallery owner, Mark Stein, to invest with him in a late-winter show. Other participants were gallery owners in Chicago, London, Los Angeles, and Paris. Each of the six would send five paintings or sculptures to be on display. The costs were tremendous—insurance, transport, advertising. A few of the artists were flying in, too, some at their own expense, and some at the expense of their hosts.

The potential to make a lot of money was great. All of the featured paintings were big ticket items, and Brooks's commission was sixty percent of whatever "his" artists took in, plus an overriding one percent of all sales for being the organizer.

Only two problems bit at him day and night, and they weren't little ones. Brooks was having trouble scraping together the upfront costs. The Rue Moderne usually netted ten thousand dollars per month, with the fall and winter months being higher. Brooks had a lot of overhead with the gallery and two homes, one in Chadds Ford and one in Manhattan, and the remaining income hadn't been enough to keep up with his part of the pre-show expenses.

Brooks'd had to resort to borrowing money from acquaintances and friends, something Shakespeare's Polonius had taught him long ago not to do. Another setback had occurred because of Blake Allmond. Brooks had planned on including one of Allmond's paintings in the show, but when two other of Allmond's paintings were stolen, Allmond backed out, claiming he had to refocus. The National Arts Club came first in Allmond's mind. That was a double-whammy for Brooks—he had hoped to advertise Allmond as a National Arts Club member and double the price of his painting.

He had promised the other dealers five Brandywine artist paintings for the exhibit, and here it was only a few months away, and all he had were three Sophia Lockwoods. Those would fetch high prices, but not enough.

With Allmond gone, so was his ace-in-the-hole. Brooks was desperate—he even considered asking his clients who owned Lockwoods and Allmonds, including the Campbells and the Bakers, if they would sell them. That option would eat into his profits, but at least he would have a full complement of paintings to show, and the Allmonds had undoubtedly risen in value since there would now be no more of them.

Brooks bent over the desk in his tiny office and held his head in his hands. There were other notable Brandywine artists, but it was almost insulting to contact any of them now, with the show just weeks away. *Damn Blake Allmond, anyway! Time and again he has ruined my plans, that little twerp.*

Yesterday at Manderley, he'd wandered from room to room, examining artwork. The Allmonds had collected many fine pieces, and he wondered how difficult it would be to get the estate to release one or two for the show. Now he had a better idea. Maybe he could get Elle Carmichael to part with one of *her* paintings. There was one in the library—pastel oils of a young woman, nursing her baby by the side of a brook. The impressionistic rapture on the mother's face was beatific, reminding him of Raphael.

Elle didn't seem to be motivated by money, but the lure of having her painting exhibited with those of Sophia Lockwood might be enough. He bet that painting would sell for at least fifteen thousand dollars.

He picked up the phone to call Elle, but put it down when he heard the tinkle of the bells on the entrance door. The prospect of a customer's buying an expensive knickknack put a spring in his step as he strode to the front of the store. When he saw who it was, though, his mood fell like a shaken soufflé. He really didn't have time for Detective Parrott.

CHAPTER 51

After the detectives left Manderley, Elle returned to the study to call the attorney, Gary Griffith. Her hands shook as she punched in the number and paced about the room while the receptionist put her through.

"Good morning, Elle. It was a beautiful ceremony yesterday, a lovely tribute to Blake. What can I do for you today?"

"Gary, the New York police detectives just left. It's a long story, but you know Detective Parrott, the Brandywine detective? He found a gun in the bathroom here yesterday, and they came out to pick it up from the county forensics department. It was the second time they've interviewed me. Both times they tape recorded, and they read me Miranda rights." She paused to slow down and take a breath. "I've done my best to cooperate with them, answer their questions. I even told them I'd authorize you to give them a copy of the will—and try to list the names of people who attended the reception—but now I think they suspect me of killing Blake. I told them I wouldn't answer any more questions today. I was hiring a lawyer." Tears welled in her eyes, and her voice rose by an octave. "Will you represent me? Please?"

"Of course. I told you yesterday I'd help you. I can certainly advise you about talking with the detectives, but I'm not a criminal attorney. We'd both have to sign conflict waivers, and if you are actually charged with a crime, we'd have to make other arrangements."

"I don't think it will come to that. How could it?" She sniffed.

"I agree it's unlikely, but if I've learned anything in this business, it's that anything is possible. Let's backtrack. Tell me the names of the detectives and the dates and times of the interviews."

Relief flowed through Elle's body, as if she'd completed penance for a confessed sin. She supplied Griffith with the information, and proceeded to explain what she knew about the gun.

"Did they say if this was the weapon that killed Blake?"

"They said they have to test it in their lab. I have no idea who hid it under the vanity in our bathroom, but Blake and I never kept guns in the house, and it's not ours."

Griffith replied, "You were right to stop the interview and say you wanted a lawyer. From this moment on, you are not to speak a word to any police personnel without my being present and authorizing you to. We need to discuss what you've already told them on the record, as well."

"Wait—" Elle said. "—did you say any police personnel? What about Detective Parrott from West Brandywine?"

"That includes him, I'm afraid. I know you trust him and his wife, but he's investigating the art theft, and you might be a suspect in that case, as well."

"Well, I've invited the Parrotts here for Thanksgiving. It would be difficult not to speak to him."

"He didn't accept the invitation, did he?"

"No-o-o, not yet."

"Elle, I know you like the Parrotts, and, having met them, I can see why. But as long as the art theft is an open case, you and Parrott shouldn't be socializing. You and the wife can get together, but don't talk about either case. I was skeptical about having them in the room for the reading of the will, but you were so insistent. In light of what you've told me about the NYPD, I need you to be more careful."

Elle exhaled. "I didn't want to be alone on Thanksgiving, so I thought I'd invite them and Alexander. I just called a little while ago. How am I going to rescind the invitation?"

"Alexander is fine. And don't worry. I'd be very surprised if Parrott accepts. That would be unprofessional, and he doesn't strike me that way." He paused to swallow something. "Listen, whenever you run into a rough spot, where you have a tough time saying something, just blame it on me. Tell people your attorney has told you not to discuss anything, your attorney has told you not to do this or that."

Having someone to watch her back was hugely comforting. Whatever it cost, it would be worth it. "Thank you, Gary. I hope I haven't made things difficult by talking to the detectives."

"We need to talk about what they asked you and what you told them. Unless and until they charge you, I won't have access to the tapes."

Elle thought about the painful insinuations and unsavory things the detectives had said about Blake and their relationship. Sharing them with Blake's friend wasn't going to be easy. She wondered how much Gary knew.

After making plans to get together after Thanksgiving, Elle said, "It's ludicrous to think I might be charged in Blake's murder. Blake was the love of my life. I never would have killed him. I could never kill *anybody*."

When she hung up with Griffith, Elle tried Alexander again. Once again the call went to voicemail, and the mailbox was full. She pulled open the heavy desk drawer to search for the Rolodex Blake had kept for many years. Maybe it would have a landline number for Melanie. She looked under Vargas, under Allmond, and finally under Melanie, before getting lucky. Hopefully Alexander hadn't disconnected it after Melanie's death.

After four rings, voicemail picked up—Alexander's voice. Elle left her message and hung up. She hoped he would accept. He hadn't shown any rancor about Blake's will. Frankly, she had been stunned Blake *hadn't* left Manderley to Alexander. It seemed only right to keep it in the family, and Alexander was a young man. He would likely have children, whose ancestors were Allmonds.

While she was ruminating about this, the phone rang. "Elle, it's Tonya. I just talked to Ollie, and he says we can't come for Thanksgiving. I'm really sorry."

Elle gave a mental nod to Griffith's prediction. She wouldn't press for a reason. "I am, too. Thank you for letting me know."

Tonya sounded dejected. "I want you to know how much we appreciate the invitation, and how grateful I am for your friendship. I've learned a lot from you, and not just about art."

"That's funny," Elle replied. "When things seem overwhelming for me, I think about *your* bravery and strength, and it helps *me*. Let's plan to get together, just the two of us, after Thanksgiving."

Elle hung up the phone, thinking how strange life could be. You could go along for years, certain in your faith and beliefs, and in an instant they could metamorphose. Blake had taken her from chrysalis to butterfly. But before that, she had been an ugly caterpillar. The past twenty-four hours had shown her Blake hadn't been perfect, but her religious studies had taught her all humans were imperfect. If Blake had had affairs with men, he had taken pains to protect her, and perhaps that didn't diminish the love they had for each other. Wasn't that what he had said in his letter and in his will?

She could forgive him. After all, she wasn't perfect, either. If she ever started to think she was, all she had to do was remember Estelle Carson.

CHAPTER 52

When five o'clock rolled around, Veronica put through a call to Alexander's burner phone from hers. Straight to voicemail, and she left a message, "SOS, call me." She paced around her tiny apartment like a caged animal, waiting for a return phone call. By six and no call, she was ready to pounce.

"To hell with it," she said aloud. Using her burner phone, she called Alexander's cell phone. When she heard, "The mailbox is full. Please try again later," she knew something was wrong. Alexander never let his voicemail messages stack up.

Maybe something had happened to him. Maybe he'd had an accident at work, or he was in the hospital, clinging to life. Forget about being discreet. He might need her. She jumped in her car and drove to Alexander's house. His car was in the driveway, a fact that calmed her fears, but angered her. Why wasn't he taking her calls? A light was on in the front room, and she could imagine him heating up a frozen pizza and sitting in front of the TV to eat.

Even though she'd convinced herself Alexander's fears and all the subterfuge with the phones were unnecessary, she drove around the block several times to make sure no one was following her or watching the house. Since she no longer worked at the bank, why did they have to worry about what she shouldn't have done when she was there?

Still, she didn't want to park her car in the driveway or at the curb in front of the house. She parked two blocks away and walked in the chilly night air with the wind whipping her long hair into her face. She was feeling less like Mata Hari and more like Poor Pitiful Pearl. She climbed the stairs to the back door and banged on the glass.

"What are you doing here?" Alexander asked when he opened the door. He pulled her inside with a roughness she wasn't used to. "I told you not to come here."

She shook him off and walked from one end of the room to the other. The house's tidiness still felt strange. "I've been trying to call you—on both phones. Why didn't you answer or call me back?"

"Look, Veronica. I don't want you to come here. I don't want you to call me. I don't know why you were parking cars at my uncle's house yesterday, but that creeped me out."

Veronica could hardly believe what she was hearing. Everything she had done she had done for him. A rage was building inside, but she wasn't ready to unleash it. Instead she sidled up to him and traced her index finger down his biceps. "But, Chachi, I love you. I've always loved you. I thought you would be pleased to see me. I was missing you so much. Didn't you miss me?"

Alexander winced, and hope flickered inside her. "No matter how much you missed me or I missed you, you did a stupid thing. What did you tell the bank?"

"They fired me. That was why I called you." Hopefully he would feel sorry for her and soften his attitude. He hadn't even asked her to take off her coat or sit down.

"Listen, Veronica. I'm sorry you lost your job, but I'm not surprised. You can't work in a bank and do crazy things. I hope you get your life back on track and find success, but you're going to have to do it without me. I'm done."

"You can't mean that," she spat. "After everything I've done for you? You told me you would love me forever. You can't just leave me like this, with no love, no job, no money."

"Don't lay the guilt on me. Everything you've done for me you did for your own satisfaction. If you need help, go to your brother. Just don't come to me anymore."

Veronica couldn't believe her ears. She had already had enough rejection for one day, and these words cut her heart into shreds. She thought of how Alonzo had instructed her to figure out a way to marry Alexander, but that door was closing, and it was almost shut.

There was no time to think. He was pushing her toward the back door, his jaw set in sheer determination. "Okay, Chachi," she shouted, as she pushed against his momentum. "I'll leave, but before I do, there's something else I need to tell you."

"What's that?" he asked, continuing to push her toward the door.

"Only that I'm pregnant. No matter how you feel about me now, you, *mi novio,* are going to be a father."

CHAPTER 53

E lle had spent the late morning and early afternoon taking care of many of the tasks on her list. Using the guest book from the funeral and reception, she typed a list of names. She would send it to Gary Griffith. If he agreed it was in her best interests to forward to Rayburn and Coleman, he would do so. She wanted the New York detectives to view her cooperation as a sign she was as eager as they were to solve Blake's murder.

Truthfully, she was. The more she thought about her situation, the more worried she became that she, herself, may be in danger. The heart of the question was why. Why would someone kill Blake? If the motive was greed, and the killer was after Blake's wealth or his paintings, it would stand to reason she would be the person he'd come after next.

Then there was the matter of the hidden Lockwood. Blake said there may be others who knew about the valuable painting. Elle had to find it. Until she did, she would be sitting on a hot potato.

She googled the value of Victor Lockwood paintings. Some had recently sold at Sotheby's in the tens of millions, far more than any of Blake's or hers, or even Charles Hawthorne's.

She abandoned her plan to go room-by-room. The attic or basement would be a more likely storage place. Changing into a pair of jeans, a sweatshirt, and some tennis shoes, basically her gardening clothes, she went in search of LeRoi.

LeRoi and Fern were collaborating in the kitchen. Fern had soup pots and sauce pans going on the stove top, and LeRoi was polishing the crystal. The two chatted in the companionable way of two old souls who worked together. The kitchen smelled of cinnamon, nutmeg, and butternut squash, and Elle was thankful for the flood of memories triggered.

When Elle walked in, they stopped talking and stared at her outfit. LeRoi said, "Isn't it the wrong season for gardening?"

Elle uttered a short guffaw, and covered her mouth, as if she had committed a sin. How could she even think about laughing with Blake gone? "Actually, I'm on a mission. I know there are paintings stored in the attic and basement, and I'm looking for some to hang in the studio for my art students to study."

"Do you want me to go with you?" LeRoi asked, wiping his hands on the polishing cloth.

"That won't be necessary, but I do have a question. Much of the attic and basement spaces are unknown to me—I just never had occasion to go there. I know about the basement under the kitchen, where the wine cellar is, but can you tell me about the other spots? They don't all connect, do they?"

LeRoi smiled. "It took me a lot of years to visit those places, myself, and to keep straight what belongs in each one. Paintings are mostly upstairs, but there are some under the living room." He pointed in that direction. "There's attic access in six different bedrooms, plus the two pull-down doors and stairs in the upstairs hallway. There's four stairs to the basement—this one in the kitchen, two outside, and one in the garage." He put down his towel and opened a drawer in a back cabinet. "Here, take a flashlight. Some of the corners are dark. Do you want keys to the outside doors?"

"No, let me get started on the inside. Paintings are probably in the more interior areas," Elle replied, opening the kitchen-basement door and skipping down the stairs. She reminded herself of Alice going down the rabbit hole, but hopefully with a more fruitful result.

Elle expected the basement to be musty and cobwebby, but it was surprisingly clean and well-organized. She suspected LeRoi had a hand in keeping it so neat. Though unfinished, the room had been cleaned and the concrete floor waxed recently. Whatever LeRoi was paid, it probably wasn't enough.

The area under the living room did indeed have family treasures—furniture, Christmas decorations, stacked boxes labeled as "records," "photo albums," "toys," and "knickknacks." The outside wall had built-in storage slats. Paintings were covered in white sheets, standing up, each in its own slat. There must have been forty of them of varied sizes, some framed and some not. Elle was both excited and dismayed. Finding a new painting was always a thrill, and there were so many. On the other hand, she was searching for a specific painting, and it would take time to get through all of these. Besides, the hints Blake provided in the letter didn't exactly fit here.

She shone the flashlight at the lower right corners of the paintings and tried to make out the artists' names. Some Allmonds, but too old to be Blake's or Melanie's. There must have been artists in previous generations. One landscape looked like a George Henry Durrie, and there were others signed by Anderson, Schanker, and Smith. Near the back of the stack, she found another Charles Hawthorne. As she shone the flashlight on it, she could see it was a scene at sunset. Her hands shook. Could this be the Hawthorne and sunsets Blake referred to?

She scoured the area for a Victor Lockwood, but ended up no closer to finding the painting than when she started. What she did realize, though, was just how vast the Allmond family collection must be. It seemed a shame to keep so many pieces of art covered up in a basement, when people could enjoy them in a museum.

When she finally stood and covered the paintings, the gnaw of hunger reminded her that afternoon had melded into evening. Only one of the storage rooms, and nine more to go. At this rate she might not find the Lockwood before the end of the year.

She took a last look around at this underground empire that had magically become hers, and she climbed the stairs, trying to dismiss the feeling she had wasted her time. When she arrived in the kitchen, Fern had gone for the day, and LeRoi was nowhere in sight. He'd offer her dinner within the next hour, but she wanted a little something now.

She opened the refrigerator and removed the half-full bottle of Pinot Grigio from the cooler on the door. She poured herself a generous glass, opened a can of cashews, and took them back to the study, where she sat at the desk, tilting her head back and closing her eyes for a few minutes.

The wine had a fruity taste, and she could identify a note of honeysuckle, as well. She jotted down the names of the artists whose work she had seen in the stacks, so she wouldn't forget. The light on the phone was blinking, but she would finish her wine before listening for messages. The person she really wanted to talk to would not be calling—anyone else could wait.

Elle pulled open the bottom drawer of the desk, where Blake's hanging file folders greeted her. Her fingers sashayed through the tabs—accountant, alarm system, insurance, keys, safety deposit box, stock broker, tickets, utilities, warranties. It looked like everything she could possibly need was filed here. She raised her glass in a toast to the imperfect Blake Allmond. Whatever his demons had been, he had taken better care of her than anyone else in her life, and she was grateful.

She glanced at the porcelain clock on the desk. She had fifteen minutes until dinner—just enough time to listen to messages and change clothes. She called the retrieval number and entered her password. "You have two new messages."

The first new message was from Alexander. In a voice she would describe as exhausted, he thanked her for the Thanksgiving invitation. "Actually, I wasn't sure what I was going to do, so your invitation came at a great time. I'd love to come to Manderley for the holiday. I wish—my uncle was going to be there, too. There are some things I wish I could say to him. Anyway, I'll see you Thursday, and thanks."

A warmth filled Elle's body that went beyond that of the wine. She would enjoy getting to know Blake's nephew. Something told her he was missing Blake, too. Maybe they could console each other.

The second message was from Rupert Brooks, the dealer at the Rue Moderne. She didn't know why, but a chill came over her every time she thought about that man, with his pointy eye teeth. She had known him almost as long as she'd known Blake, and both she and Blake had sold paintings through his gallery. He'd always treated her with extreme politeness, obsequiousness, almost. She'd told Blake her theory that he'd never gotten over Melanie, and Blake had agreed.

Today he wanted to talk to her about an art exhibit he was hosting in New York in a couple of weeks. "I apologize for contacting you so soon after the funeral. I know you must have a lot on your plate, literally and emotionally. The fact is, though, I am in need of two paintings of high value by known artists. Blake was going to help me, but his paintings were stolen, and—" His voice broke into what sounded like a sob. "Anyway, I would be most grateful if you would return my call this evening. It's urgent I speak with you."

Elle shook her head at the irony of it all. He needed paintings of high value, and she was sitting on a Victor Lockwood—if only she knew where it was.

CHAPTER 54

When he'd walked into the Rue Moderne, Parrott had intended to chat Brooks up about the upcoming New York exhibit, and then work his way around to questioning the art dealer about the National Arts Club and the specific paintings stolen from Allmond.

But Brooks was wearing impatience in the lines around his mouth and exhaustion in the brownish wells under his eyes.

"Can you give me a few minutes?" Parrott asked. "We don't even need to sit down. Just a couple of things."

"Uh okay," Brooks replied. He'd thrust his weight onto one hip, and his fists on the backs of both. "I'm working on a very important project right now, so it will have to be quick."

"The Sophia Lockwood Exhibit in New York?" Parrott replied, gratified when Brooks's eyes lit up. "That's part of why I wanted to talk to you. I'm planning to attend, but I'm not familiar with all the protocols. How does it work?"

Brooks filled him in on the exhibit. "You can purchase tickets here or online, after December 1."

"Do people come to look at the paintings, or buy them?"

"Both. In the case of Sophia, for example, there is a lot of curiosity, because she's a debut artist, and heir to the Lockwood talent. People will compare her work to that of her father, grandfather, and great-grandfather. The show will bring buyers, too. Anyone who purchases a painting will leave it on display until after the show."

Parrott took the pictures of the stolen Allmonds from his pocket. "Would these paintings of Allmond's have been worthy of being in your show?" He unfolded the paper Allmond himself had sent him.

Brooks glanced at the paper and did a double-take. "Those are the ones stolen. Where did you get that? Did you locate the paintings?"

"Mr. Allmond sent it to me after the theft." Parrott folded it up and returned it to his pocket. "Would these paintings fit in with your collection?"

Brooks gave a snort. "I begged Blake to let me show those paintings, but he turned me down flat. Said these were going to the National Arts Club, non-negotiable. They were stolen shortly afterwards."

Parrott raised an eyebrow. "I guess he would have rather had them in the show than be taken away. It's strange how things work out."

"I've asked Elle to let me exhibit some of the paintings from Manderley. Hoping to hear back from her today. If not, I'll just drop in."

"Elle's pretty busy right now. Don't you think she has enough on her plate?" Brooks was starting to get on Parrott's last nerve.

"The person who's got a lot on his plate is *moi*. I've got a lot invested in this exhibit. If I don't find two great pieces of art in the next little while, I'll be the laughingstock of New York City." He shifted his weight to the other hip. "If that's all, I really need to be getting back to my work now."

It was not the first time Parrott had been brushed off by a pretentious socialite type, but the seeds of fury were sprouting inside of him. An idea was germinating, as well. Abandoning the questions about the Arts Club, Parrott replied, "Well, I guess I'll be on my way then. But before I go, may I use your restroom?"

The only restroom was in the back next to Brooks's office, a fact Parrott had gleaned from previous visits. It was a risk worth taking. Brooks could always say the restroom was off limits to patrons, but he seemed so happy at the prospect of getting rid of Parrott, he bared his teeth in a semi-smile and said, "Certainly."

When Parrott entered the tiny lavatory and locked the door behind him, he found what he was looking for. It hadn't been a waste of time to come here, after all.

CHAPTER 55

The next morning Tonya and Parrott got up together. It was the day before Thanksgiving, and Uber was coming in a half hour to take her to an appointment with the counselor at the VA. He'd fixed the coffee, and she'd fixed instant oatmeal one-handed.

Horace perched on the counter, looking from one to the other of them. They ate, mostly in silence. Parrott was gratified with the progress Tonya had made in adjusting to her handicap. Except for writing, cutting up vegetables, and driving, she was managing to do almost everything she used to do, except maybe a little more slowly.

"I'm sorry about Thanksgiving," he said. "I know you wanted to go to Elle's."

"Yeah, I did. I really dig that lady. I get the sense she's a lot like me—not just the art—she's tough, and she's been through a lot. I learn something new from her every time I see her. She's also the least prejudiced person I know."

"I admire her, too, but you have to understand—"

"I know. It's an open case. I get it."

"Not just that. I've been trying to find a good way to say this, but there isn't one. And what I'm about to say is for your ears only."

Tonya chuckled. "I just saw Horace tilt his head. Don't say anything you don't want him to repeat."

"Unfortunately," Parrott said, his brows drawn close together, "this is no joke. Elle may be a serious suspect in Allmond's murder."

"What? That's the most ridiculous thing I've ever heard. Elle is the least violent person I've ever met in my life. Besides, she loved him."

"I didn't say she did it. I said she is a suspect. Those are two very different things."

"Why would anyone suspect her? Because she inherited the most? That's totally lame, and you know it."

Parrott could see this line of conversation was triggering strong feelings. It was exactly what he had been hoping to avoid. "I only told you because I want to protect you in case things get ugly for her. Please don't shoot the messenger."

Tonya took a few deep breaths. "Okay, I get your motive, but I need you to get mine. I've agreed not to go there for Thanksgiving, but I'm going to keep going to Manderley for art classes and visits whenever Elle invites me. She's a good and loving friend, and I'm going to support her a hundred percent. Elle is the last person on earth I'd suspect. I'll bet she's never done a single wrong thing in her whole life."

Parrott wiped his mouth with a napkin and cleared the table of dirty dishes. He held back the retort that filled his mind. *I used to be able to say things like that about people I knew, but since becoming a cop, I know better. Nobody, but nobody, is that perfect.* Instead, he kissed Tonya on the top of her head. "You're the loyalist friend anyone could ever have, baby. And I'm the luckiest husband on earth."

Now that Jerry had skin and hair samples from the art studio, Parrott was ready to hit the accelerator. If he could rule out the people who had a legitimate reason to be in the art studio, he'd be well on the way to finding the thief—and, if lucky, recovering the paintings.

Normally, he'd have a hard time selling the chief on running DNA tests for a burglary, but this case was no ordinary burglary. The value of the paintings made it felony theft, but the murder, coming so quickly after the theft, upped the stakes. If Schrik balked, Parrott was sure Elle would pay for them, but he didn't think it would come to that.

It was a shame Blake Allmond wouldn't be there to get his paintings back, but he figured Elle might honor his memory by donating them to the National Arts Club, just as planned.

He shook his head at his mini-daydream. It wouldn't do to get too far ahead of himself. Then there was the possibility the art theft and the murder were committed by the same person. Parrott would give his eye teeth to be in on solving that murder, despite the jurisdictional prohibitions, real or imagined. Finding the gun, if it turned out to be the weapon that killed Allmond, was sheer serendipity, but it would mean New York owed him.

"First things first," Mama always said. Parrott curbed his enthusiasm and called Elle. He remembered his conversation with Tonya, and decided it best not to mention Thanksgiving. When she answered, he said, "I hope I'm not disturbing. I'm sure you have a lot to do this morning."

Elle sat cross-legged on her unmade bed, the letter from Blake open on her lap. She had read it so many times, she had the whole thing almost memorized now. "Nothing more important than talking to you. How can I help you?"

"We've got some skin and hair samples from the studio that might link up to the thief. It could be an important lead, but we need to exclude the people who might have been in the studio legitimately. I need your help to do that."

"Sounds like good news on this cold and cloudy day. How do we exclude? And whom?"

"We already have DNA from Mr. Allmond. Ideally we need samples from you, LeRoi, everyone who works at Manderley, the students in your class, and anyone else you can think of who visited the studio."

"That's quite a long list. There are five students. Three, four, and six, ten employees. But not all of the employees work inside, and some don't come into the studio."

"Doesn't matter. We want them all, just to establish a database. Problem is, we can't mandate. All we can do is ask and hope they cooperate. That's why I need you to propose it to them." Parrott crossed his fingers. He felt certain Elle and LeRoi would come along, but the others were iffy. "I'd like to get them to come into the station today, if possible. I know that may be difficult to arrange before the holiday."

"Easier today than tomorrow, at least for the people who work here. The students may be out of town. That could be problematic—except for one of them."

Parrott smiled at the allusion to Tonya, but ignored it. "How soon do you think you could assemble them? All we need is hair from each person. It shouldn't take much more than a half hour of their time."

"Let me get with LeRoi, and I'll call you back." Parrott could hear her jumping into action.

It wasn't even nine a.m., but the day was shaping up to be productive. It felt good to flex the ol' mental muscles.

CHAPTER 56

Things were hopping even more when Parrott returned to the station. Detective Rayburn had called Chief Schrik to say the Beretta pistol was the weapon that killed Blake Allmond. Two bullets had been recovered from the victim's body, one in good enough condition to match the rifling.

Parrott, sitting in front of Schrik's desk, punched the air above his head and shouted, as if his team had made a touchdown.

Schrik shot him a squinty-eyed look. He fiddled with a paper clip and waited.

"Okay, okay. It's not our case. But chalk one up for the good guys, anyway."

Schrik went on. "If that weren't enough, they had more news. The gun was registered to Blake Allmond."

This was not good news, Parrott thought, for clearing Elle of suspicion. She would have had access to a gun owned by her partner, and she would have lied when she said they didn't own guns. Not to mention the weapon's having been found in the bathroom at Manderley.

"Rayburn said they'd ruled out suicide, based on angles and trajectory, and, besides, they believed Allmond was shot in the living room and dragged to the shower post-mortem. So someone used Blake Allmond's gun on him."

Parrott said, "All very interesting. They share anything about *our* case?"

"Don't be sarcastic. It was a lot for them to open up this much. If you hadn't found the gun and preserved chain of custody, I don't think they would've said a word."

"No, but when we solve our case, they'll be all over us for information." Parrott sighed. "Guess I don't blame them. The job's hard enough even when you have all the puzzle pieces, which is hardly ever."

"Speaking of our case, want to give me a run-down?"

"Sure." Parrott stood and paced, collecting his thoughts. "You know we have forensic evidence from the art studio. Jerry and his team came through for us again. Elle is asking ten employees to come here this afternoon to give hair samples." He paused to make eye contact with his boss. "If the testing is too expensive, she offered to pay."

Schrik waved a hand in the air. "Not a problem. Let's hope we can rule them all out. Do you have any suspects, if we do?"

"I've got a few ideas, based on the method used to bypass the security system. But I've got a lot of questions, too. Why were just those two paintings taken? The studio is full of artwork, some of it very valuable. What does the thief intend to do with them? Where might they be stored that wouldn't put the thief in jeopardy?

I also want to know why Allmond was killed. I know—that's not our case—but I want to know whether the art theft had anything to do with the murder or vice versa. Can't be sheer coincidence that one happened on the heels of the other."

Schrik slid the paper clip through his fingers and tapped it on the desk in a kind of hypnotic rhythm. "Rumor has it Allmond was gay. Think that plays a role?"

Parrott grinned playfully. "In our case or theirs?"

"Don't be a smartass. In both. Either."

"I don't think he was gay. Maybe bi. His will leaves most everything to Elle and his nephew, so I don't think he had any serious attachments to other men." Parrott sat again and stretched out his legs. "As for playing a role, maybe. Anytime someone leads a double life, it exposes him to life's ugliness—blackmail, theft, even murder. Doesn't always happen, but the potential is there, like a coiling snake, ready to strike at any time."

"Pretty profound coming from a young guy like you," Schrik replied. He walked around the desk and patted Parrott on the back.

"Don't let my age fool you. I've seen a lot in my life."

"I know, Parrott. That's what makes you a great detective."

CHAPTER 57

Dragging to the police station to give hair samples had triggered bad memories, as Elle had known it would. From the moment Detective Parrott had asked her to do it, she had begun quivering inside. She didn't want to disappoint him. He was so sincere about wanting to solve the mystery of the theft, and she respected the way he had handled the gun—without alarming everyone in the house. Besides, Tonya and he reminded her of herself and Blake.

Of the ten people she had asked to come with her, only eight complied. They were LeRoi and Fern; Hallie, Patrice, and Clara, the housekeepers; and Raymond, Harold, and Ebby, the groundskeepers. Groundskeepers Alonzo and Manuel had declined, and she hadn't bothered to ask the chauffeur. Elle didn't press them, since Parrott had made it clear it was voluntary.

Police stations brought back memories it had taken decades of praying and art to soften. And Blake. He had seen her inner palette with its dark colors and rough textures, and he had helped her add smoother and brighter layers. But the base would never go away.

She didn't know if her DNA was on file in New York, but her fingerprints were. She didn't bother to mention this. They would figure it out soon enough. Visions of her father, mother, and precious sister floated in her mind, bringing the sting of tears.

Elle introduced the group from Manderley to Officer Barton and Detective Parrott, who escorted them to a small room on the first floor with a window overlooking a playground. Parrott made a short speech, thanking each person for doing his civic duty of his own free will. "We all appreciate your assistance. Hopefully, we can get you going as quickly and painlessly as possible."

One by one, each of them allowed five or ten hairs to be pulled from the head, so the follicles would remain intact. Strict protocols required each person's sample hairs to be collected and preserved in a separate kit. The women had an easier time, Elle thought, since Barton or Parrott could grab a switch of hair, wind it around his fingers, and give a quick jerk. The short-haired men had to have their hair tweezed, a process that took ten times as long.

No one complained, though, and within an hour the two vehicles were on their way back to Manderley. It was the day before Thanksgiving, and everyone was in a hurry to finish his work. Elle had cash envelopes with bonuses ready for them. They had all been so helpful with the funeral reception, and they would likely appreciate having extra money for the holiday.

When Elle got home, she took a cup of hot cinnamon-apple tea to her room and closed the door. The shivering had subsided into the general feeling of malaise that overcame her whenever she revisited the trauma associated with her alcoholic father and her innocent sister. She pulled her sketch pad and Blake's letter from the closet and sipped her tea as she reviewed the contents of both.

The drawings were good, some even better than good. A few captured the light within her subjects in a way that was life-affirming. She doubted she could have done them now, after losing Blake. Then again, she had felt the same way after losing Charlotte. She crossed herself and prayed for Blake's soul and for her own comfort.

She was glad Alexander would join her for Thanksgiving. Blake's death had made her realize how isolated her life was. It would be a tiny gathering in the huge Manderley dining room, but at least she and LeRoi would have company. She put away the letter and sketch pad and changed into gardening clothes to do more attic searching. What mattered most to her? She grabbed at thoughts as they circled in her mind, like a word carousel. Faith, love, art—of course—but a new idea emerged as well. What she also needed was a sense of purpose, and that meant finding Blake's hidden painting.

CHAPTER 58

The Parrotts and Horace, the cockatiel, had their own tiny gathering for Thanksgiving. Tonya's injury prevented them from traveling, and, anyway, it was their first Thanksgiving together as a married couple. Parrott had ordered turkey and all the trimmings from Boston Market, and, for dessert, he splurged on a Pumpple Cake from Flying Monkey Bakery.

Having a day without appointments or work duties was rare, so the newlyweds pledged to spend it wisely and together. After sleeping late, itself a rarity these days, they dressed in jeans, sweaters, boots and jackets, and took off for a day's hike at Longwood Gardens and the Conservatory. The crisp air cooled their faces and hands, but there wasn't a cloud in the sky. The scenic walking areas were decorated in the season's natural glory, but Thanksgiving was opening day for the Christmas spectacle, "A Longwood Christmas," so the gardens' fountains, thousands of blue and white twinkling lights, colorful seasonal plants, and Christmas trees, glistening with icicles and fountain-inspired decorations, provided an incredible feast for their souls.

Holding hands as they moved from one fantastic scene to another, they forgot about PTSD and thefts and murders. When they reached the Italian Water Garden, where a twenty-foot lighted tree display welcomed them, they found a bench and sat.

"I've a lot to be thankful for," Parrott said, as he nuzzled his wife's neck, pushing aside her braids. "It was my luckiest Sunday, meeting you."

"I thought it was a Tuesday," she replied, showing the gap between her front teeth with a grin. "You were wearing a blue shirt."

"Maroon. And definitely Sunday. You were wearing a white halter top that showed off your shoulders."

"Nope. I distinctly remember wearing jeans and a lavender hoodie."

They both broke out into the chorus, "Yes, I remember it well." And then they laughed and hugged as tightly as possible, considering the immobilizer.

Tonya leaned her head on Parrott's chest. "Sorry not to be cooking on our first Thanksgiving."

"Not this year. We'll have many more Thanksgivings, and we can cook for every single one from now on."

"We?" Tonya played with the knuckles on Parrott's hand.

"Yes, ma'am. We are equal partners—in the kitchen, and in the bedroom." He wiggled his eyebrows.

"Ollie, thank you for this beautiful day, and thanks for being my life partner. I'm the one who lucked out, getting you."

"Yeah, we both lucked out. We could've both ended up with real turkeys."

Alexander showed up at Manderley in tan slacks, a light blue button-down shirt, and a navy blazer, no coat. Clean-shaven and sporting a fresh haircut, he smelled like spicy grasses and woods. He carried a bouquet of sunflowers, lilies of the valley, and chrysanthemums, yellow, orange, and purple. A box of See's chocolates was tucked under one arm.

Elle was impressed. He'd gone to a lot of effort. But something in his posture, his demeanor, was off. She couldn't put her finger on it. Elle greeted him at the door, herself, because LeRoi was in the kitchen, warming the food.

"Do you mind tending bar?" Elle asked, leading him to the den. "We have almost anything back there, I think."

Alexander walked around the walnut and soapstone counter and gazed at the bottles decorating the mirrored and glass shelves. The refrigerator was well-stocked, as well. "I usually drink beer, but in honor of the occasion, I'll have a martini. What can I get for you?"

"I'll stick with Dewars on the rocks." She pulled out a vase and arranged the flowers while Alexander poured. The room reminded her of a New York pub, comfortable, quaint, but not tacky. "Let's sit here a while and talk before LeRoi comes to get us."

Alexander apparently had some experience with bartending, because the drinks were perfectly prepared and in the correct glasses, just the way Blake had done. In fact, when Elle squinted, she could almost make out Blake's handsome features in Alexander's face. It was a comfort.

"Why don't you tell me about your job?" Elle asked, thinking that might be a safe conversation starter. She really didn't know much about Alexander, and with no one else to carry conversation for hours, it could become awkward. She wasn't very good at this.

He told her about the current project, and wove in information about a few previous ones. "I'm getting great experience, and growing my knowledge. I've got the talent for it, you know, like you and Uncle Blake and my mother have the talent for art. I'm thinking maybe I can own my own construction company one day."

"Everyone has his own gifts. It's a wise man who knows what they are and uses them. Your uncle would be proud of you."

Was it her imagination, or did Alexander tense up at the mention of Blake?

As they consumed their drinks, they talked about the Brandywine art community and various artists currently painting. "There's going to be an exhibit of Sophia Lockwood's paintings in New York in February. She's the granddaughter of Victor Lockwood."

"Guess that name will open doors for her. The Lockwoods sort of dominate the art world in these parts, don't they?" When Elle nodded, Alexander said, "My mom knew him well. She's told me stories—"

"—Time for dinner," LeRoi sang from the doorway, tapping the melodious chime at the same time. "Everything's on the table in the dining room."

As the three diners, none of them related, but bonded together by Allmond, walked toward the feast, sweet and savory aromas surrounded them. Despite Elle's earlier lack of hunger, her mouth watered. Nobody made sweet potato soufflé like Fern. The table for six had been set for three, with the remaining space taken up with dishes of culinary delight—turkey, oyster dressing, sweet potatoes, grilled vegetables, potato rolls, cranberry relish, spinach salad, and Santa Margherita Pinot Grigio.

Elle led them in prayer, and for several minutes the only sound was that of silverware against plate. "Delicious," Elle said. "Fern has outdone herself."

"Save some room for dessert," LeRoi said. "It's equally amazing."

Alexander wiped his mouth with a napkin and leaned back in his chair. "Too late. I'm so full. I've eaten like a…"

"Construction worker? You must work up a real appetite with the work you do."

"Yeah, but I don't usually get to eat like this. What a meal."

Elle put down her napkin and said, "This is the part of the meal when Blake and I usually make little speeches about what we are grateful for." Her throat threatened to close with the pain of his absence. "So even though Blake's not sitting at the table, I'd like to continue the tradition. Will you join me?"

LeRoi nodded, and Alexander murmured agreement.

Elle poured more wine into her glass and held it aloft. "It's a struggle to feel thankful when the person you love most in the world has been taken from you, and in the worst way, but I know Blake would tell me to find my joy and carry on. So I'm very thankful to share Thanksgiving with two others who loved him. I appreciate your company, and I wish both of you health, happiness, and peace."

Everyone clinked glasses and drank. "That was beautiful," Alexander said. "My turn?" He paused to fill glasses. "I'm thankful to be included in this wonderful celebration. Thanks to you, Elle, for inviting me, and to you, LeRoi, for your part. Mostly, I'm grateful to my uncle for being a role model and a benefactor in my life." He stared at the tablecloth. "I wish I had been a better nephew."

Elle wondered why Alexander harbored those feelings, but this wasn't the time to find out. Instead, she turned to LeRoi.

The older man's eyes were wet as he picked up his glass. "Most people who do what I do never get to live in a palace like this, and for sure never get to sit at the Thanksgiving table with its owners. I'm thankful to the Allmond family for sharing their Thanksgiving table with me all these years, and to you, Miss Elle, for keepin' up the tradition. It was my honor to take care of Mr. Blake, and I'm goin' to keep takin' care of you as long as I can." He stood and began clearing the table. "And now, let me get ready for dessert."

Alexander jumped out of his seat to help, and Elle laughed. "I'm not going to sit here like Cleopatra and be waited on. I'm helping, too."

After coffee and dessert, consisting of key lime, pumpkin, and pecan pies, Elle and Alexander adjourned to the library, where he lit a fire. The burning wood released a piney smell, both homey and tranquil. Alexander's worry lines were gone, and Elle felt happy about that.

"Would you like an after-dinner drink?" Elle asked, pointing toward an antique cupboard, built into the wall. "We've got brandies and port, and I don't know what else."

"I don't think so. I have to drive home." He leaned back on the love seat and laced his fingers behind his head.

"Do you have plans for the rest of the weekend?"

"Not really. I was thinking of taking in a movie or something."

"Not meaning to pry, but anyone special going with you?"

The wince on his face spoke volumes.

As soon as she asked the question, she wished to call it back. "I'm sorry. You don't have to answer that."

"No problem. It's just—I have—had a girlfriend. We just broke up." A twitch under his eye gave away more emotion than his voice.

"You love her still?" Elle whispered.

"It's complicated. I love her, but—she's gone weird on me." The fire crackled and glowed neon orange.

"Do you want to talk about it?" She smiled and winked. "They say ex-nuns make the best listeners."

He smiled back. "Just weird, unpredictable. For example, she actually showed up here the other day, disguised as a car parker."

"What? How did she manage that?" Elle thought the valets had all been the groundskeepers, but now she remembered Alonzo's request to bring in extra staff.

"Her brother works here, Alonzo Espinosa. Big, husky guy, sideburns and mustache."

"Yes, I know Alonzo. I didn't know he had a sister. Why would she do something like that?"

"Who knows? She said she wanted to see me. She even took the day off from work."

"What does she do?"

"Teller at Lyons Bank in South Philly—or at least she was. Anyway, I broke up with her." He stood and walked back and forth in front of the bookcases, like an English professor ruminating over a trope.

"But you still love her. It's written all over your face."

"Like I say, it's complicated. She might be pregnant."

"Oh, you poor boy." Elle fought the impulse to run over to hug him. "No wonder you say it's complicated." She clasped her hands and squeezed. "Why do you say, 'Might be?' Doesn't she know for sure?"

"I probably shouldn't have told you all this. But you asked, and I—it feels good to talk to somebody about it. My mother's gone, and my father and I haven't talked in years."

"Well, if you're asking my advice, I'll say you need to find out for sure if she's pregnant. Once you have all the facts, you can make an intelligent decision. Of course, I'm biased, but that's a topic for another day."

Alexander thanked Elle, and she thought he meant it. An inner glow warmed her chest, the kind that always came with the satisfaction of helping someone out.

Somehow they got on the subject of Melanie's artwork. Alexander talked about the oil painting of Manderley that hung in his living room. "You should come see it. It gives the house an ethereal quality, without being too sentimental."

"We have a few of your mom's paintings here, too, you know. Two in the living room, and another in the studio behind the house. I took it there to use in a recent lesson."

"I'd like to see them sometime. I think I remember one in the living room—it's mostly mauve and gray, right?"

Elle nodded. "Do you want to look at them now? That might be a fitting activity for Thanksgiving." Elle looked at her watch. It was almost ten.

"Let me just tamp down this fire, and we can go. It's getting late, anyway."

As the tall man and the petite woman moved through the rooms toward the living room, Elle noticed LeRoi had straightened up and gone upstairs to bed. They turned on the lights in the living room, including the small lamp over Melanie's painting. They admired it in silence. A tear glistened on Alexander's cheek. A few minutes later, Elle led the way down the path outside to the studio, key in hand.

"I hate to trouble you this way," Alexander said, as they arrived at the well-lit entry door.

"It's no trouble at all. Let me just open the door and turn off the alarm. LeRoi arms it when he goes to bed each night." She wrestled with the key in the lock. When the door swooshed open, they were greeted by a silent, dark, and cool front room. "That's funny. The alarm should have been on. I guess LeRoi didn't set it."

Elle flipped on the lights in the front two rooms. "Let's go this way. Your mom's still life is stacked in the corner."

They didn't get more than ten steps into the big room before something caused Elle to gasp and dart over to the first table. Lying flat, side-by-side, in exactly the position Blake had left them, were the two stolen paintings.

CHAPTER 59

After spending the day at Longwood Gardens and the evening feasting and cleaning up the kitchen, Parrott had suggested some quiet time, reading. Tonya sat on one end of the sofa, her legs wrapped in a chenille afghan, and reading a news magazine, while Parrott sat at the other with a Harry Bosch bestseller.

Quiet and cozy, they both jumped when Tonya's cell phone rang at ten thirty. Parrott reached it on the table first and saw E CARMICHAEL on the screen. "Should I answer it, or do you want to?"

"Go ahead," Tonya said, putting down the magazine.

Elle's voice sounded strong. "Hope you don't mind my calling this late and on Tonya's phone, but you won't believe what I just found." She proceeded to describe the scene at the studio.

"Don't touch anything. I'm coming right over."

"Are you sure? It could wait until tomorrow. Blake's nephew Alexander is here with me, and he was getting ready to go home."

Parrott thought for a minute. He wasn't thrilled about disrupting the cozy ending to a wonderful holiday with his wife to go out into the cold night, but his mother's saying about not putting off until tomorrow was running through his head. He had to go. "I need to stop at the station to pick something up before I come over. It'll take me at least an hour. Alexander can go ahead and leave. We know how to find him if we need him."

Parrott kissed his wife, telling her not to wait up for him. He needed the letter Allmond had sent him with pictures of the stolen paintings, and he wanted to grab a forensics kit. He doubted there would be much trace evidence, and he didn't want to call Jerry this late on Thanksgiving night. Besides, if the actual paintings had been returned unharmed, his case could come to a screeching halt.

Elle was waiting for him at Manderley's front door. Circles under her eyes betrayed the stress of all she had been through, but she looked remarkably unruffled. "Thank you for coming. LeRoi is upstairs in bed, and I told him to stay there. He set the alarm for the studio at around nine, but when I went there at ten, it was disarmed."

"Same as—"

"Exactly. Someone knows how to go in and out without tripping the alarm."

"Let's check it out." Parrott followed Elle along the path, illuminated by a flashlight and the stars of Andromeda. The outdoor light over the studio door was on, casting a yellowish cone onto the doorstep.

Once inside, Parrott handed Elle a pair of plastic gloves and booties to cover her shoes. He donned similar accessories, and the two of them walked to the table where the paintings lay, side by side. Parrott removed the letter from his coat pocket and unfolded it. These looked like the same paintings, at least to his untrained eye.

"Do they seem the same to you?" he asked.

"Oh, yes. I never thought they might not be."

"They've been gone more than ten days. Is that long enough for someone to make copies and substitute them for the real thing?"

Elle held a hand to her cheek. "I don't know. I suppose it could be done. But look at the texture of the paint, especially here." She pointed to the lifelike depiction of a creek in the woods, thick with shiny silver dots. "Blake was so proud of this technique. It *made* his career." She bit her lip when she said this, and Parrott wondered why.

"How could we go about authenticating the paintings?" he asked.

"Rupert Brooks could do it. He's familiar enough with Blake's work, and he has the appropriate certifications. He called me earlier anyway. He's pressuring me to exhibit one or two valuable paintings for the Lockwood show. He sounded rather desperate."

It seemed late to be trying to find paintings to show in just a few months' time. "If you show him these, he may want you to let him sell *them* in the show."

"Then I would have to say no. Blake wanted these to go to the National Arts Club. I have to honor his wishes."

Parrott was struck again with admiration for Elle. She might be diminutive in stature, but she had a firm sense of right and wrong, and her love and respect for Allmond was at her center.

"Let me ask you a question then. If these turn out to be Mr. Allmond's original paintings, and we are able to find the thief, how interested are you in seeing him brought to justice, and how willing are you to give testimony in court? You don't have to answer tonight—sleep on it and tell me tomorrow." He opened the forensics kit and prepared to vacuum the table and floor around the paintings. "Secondly, if you ask Brooks to come out here to authenticate the paintings, do you want me to be here with you? Maybe he won't pressure you so much to sell if I'm here."

Elle chuckled, and an Irish lilt hung in the air. "I'm a big girl, detective. Rupert Brooks doesn't scare me in the slightest." She sat down, still wearing gloves and booties, and watched while he examined the scene. "As for testifying, I'm not a vindictive sort of person, and I wouldn't want to see the person given some extreme punishment, especially now that we may have the paintings back. On the other hand, the theft caused Blake a lot of aggravation and grief. I resent that, and I'd hate to see the person get off without consequences. I'll think about it some more, but at the moment I'd say, yes. I'll testify."

Parrott completed his forensics work. The most promising result was a partial fingerprint—that and the contents from the vacuum sweep. He would take it to Jerry in the morning and see if it was good enough to run through the database of people with prior arrests. Maybe there would be something to match the samples taken after the first break-in. And maybe eventually there'd be a DNA match from the people sampled.

As he was packing up and getting ready to leave, Elle asked, "Why do you suppose a person would steal the paintings, only to return them?"

"Only thing I can think of," Parrott replied, "is cold feet."

"Cold feet?"

"Whether we realize it or not, we must be getting close to discovering who did it. Maybe it was doing the DNA tests— maybe something else. Whatever it is, the thief decided it wasn't worth it to hold onto the paintings any longer."

"So he's running scared?"

Parrott smiled. "Something like that. And you know what? People who are running scared are a whole lot easier to catch."

CHAPTER 60

Friday morning Elle slept past her usual seven a.m. wake-up time. Fragments of a dream about paintings clung to her, but try as she might, she couldn't retrieve the details. She stretched and looked at the unused side of the bed. The stab of realization Blake was gone hit her once more, but today it was followed by a new realization—the missing paintings were back. The latter was no consolation for the former, but there was a certain satisfaction in knowing she could carry out Blake's wishes in donating them.

As she jumped out of bed, she was already making a to-do list in her head. She would call Rupert Brooks about authenticating them first. Next, she wanted to spend more time looking for the Victor Lockwood painting. She was sure it was close by, and her determination to carry out this other wish of Blake's had become almost a sacred duty.

She had planned to have Tonya over for tea today, but with all the leftovers, maybe she should see if she could come for lunch instead. She'd still have a couple of hours to search for the painting first. She still felt a little guilty having called Parrott away on Thanksgiving night. Hopefully Tonya wouldn't hold it against her.

Elle said her morning prayers, completed her personal grooming, and threw on some clothes. When she arrived downstairs, LeRoi was in the kitchen.

"I'm getting a late start today," he said. "I was just thinking about breakfast."

Elle smiled and patted him on the forearm. "Nothing too heavy after last night's meal. Maybe just tea and toast. Do we still have those home-made preserves?"

LeRoi nodded and pulled the jar of lemon-thyme preserves from the cupboard.

"How are we fixed for leftovers? I'm thinking of inviting Tonya Parrott over for lunch."

LeRoi walked to the SubZero and opened it. "Plenty left, and I'm good at fixing meals with leftover turkey." His eyes lit up, perhaps for the first time since Blake had died.

"What's the deal with Hoke? Is he working today? If she accepts, Tonya will need a ride because of her shoulder."

"Yes, ma'am, he's on the grounds, prob'ly out there in the garages, washing the cars."

By now, LeRoi had filled a tray with rye toast, butter and preserves, and a cup of Earl Grey. "Where would you like to be served?"

Elle sat down in the breakfast room, opposite the cow mural. She put her napkin on her lap and sipped from the tea cup. *Just on the good side of bitter.* A bite of toast, another swig of tea, and she took out her cell phone to call Tonya. After a brief conversation in which Elle apologized for calling so late last night, Tonya agreed to come to Manderley for lunch at noon.

Elle finished her breakfast and let LeRoi know she would be doing some more work in the attic and basement. She picked up in the basement under the center of the house, where she had left off on Wednesday. If she didn't stick with spatially sequential order, she was afraid she would lose track of where she had or hadn't been.

Again, she was impressed with how neat these storage areas were kept. There were so many possessions in this house, some centuries-old, she was sure. One area had a whole wall of clothes hanging in see-through quilted and zippered bags. The opposite wall had a cupboard for hats. Perhaps a museum would be interested in some of them—or maybe a theatre. Such a shame to keep everything hidden below ground, when it could have meaningful use in the world.

As she searched, she thought again about the returned paintings. Consulting her watch, she determined Rupert Brooks would be at work by now. Having left her cell phone in the breakfast room, she used the servants' staircase to get to the games room, where she picked up the land line to call. As she listened to the ringing, she rolled her fingers over the cool marble notches of the rook, her favorite chess piece. She remembered having tried to teach Charlotte to play chess, before she'd understood her sister was incapable of learning the game.

He answered on the fifth ring. "Rue Moderne. How may I help you?"

After the preliminaries, Elle got right to the point. "The two paintings stolen from our studio have been returned. I'd like you to authenticate them. Can you prove they are Blake's?"

"Yes, of course, I can. Do you have the letters of provenance? Photographs of the originals?" When Elle answered in the affirmative, he continued. "And if they are, can I prevail upon you to let me exhibit them in my show?"

Elle cringed. She knew he would connect one favor to the other, and she had no intention of having Blake's paintings go anywhere but the National Arts Club. "They've been promised elsewhere, you know. Blake was never one to renege on a promise, and neither am I."

"Well, if not those, I'm sure you have other suitable paintings in that huge mansion. Would it be all right if I took a look around when I come over?"

The way he said it gave Elle a shiver, but she wanted to appease him. He was doing her a favor, after all. "Sure. We can talk about it. When can you come?"

"Time is of the essence. How about this evening? I'll stop by as soon as I close the shop at five." Elle thought she could hear him rubbing his hands as they disconnected.

"Thank you for the amazing lunch," Tonya said, rubbing her thumb along the handle of the china cup on the table next to her.

"I don't know when I've been this relaxed." They had adjourned to the library to take their tea.

Elle returned the smile. "I enjoy being with you, too. You're the first Navy SEAL I've had as a student."

"Your other students probably aren't as messed up, either. I've got some bad stuff floating around in my mind from the last tour of duty."

"You'd be surprised. Most of my students are there because art soothes the soul. It's true for me, as well." That last part slipped out. Elle wasn't used to revealing personal information, but her comfort level with Tonya was high, or maybe it was the pine-scented fire.

"You? You're probably the calmest person I know."

"Hah," Elle replied, sounding more like a tinkle than a snort. "Our paths are crossing many years after my own traumatic events. I've had a lot of time to think and pray and paint and love. One day someone will tell you you're the calmest person she knows, too. When it happens, think of me."

Elle wanted to say more, to do more, to pull the seeds of trauma from Tonya's mind and use a magic elixir to make them disappear. But she knew there was no possibility of that, no magic. What she could do was what she was doing, being a friend. Somehow she felt a strong connection with Tonya, and with Parrott, too. She couldn't explain it, but comforting Tonya brought comfort back to her.

Tonya strolled around the library, touching the spine of a book here and there. "This is the nicest library I've seen since college. It would take decades to read all of these beautiful books. Are you an avid reader?"

"I love to read, yes. It's good for the soul. I think many of these books have never been touched. I told Blake I was going to take one shelf at a time, until I had read them all. I haven't made a dent." Elle gazed at her hands in her lap. "If you see something you'd like to borrow, feel free."

Tonya moved from shelf to shelf, wall to wall. When she got to the picture window on the western wall, she stared at the beautiful landscape. Even in late autumn, the view was magnificent, as the fading sunlight wrapped its rays around the vegetation. A young deer skittered across the lawn. "You must have magnificent views of the sunset from this window."

Elle came over to see what Tonya was looking at. She hadn't been in the library at sunset for a long time, but it was true—when she had, the view had been spectacular. "It is lovely."

Tonya reached up to pull a book from a shelf next to the window. "*The Scarlet Letter*, one of my favorites. Most of my high school friends hated it, but I loved every word. I especially liked Hester's spunk. It took guts to stand up—"

Elle stopped paying attention to what Tonya was saying right after the title. Cold prickles covered her neck and arms, and she took note of the closest painting on the wall. It was one she had painted of the Delaware coast.

"—Would it be all right if I borrowed this?"

Tears filled Elle's eyes, and all she could do was nod. How grateful she was to Tonya. Sunsets, Hawthorne, and my favorite artist's painting—Elle was sure she had found the Victor Lockwood.

CHAPTER 61

The day after Thanksgiving was a holiday for Alexander. He wished he could spend it relaxing, but he had a lot to do—groceries, laundry, shopping for a new cell phone. He had an idea about signing up for a community college class on financial planning. He didn't know enough about investing money, and he wanted to be proactive. A million-dollar bequest was a once-in-a-lifetime opportunity. He didn't want to waste it.

Also, he couldn't stop thinking about Veronica. He'd been gob-smacked by her pregnancy announcement. Certain she'd been taking birth control pills, even seeing them in her bathroom, he'd never considered the possibility. At the beginning he'd used protection, but she'd told him it wasn't necessary. Whether she had slipped up by accident or on purpose, it gave him one more reason to resent her.

If she was pregnant, it threw a wrench into their break-up, big-time. It cast everything in a whole different light. Alexander didn't consider himself a right-to-lifer, but the thought of aborting his child struck him as selfish in the extreme. Other options didn't appeal to him, either.

Elle's advice about verifying the pregnancy echoed in his head. He concocted a plan, making the drug store the first stop on his errand list. He stood in the too well-lit pregnancy test aisle, comparing claims on the boxes to see which was the most accurate. He wondered how many purchasers of these things were men.

The most expensive kit claimed to be reliable at six days after conception. It had been longer than that since they'd had sex. He stuck the box under his arm and slunk to the checkout counter. After paying for it, he asked the clerk where the nearest pay phone was.

By luck, there was one twelve blocks away, but on the way to Veronica's. He'd driven past it often, but owning a cell phone had made it irrelevant until today. The chilly wind whipped around him as he stuffed coins in the slots. He'd memorized Veronica's burner phone number, and he dialed it.

She answered with a nasal-sounding voice. Had she been crying? His heart tugged, despite himself.

"It's me, Alexander. Okay if I come over in a few minutes? We need to talk."

A blowing of the nose, definitely crying. "You're coming over? R-really?" He pictured her brushing tears away and rocking her torso from side to side. "I agree we need to talk. Come on over now."

The happiness in her voice almost broke his heart. There was a time, not too long ago, when he would have believed anything she'd said in that tone of voice. He *had* loved her—he was sure of that—but now, well, a lot was riding on the little pink box in his coat pocket.

When he arrived at Veronica's door, she greeted him in the usual way, clinging and pressing against him, the silky fabric slipping to reveal more than he cared to see, at least today.

"Oh, Chachi, thank you for coming back to me. I love you so much. You had me so worried." Her baby-talk purred in his ear, and he had to remind himself why he had come.

"Listen, Veronica. We need to have a serious conversation." He pushed himself back from her and flopped down on the couch.

She pouted, but sat across from him. "Okay, talk."

"You say you're pregnant? How and when did you find out?" His voice sounded accusatory, even to his own ears, but he steeled himself to stay the course.

"I took a home pregnancy test last week. I threw it out, or I'd show you. It surprised me, too, Chachi. You know I'm on the pill."

"I thought birth control pills were almost infallible. Did you miss taking them?"

Veronica jumped up and ran to the bathroom to get her pill dispenser. She held it out to show him. "See, I took all of the pills for that cycle. I don't know how it happened." She looked down at her bosom and buttoned two more buttons.

He glanced at the empty container and then at her shiny dark eyes, wondering that she would save the empty birth control dispenser, but not the positive pregnancy test. "I hope you won't mind taking another test today. I need to see it with my own eyes." He pulled the test kit out of his pocket and dropped it on the coffee table between them.

Her eyes grew rounder, and he could see her struggling not to flinch. "You saying you don't trust me?"

"Interpret it however you'd like, but I'd like you to do me this one favor." He picked up the box and handed it to her. "Now. While I'm watching, please."

Veronica shot him a hard, squinty look and grabbed the box from his hand. She held it by the edges, as if it were hot. "I can't believe you don't believe me, Chachi. I thought you loved me, too." She dropped the box and cozied up to him, grabbing the lapels of his coat and pulling him into her.

Repulsed, Alexander wondered how he had ever fallen for her seductive ways. He pushed her away again and mustered his sternest tone of voice. "You can't distract me this time. I need a scientific answer to a scientific question."

"Okay, Chachi. Come with me to the bathroom, but you're not going to watch me pee." She led the way to the bathroom and tried to close the door.

"No, *sweetheart*, the door will stay open. I'll turn my back while you pee, if you wish."

She shrugged, her expression one of a trapped animal. She read the steps diagrammed on the box, then began to follow them, her eyes unreadable. She urinated on the plastic stick for five seconds, shook the indicator, and placed it on a tissue on the vanity counter. "Now we wait. Three minutes." A plastic clock ticked away the seconds.

Within seconds, a single pink line showed the kit was working. Alexander stood next to her as she dressed herself, staring at the clock and the indicator. Tiny beads of moisture dotted her upper lip.

At the end of three minutes, he picked up the indicator and held it to the light. Turned this way and that, the result was still the same—no second line—no pregnancy.

CHAPTER 62

Parrott sat at his desk with a cup of black coffee, steaming and aromatic. He felt like a tiger who could smell his prey, but didn't yet know which way to pounce. Now the paintings had been returned to Manderley, Parrott had a new lens through which to view his case. Whoever took them—and Parrott's radar was on full alert now—the thief had been sufficiently unnerved by the DNA testing to return them. That didn't exonerate him, but it did offer mitigating circumstances that would probably lighten the sentence when brought to justice.

If Parrott was right, the thief had to know about the DNA testing, and that limited the field of suspects considerably. He had DNA from most of the people at Manderley, but some workers hadn't chosen to be tested. The hair he had taken on impulse from the bathroom at the Rue Moderne hadn't been tested, and probably wouldn't be, since he'd taken it without due process, as an insurance policy. It was noteworthy that Alexander Vargas had been on the premises for Thanksgiving. He might've had the opportunity to return the paintings before showing up at the house for dinner, and he might've feigned surprise when they were discovered.

Bypassing the alarm system twice added another clue. It wasn't a matter of knowing the code to disarm it—no warning beeps had sounded. The thief owned or had access to an expensive jammer and had used it at least twice at the studio.

Finally, if the partial fingerprint he'd picked up from the studio and dropped off at forensics this morning bore fruit, he'd be well on his way to solving the art theft. He remained convinced, though, that the theft and the murder were somehow linked. He wished for a better pipeline to the New York case, but as much as it frustrated him to be left out of their case, he understood the hierarchy. What he could do, though, was call Detective Rayburn. The return of the paintings gave him an excuse.

"...What dya know? I'm sure you realize how infrequently that happens," Rayburn said, "I've actually never heard of stolen merchandise being returned. I think you're right about being close to catching the guy."

"Thanks. How're things going with the murder, if you don't mind my asking?"

Rayburn hesitated. "Moving forward. You know how it is, one step forward, two steps backward." Parrott could hear papers being shuffled in the background. "Listen, let me ask you something since I have you on the phone. How close have you been able to get to the girlfriend?"

"Elle Carmichael? Pretty close. You don't still suspect her, do you?"

"I'm sitting on a full dossier here. All I'll say is there's more than meets the eye with her. Don't let the nun thing blind you. There were reasons she went into the convent to begin with."

Parrott couldn't believe what he was hearing. His mind told him anyone could have secrets, and anyone could make mistakes. But his heart told him whatever Elle had done in the past, she was incapable of having murdered Blake Allmond. "Without knowing the details, all I can say is I think you're barking up the wrong tree if you have her pegged for murder."

"Maybe you're right, Parrott. Maybe you're right. But maybe if we keep barking, she'll shake lose, just like the perp in *your* case. Best of luck to both of us."

As Parrott hung up the phone he tried to shake off the feeling Elle was in danger, and he would need to be the one to protect her.

CHAPTER 63

It was all Elle could do to contain her excitement until Tonya left, and she could get back into the library alone. The three clues lined up like mermaids on a slot machine, and she was positive the Victor Lockwood was hidden somewhere nearby. There was no closet in the room, just a fireplace, a mantle, a long window seat, a picture window facing west, and cases of floor-to-ceiling bookshelves, a few of which contained storage compartments beneath the bottom bookshelf. All the paneling and bookshelf material was solid cherry, dark, with a gleaming patina.

Elle's hands shook as she started pulling out the drawers, although it didn't make sense that an oil painting could be stored in any one of them. Around the room there were six cabinets with drawers beneath them. Most were empty, but a few had items from other decades—ash trays, fancy cigarette lighters, a silent butler, but nothing resembling a painting.

Concentrating her attention on the cabinets on the west wall, on either side of the window, Elle removed books from the shelves she could reach and stacked them on the floor nearby. The shelves were dust-free, and she wondered again at how much maintenance was required to keep this home in such pristine condition. Carrying heavy books was a big job, and Elle's face and hands were covered with a fine moisture.

She considered asking LeRoi or one of the housekeepers to assist. That would lead to questions, though, and if she were lucky enough to find the painting, she wasn't sure she wanted anyone else to know.

She gazed at the upper shelves. She would have to use the rolling ladder to reach those books, and moving them to the floor would require a lot of tedious ups and downs. Before she tackled that, she examined the cabinet to the left of the window. She tried pressing and sliding. She looked for seams where one panel met another. Nothing gave way, and nothing moved, except one of her fingernails, snagged on the edge of the shelf.

Shaking her hand and making a whistling noise from the pain, Elle moved to the cabinet to the right of the window. This one was closer to the spot where her painting hung. She crossed herself before running her hands over the wood, feeling for anything unusual. There was nothing on the shelves, the backs, or the sides of the cabinets.

Discouraged, she eyed the next stack of shelves to the right, sighing at the prospect of removing another fifty or more volumes. The broken fingernail throbbed, and when she looked down to study it, she noticed an anomaly in the edge of the shelf. It was a diagonal line where two pieces of wood came together.

She ran back to the first cabinet, almost afraid to see if there was a corresponding line there. She squinted and ran her hands over the cabinet's edge, but the construction there had no diagonal lines.

If Alexander were here, he would know better than she, but common sense told her there had to be a reason for the mitered edge. Those two sections joined by the line had to separate. Mindful of the weight of the books on the upper shelves, she threw herself against the shelf's edge. Nothing budged.

There was nothing to do but climb the ladder and bring down the heavy books, one armful at a time. Not surprisingly, the higher tier of books hadn't been dusted in a long while, so the air was filled with streamers of fine confetti-like particles that danced in the light and almost gagged her with their paper-and-leather smell.

When she had cleared the shelves, she wiped her hands on her pants and squatted to put herself at eye level with the seam. She placed one hand on either side of the seam and pushed against it with all her strength. Nothing moved, but when she let go, she heard a click.

Sure enough, the seam had opened a tiny crack. Now she pushed against both sides of the crack, and the bookcase swung slowly open, revealing a black hole. Amazement flooded her like a clear, cold spring, overflowing its banks. Standing and holding the edge of the bookcase with one hand, she peered into the space. As her eyes adjusted to the darkness below, she made out a wall, a staircase, a banister, and a light switch.

Shaking all over with wonder, she flipped the switch and darted down the stairs. The concrete room below was smaller than the library. No doors or windows connected it to any other areas. It had obviously been designed as a hidden room for valuables, isolated and obscure. Unlike the other basement areas Elle had visited, this one had no built-ins, no clothing racks, no accumulation of family heirlooms. In the corner on a two-foot riser sat a rusted metal safe with a combination lock. The door to the safe was partially open, and nothing was inside.

Further back in the room stood an easel, covered by a white, dusty sheet. Elle closed her eyes and said a Hail Mary, as she flung the sheet aside, casting dust everywhere. Underneath sat a 36" x 48" painting that stung her eyes and took her breath away.

A young Adonis stood in the morning light, next to what looked like the Brandywine River. The water glittered with reflection of the sun's rays on its purplish depths. The boy shaded his eyes, as if the scene were too glorious for human eyes. A smile played on his lips, making him look—what? Confident? Satisfied? Complicit in a secret?

The corner bore the signature, V. Lockwood. Even without Blake's letter, Elle would have recognized the subject as a young Blake, handsome and healthy, almost regal. And her artist's heart told her the painter was in love with the model. A hundred little touches spoke to that. She could see why Blake had kept this masterpiece to himself. It revealed too much.

At this moment, Elle felt closer to Blake than she ever had in life. He had entrusted her with this exquisite treasure. He wanted her to do what he could not do, himself. She gave thanks to God for allowing her to escape her past, to serve the good children through her life in the convent, to meet Blake and reinvent herself as an artist and teacher, and to find this magnificent work of art and play a significant role in its deliverance to the world.

CHAPTER 64

Alexander stormed out on Veronica, slamming the door behind him. In his last view of her, she was covering her face with her hands and sobbing. Lying about a pregnancy was the last straw. He would never be able to trust her again.

The wind scrubbed him of excess emotion, though, and as he dashed to his car, he felt twenty pounds lighter. He turned on the radio, and as he drove to T-Mobile, he hummed along with Cee Lo Green's "Forget You."

After he purchased the latest Samsung phone and a new number to go with it, happy his credit card company approved the charge, and looking forward to the time when he wouldn't have to worry about such things, he took off for the main campus of Community College of Philadelphia on Spring Garden Street. He'd always admired the stately Mint building with its Doric columns and elaborate gingerbread. His mother had wanted him to take courses there immediately after high school, but the offer of a decent hourly wage doing something he enjoyed had lured him away.

There was a course in the catalog called Personal and Consumer Finance, taught two evenings a week. If he liked it and could manage to study while working full-time, who knows? He might keep taking courses and get an associate's degree.

He entered the Mint building and whistled at the beauty of its rotunda. He passed the library, where a few people were reading or milling about. He imagined there were fewer than normal students on campus today because of the holiday. Signs for Enrollment Central led to the adjoining Bonnell Building.

The door to the enrollment office was open, and the lights were on, but no one appeared to be staffing the front desk. Maybe this wasn't the best time to come, but Alexander couldn't delay if he wanted to get into the January semester.

"Hel-lo?" he said, looking around for anyone who could help.

A slender, pink-cheeked girl with hair the color of marigolds rushed toward the counter, slightly out of breath. "Huh, I'm, uh, sorry. I'm the only one here today, and I had to take a nature break. You know. How can I help you?"

She looked to be barely out of high school, herself. Pretty, though. "I'd like to see about enrolling in a night class. Personal Finance."

"Come around the counter and have a seat. I'll give you an application and all the materials you need. Have you taken any college courses before?"

As he rounded the corner of the counter, he noticed her name tag, "Wren," and he noticed two very shapely legs, as well. "No, this will be my first."

"Well, you know you'll have to take an English class, too. Either first, or concurrently. We want all students to pursue programs, instead of taking a course here and a course there. Make sense?"

"I guess I could take two classes, as long as they're both offered in the evenings. I work construction full-time." Now he was free of Veronica, he wouldn't have anything to distract him in the evenings.

She smiled, and her eyes lit up like sparklers. "My dad owns an electrical supply, and I help him out in the office on weekends. Construction is a good career."

"You take classes here, too?" He crossed his fingers, mentally, hoping he'd run into her outside of this office.

"Yeah. I work here part-time. I get a tuition reduction and a little bit of change. I like it a lot."

Was it his imagination, or had Wren winked at him? "Your enthusiasm is contagious. I'm starting to like CCP already."

Alexander completed the registration and paid the tuition by credit card, wondering how soon his inheritance would be released. His new life as a millionaire-construction worker-college student felt better than a new outfit and a new pair of shoes. He had a feeling his mother would be proud of him. And that thought led to a strange urge to call Elle.

One thing was for sure. He would find a way to double back to the enrollment office to say hi to Wren.

CHAPTER 65

D NA tests in murder cases would always go to the front of the line, but in thefts, they might take a couple of months to process. It was a fact of life Parrott had to live with, but he felt sure the testing had already served its purpose by prompting the thief to return the paintings. Now he had a few questions about the two groundskeepers who had declined to participate.

He sat at his desk on this quiet Friday afternoon and turned things over in his mind, things from his case, and things Rayburn had told him. He wondered again what NYPD had in its dossier on Elle. Whatever it was, Tonya hadn't picked up on anything, and Tonya was a great judge of character. The two of them had eaten lunch together today, in fact. Their blossoming friendship still made Parrott feel a little uncomfortable with an open case, but it had come in handy, and, so far, no serious conflicts had arisen.

It was three o'clock. He would have to act quickly if he wanted to put his plan in action. He called Tonya to make sure she was back at home before he headed out to Manderley.

"Yes, I'm home, stuffed tighter than yesterday's turkey. It was a nice luncheon, and I enjoyed being chauffeured, too."

"Glad you had fun. By the way, has Elle ever told you anything disturbing about her past?"

"No-o-o, not really. She's alluded to some trauma long ago, just like me. Why?"

"Just curious. I'm going to head over there now. I'll see you for dinner, but I might be late."

"Okay, but the way I feel now, you'll be the only one who's eating."

When Parrott arrived at Manderley, LeRoi ushered him in. "Let me tell Miss Elle you're here. I believe she's in the library."

Elle strode into the living room, looking a little bedraggled, but with a jubilant expression on her face. She wiped her hands on her pants before shaking Parrott's hand and sitting across from him. "I'm sorry you've caught me at the tail end of something. What can I do for you today?"

"I'd like to interview the two people who declined to do the DNA test. I believe they were groundskeepers?"

"Yes, Manuel and Alonzo. I did tell them the test was voluntary."

"I know, and it was, but I still would like to interview them, separately. Are they working this afternoon?"

"They should be. There's always something to do here with forty acres of land. LeRoi can contact them, and you can interview them in the outbuilding next to the studio, if you'd like. They use that as a sort of office." Her brow crumpled, as if she were worried, and she said, "There's something I probably should tell you. It's about Alonzo."

Parrott nodded and leaned forward in his chair.

"You know, Alexander was here for Thanksgiving dinner. Was that just last night? While we were talking, he mentioned he's been dating Alonzo's sister."

"Strange coincidence, don't you think?"

"Yes, and he also said the sister was here the day of the funeral, dressed as a man, and parking cars. It doesn't sit well with me."

"Or with me. Is this a casual dating relationship or something more?"

"That's the other thing. Alexander didn't swear me to secrecy, but he told me something rather private—he's been trying to break up with her, but she told him she was pregnant."

"Is she? Pregnant, I mean?"

"He didn't know, but I told him to make sure before he made any important decisions. I worry about him."

"Well, first things first. Let me interview Manuel and Alonzo, and then we'll take it from there. Oh, one more thing. The day of the funeral reception, when Alonzo was parking cars, might he or any of the car parkers have come into the house to use the bathroom?"

"Hmm, I didn't see any of them inside the house, but except for the one in the studio, which was locked, the only other toilet they might use is a good five to ten minute jaunt from the front of the house. Maybe in the interest of time, somebody popped in and out." As she spoke, a wave of understanding passed over Elle's expression. "Oh, I see why you're asking." She covered her mouth with her hands.

"I'm going to meet with the guys now."

"Do you need me to be present? I've got to get cleaned up and grab a bite to eat. Rupert Brooks is coming over around six to look at the returned paintings."

At the mention of Brooks, a chill flashed through Parrott's torso. "Glad you mentioned that. Are you sure Brooks is the best person to authenticate the paintings?"

"You don't suspect Brooks of having stolen the paintings, do you? I can't imagine he'd do anything like that."

Parrott shook his head. "Just trying to cover every possible angle. He told me he had begged to have the stolen paintings in his show, and they were stolen shortly after Mr. Allmond turned him down. He also told me he hopes you'll let him show some of the paintings from Manderley."

"Hmmm, you've given me something to think about, but it's too late to cancel the appointment with him. Don't worry. I have no intention of letting Blake's artwork to go anywhere other than the National Arts Club. Mr. Brooks will have to find someone else's paintings for his show."

The interview with Manuel went down with no glitches, except his limited English and Parrott's limited Spanish made for a few impediments. He hadn't seen or heard anything related to the theft of the paintings. He didn't know anything about the alarm system in the studio. He was a groundskeeper, he liked his job, and he wanted to keep it.

Alonzo came in next. He was a husky guy with hands like mallets, spotted with dirt that looked permanent. Facial hair covered his cheeks and upper lip. Parrott could tell he wasn't thrilled to be here.

He sat down in the folding chair opposite Parrott, laced his fingers in his lap, and stared at them, waiting.

Parrott asked if he was Alonzo Espinosa. He nodded. Parrott launched into the Miranda rights, and watched as a look of terror flickered in Alonzo's eyes. When he was finished, he asked if it would be okay to tape record the interview.

"What for? What did I do wrong?" The groundskeeper clutched the seat of his chair on both sides, as if expecting it to rise and carry him on a bumpy ride.

"I'm not accusing you of anything. I'm merely gathering evidence. Do I have your permission to record this conversation, or not?"

"If I have a choice, I'll say no." He stared at Parrott with eyes that smoldered.

"Okay." Parrott put away the recorder and tried to look friendly. "Mr. Espinosa, how long have you been employed here at Manderley?"

"Almost a year. Hired last winter. There's much to do in winter to get ready for spring."

"How much contact have you had with Blake Allmond?"

"Not too much. Mr. Allmond, he signs the paychecks, but most of the time we deal with LeRoi."

"Were you aware Mr. Allmond was a well-known artist?" Alonzo nodded, and Parrott continued. "Were you aware the building next to this one was being used as an art studio?" More nodding. "Have you ever been inside the building used as a studio?"

Alonzo's eyes darted from side to side, as if looking for a safe place to rest. "I don't remember," he replied.

Parrott felt sure the threat of collected DNA was hovering, making Alonzo flinch. "You don't remember whether you've been inside the studio in the past year. How about in the last three weeks? Surely you'd be able to remember that."

Alonzo hesitated, but replied. "I don't think so." He brushed at his jeans, avoiding eye contact. "We don't go inside the buildings, except this one. Our work is outside."

"And you can't recall Mr. Allmond or Ms. Carmichael or Mr. LeRoi asking you to do anything inside the art studio during the last three weeks?"

"No."

"Mr. Espinosa, where were you yesterday afternoon and evening?"

"Yesterday was Thanksgiving."

"I know that. But where were you?"

"I was with my family. We go to my mother's in South Philly."

"What were the hours during which you were at your mother's yesterday?"

Alonzo's eyes rolled to the ceiling. "Three o'clock until ten, maybe."

"Can anyone substantiate you were at your mother's in South Philly without leaving during those seven hours?"

"Hey, man, what you want to know for? We wasn't looking at no clocks."

"Are you married? Do you have a family?"

"No."

"Where do you live?" Parrott opened his iPad mini and prepared to take notes.

Alonzo gave an address in South Philly. "It's an apartment. First floor."

"And what is your mother's address?"

"I'll give it to you, but please don't drag my mother into anything. She gets too upset if the po-lice come around. She's a quiet lady."

Parrott took down the second address. "Let me ask you something else, Mr. Espinosa. Can you tell me why your sister was parking cars here the day of Mr. Allmond's funeral reception?"

Alonzo's face turned the color of parchment. "My sister, she needed some extra money. I told her she could help out with the parking. She wouldn't get paid, but she'd pick up some tips."

"Didn't the other parkers object to having an extra person siphoning off tips?"

"The other parkers? Naw, it was just me and Manuel. He didn't mind."

"It wouldn't have anything to do with the fact Mr. Allmond's nephew, Alexander Vargas was her boyfriend, would it?"

"That prick? He's not her boyfriend anymore. He used her. He used her, and then he dumped her." His fists clenched into strings of white knobs, and his jaw clenched. "Don't ask me nothing about him. I ain't got nothing good to say." Swiping the back of his wrist against his forehead, he asked, "How much longer we got to sit here? I got to clean up, and it's past quitting time."

Parrott thought for a minute, more to see if delaying would provoke more tension than for any other reason. Finally, he said, "Okay, you can go. No more questions—at least for now."

CHAPTER 66

Parrott was on a roll, and he didn't want to stop the momentum. When he left Manderley after interviewing Alonzo, he took his cell phone off of airplane mode and checked for messages. Sure enough, there was one from Jerry.

He called back immediately. "You got something?" he asked.

"Yes, indeed. The partial matches a guy with a couple of B&Es. The name's Espinosa. Alonzo Arturo."

Parrott's heart skipped a beat. Alonzo had just told him he didn't remember going into the studio, and he had been there last night. He felt like singing from the top of a mountain. "Jerry, you're the best. You've just made my day."

Parrott raced back to the office to prepare materials for a search warrant, including a probable cause affidavit. He wanted to search Alonzo's apartment for a security bypass device. If he found it, he would make the arrest.

One of the local judges was a distant relative of the Campbells, and he had told Parrott to call him any time he could help with signing warrants. This would be the first time Parrott would take advantage of the offer. He wanted to get to Alonzo's place in South Philly before the groundskeeper could get rid of the evidence.

Alonzo's refusal to submit DNA couldn't be used to incriminate him, but the fingerprint on the picture frame was a solid indication he might have been the one to take and return the paintings. Most likely he'd cooked up a plot to steal Allmond's paintings as a get-rich scheme. Perhaps he intended to ransom the paintings, but when Allmond was killed, he decided to scratch that. Or if he was the killer, possession of the paintings would be too big a liability.

If Alexander had dumped the sister, that probably meant she turned out not to be pregnant. Alonzo's flimsy excuse for having the sister park cars at the funeral was transparent. There was too much involvement of the Espinosa siblings in the Allmond business to be innocent.

The way Parrott saw it, Alonzo had motive and opportunity to steal the paintings, and also to return them when the case grew hot. If he could prove Alonzo also had the weapon, as in the disarming device, he would solve the theft.

Whether or not Alonzo also was the one to plant the gun in the bathroom at Manderley, Parrott was going to proceed with his own case. His agenda for the next two hours was to deliver the warrant application to Judge Manetti, wait while he read and hopefully signed it, show up to search the premises, and, if he still had time, stop by Alonzo's mom's address to see if anyone could blow a hole in Alonzo's statement that he was there until ten p.m.

It was a lot to accomplish before going home for dinner, but Parrott was confident he could do it.

Elle had just finished closing the bookcase and returning books to the shelves when Parrott rang the doorbell. Her elation at locating the Lockwood painting was tempered by her need to keep the treasure under wraps a little longer, at least until she could make proper arrangements for it to be valued and sold.

She knew Lockwood's paintings sold in the many millions of dollars, and this was perhaps the most spectacular of them all. Blake's letter had implied others may know of the painting's existence. Who those others were, and whether they were friendly or not, remained a mystery, but regardless, she knew enough about art to know this painting merited serious treatment by one of the big auction houses, like Sotheby's or Christie's.

Now Parrott had left, she had a few minutes to get cleaned up and maybe grab a bite to eat before Rupert Brooks arrived. While she showered, put on makeup, and dressed in a wool pantsuit, she thought about her visit with Tonya Parrott. The more time they spent together, the more Elle saw commonalities between

Tonya's PTSD and her own. Whatever serendipity had brought them together in this world, Elle was grateful. If it hadn't been for Tonya, she might never have found the Lockwood.

Her mind drifted to what price the Lockwood might fetch. Whatever it was, it would only be money. It wouldn't undo the horrible events of the past. It wouldn't assuage the guilt she carried in her heart. It wouldn't bring Blake back. If and when the painting sold, she promised the Blessed Mother she would find a way to do good with it.

The doorbell rang, interrupting her thoughts. *There goes dinner*, she thought, as she dropped her cell phone in her pocket and descended the stairs, ready to meet with the art dealer.

CHAPTER 67

It was already dark, and tiny snowflakes were dancing in the air when Elle met LeRoi at the door to greet Rupert Brooks. The art dealer had aged in the few days since the funeral. Purplish circles underscored his eyes, accentuating the crow's feet on either side. He stamped his feet on the welcome mat and brushed the shoulders and arms of his all-weather coat with gloved hands.

"Thank you for coming out," Elle said.

Brooks stepped over the threshold and started removing his scarf and gloves, but Elle stopped him. "Why don't I get my coat on, and we can go right to the studio to look at the paintings? Then we can come back here for tea and a light supper."

"That's fine," Brooks replied, putting his gloves back on. "No sense in wasting time."

LeRoi stayed behind to prepare the repast, while Elle led the way, past the groundskeepers' building, to the studio. Elle used the key to open the door, and she slipped inside to disarm the security system, while Brooks remained outside.

"Come on in," she said, motioning. "I apologize for how cool it is inside. We keep it this way when we're not using it. Better for the paintings."

"It's not uncomfortable," Brooks replied, looking around with the expression of a squirrel hunting an acorn. "It's been years since I was here last. Maybe ten. When was it that I showed Blake's paintings at the gallery?"

"Seems like yesterday to me," Elle replied. "Let's go into the next room." She led him to the large room, where the paintings had been moved to a back table, and the fingerprinting mess cleaned up. Each of the two framed paintings sat on its own table, propped on a short easel. Elle imagined viewing them for the first time, as if she were an art critic at a museum. The quality, the vibrancy, stood out, and she knew in her heart these were Blake's originals. Still, she was eager to hear Brooks's confirmation.

Brooks removed a pair of magnifying eyeglasses from his coat pocket and put them on. "There would be no sense in carbon-dating these paintings, since they are relatively new. What I'm doing, instead, is a Morellian analysis, looking for specific criteria we know to be in Blake's paintings. His formula for depicting water, for example, is difficult to replicate, so it shouldn't be too hard."

Elle watched as he pointed out various details, tiny beading, swirls to the left at certain angles, feathery lines representing shadows. All artists used similar techniques, but Brooks was right—these particular characteristics were part of Blake's personal style.

Brooks's voice became louder and his gestures more exuberant as he talked about the way Blake had depicted the water in both paintings. "Brilliant, absolutely brilliant. No one does water the way Blake does. Others try to emulate it, but they never get quite the same sparkle. When it comes to water, Blake is the master."

"So you think these are Blake's paintings, not replicas?" Elle wanted to push this along. She was cold and hungry, and Brooks was starting to annoy her.

"Most definitely," he replied, removing his glasses and putting them away. "I'll put it in writing for you in the next day or two. Let me take a few photos to help me remember the particulars." He snapped a few pictures of the two paintings with his cell phone. "I could fetch a pretty penny for these if you'd let me exhibit them with Sophia Lockwood's." He smiled, showing his pointy eye teeth, one eyebrow cocked.

Elle turned away. "Let's go back to the house. We can talk more over tea." She had no intention of agreeing, but she didn't want to get into that right now. She scrambled, mentally, to find a way to turn him down without destroying the relationship she, and especially Blake, had had with him for so many years. He had shown and sold a lot of their paintings, and he had almost been a member of the family. She remembered the photo of him and Melanie at their engagement party.

When they arrived back at the house, LeRoi had set a lovely table for two in the library. Elle cringed inside. She hoped she hadn't left tell-tale signs of her discovery there a few hours earlier. Even if she hadn't, her heart beat faster, knowing the Victor Lockwood painting was so close by.

Elle left her coat for LeRoi to hang up, but Brooks insisted on keeping his, claiming to be chilled to the bone. Inside the library, the crackling of a cozy fire greeted them. "One of my favorite rooms," Brooks said, as he strutted around, peering at books on the shelves and artwork on the walls. He stopped to admire Elle's painting of the Delaware coast, and Elle held her breath. *So close to the hiding place.*

"You know, this painting is quite good," Brooks said. "If you ever want to sell it, I know someone who would adore it." He continued to walk around the room, scrutinizing artwork, as if he were at a market, instead of a private home.

"Why don't we sit down?" Elle said, moving to the small table. LeRoi's creative recycling of Thanksgiving leftovers made her smile. She hated to waste food, and Fern's dishes always seemed to improve with age, at least for a few days. "Shall I pour you some tea?"

Still wearing his coat, Brooks helped himself to a few hors d'oeuvres—bacon-wrapped turkey bites, sweet potato puffs, and zucchini squares—and sipped from his porcelain teacup. His demeanor was anything but casual, though. His fingers drummed the tablecloth, and he kept shifting in his chair.

"Pardon me for saying so," Elle said, "but you seem a bit antsy. Don't you want at least to take off your coat?"

"No, thanks. I'm still cold. As for being antsy, I guess I should get to the point. I'm in a very tight spot right now, and I need your help. The Lockwood Exhibit is only weeks away, and advertising needs to go out in just a few days. I'm at my wits' end, trying to identify some paintings to show." His lips pulled back to show his vampirish teeth, and Elle recoiled inside.

"How do you imagine I can help you? If you mean the two returned paintings, Blake made it clear those were to go to the National Arts Club. I can't go against his wishes."

"Blake, Blake, Blake. Never was so much made over *my* wishes. How about the wishes of others? Blake isn't the only one who had wishes. How about your wishes? My wishes?" He jumped up from the table and started walking in circles around it.

Shocked by this diatribe, Elle wished she hadn't invited Brooks over at all. "I thought you and Blake were good friends. I had no idea you felt this way."

"Good friends? You might say we were good friends. I've known Blake all of his life and most of mine. I was once almost his brother-in-law, you know." He stomped around, lost in his own words. "And I would've been if it hadn't been for that little rat, spoiling everything."

"What do you mean? How did Blake ruin your engagement?"

Brooks looked at Elle as if just realizing she was in the room. "Do you really want to know? It might blow your image of perfect little Blake."

At that moment, Elle was struck by a bolt of insight. *I'll bet he's going to tell me something about Blake's involvement with Victor Lockwood.* Her hands flew to her ears, as if she were the "hear no evil" monkey.

Brooks continued, as if she had responded in the affirmative. "It all goes back to Victor Lockwood. He was not only a phenomenal painter, but also a charismatic person. All of us kids were mesmerized by him—we followed him around in hopes of receiving a moment's attention, a kind word, a loving touch."

Elle's hands moved from her ears to her eyes. She knew what was coming, but she didn't know how to stop Brooks. His voice had an otherworldly timbre, and his recital had become almost emotionless.

"We all had our day with him, or should I say, he had his day with each of us? But Blake was clearly his favorite. He was the youngest by far, and perhaps the most pliable. Having the famous Victor Lockwood fall in love with you—it was like being chosen from among the constellations in the sky to be *the* star."

Elle could understand how a young boy interested in art would be flattered—honored, even—to be fawned over by someone of such stature in the artist community. But she also understood what a gross abuse of power Lockwood's seduction of young boys had been.

"So," Brooks continued, "having such an early taste of Lockwood's love put us all into a kind of fraternity. There were six or seven of us. We all knew delicious secrets about one another, all held in a giant net over the mundane world, like balloons over a dance floor in a fancy ballroom, ready to float down at Lockwood's whim. It spoiled us for the ordinary kind of first love. Girls our ages seemed plain and uninspiring."

Elle thought of the painting, just a few feet away, and what a story it told. "I'm getting the picture, but how did *Blake* ruin your engagement to Melanie?"

Brooks stopped pacing and looked into Elle's eyes. "He told her. He broke the code of silence and told her I was in love with Lockwood, in love with men." His voice choked, and tears stood testament to the depth of his loss, even so many years later.

Elle might have felt sorry for him, had it not been for the wild-eyed and twisted expression on his face. Prickles of fear were sprouting at the base of her spine and moving upward.

"I loved Melanie, and she loved me. We could have had a wonderful life together, better than either of us had apart." He sat down with an abruptness that stunned Elle, and he put his face into his hands. "Oh, I forgave Blake. He was just a boy when he turned his sister against me, and I don't think he realized how his actions would devastate our lives, or that he would also fall victim to a similar position when he married Susan. I could have retaliated and told Susan, but I kept my mouth shut. But I never forgot, and there's something else I never forgot, as well."

Elle sucked in a breath. "What is that?"

Brooks's eyebrows drew into inverted "v's." "Did Blake ever show you the painting Victor Lockwood gave him? It was a love-gift, an exquisite portrait of Blake by the banks of the Brandywine. It's worth many millions of dollars, and I want it for my show."

A cold hand squeezed Elle's heart. Blake's admonition about others who may know about the painting was taking human shape.

Elle knew she had to protect the painting, but she wasn't sure how. Sitting here in the library, with the painting so close, it seemed like a bizarre game of keep away. "I don't know what painting you are talking about," she replied. "Blake never showed it to me."

"You're lying. Blake wouldn't have kept such a valuable painting a secret from you. I know it's here, and I need it for my show. If you let me exhibit it, it will benefit everyone—you, me, the world. I'd go so far as to say it would expiate the sin Blake committed against me years ago." He stormed over to Elle and grabbed her by the shoulders, shaking her. "Where is it?"

Any form of violence like this reactivated Elle's PTSD by reminding her of her abusive father. She struggled to keep her eyes focused straight ahead, but she was hyperventilating and feared she would pass out.

"You don't even have to sell it—just let me exhibit it, let me introduce it to the world. It would be so appropriate to show her grandfather's painting with Sophia's." He held Elle's shoulders as if she might evaporate.

"Please, I don't know about this painting. I can't help you." She wrestled from Brooks's grasp and made for the door, looking for LeRoi.

"Somehow I don't believe you. I believe you know about the painting, and you even know where it is in this house. That painting could make us both very happy. You could become very rich, and I would have important standing in the art community. I was hoping you would see things my way, but if you don't, I will have no choice but to—"

"Stop it," Elle said, her voice echoing in the quiet of the room. "Why are you threatening me?"

Brooks lowered his voice in tone and volume. "I. Need. The. Painting. This show is *my* masterpiece, and without a substantial showpiece, it will be a failure. Can you understand my position? If this show flops, I will be ruined—financially, professionally, and socially—just as I was ruined when Melanie refused to marry me."

"Why did you arrange for this exhibit without having secured the art? Why did you put yourself in this position?" Elle's question was innocent, but the effect was as if she had stabbed him in the heart.

"You don't understand at all. Once I had Sophia Lockwood's paintings in place, I thought Blake would see the beauty of it— the renowned grandfather, the talented granddaughter—I thought Blake would contribute the painting. I was trying to—"

"—You were trying to pressure him, as you're trying to pressure me?" Elle clenched her fists and took a few deep breaths. "What if I don't know where this painting is?"

"I'll have no choice but to make public the ugly things I have researched about you. You see, I have friends in high places in the NYPD. I held back on ruining Blake's reputation, but I won't hold back anymore. If I'm going to be ruined, so will you. The genteel society of Brandywine Valley would not be happy to know there was a criminal in its midst. Maybe that will motivate you to find the painting."

At that moment, LeRoi appeared at the door. "Have you finished with your meal?"

Brooks replied to LeRoi, while burning his eyes into Elle's. "I really must go now. It's late, and you can sleep on my proposition. However, I will be back tomorrow. We have some unfinished business to complete, right, Ms. *Carson?*"

Elle remained silent, while LeRoi escorted Brooks out.

The man is completely mad. He'll never leave me alone unless he gets the painting. Elle closed her eyes and began saying the rosary, her thumb moving imaginary beads. By the time she got to the third Hail Mary, she was breathing better, and after the tenth, she had formulated a plan. She took her cell phone out of her pocket and pushed a number.

CHAPTER 68

It only took Parrott forty-five minutes to get the search warrant and head out to Alonzo Espinosa's apartment in South Philly. Even at this early hour, the night was inky, and tiny snowflakes landed on Parrott's windshield and melted, forming wet pinpoints.

His stomach growled, and he yearned to be at home with Tonya, eating leftovers, but duty prevailed over pleasure every time, and there was a special pull when the task at hand would most likely solve the case.

He had arranged for the South Philadelphia police to meet him there, as safe searches required at least two people. For one thing, someone had to keep Alonzo out of the way and under control. When he pulled up to the apartment complex, he saw two officers sitting in a cruiser, on the side street next to Alonzo's front door. He climbed out of his car and walked over to introduce himself.

Officers Sims and Jackson seemed friendly enough. Parrott briefed them on Alonzo, his priors, his partial fingerprint on the picture frame. "I'm looking for a jammer. Could be on his person, but probably in a hidey-hole, a drawer, cabinet, or closet. Might also find a face mask, if we're lucky."

Sims replied, "I'll babysit the suspect, while the two of you look around. I'll bring him outside, until you clear the front room. Then we'll stay there, while you do the rest of the apartment. Shouldn't take too long. Not a big place."

Parrott stared at the apartment building, one of four in a row, identical in size. Outdoor lights tried but failed to improve their appearance. The windows and doors were old and weathered, and the paint was peeling. A light went on in the front, first-floor apartment, Alonzo's.

"Appreciate the help, guys. Let's roll." Parrott led the way and pounded on the door. After a minute they heard footsteps, and someone turned on a porch light. Parrott imagined Alonzo's heart racing when he recognized Parrott standing in front of two uniforms.

The door cracked a couple of inches, the amount allowed by a brass chain. "What you guys want?"

Parrott held the search warrant open, so Alonzo could see it. "Alonzo Espinosa, I have a warrant to search your house. Please step outside, so we can conduct the search."

Alonzo unhooked the chain and opened the door wider. He ran his hand through his hair and beard, and his eyes shifted from side to side, as if looking for a place to hide. "Can I get a jacket?"

"We'll get it for you. Tell us where it's at. Anyone else in there besides you?"

"No, I live alone." He stepped aside and held the door open, so the trio could enter. Behind the door was a closet, where a puff jacket hung on the doorknob.

"This the jacket?" When Alonzo nodded, Sims examined it for contraband and, finding none, handed it over. Alonzo stuffed his arms into the coat and zipped it up. He stepped outside onto the porch without another word.

Sims nodded to the others and followed Alonzo out. Parrott and Jackson gloved up. They wasted no time in searching the front room, a twelve by sixteen combination living room and dining room, with a couch, TV, table and four chairs, all having seen better days. The couch pillows and frame yielded more than its share of dirt, food crumbs, loose change, but no jammer. Nothing underneath it either.

Parrott called Sims and Alonzo to come back inside, where it was warmer, stifling, even. The two still weren't chatting. He and Jackson moved on to the kitchen. The jammer would be slightly larger than a pack of cigarettes, so it would easily fit into any of the cabinets, the refrigerator or freezer, or oven. Parrott took one side of the kitchen, and Jackson took the other, but aside from a few groceries, some dirty dishes piled in the sink, some empty beer cans, the kitchen was clean, too.

Next came the bathroom, too small for two. Jackson agreed to take it, while Parrott moved on into the single bedroom. Parrott flipped on the lights and started with the bed, systematically removing one layer of bedding at a time, emptying the pillow cases, sliding his hands under the mattress all around, and peering underneath. He did the same with the rank-smelling pile of clothes in the corner of the room. Nothing remarkable. No signs of a second person living here, either.

Next, he checked the six drawers of a tall dresser. Shirts, underwear, socks. The bottom drawer held miscellaneous items— gloves, caps, two ratty-looking scarves, and, at the very bottom, a knit face mask, black with red-trimmed eye and nose holes. Not, in and of itself, indicative of anything, but possibly used in case there were security cameras at a target. The jammer interfered with the alarm signals, but wouldn't do anything to prevent pictures being taken of the thieves. That there were no cameras at Manderley made the find irrelevant, though.

Moving on to the closet, Parrott slid all of the hangers toward the front, leaving the back third of the closet bare. If something were stowed in a closet, it would typically be there. Two shoe boxes on the floor in a back corner grabbed Parrott's attention. The first had papers—some in Spanish—probably birth certificate, school documents, some newspaper clippings. Interesting, but not what he was searching for.

The second shoe box contained a pistol. Parrott sensed he was getting hotter. He bagged the weapon and put it in his pocket. He ran his hands down the length of every clothing item hanging in the closet, hoping to find the jammer in a pocket or lining, but no luck.

Jackson had finished in the bathroom, and they had run out of rooms to search. Alonzo, still sitting in the front room with Sims, had started talking in Spanish. The only words Parrott could make out were curse words, but he took this as a sign to move along. He wanted to make the arrest, with or without the jammer, but he knew it would be a stronger case with.

Disappointed, Parrott shrugged at Jackson and motioned toward the front room, allowing the officer to go first. As he walked into the sparsely decorated room, he cast his eyes about, looking for potential hiding places. Alonzo was on the couch, still wearing his jacket, arms crossed and muttering to himself.

Parrott held up the bagged pistol and said to Alonzo, "I found this in your closet. I assume it's yours. Do you have a permit for the gun, and do you have an owner's license?"

Alonzo grunted.

Parrott turned to Sims and said, "I've got no interest in the gun. If you guys want the bust on the weapon, it's fine with me."

"Sure, we'll take him in and let our detectives decide what to do." Jackson cuffed him, while Sims started Mirandizing.

Parrott's eyes landed on a potted plant in the corner of the living room. It seemed out of place in this grubby bachelor's apartment, maybe a cutting taken from the grounds at Manderley. Still, it was the only decorative item in the place, and, groundskeeper or not, he didn't make Alonzo to be the houseplant type.

"Hold on a minute, guys," Parrott said. "There's one more place I want to look. Sims, can you and Mr. Espinosa step outside again?"

Alonzo shot Parrott a squinty look, muttering, "*Hijo de puta.*"

When Alonzo and Sims were gone, Parrott said, "Let's dig up this pretty plant. My gut tells me the jammer might be buried here." Jackson held the pot steady while Parrott dug into the loose, dry dirt with his gloved hands. After six or seven handfuls of dirt had been removed from the edges, Jackson was able to lift the plant, roots and all, and place it on the carpet next to the dirt. Parrott dug further, toward the bottom of the pot, until his fingers hit something hard and rectangular. He brushed aside the dirt to reveal a silver and black box, exactly what he was looking for.

Jackson whistled. "Man, you're a genius. I never woulda thought to look in the plant."

Parrott smiled, as he bagged the jammer. "Guess you could say we hit paydirt—literally." Parrott bagged the jammer and put it in his coat pocket. "We can go now. Tell your detective if there's a weapons violation, I'd be grateful to have him charged. When do you think he'd make bond court?"

"Could happen tonight."

"How about slow-walking him through it, so he doesn't go anywhere until tomorrow. I've got him on my theft, but I need some time to get the warrant signed."

"Not a problem, far as I can see. Gimme your card, and I'll call you if there's a wrinkle."

Parrott followed Jackson out, turning off the lights and locking the door behind him. He kept his face impassive as Officer Jackson made the arrest, and Officer Sims cuffed Alonzo and put him in the cruiser.

Parrott's heart was bursting with the same explosive pride he used to get from making winning touchdowns in his days at Syracuse. This time there was no rush of players, slapping him on the back or escorting him off the field, but it was no less satisfying. He had solved the case of the stolen paintings.

CHAPTER 69

If he had been hungry before he went to Alonzo's, Parrott was voracious now, and he abandoned all hope of getting home before midnight. He called Tonya to tell her what was going on, and he looked around for a drive through. He didn't want to get out of the car until he got to the station with the jammer. No sense risking its being lost, damaged, or stolen after all this.

He swung into the Burger King on Christopher Columbus off of I95 and ordered a Whopper, fries, and a shake. While he was waiting to pick it up, he got an incoming call from Elle Carmichael.

"I hope you don't mind m-my calling this late." Her voice sounded timid.

"Not at all. In fact, I was going to call you once I got to the station. We're close to wrapping up the case of the stolen paintings. The thief is your groundskeeper, Alonzo Espinosa."

"Alonzo? But how did he get into the studio?"

"He had a jammer device that bypassed the alarm system. Maybe he picked up a key somewhere, or picked the lock without leaving a trace. Anyway, it's not his first breaking and entering job, and he left a fingerprint on one of the frames, so I'm sure it's him."

"Well, I'm glad he returned the paintings unharmed." Elle paused for a few seconds. "Do you think his sister had anything to do with it?"

"It's possible, but I doubt it. There's no evidence linking her, anyway." Parrott picked up his meal and parked in the lot to eat it. "Sorry if you can hear me chewing. I'm just getting dinner."

"You poor thing. It's already after ten."

Parrott munched on some fries and took a large gulp of the shake. "Which brings me to ask why you're calling."

"I've had an upsetting experience with Rupert Brooks this evening—a long story, and it's not over yet. I was wondering if you could stop by sometime tonight. I know it's late, and I might not be thinking straight, but among other things, I'd like to get a protective order against Brooks."

Parrott set his burger down on the paper wrapper and swallowed. "Did he hurt you? Threaten you?"

"Not really. It'll take a while for me to explain it to you. Mostly I feel some *paintings* are in danger from him. I need to protect them."

Parrott rubbed his eyes. He was looking at a long night's work, even without Elle's request, but he knew she wouldn't have called for something frivolous. Truthfully, the last time he'd been at the Rue Moderne, Brooks had given him the creeps, too. "Tell you what—I'll come by as soon as I take care of the paperwork on Alonzo. An hour or so?"

Elle exhaled. "I'll be waiting with a pot of coffee. LeRoi's gone to bed with the sniffles, so I'll meet you at the door."

"So glad you're here," Elle said, as she opened the door to Parrott at 11:20 p.m. She led him to the breakfast room and offered him a seat at the table where placemats, napkins, and silverware had been set for two. "We could go to the library, but that's where Brooks and I were, and the dirty dishes are still in there." She walked toward the kitchen. "How do you take your coffee?"

"Black is fine," Parrott replied. He was going to need the coffee to stay focused. While he waited, he texted Ton-ya, even though she was probably already asleep.

Elle walked back in with two steaming coffee mugs. She set them down and took her own seat. "I'll try to make this as concise as possible."

"Take your time," Parrott said. "Don't want you to leave out anything important." He tasted the coffee and gave a thumbs up sign." He could work all night, as long as he had strong, black coffee.

"All right. Do you remember when Gary Griffith was here to read Blake's will?"

"Sure do."

"Afterwards, Griffith gave me a letter from Blake. Among other things, Blake wanted me to know about a painting Victor Lockwood had done and given to Blake as a gift. Blake had hidden it away for personal reasons, but after his death, he felt it should be auctioned, so the world could enjoy it."

Parrott nodded. He could see why Rupert Brooks would be interested.

"He gave me clues to its location, and I spent days searching for it, but I didn't find it until today, just after Tonya was here. It is truly a masterpiece, and I intend to follow Blake's instructions."

Questions were rolling around in Parrott's mind, but he didn't want to interrupt. Elle would tell him what she wanted him to know.

"Brooks came over to authenticate the two paintings that had been returned to the studio. I never should have called him to do that, although I knew he was familiar with Blake's work. He was satisfied they were the originals and said he'd put it in writing. Now you've caught the thief, and once I get the authentication, we can proceed with the donation to the National Arts Club. I know Blake would want that."

Elle nodded, as if to herself, and took a sip of coffee. "Brooks and I had supper in the library, and he started in on me about the Sophia Lockwood exhibit. He was insistent about filling the show with Blake's returned paintings, and when I refused, he mentioned the Victor Lockwood."

"He knew about the hidden painting?"

"Yes, he knew all about it, knew Blake had been sitting on it all these years. He said he had asked Blake to let him exhibit it, but Blake refused. Now Blake is gone, he's pressuring me."

"What did you tell him?"

"I said I didn't know anything about the painting, and he called me a liar. He made all sorts of propositions, but they seemed like threats. They made me wish I hadn't found the painting at all."

She shivered. "Really, he was most unpleasant. He told me Blake had ruined his life by instigating the breakup of the engagement between him and Melanie, Blake's sister." With that, Elle began to cry, a quiet, steady cry that reminded Parrott of a summer rain. "I might as well tell you the whole story. The predicament won't make sense to you without it." So in a soft monotone, in this late-night *tete-a-tete*, she revealed Blake's darkest secrets to the detective who had become her friend. She recounted what Blake had told her, and what Brooks had told her—about Lockwood's exploitations, his attachment to Blake. Whenever she mentioned Brooks, she bit her lip.

"Now Brooks thinks he's entitled to the painting. Perhaps not to own it, but to show it, maybe to sell it and get the commission. He's adamant and says he will be back tomorrow. Is there any way I can get a protective order to keep him away from Manderley?"

Elle's story had caused some cylinders to click in Parrott's mind, although he was sure she had held back on something. Now it was his turn. "You and Brooks had this discussion in the library, you say?" When Elle nodded, he said, "Let's go into the library, if you don't mind."

When they reached the library, Parrott walked around, imagining the bitter conversation Elle had had with Brooks. He noticed the table with uneaten food, dirty dishes and silverware, teacups, and it gave him an idea.

"Elle, are these the dishes you and Brooks ate from?"

"Yes, I'm sorry they haven't been cleared yet. LeRoi wasn't feeling well, and I was too upset."

"Can you identify which dishes were yours, and which were Brooks's?"

"Of course." She pointed to hers and then his. "Why do you ask?"

"I'd like to bag them and take them with me this evening, with your permission." Parrott circled the table, thinking. "Also, I'd like for you to show me in this room, what Brooks said and did to you. Where you were at the moment, whether he touched you, and how. If you could sort of act it out for me, it would be helpful."

Parrott went to his car to get evidence bags, which he filled and labelled with Elle's and Brooks's names, respectively. After Elle demonstrated how Brooks had grabbed her by the shoulders, and he had determined how afraid she was of his return, he explained the procedure for applying for an emergency protective order. "We can fill out the paperwork tonight, and it will go into effect on a temporary emergency status, but you will need a Chester County attorney to represent your interests in county court, where a judge will review it. Then it's another forty-eight hours before it goes into full effect."

"I guess I could call Gary Griffith to ask for a referral to a county attorney." She glanced at her watch. "I'll have to wait a couple of hours, though."

"Well, let's get the paperwork started tonight. And make sure LeRoi knows Brooks is not to come inside Manderley under any circumstances."

"I'm so relieved—I can't thank you enough for helping me. I'm going to spend the next few days arranging for transport of the paintings to the destinations suggested by Blake. The sooner I get them off the premises of Manderley, the safer they will be."

It was past one when Parrott took his leave and headed back to the station with the dishes. A text from Tonya said she'd gone to bed around midnight. He kept reviewing what Elle had confided in him about Blake Allmond's past. It answered a lot of questions, but not the one question that annoyed him like a burr between his toes. *What has Elle done in her past life to cause the New York detectives to think she could be a murderer?*

CHAPTER 70

The coffee Elle had served him was wearing off by the time he got back to the station, but he didn't want to drink any more. He put the bagged place settings and teacups in the evidence room. The Alonzo arrest warrant needed to be prepared, and that was top priority. He'd make sure it was submitted by seven a.m. to whatever emergency judge was on duty, this being Saturday. Then he dotted some "i's" and crossed some "t's" on the protective order, and tried to get a few hours' shuteye on the army cot in the utility room. He wanted to call Coleman and Rayburn first thing in the morning, but tomorrow was going to be a busy day, and it would be here in a few short hours. There was no point in going home.

Parrott slept fitfully for five hours amongst the dusty boxes and old gym equipment in the station's utility room. He would've preferred by far, sleeping next to Tonya, even if she'd kicked him during a nightmare. Still, he'd saved time, and he woke up, if not refreshed, at least ready to hit the ground running. A travel toothbrush kit and a change of clothes kept in his office helped.

He put up a pot of coffee, finding a small measure of joy in the fact that he could make it as strong as he liked. It was a few minutes past seven, so he called Tonya. "Hope I'm not waking you."

"No, I'm just waking up Horace and cleaning his cage." She yawned. "Missed you last night."

"Me, too. Sorry I'm not there to take care of the little man, but maybe I'll get home late this afternoon. I'll keep you posted."

"I hope you got some sleep. Twenty-four-hour work days do not healthy detectives make. When I was on the tour of duty, all-nighters were my least favorite part."

Parrott changed the subject before Tonya started thinking too deeply about her tour of duty. "Hey, a question for you, the day of the funeral, did you see any of the car parkers using the bathroom at Manderley?"

"Not that I can think of. Maybe ask LeRoi. He's got a pretty good grasp on everything over there."

"Okay. Listen, I've got to get rolling. The sooner I start, the sooner I can come home. Love you, wife."

"Love you, too, detective. Good luck with everything."

By a stroke of good fortune, Judge Manetti was on emergency duty, so Parrott didn't have much to do to bring him up-to-date. By seven-thirty a.m., Parrott had the judicial signature on the warrant for the arrest of Alonzo Espinosa, and he faxed it to South Philly before the appearance in bond court. South Philly would, no doubt, send Alonzo's weapon for ballistics to see if it matched any open cases, but hopefully Parrott's warrant would give the district attorney a reason to dismiss the unlawful use of weapon charge and send Alonzo off to Brandywine. If the gun turned up dirty, they could always come after him there.

By nine-thirty, Alonzo's UUW case was dismissed, and he was ready to be picked up by West Brandywine. On the way to pick him up, Barton drove the cruiser, and Parrott rode shotgun.

As he drove, Randy asked, "Think this guy'll get off easy since he returned the paintings?"

"Interesting question. *He* probably would've been better off not returning them, since the partial fingerprint is how we nailed him. Of course, it's better for Elle and the National Arts Club that the paintings are back. Now they can go where Allmond intended, and the sentencing will probably take that into account."

Parrott rode some minutes in silence. There were only two questions on his mind: was Espinosa's sister an accessory to the theft, and had he used the bathroom at Manderley the day of the funeral reception. Asking Espinosa would do no good. Parrott already knew the answers to both questions would be no. *One thing at a time.*

South Philly had no problem releasing Alonzo into Parrott's custody. His theft charge trumped their weapons charge. Parrott thanked Jackson and Sims again for helping with the search and arrest, and Barton cuffed the prisoner and put him into the back seat.

On the way back to the station in Coatesville, Alonzo kept his mouth shut. In Parrott's experience, guys with priors tended not to talk much. They realized talking could only get them into more trouble. Parrott had no problem with that. He rode along quietly, his arm resting across the top of the seat, his body angled so he could watch the prisoner.

About fifteen minutes into the ride, Parrott said to Barton, "You know, we may not be keeping Alonzo with us any longer than they kept him at South Philly."

"Oh, yeah?" Randy played along. "Why not?"

Parrott watched Alonzo's face. "NYPD may arrest him for the murder of Blake Allmond. They've felt all along the theft and the murder were related. If they can prove it, they'll have precedence."

Alonzo's eyes opened wide, and his jaw clenched so hard, Parrott thought he could hear it crunch.

"A lot will depend on whether Alonzo's fingerprints or DNA is anywhere in a certain bathroom at Manderley. Of course, that's not our case, so I don't know much about it, but if he offed Blake Allmond, I guarantee you they'll lock him up and throw away the key."

Alonzo grunted and sputtered. "For what, man, going to the john? I didn't kill nobody. So what if I used the bathroom the day of the funeral? Allmond was already dead."

Parrott exchanged glances with Barton and grinned. He looked back at Alonzo, who stared out of the window with a stony expression on his face. Parrott replied, "Very true. Allmond was already dead."

When they got back to the station, Parrott let Barton take care of Alonzo. The day was slipping by too quickly, and Parrott's eyes were starting to feel gritty. He wanted to call the New York detectives. He had a feeling they were going to be interested in what he had to say, but first he stopped by Chief Schrik's office on the off chance he would be there on a Saturday. One of the reasons Parrott and Schrik got along so well, he was sure, was because Parrott kept his supervisor informed, especially when something was going on outside of the sphere of West Brandywine.

Schrik's office was dark, though, and Parrott felt this couldn't wait. He strode into his own office, shut the door, and called Detective Rayburn's number.

It took Rayburn several rings to answer, but when she did, she sounded friendly. "Detective Parrott. What's happening at your end of the world?"

"I've got some news, but before I tell you, I've got a question about your case, if you don't mind." Hearing no objection, he went on. "Have your forensics turned up any DNA?"

"Funny you should ask. Nothing on the gun, nothing on the body. Perp must've worn gloves. Maybe even vacuumed afterward and taken the bag. But we got lucky with the outside glass wall of the shower."

"A print?"

"No, not unless you call the mark of a forehead a print. Carrying Allmond's dead weight must have been taxing, and the guy was sweating. His forehead must have touched the glass without his noticing. But he left a calling card, and the DNA didn't match Allmond's."

"I noticed you said, 'He.' Have you ruled out Elle Carmichael then?"

"On the contrary, we still like her for masterminding. DNA is definitely male, and she's too petite to have dragged the body, but that doesn't mean she didn't plan the whole thing."

"Well, here's why I called. We've arrested the perp in the art theft. Guy left a partial on one of the frames when he returned the paintings, and I found the jammer he'd used to get into the studio. Name's Alonzo Espinosa. He was a groundskeeper at Allmond's home."

"Espinosa? Is he related to Veronica Espinosa who dates Allmond's nephew?"

"One and the same. She's his sister."

"Yeah. We interviewed her at Lyons Bank. She put her nose into Allmond's financial business prior to the murder. We knew she was shady, but we came up dry."

"Anyway, Alonzo and the sister were parking cars at the house the day of the funeral reception. Either of them could've sneaked the gun into the bathroom, but that's not what I'm thinking."

"Go on."

"What do you know about Rupert Brooks, the owner of the Kennett Square art gallery, Rue Moderne?"

Rayburn inhaled, and, when she replied, her voice was wary. "What should I know?"

"He's a long-time friend of the family, bears a grudge against Allmond for breaking up his engagement to Allmond's sister. He pressured Allmond to give him a painting to exhibit in a New York show, and Allmond refused, so now he's pressuring Elle. He was at the funeral reception—could've sneaked the gun in to frame Elle."

Rayburn laughed. "Sounds like you've been working our case just as much as yours."

Parrott thought of the chief's admonitions. "Not intentionally. Just a lot of crossover. Last night Brooks frightened Elle, and she asked me to get a protective order against him. When I went over to interview her, I saw dishes and tea cups they had used. I bagged and labeled them just in case, and I've got 'em here in evidence. You interested?"

"You've got DNA from Elle and Brooks?" Rayburn laughed again. "Yeah, we'd be interested. I'll send an evidence technician to pick them up. Maybe the two of them collaborated to get rid of Allmond."

"You've really got it in for Elle, and I just can't see it. What do you know about her past that I don't know?"

"I'll tell you. It was a juvie incident, here in New York, some years ago, and under a different name. Records are sealed, so we can't use it in court, but we got access. Basically, she set fire to the garage while her father was in it. Old man died. She was charged, tried, and acquitted. Justifiable circumstances. She might seem holier than thou, but someone who has that much anger and hate might have acted out again."

Parrott's stomach turned at the thought of Elle's having gone through so much as a kid, but he remained convinced she wasn't the killer type. Whatever justifiable circumstances there were, they probably constituted the "traumatic events" she had alluded to when talking with Tonya. Living with a person who had PTSD had altered his perspective. Also, there was nothing in this case that caused him to think there'd been anything but a loving relationship between Elle and Allmond.

"Well, I'd bet my last paycheck Elle isn't collaborating with Rupert Brooks on anything. Least of all, murder."

CHAPTER 71

Saturday was the busiest day of the week at the Rue Moderne, which was why Rupert Brooks didn't go back to Manderley first thing in the morning. When he returned, he knew he could persuade Elle to let him show the Victor Lockwood. He knew she was lying when she said she didn't know anything about it. The painting was too valuable for Blake not to have mentioned it in his will. Lockwoods were selling in the multiple million-dollar range, and that one, beautiful as it was, would bring glory and fame to whomever showed it. The mere thought sent Brooks's mind reeling.

He had only seen the painting once, before Lockwood gave it to Blake. But once was enough to burn its evanescence into his memory. It was that good. Over the years, Brooks had urged Blake to sell it. Once they'd argued so much over it they had gone several years without speaking. To Brooks, the painting was a masterpiece, deserving of its opportunity to be admired, studied, emulated, even. To Blake it was a reminder of things best forgotten. Brooks had finally given up on pressing Blake. He had been satisfied with showing and selling Blake's own paintings and some of Elle's, and he had even stopped lusting after the hidden Lockwood.

Then Sophia Lockwood had appeared on the Brandywine art scene. Her grandfather's talent, filtered through her father, and running in her arteries like ordinary blood, shone through in her work. Sophia was only twenty, but already she had a body of work that glowed and shimmered and would draw attention to Brandywine. Brooks was so enamored of her work and so flattered she had given him the first look at it, he had rushed to convince the New York gallery owners to exhibit with him.

It was a perfect segue to re-opening talks with Blake about the grandfather's painting. Brooks had been confident. Surely enough time had passed by now. Surely Blake would realize that showing and selling the painting would be of a huge benefit, not only to him, but to the art world as a whole. When Blake had invited him over for drinks and dinner in Gramercy Park, it was the perfect setting.

Brooks hadn't counted on Blake to be so stubborn, so impervious to reason. It hadn't gone well, to say the least. And now here it was, weeks until the show, and he was left trying to fill prime spots. He simply must have the Victor Lockwood. He had come too far to turn back now.

If yesterday's threats hadn't worked, another brilliant plan for convincing Elle had come to him in his sleep last night. After he closed the shop for the day, he would go to Manderley and make her an offer she couldn't refuse.

Once Alonzo was in custody in Brandywine, Parrott turned his attention to making sure the protective order was set to be served to Rupert Brooks. It wouldn't take effect legally until then. It was a good feeling to wrap up a case, but solving the theft still left Parrott feeling as if he'd left a pot boiling on the stove's back burner.

NYPD was close to solving the Allmond murder, too, but the things Rayburn had told him about Elle were sticking in his mind like fresh-made taffy. Could it be true Elle had killed her father?

Parrott picked up the phone and called Tonya. When she answered, he could hear water running in the background. "Washing dishes?" he asked.

"No, I'm giving Horace a shower. You know how he loves it."

Parrott could hear the flapping of wings and the chirping that sounded like, "Oh, boy."

"Sorry to interrupt all the fun, but I have a question about Elle."

He could hear the smile in Tonya's voice. "I don't know if I can answer, Detective. Conflict of interest with my friendship, you know."

"You wound me. I thought our vows were to love, honor and obey."

"I must have missed the obey part. What's the question?"

"Where did Elle grow up, do you know?"

"That all? Queens. Lived there until she entered the convent in Philadelphia and started working with Don Guanella. Why do you ask?"

"Can't answer. Conflict of interest." He chuckled. "Thanks for the info, and pet Horace for me—after his shower, of course."

Parrott spent the better part of the next half hour searching the internet for fires with fatalities in New York three decades ago. It turned out to be easier than he'd thought, especially when he used the keyword, "Carson." The first mention was in the *Queens Times*, a two-inch article headlined, "Garage Fire Claims Life of Harry Carson, Auto Mechanic, 43." Once he had a name, he searched for the obituary. Short and to the point, but the list of survivors were Harry's parents, Phyllis and Harold Carson, wife Edith, and daughters, Estelle and Charlotte. It was enough to convince him Rayburn's story about Elle had, at least, a germ of truth. He'd been hoping for something different.

He still didn't make Elle for the murder of Blake Allmond, but he didn't like it that Rayburn and Coleman had her in their sights, either. In his opinion, it was distracting them from the real murderer.

At three p.m., a tall, slender man wearing a wool-lined London Fog coat and dark sunglasses entered the Rue Moderne. He didn't look like the typical Saturday afternoon customer. His eyes, as he gazed about the front room, failed to stop on any of the elegant objects of art, a sure sign he wasn't shopping.

An odd sensation came over Brooks as he watched via the security camera in the back of the store. The two nearly collided as they met at the door to the second room.

"My apologies," Brooks said, brushing the sleeves of his sport jacket. There was a distinct odor of tobacco emanating from the visitor. "How may I assist you?"

"Are you Rupert Brooks?" the man asked, his voice laced with a heavy New Jersey accent. His arms were crossed over his buttoned coat.

"Yes. And you are?"

The man uncrossed his arms and unbuttoned his coat. He pulled a rectangular envelope from his waistband, as if he had done this a million times. Handing it to Brooks, he said, "This is an order of protection, and you have now been served." He turned on one heel and headed back toward the front door, without waiting for Brooks's response.

Dumbfounded, Brooks muttered, "What the hell is this?" He ripped the perforated strip of the envelope and stared at the document. He couldn't imagine why he was being ordered to stay away from Elle Carmichael, LeRoi Hawkins, and Manderley, but as he read the words, his stomach filled with a thick, bitter syrup. He knew one thing, though. He wasn't going to let a piece of paper keep him away from the Victor Lockwood. As soon as he closed the shop, he would go talk sense into Elle Carmichael, order or no order.

Parrott had spent a few minutes in the afternoon filling Chief Schrik in by telephone on Alonzo's arrest and the status of his communication with NYPD about Elle and Brooks. Schrik was in bed with a sore throat and fever, but he was delighted to hear the theft was closed.

"You're not getting too involved with the New York case now, are you?" he asked, congestion obviously not changing his attitude any.

"No worries," Parrott replied. "Whatever I've done, I don't think they'll complain."

After he hung up, he cleared his desk of paperwork that had accumulated over the past few weeks. The fatigue from lack of sleep had permeated his brain, despite several cups of coffee, and he was more than ready to call it a day. At 4:45 he grabbed his dirty clothes and started to turn off the light in his office, but he stopped at the sound of his cell phone. Dropping the clothes on the desk, he glanced at the screen—it was Detective Rayburn.

"Sorry to bother," she said, "but the sample you gave us from Brooks was a match to the perspiration on Allmond's shower. We lucked out. Our best lab tech was on duty, and there was a lull in his job queue today. Thought I'd give you a courtesy call that we're on our way to Brandywine. Can you round up a judge to authorize the warrant, and then go with us to make the arrest?"

Sunshine replaced the fatigue in Parrott's head, and he punched the air with a fist. "I sure can. That's great news." He imagined sharing the news with Tonya, maybe stopping to buy a bottle of champagne on the way home, now realizing that might be hours away.

Parrott gave Rayburn the necessary information and offered to meet her and Coleman at Judge Manetti's. "I'll call you back if he isn't available." Then he realized something. "So the DNA matched to Brooks. Does that rule out Elle?" He held his breath, waiting for the answer.

Rayburn's laugh was low and a little hoarse. "You know we're going to look for collusion, Parrott. We'll try to get Brooks to flip on Allmond's girlfriend."

Parrott called Manetti back. "Hope I'm not wearing out my welcome, Judge. I wouldn't be calling if it weren't super important." He explained the situation, the same person served by the injunction, the DNA, and the NYPD warrant.

Manetti laughed. "You've just given me the excuse I need not to go to my wife's charity auction. Probably saved me a couple of C-notes, too. C'mon over whenever you want."

Parrott threw his clothes into the trunk of his car and headed toward Manetti's. He'd have an even better reason to celebrate by the time he got home. He was pulling into Manetti's neighborhood when his cell phone rang again. It was Elle.

"I didn't know who else to call. Is the protective order in effect? Rupert Brooks pulled up into the driveway, and he's banging on the front door. What should I do?"

"Don't let him in, no matter what he says or does. Let me handle it. I'm on my way now." Parrott took a deep breath and exhaled, adrenalin pumping. Before he put the car in gear, he called Rayburn. "Brooks is at Manderley, despite the order of protection, and I'm on my way to apprehend him."

"Thanks for the heads up, Parrott. We're a couple or three hours out. Be sure you have backup. He's dangerous and sounds like he may be desperate."

Thankful for the Bluetooth, Parrott called for backup, then called Judge Manetti back, while switching directions and heading for Manderley. He explained the circumstances. "Sounds like you might be able to go to that auction after all."

"No, thanks. I'll wait here till you get your guy. Pat's already gone to the affair without me, and I'm relaxing in my chair. You be careful out there."

Parrott chewed on the irony of it all. Everyone was warning him to be careful as he dealt with a suspect—and this wasn't even his case

CHAPTER 72

Darkness and patches of fog were enveloping Brandywine Valley, and as Parrott drove up the winding drive to Manderley, he thought, for all its magnificence and rich history, it wore a cloak of sadness. As he pulled into the circular driveway, he parked behind a black Lexus with tinted windows, probably Brooks's. The man was nowhere in sight. Had Elle or LeRoi let him in, or had he broken in?

His cell phone was down to one bar, the victim of his having worked for two days straight without charging it. He used it, though, to call Elle. "I'm outside in front. What's the status?"

She whispered. "I don't know. He pounded on the door for what seemed like hours. LeRoi and I moved upstairs. We didn't answer the door and didn't want him to see us through a window. We thought he might figure no one was home and leave, but no. He kept yelling and ringing the bell and banging on the knocker. Then, about five minutes ago, everything got quiet. But his car's still here, so he must be here, too.

He kept saying, 'All I want is to show the painting. If you let me exhibit it, I promise I'll leave you alone.' Maybe I should just give it to him. Nothing is worth all this harassment."

The fear in Elle's voice was palpable, and Parrott recognized it. It wasn't unlike the tone in Tonya's voice the night she'd driven off and run into a deer. "Listen to me, Elle. This is important. Rupert Brooks is a dangerous man, and he is not to be trusted. Do not even think about giving him the painting. Do not open your door. Do not engage in a conversation with him. You and LeRoi stay upstairs and away from the windows. You need to be smart and strong, and you'll get through this."

"Okay. I'm listening, and thank—"

"—Save thanks for later. I'm hanging up now. I need to save cell phone juice. Hang in there." He disconnected and stuffed the phone low in his pocket and removed the .40 caliber Baby Glock he wore at his waist. He checked to make sure it was loaded and removed the safety. He hoped he wouldn't have to use it. Firepower was an occasional necessity in this line of work, but brainpower was even more important.

He was probably fifteen minutes away from the arrival of backup from West Brandywine, but right now it was just he and Brooks, and a lot of wide open spaces and nooks and crannies of a few outbuildings.

He tried to think like the art dealer, desperate for a painting and furious at having been denied something he considered himself entitled to. When pounding on the door hadn't done any good, what would he do next? Try to find the painting himself?

Parrott had a feeling Brooks was at the studio, intent on breaking in. It was as good a place as any to search for him, so Parrott took off for the back of the house, staying as close to the structure as possible, so as not to be spotted first. Parrott's youth and athleticism gave him an advantage over Brooks, who was more than twice Parrott's age, but an unstable person sometimes drew extraordinary strength. Parrott wouldn't take anything for granted.

As he approached the groundskeepers' building and then the studio, he thought of how much had transpired since his interview of Alonzo yesterday. The fronts of the two buildings were quiet and dark. Parrott slipped between the two buildings, using one to cover him. He ran toward the back of the studio and rounded the corner, still seeing nothing out of the ordinary. When he rounded the next corner, though, the sound of footsteps on gravel assaulted his ears.

He kept going, and when he rounded the next corner, he was back at the front of the studio. Peering into the window was a tall, thin man in slacks and a sport jacket. As he drew closer, he recognized the art dealer's eyeglasses on a chain, resting on his chest.

The light over the entrance to the studio clicked on, probably on a timer, and it bathed Brooks in an unflattering yellowish glow.

"Detective Parrott," Brooks called out, "perhaps you can assist me. It seems no one is at home, and I came to get a painting I'm going to exhibit in New York. I need to—" His voice broke off, perhaps because he saw the gun Parrott had fixed on him.

"You aren't supposed to be here, Brooks. You've been served with an order of protection." He waved the gun toward the main house. "I think we'd better go to the front of the house now."

"I'm not leaving without the painting. I'm not here to hurt anyone, but I must have the painting." His voice was pitched higher than usual, the ravings of a madman.

"You're not making sense, Brooks. You can't take a painting nobody has given you. You can't be here. Let's go to the front of the house now." Hopefully, by the time he could get Brooks to the front of the house, there would be help to subdue him.

"You don't understand. You just hold that gun on me and think you can tell me what to do. Either I get into this studio and get my painting, or I *will* cause mayhem. Maybe I'll set fire to it." Brooks pulled a cigarette lighter out of his pocket and flicked it on, waving it around in the evening like a child with a sparkler.

Parrott didn't think a cigarette lighter could set a building on fire without an accelerant, but he didn't want to stick around to find out. "Put that down and let's talk, Brooks. I understand you need a painting, but why does it have to be a specific painting? Surely it's not worth going to jail, is it?" The more he babbled, the less, it seemed, Brooks was listening.

Brooks screamed, "You don't understand. That painting is extraordinary. It belongs in my show." So agitated, he moved about in a macabre dance and finally shut the lighter off and took off into the darkness at a run.

With over forty acres of land, there was no telling where he would end up, but Parrott didn't want to shoot him. Instead, he fired a warning shot into the air, yelling for Brooks to stop. He considered running after him, but now it was dark, and there could be all sorts of unseen dangers out there. He knew where to find Brooks, even if he and the New York detectives had to wait until tomorrow—his car was here, and he wouldn't go far.

For a few minutes, he could hear the swishing of Brooks's feet through the grassy lawn as he ran toward the next farm, several miles away. Then he heard nothing for another minute. Aiming to turn around and go back to the house, he heard a long, high-pitched scream, coming from the same direction Brooks had run toward. It sounded like a wounded animal.

By this time, Randy Barton was running toward Parrott with flashlight waving, and Parrott had the feeling of being in the center of a fourth down, all or nothing, play. Parrott waved in the direction of the screaming. "That way. About two minutes away before something happened to make him yell. Bring the flashlight, and let's go."

"Is he armed?" Barton asked, catching up to Parrott and moving ahead at a light jog.

"Not unless you call a cigarette lighter a weapon. He's crazed, though. No telling what he'll do when he sees us ganging up on him—if he's still alive, that is." Parrott didn't want to get too far ahead of himself.

The flashlight made a pattern of arcs as law enforcement chased prey, most importantly, keeping their footing sure. Parrott couldn't imagine how Brooks had done it in the dark. Now there was moaning straight on. They slowed their pace and focused the flashlight on the ground ahead.

At first the globe of light picked up a body in slacks and a sport coat, lying on its side and writhing in pain. No apparent cause—no blood, no other animals, no obstruction of any kind. Guns drawn, they approached.

Parrott took the lead. "Brooks, are you conscious? What's happened?"

More moaning, and a flashlight on the face showed Brooks gritting his teeth and squeezing his eyes shut.

"It's a ha-ha," Barton said, running his hands along the foot-tall invisible fence. "There are tons of these out here in the country. Built to keep cows corralled without messing up the landscape views. I've tumbled over a few in my time, too."

Barton shone the light along Brooks's body, searching for the wound, and finding it. His right leg was broken and angulated awkwardly.

"He must've hit that wall with a lot of speed—either that, or his bones are weak. He's not going to be able to walk on that.

Better call EMS." Parrott took out his cell phone to make the call, but the power bar was on red now. "Can you make the call?" he asked Barton.

He squatted next to Brooks and spoke in a matter-of-fact tone. "Brooks, we're calling EMS to take you to the hospital. You ran into a wall, and looks like you've broken your leg pretty badly. Also, you are under arrest for violating the restraining order placed on you. You have the right to remain silent..."

Things started moving quickly then. Barton remained with Brooks and accompanied him to the hospital in the ambulance, where he would babysit him until he could be arrested on the second warrant. Parrott ran back to the house.

Parrott tried to use his cell phone to call Elle, but the power indicator was on red, and he couldn't make the call. Cursing himself for not keeping his phone charged, he dashed to his car and grabbed the charger from the glove box. He started the car and hooked the phone up. Then he called Elle. She picked it up on the first ring.

"Parrott? What's going on?"

"You can relax now. Brooks is under arrest for violating the injunction. He's lying out there on the grounds, waiting for EMS to come get him. He's got a bad break in his leg."

"He must've stumbled over the ha-ha fence," she replied.

"How did you know that?" Parrott asked.

"It just occurred to me. Alonzo and Manuel built that fence a few days ago, the day the rest of the groundskeepers had their DNA tested."

The irony was not lost on Parrott. By evading the DNA test, Alonzo had helped apprehend Blake Allmond's killer.

Parrott had held back on telling Elle that Brooks was also the murderer. He hadn't wanted to frighten her even more when Brooks was trying to gain access to Manderley. He also had wanted to tell her face-to-face, but it was getting late, and he needed to keep moving. "There's something you need to know—and we can talk about it more later—but Rupert Brooks is going to be charged with Blake's murder. His DNA was found on the shower in the Gramercy Park apartment, and he also must have been the one who planted the gun in your bathroom the day of the funeral."

Elle took the news with amazing aplomb. "That doesn't surprise me."

The rest was mechanics. Judge Manetti signed the warrant. When Rayburn and Coleman showed up, Parrott accompanied them to the Brandywine Hospital, where Brooks's leg had been casted by the doctors and his hands cuffed by Barton. He had chosen to remain silent, but that might have been more from the pain medication than good sense. Parrott made the arrest for murder, and transferred Brooks to the West Brandywine jail, awaiting extradition to New York.

The exhilaration of wrapping up a case felt something like Parrott imagined opening a bottle of champagne inside one's body might feel. Pleasant tingles radiated inside him, doubled, because there were two cases in the books. It was two-thirty a.m. by the time everyone dispersed from the hospital, and now Parrott sensed the utter exhaustion that came from lack of sleep. His eyes burned, his legs wobbled, and his head felt fuzzy. Three words repeated themselves in his head as he drove home, and they had nothing to do with theft or murder. They were—home, bed, and Tonya.

CHAPTER 73

Parrott and Tonya stayed in bed until almost noon, when she got up to fix some bacon and eggs, and he called Chief Schrik. Barton had already completed the paperwork and given Schrik the run-down, and Parrott didn't have much to add. "I might go in for a few minutes later today." He yawned. "Catching up on my sleep."

"It's Sunday, Parrott. Stay home and relax. You've more than earned it." Schrik's voice had that timbre of a proud papa. "You won't miss anything much, unless you have a burning desire to say bye-bye to Brooks. His lawyer convinced him to waive extradition. He's being moved in a couple of hours."

Parrott declined the honor and hung up. He put on his terrycloth bathrobe and padded into the kitchen, where he uncovered Horace's cage and gave the little guy some attention. Then he sidled up to Tonya at the stove and nuzzled her neck.

"After breakfast, let's go back to bed."

"I'll have to consult my busy schedule." She slid the eggs onto plates that already had buttered toast and crispy bacon on them.

"You've gotten pretty smooth with cooking one-handed."

"The better to feed you with, my dear," she replied, giving him a long kiss. "Now eat, before it gets cold."

As they finished eating, the landline rang, and Elle's name showed on the caller ID. When Parrott put her on speakerphone, she said, "Oh, you're at home. I didn't expect to catch you, but I didn't want to call too early."

"You're fine. How are you doing today?"

"I'm grateful. It's like coming out of a dark cave and seeing the first glimmers of light in days. Of course, I miss Blake. I'll never stop missing him for the rest of my life. But now I can honor his wishes and continue to take care of things the way he would want me to." She paused, and Parrott imagined she might be saying a prayer.

"Anyway, the reason for my call is this. Now the case is over, can you and Tonya come here for dinner? Fern is cooking a special meal, and LeRoi is feeling better, so I thought we could celebrate. Seven o'clock?"

Parrott gave a little shrug and looked at Tonya. Together they said, "Sure."

Before they went to Manderley for dinner, Parrott called Detective Rayburn. "I hear Brooks is on his way to the Big Apple. Mind giving me an update?"

"Sure. We've got Brooks every whichway. His DNA turned up on the grip of the pistol, too."

"What about your theory he was working with Elle Carmichael?" Parrott held his breath.

"Nothing to substantiate it at this point. We've checked phone records, emails. Both his and hers. You may be right about her after all."

Parrott felt like he had after making a fourth quarter touchdown, but he kept his voice even. "Sometimes gut instinct pans out, and sometimes it doesn't. Anyway, I'm glad you got your killer."

"Thanks, in no small part, to you. If you ever need a favor—"

"—The offer is mutual."

Fern's dinner menu was Thanksgiving, part deux. Beef tenderloin, potatoes au gratin, artichoke bottoms stuffed with petite peas in lemon butter, Brussels sprouts with walnuts, and a chocolate-raspberry-whipped cream cake for dessert.

Throughout dinner the conversation had been about art, Manderley, the Allmond family—nothing heavy or sad—but after dinner, when LeRoi excused himself to clear the table, Elle looked at Parrott and said, "I know the New York detectives suspected me of killing Blake. If it weren't for you, I might be sitting in some jail, instead of Brooks. It was the DNA from the teacups you gave them that gave them the match, right?"

"Yes, I think so, but it seemed to me you were never a serious suspect. Beyond the fact that you inherited the most, there wasn't much to go on."

"No, don't forget about the gun in my bathroom, and then there was my past—" Elle's voice croaked the last word, and she looked down at her lap.

Tonya filled the silence that followed. "We love you, Elle, no matter what happened in the past."

"I want to tell you about it. Confession is good for the soul, and besides, I want you to understand why the NYPD suspected me, as they did.

When I was a kid, I had a sister named Charlotte. She was three years older, much prettier, and the sweetest person you could ever meet. She was also mentally handicapped. Despite being younger, I don't remember a time when I didn't feel responsible for my sister. I helped her do everything. I spent lots of time with her. I really loved her, and she loved me.

As we got older, there were times I found myself defending her, protecting her. It made me feel strong and capable. Our mother was a quiet woman. I felt later Mother's personality had been subdued by having a handicapped daughter. The worry and required energy from that took its toll on her, but also our father was demanding and demeaning. When we were about thirteen and ten, Dad started coming home loud, pushy, and drunk."

Parrott cringed inside. He knew numerous versions of this story from people in his own neighborhood, growing up, and he also knew from his conversation with Detective Rayburn how this particular story would end. He glanced at Tonya, whose face was fixed on Elle's, and whose eyes were shiny.

"I won't bore you with the details, but Dad needed someone to push around, someone who wouldn't push back, and, after Mother, Charlotte was an easy target. He'd yell at her and shove her, sometimes causing bruises and scrapes. Charlotte wouldn't talk back to him, but I would, every time.

A few years went by, and while I was at school or out of the house, Charlotte wasn't. One day I came home to find my sister bruised and bloodied, and that day I learned my dad had found a new way to abuse her. I was afraid to report this. If child protective agencies learned about it, they would take us away, and maybe separate us by putting Charlotte in a group home.

I thought I could bully my dad into stopping, but nothing I did made a difference. Finally, when I was thirteen, I came home from school to find Charlotte with a black eye and a long cut down the side of her face. Her arm was in a sling, too.

I went ballistic. I wanted to hurt Dad the way he was hurting my sister. I ran into the garage, looking for trouble, and I found it. His toolkit had a book of matches in it, and there was a can of gasoline he kept for the lawn mower. I wasn't thinking, just acting in a mean, vengeful stupor. I poured gasoline all over the place and set the garage on fire."

Tonya gasped, and she looked at Parrott, as if for help to breathe. He reached for her hand and held it, tight in both of his.

"Everything that happened then is a blur. Dad ran into the garage, trying to save his car and his tools. They meant more to him than his family. The flames reached the gas tank and exploded, killing him instantly."

"You poor thing," Tonya said, letting go of Parrott's hands to grab Elle's.

"I was charged with murder, but I was a juvenile. When it went to trial, the judge ruled not guilty, due to mitigating circumstances. The record was supposed to have been sealed, but somehow the police found it. Anyway, the guilt is with me always—nothing can take that away."

Tonya asked, "What happened to Charlotte?"

"She died before her nineteenth birthday, and Mother died the next summer."

"So you were sixteen years old and all alone in the world?" Tonya wiped at a tear.

Elle smiled, what seemed to Parrott to be the smile of a saint, pained, but patient, and other-worldly. "We are never all alone in the world, my dear. All we need do is reach out to help others, and we will be helped, ourselves. I'd always been fascinated by the work of the Don Guanella religious orders — the sisters of the Daughters of St. Mary of Providence and the priests and brothers of the Servants of Charity — to work with children with physical and intellectual disabilities. After the fire, Charlotte went to a day program at their facility for girls and women. They treated her with the kindness and love she deserved."

"And that's the order you joined?"

"Yes, it seemed like the best way for me to live the rest of my life, dedicated to serving God's children, children like Charlotte. I was able to use my talent for art to reach them." She sighed and wrung her hands. "And I think you know the rest. I hope this story doesn't make you hate me."

Parrott hesitated for a few seconds before speaking, and when he did, his baritone voice was subdued. "I'm no authority on what constitutes murder from a spiritual standpoint, but from a legal standpoint, you're not guilty of murder any more than a policeman who kills someone in the line of duty. You were a child, but even if you hadn't been, your intent was to punish your father, not to kill him. The fact you were acquitted tells you it wasn't murder."

In a cheery tone, Tonya said, "How about we change the subject? Have you had time to think about your immediate plans? When will the classes start up again?"

"I'm glad you asked. I think we can start classes again next Wednesday. It'll be good for me to get back into the studio and set up the lessons. I may start a painting, too. I've got a few ideas for a portrait of Blake to hang in the library."

Elle stood up and stretched. "Speaking of the library, I have something to show you in there. Let's go."

The lights in the library were on, but the door to the hall was closed, so Tonya and Parrott had no idea what they were about to see. After talking so much after dinner, Elle gave no preliminary explanation. She just opened the door and motioned for them to enter before her.

Tonya walked in first, so she was the first to see the back of the framed painting, resting on a large easel. She led the way into the room and around the easel, where she could see the painting itself, and she gasped.

Parrott took in the masterpiece, and it was as if he had swallowed it whole. It filled his brain with color and composition, but it filled his heart with something else. He was reminded of a quote by Andrew Wyeth he'd seen at the Brandywine River Museum. "One's art goes as far and as deep as one's love goes."

Tonya walked around the painting, admiring it from different angles. "This is magnificent," she said finally. "This must be the painting Rupert Brooks wanted so badly—"

"—So badly, he killed Blake. When he couldn't get Blake to let him exhibit it, he killed him and started working on me." Elle began to lose her composure, but she took a deep breath and closed her eyes, then crossed herself. "You asked me a few minutes ago what my plans were. I've had someone at Sotheby's agree to come evaluate it. I'm going to transfer the two paintings of Blake's to the National Arts Club straight away, and I'm going to auction this painting through one of the large brokers, just as Blake suggested. As beautiful as it is, it holds bad karma for me and this house. Victor Lockwood's masterpiece needs to be outside of these walls, where the world can appreciate it."

EPILOGUE

Rupert Brooks's exhibit of Sophia Lockwood's paintings went on without its organizer. Somehow the other gallery owners found enough works of art to fill in the gaps, and, thanks to great publicity in the *New Yorker* and the *Times*, it was well-attended. Elle went in with Caro and John E. Campbell, who purchased one of Sophia's charming landscapes for their dining room.

Alonzo Arturo Espinosa, an excellent groundskeeper, but a sloppy art thief, was convicted of felony theft and sentenced to three years in prison. His prior record hurt him, but the fact he'd returned the paintings helped him in the sentencing phase of his trial. His sister, Veronica, testified as a character witness, but the testimony of an unemployed relative did little to convince the jury of his innocence.

Because Blake Allmond's murder was a high profile case, and because the evidence against Brooks was iron-clad, his attorney advised Brooks to plead guilty to first degree murder in hopes of reducing his sentence from life imprisonment without parole to a twenty-to-twenty-five-year sentence. The Manhattan District Attorney had received blessings from both Elle and Alexander to make the deal. If he lived long enough, Brooks would be more than eighty years old when he got out.

The Rue Moderne was sold, and its assets used to pay for Brooks's defense. The new owners changed the name to The Valley Gallery and broadened the inventory to include jewelry and other craft items.

Alexander earned "A's" in both of his college classes, so he signed up for two more in the summer semester. He and Wren were frequent visitors at Manderley, where they enjoyed Fern's cooking and Elle's company.

Gary Griffith and Cecil Pennington, Blake's lifelong friends, helped Elle manage the estate. They put her in touch with competent financial planners and other professionals, but they all agreed she was one strong, clear-minded individual, down-to-earth and sure-footed. Griffith assisted her with a consignment contract with Sotheby's to auction the Victor Lockwood. The painting had been appraised for seventy-five million dollars, based on the prices other Lockwoods had fetched in the past, the novelty of its discovery so long after it was painted, and recent auctions of paintings by other American artists. Elle couldn't fathom that much money being paid for a single painting, but she hoped the painting would end up being cherished, wherever it was hung.

The evening of the auction at Sotheby's, Elle met Gary and Kim Griffith, and together they went to the seventh-floor saleroom on York Avenue. She didn't have to be there, but she wanted to observe the bidding. As the painting opened for bids, she held her breath, but one-by-one, anonymous bidders called in higher and higher amounts. At the end of the evening the painting sold for a hundred and fifteen million, almost five million more than the highest price ever paid for a painting by an American artist.

Afterwards, Elle and the Griffiths went out to celebrate at the National Arts Club, where Blake's posthumous membership gave Elle privileges. The water in Blake's two paintings shimmered behind their table, and Elle had the feeling Blake was sharing in the toast they made. Gary asked Elle what she planned to do with the money from the painting. She pulled a hand-written list from her handbag and began reading aloud.

"Expand the studio at Manderley to include a facility for daytime educational and social activities for mentally challenged girls and women in association with the Don Guanella Villages. The facility will be named the Charlotte Carson Learning Center. The chief contractor for this project will be Alexander Vargas of the recently formed construction company, AV Construction, of Philadelphia. (Please note: I intend to write a will that bequeaths Manderley to Alexander Vargas, assuming LeRoi Hawkins and I predecease him, and to his heirs, if not. Manderley should continue in the hands of family.)

Establish an educational scholarship foundation in memory of Blake M. Allmond, providing a full four-year scholarship for a deserving art student to attend the Pennsylvania Academy of the Fine Arts in its Bachelor of Fine Arts program. A new student will be selected every four years by an impartial committee. I will endow the foundation with ten million dollars.

Bestow a one-time tax-free gift of ten million dollars to—."

Griffith's eyebrows rose sky-high. "Say no more. Before you start giving away gifts, to anyone, let me do some research."

Elle had expected the objection, but she smiled and said, "Perfectly fine. Do your due diligence. But my mind is made up about this."

The next evening Tonya and Parrott received a phone call from Gary Griffith, telling them Elle had authorized him to give them a one-time tax-free gift of ten million dollars. Now they were in bed after having celebrated their good fortune with a champagne dinner at home. "I can't believe we're multi-millionaires," Tonya said, giggling. "What would the kids in the 'hood say about that?"

Parrott traced an imaginary line along his wife's jaw, neck, and shoulder. "Why do they get to say anything at all about it? Why can't it be our little secret?"

Tonya pulled back from her husband and looked him in the eyes. "Ollie? Are you ashamed of having money?"

"No, not ashamed, exactly. Maybe uncomfortable."

"Would you feel the same way if you had earned it, instead of its being a gift?"

Parrott stretched his long body alongside Tonya's, careful not to press on her bad shoulder. "That's the point. There's no way I could earn that much money. Remember how excited we were when I made detective? We've been thinking we're rich all along. Now we have to readjust everything."

"Who says so?"

"I've been working cases involving people in the one percent. I used to think they were snobby and shallow. Then I learned they were just people, like anyone else. And now I am one of them. It'll take some getting used to."

"You don't see Elle becoming snobby and shallow, now she's inherited money. She's still the same kind, generous person she was before."

Parrott propped himself on an elbow. "Yeah, but we're young. And I love my job. I want to keep working, keep contributing."

"Nobody's telling you to quit working, Ollie. You've got a gift. You should keep on using it. You know how much Chief Schrik appreciates you."

"He does, and I enjoy working with him, too." Parrott was quiet for a while, thinking. "Remember the police chief and his wife we met in Galveston?"

"Gonzalez? Sure. Why?"

"I helped him solve a case, and he's been making noise about me coming down there to work, maybe being in line to replace him when he retires. It would mean starting all over in police academy, though."

"Well, Detective Oliver Parrott, excellent case-solver, wealthy man, and incomparable husband—you have a lot of things to think about."

"And a lot of time to think about them. Right now I've got one thing on my mind."

"Mmm, mmm. Let's see if I can guess what that is." Tonya reached over to switch off the lamp.

Parrott let all thoughts of PTSD and theft and murder and money and jobs drift away for now. The one thing he was sure of was right there next to him.

ACKNOWLEDGMENTS

I am deeply indebted to the following people, who assisted with authenticating information for this novel: Father Frank Fabj, Ed Richard, David Richard, Carol Cukierman, James Robertson, Lisa Windsor, Marvin Langston of Hometown Bank, Lee Walasavage of Terry Funeral Home, Michelle Thackrah of Archer and Buchanan Architects, Lieutenant Destin Sims of the Galveston Police Department, John Selig, Linda Hiles, Nancy Hughes, Susan Tyler, Scott Richard, Mamie Duff, Susanne Pagano of *Delaware Today*, Jessica Stryker of *The Hunt*, and the West Brandywine Police Department. Thanks also to the many readers of Murder in the One Percent, the first in the Detective Parrott series, who insisted I bring Parrott and Tonya back for another case in Brandywine Valley. I am grateful to Palm Circle Press and Rebecca Evans; to Susan P. Baker and Phyllis H. Moore, for their constructive criticism; to Maureen Patton and The Grand 1894 Opera House and Rozanne Rubin for their generous support; to Tina Benkiser; and to Caitlin Hamilton Marketing. Most of all, thank you, Readers. The joy of writing comes through each and every one of you. If you enjoyed *A Palette for Love and Murder*, please rate and review it.

ABOUT THE AUTHOR

Saralyn Richard writes award-winning mysteries that pull back the curtain on people in settings as diverse as elite country mansions and disadvantaged urban high schools. An active member of International Thriller Writers and Mystery Writers of America, Saralyn teaches creative writing and literature. Her favorite part of being an author is connecting with readers. Please subscribe to her monthly newsletter at the website, www.saralynrichard.com.

Photo by Jennifer Reynolds